The window exploded. Starbuck reacted on sheer instinct and threw himself backward in his chair. He crashed into the wall, pulling his Colt as the chair collapsed and he toppled to the floor. Hoyt jackknifed to his feet and gaped at two men dimly visible through the shattered window. Then the men opened fire with sawed-off shotguns.

Starbuck levered himself up on one arm before the men could reload. He sighted on the shadowy figures and thumbed off a hurried snap shot. One of the men screamed and dropped his scattergun. Starbuck triggered another shot and then realized he was firing at an empty window. The men were gone, and in the sudden stillness he heard pounding footsteps on the boardwalk. Starbuck cursed the darkness and his own shooting. The man he'd hit wasn't wounded seriously, for they were both running at top speed.

A look around confirmed what he already knew. George Hoyt was dead, and with him had died any hope of a quick break in the case . . .

THE
JUDAS TREE

Matt Braun

St. Martin's Paperbacks

THE JUDAS TREE / THE LAST STAND

The Judas Tree copyright © 1982 by Matt Braun. Published by arrangement with Signet, an imprint of New American Library, a division of Penguin Books USA Inc.
The Last Stand copyright © 1998 by Winchester Productions, Ltd.

Cover photo © Comstock Images.

ISBN: 0-312-94605-8
EAN: 978-0-312-94605-0

Printed in the United States of America

The Judas Tree first Signet paperback edition / June 1992
St. Martin's Paperbacks edition / October 2003

The Last Stand St. Martin's Paperbacks edition / June 1998

St. Martin's Paperbacks are published by St. Martin's Press, 175 Fifth Avenue, New York, NY 10010.

10 9 8 7 6 5 4 3 2 1

To
Ron
Marty and Marnie
Milt and Peter
A team with vision and
All Westerners at heart

Author's Note

The *Judas Tree* is based on a true story.

The mining camps of Montana Territory were hellholes of depravity and lawlessness. None was more infamous, or alluring, than Virginia City. There, deep in the wilderness, one of the great gold bonanzas of all time was discovered. Thousands of miners were drawn by the promise of riches; not far behind them were the scavengers of the frontier, the saloonkeepers and gamblers and whores. Yet it was the outlaws and road agents who posed the gravest threat along Alder Gulch. Human predators, they robbed and killed with a savagery unequaled in the annals of the Old West. Their reign of terror ultimately claimed the lives of more than one hundred men. Wholesale murder was the order of the day in Virginia City.

Where violence flourishes there are always men willing to take the law into their own hands. Vigilante movements were common in the Old West, and justice was seldom tempered by mercy. Such was the case in Virginia City, where unchecked lawlessness gave rise to mob rule and summary execution. Not infrequently, the leaders of vigilance groups were as ruthless and coldblooded as the outlaws they hanged.

Anyone familiar with the history of Montana Territory will recognize *The Judas Tree* as a work of fiction based on fact. Some license has been taken with events and dates, and the names of certain historical characters have been changed. Yet the truth of that long-ago time has been depicted with accuracy and realism. Documented fact rather than invention forms the cornerstone of the story.

Luke Starbuck undertakes a hazardous assignment in *The Judas Tree*. His reputation as a detective and mankiller precedes him wherever he travels on the western frontier. All his talents as an undercover operative and a master of disguise are tested to the limit in Virginia City. His mission pits him against corrupt politicians, vice lords, and a murderous gang of robbers. The ultimate challenge, however, involves a confrontation with the band of stranglers who called themselves vigilantes. His investigation brings to light the volatile world of a lawless mining camp.

The Judas Tree, in the end, depicts a tale of men brutalized by events. Luke Starbuck saw it happen very much the way it's told.

THE
JUDAS TREE

Chapter One

The trolley car stopped at Seventeenth and Larimer. Starbuck swung down, waiting for a carriage to pass. Then he crossed to the corner occupied by the Windsor Hotel. His office was on Seventeenth Street, halfway down the block. He strolled along at a leisurely pace.

Denver basked under a bright August sun. To the west, the Rockies jutted skyward, still capped with snow. The air was crystal clear and the afternoon moderately warm. Starbuck's attire was casual, suitable to the weather. He wore a light corduroy jacket, a linen shirt open at the neck, and a low-crowned Stetson. Under the jacket, snugged tight in a cross-draw holster, he carried a Colt .45 at waist level. Even in Denver, he always went armed.

The office building was directly behind the hotel, across the alley. He mounted the stairs to the second floor and proceeded along a hallway. Several years ago he had established headquarters in Denver. As his business expanded, his office had grown from a modest cubbyhole to a two-room suite. His caseload generally kept him on the move, and his visits to the office, even when he was in town, were sporadic. He turned into a doorway marked by a simple brass placard:

**LUKE STARBUCK
INVESTIGATIONS**

Verna Phelps, his secretary, was seated behind a desk in the outer room. She was a spinster, pushing forty, and seemingly resigned to the life of an old maid. Her hair was pulled back in a severe chignon, and pince-nez glasses dangled from a black ribbon around her neck. She greeted him with a perfunctory nod.

"Good afternoon."

"Afternoon, Verna." Starbuck nailed his hat on a halltree. "What's on for today?"

"Where shall I start?"

"That bad, huh?"

"You have a full schedule."

"Well, like they say . . . no rest for the weary."

"Humph!"

Verna clamped her pince-nez on the tip of her nose. She took great pride in his work as a detective. She even derived a certain vicarious satisfaction from his notoriety as a mankiller. Yet she viewed his personal life with prim disapproval. Between cases, he devoted his nights to Denver's sporting district and seldom rose from bed before noon. His general attitude was that a man who worked hard was entitled to play hard. The upshot was what Verna considered a mild form of debauchery. She thought it scandalous behavior for a man in his position.

"Perhaps a *decent* night's sleep"—Verna gave him a vinegary glance—"would leave you less weary."

Starbuck yawned. "I like the indecent kind lots better."

"No doubt!" Verna flushed and handed him a stack of papers. "Here's your correspondence and the monthly report from your banker."

"Anything else?"

"You have a two o'clock appointment with Horace Griffin of Wells Fargo."

"Since when?"

"He sent a note over this morning."

"What's it about?"

"I have no idea," Verna replied. "His note simply requested an appointment."

"Here or there?"

"Here." Verna squinted over her glasses. "I thought it safe to reply you would be available—by two o'clock."

"Ouch!" Starbuck met her frosty look with a grin. "No need to draw blood."

"I merely deliver messages, nothing more."

Starbuck laughed and moved through the door to his private office. Nothing fancy, the room contained a desk and several wooden armchairs. On the far wall was a large double-door safe where confidential records were stored. He seated himself in a swivel chair behind the desk and lit a cigarette. Then, with no great enthusiasm, he began riffling through the correspondence.

The letters were routine requests for his services. So far, 1882 had proved to be a banner year. He had played an active part in the death of Jesse James, and he'd broken a criminal conspiracy in Deadwood, Dakota Territory. The cases garnered national attention, and the resulting publicity had boosted his already formidable reputation as a private detective. The volume of mail increased accordingly, and he was now being offered work from every corner of the West. Several firms had even proposed placing him on a yearly retainer. Those letters were the first to hit the wastebasket.

One thing Starbuck prized above all else was independence. His list of clients included railroads and stagelines, mining companies and banks. Yet he was extremely choosy, and money alone was never the determining factor. He accepted an assignment principally for the challenge involved; a run-of-the-mill case was simply passed over without consideration. He could afford to pick and choose by virtue of a sizable investment portfolio. The monthly statement from his banker indicated diversity and sound judgment. He owned substantial blocks of stock in railroads and mining companies, along with municipal bonds and select parcels of real estate. His total worth was approaching three hundred thousand dollars, and dividends alone provided a comfortable income. He enjoyed his work and he took pride in his craft. But he accepted an assignment only when it intrigued him. The wastebasket was constantly full.

Today was no exception. One letter out of the entire stack was set aside for reply. Then, with that bothersome chore completed, he leaned back in the swivel chair. His mind turned to Horace Griffin and the upcoming appointment. He quickly sifted through his mental catalogue on the Wells Fargo division superintendent.

Griffin had first hired him the fall of '81. The assignment had taken him to Tombstone and pitted him against Wyatt Earp. In the course of his investigation, he had established that Earp was a coldblooded murderer and the ringleader of a gang of stage robbers. The outcome, in his view, was the one black mark on his record. Try as he might—and he'd tried very hard—he had failed to kill Earp. A slippery character, Earp had refused to fight, and therefore escaped Arizona alive. His present whereabouts was unknown, and of no interest to anyone.

Still, even though Starbuck considered the job only half done, Wells Fargo had been appreciative. After Earp's departure, stage robbery had all but ceased in the Tombstone district. Griffin had put through a request for a bonus, and the head office in San Francisco had approved it without hesitation. Since then, Wells Fargo had been instrumental in steering several clients to Starbuck's doorstep. One assignment had taken him to San Francisco itself, and another had put him on the trail of Jesse James. The cases, in both instances, were unusual and challenging. So far as Starbuck was concerned, Wells Fargo was a regular tapspring of interesting work. He liked the brand of trouble they sent his way.

Some while later, Verna ushered Horace Griffin through the door. The Wells Fargo superintendent was accompanied by two men, and they trooped into the office like a trio of gravediggers. Their expressions were curiously somber, and Starbuck sensed an undercurrent of tension. Griffin made short work of the introductions.

"Luke, I'd like you to meet Munro Salisbury and John Duggan." While a round of handshakes was under way, Griffin went on. "Mr. Salisbury is senior partner of the Gilmer and Salisbury Stage Line. Mr. Duggan is president of the Virginia City Mining Association."

"Nevada?" Starbuck inquired. "Or Montana?"

"Montana," Duggan responded with a marled stare. "So far as we're concerned, it's the *only* Virginia City!"

"I admire your civic spirit, Mr. Duggan."

At Starbuck's invitation, the men took chairs in front of the desk. He was unaccustomed to dealing with committees, and he warned himself to proceed with caution. The nature of his work, which was largely undercover, demanded the utmost secrecy. For all their sepulchral mood, the delegation before him was an unknown quantity. He nodded and smiled.

"What can I do for you gentlemen?"

Griffin took the lead. "Before we get down to cases, let me fill you in on the details. Several years ago Gilmer and Salisbury bought out Wells Fargo's interests in Montana. We have an express contract with them—primarily gold shipments—but that's it. We don't actually operate the stageline ourselves."

"Sounds like a profitable arrangement."

"It was," Griffin remarked stiffly. "Up until a year or so ago. Then the holdups started, and things have gone downhill ever since."

"Oh?" Starbuck said evenly. "How many hold-ups?"

"Three or four a month, and that's just the stage-coaches! Some miners transport their bullion themselves, and they've been hit even harder. We're talking about an epidemic, Luke. Wholesale robbery!"

"And murder," Salisbury interjected gravely. "At last count fifty-six men had been killed. Twelve were stage employees or passengers, and the rest were miners."

"I'll be damned!" Starbuck suddenly looked interested. "What about the law? Why hasn't your sheriff cracked down?"

"He has!" Salisbury said hastily. "We couldn't ask for a better sheriff than Henry Palmer. In the last year alone, he's captured eleven bandits and killed four more. I might add we tried and hanged ten of those he captured. But, as Mr. Griffin told you, it's an epidemic! No peace officer can be everywhere at once."

John Duggan cleared his throat. "Are you familiar with that part of Montana, Mr. Starbuck?"

"No," Starbuck admitted. "I've only been through there once, and that was by train."

"It's rough country," Duggan explained. "Only two roads in and out of Virginia City. One to the railroad at Dillon, and the other to Butte. All of it's mountainous and heavily wooded. Perfect for outlaws—and a nightmare for lawmen."

"Offhand"—Starbuck paused, an odd smile at the corners of his mouth—"I'd say it's a matter of the wrong people getting killed."

The words were spoken in a pleasant voice. Yet

none of the men missed the quiet deadliness underlying the statement. Starbuck stared back at them with eyes that were uncommonly blue and deceptively tranquil. He was tall and wide through the shoulders, and his features were ruggedly forceful under a thatch of sandy chestnut hair. Over one eyebrow was a jagged scar, and his nose was crooked a hair off center. He looked like a blooded veteran, cold and dangerous. His moderate tone somehow underscored the impression.

Horace Griffin thought the statement revealed much about the detective. Starbuck was as deadly as the outlaws he hunted—a mankiller—the very attribute needed if ever law was to be brought to Virginia City. At length, the Wells Fargo superintendent shifted in his chair. He looked Starbuck straight in the eye.

"We'd like to retain your services, Luke."

"Why?" Starbuck asked deliberately. "From what you say, you're up against a regular army of robbers. What makes you think I'd do any better than your sheriff?"

"The sheriff's too well known for what we have in mind." Griffin hesitated, took a deep breath, and let it out slowly. "We have reason to believe the stagecoach robbers are an organized gang."

"How so?"

"The holdups appear to be planned. We think that would require someone with inside information—a Judas."

"Any idea who's behind it?"

"None whatever." Griffin frowned, shook his head.

"But if we're right, then what we need is an under-cover operative. Someone who can get to the bottom of it—and stop it."

Starbuck understood the message. He was being asked to infiltrate the gang and dispense summary justice. The gang leader—and the Judas—were to be killed. He mulled it over a moment, intrigued primarily by one aspect. He wondered why the robbers murdered their victims so casually, and so often. Then, abruptly, he turned to Duggan.

"What's your part in all this?"

"I don't follow you."

"It's simple enough," Starbuck said bluntly. "Griffin and Salisbury want the stage holdups stopped. What're you after?"

"Law and order," Duggan informed him. "At this very moment, Virginia City is on the edge of anarchy. Too many miners have been murdered, and there's no end in sight. It has to stop!"

"What do you mean . . . anarchy?"

"Vigilantes," Duggan said grimly. "One of our local hotheads is beating the drum for a vigilance committee. Unless you put a halt to these murders, he'll get his way."

"What's his name?"

"Lott," Duggan said with a grimace. "Wilbur X. Lott. He's politically ambitious, and he's using the vigilante issue as a soapbox. People are starting to listen—and that's dangerous."

Starbuck fixed him with a speculative gaze. "Do you think there's some connection between the stage robbers and whoever's robbing the miners?"

"God, I hope so!" Duggan said vehemently. "If there's not, then there's no stopping the vigilante movement!"

Starbuck was thoughtful for a time. His expression was abstracted, and he appeared to be debating something within himself. Then, at last, he looked at Griffin.

"Does anyone know you've approached me? Any of your associates, the sheriff, anyone at all?"

"No one," Griffin assured him. "These gentlemen arrived in Denver only last night. They asked my advice, and I recommended you as the man for the job. That's as far as it's gone."

Starbuck regarded him with great calmness. "I'll take the assignment on two conditions. First—I do it my own way, no questions asked. Second—all three of you button your lip till the job's done. Anybody talks out of school and I'll know where to look."

Duggan stiffened. "That sounds like a threat!"

"Take it any way you want," Starbuck said flatly. "It's good advice . . . the best you'll ever get."

"Indeed it is," Griffin broke in smoothly. "Now, what about your fee, Luke?"

"Same as last time," Starbuck said without inflection. "Five thousand down and five thousand on delivery."

"One question, Mr. Starbuck." Salisbury cocked his head with a quizzical look. "How will we contact you, once you've undertaken the job?"

"You won't." Starbuck's eyes were hard, impersonal. "You'll get a report when the assignment's completed, not before. That's the way I work."

Griffin smiled and rose to his feet. "We'll wait to hear from you, Luke."

"Depend on it, Horace."

When they were gone, Starbuck walked directly to the safe. He spun the combination knob and swung open one of the doors. On an inside shelf were four leather-bound ledgers. He took out the ledger stenciled *G-L* and returned to his desk. After lighting a cigarette, he opened the ledger to the section flagged with the letter *L*. He began thumbing through the pages.

The ledgers were a rogues' gallery of western outlaws. Almost a year ago, he'd begun collecting information on the Who's Who of the criminal element. Correspondence with peace officers and U.S. marshals across the frontier provided him with hard intelligence. Added to newspaper clippings and material gleaned from wanted dodgers, it gave him a quick and ready reference whenever he undertook a new case. He now had dossiers on more than three hundred gunmen and desperados.

A few moments later he stubbed out his cigarette. There was no page on Wilbur X. Lott, the aspiring vigilante leader. Nor was there any cross-reference indicating an alias. He'd thought it a long shot, but nonetheless worth a try. All things considered, though, it was no great loss. He was accustomed to working in the blind.

Lost in thought, he replaced the ledger and locked the safe. Then he wandered into the outer office. Verna looked up, and he stopped beside her desk.

"I took the assignment."

"So I heard."

"Eavesdropper." Starbuck smiled, nodding absently. "Check out the train schedule. I want to connect with the stageline at Dillon. That's somewhere in western Montana."

"When will you leave?"

"Couple of days ought to be soon enough."

"I'll see to it right away."

"Good." Starbuck turned toward the door. "Guess I'll call it a day. All that paperwork tuckered me out."

Verna sniffed. "Don't forget your theater tickets. A messenger brought them from Mr. Rothacker while you were in conference."

"Hell's bells!" Starbuck grumbled. "I forgot all about that!"

"No doubt you wanted to forget."

Verna extended an envelope, and he stared at it a moment. Orville Rothacker, publisher of the morning *Tribune,* was one of his few friends in Denver's society circles. He had accepted the invitation more than a week ago, and there was no way out of it now. With some reluctance, he took the envelope. There were two tickets inside.

"Who's playing, anyway?" He suddenly remembered, and frowned. "It's whatzizname—the Irish poet?"

"Oscar Wilde," Verna said sharply. "And it's neither a play nor poetry! Mr. Wilde will deliver a lecture on interior house decoration."

"No kidding?" Starbuck watched her with an indulgent smile. "A poet and a house decorator! What's he do for an encore?"

"Really!" Verna said with feisty outrage. "Some people consider Oscar Wilde a genius. You might very well be surprised!"

"Nothing surprises me." Starbuck's features mirrored cynical amusement. "Course, lots of things surprise Lola. She'll probably enjoy it."

"You're taking *her?*" Verna asked querulously. "To see Oscar Wilde?"

"What the hell!" Starbuck gave her a satiric look. "They're both in the show business . . . her and Oscar."

Verna appeared mortified. She merely stared as he chuckled and walked out the door. Her mind was reeling with the thought of him and his hussy—at the Tabor Grand Opera House!

She suddenly felt faint.

Chapter Two

Lola Montana was a vision of loveliness. She wore an exquisite gown of teal blue and a pearl choker with a sapphire in the center. The bodice of the gown was cut low and cinched at the waist, displaying her sumptuous figure to full advantage. Her flaxen hair was upswept and drawn back, with a soft cluster of curls fluffed high on her forehead. She looked at once regal and sensual.

Holding her arm, Starbuck was attired in a cutaway coat and black tie. Orville Rothacker and his wife, directly ahead of them, were following an usher down the aisle. The opera house was packed to capacity, and their entrance caused a sudden stir of commotion. Heads craned and the audience buzzed, all eyes turned in their direction. Starbuck was amused by the reaction, his face fixed in a nutcracker grin. He looked proud as punch.

Certain conventions were normally observed at the Tabor Grand Opera House. The boxes and all of the orchestra were reserved for the elite of Denver society. The sporting crowd and other assorted riffraff were consigned to the upper balcony. Tonight, for the first time in memory, the customary order of things had been breached. Yet no one in the audience raised a cry, and none would dare reproach Orville Rothacker. The publisher knew where all the skeletons were buried, and the lorgnette set of Capitol Hill lived in fear he would unearth the darker secrets of their past. Scandal, despite Denver's cosmopolitan airs, was still very much in vogue.

In truth, Rothacker cared nothing for their conventions or their secrets. He considered himself a newspaperman, and his friendship with Starbuck stemmed from a series of interviews over the past several years. He'd always found the detective forthcoming, however sensational the case, and the interviews never failed to boost circulation. Only on one subject had they come to an impasse. Starbuck either deflected or ignored any question as to the number of men he'd killed. Rothacker privately speculated that the number was twenty or more, perhaps many more. He hoped one day to print the full story, for he believed Starbuck deserved all the credit normally accorded sworn lawmen. Tonight, however, there was no thought of a story. He was content to enjoy the manhunter's company.

The houselights dimmed as the usher seated them. Lola squeezed Starbuck's arm and snuggled closer. She was a tawny blond cat of a girl, with bold eyes and enchanting verve. Her evenings were usually spent prancing about the stage of the Alcazar Variety Theater. The star of the show, she belted out songs in a husky alto and bewitched the crowd with her sultry good looks. The combination had made her the toast of Denver's Tenderloin district, and every man's fantasy. Yet she was one man's woman, and never prouder of it than now. Tonight he'd flaunted her before the society swells, which amounted to a public announcement. She was Luke Starbuck's woman. His only woman.

The curtain rose to reveal a lectern positioned stage center. Then a spotlight flared and Oscar Wilde walked from the wings. He was a short, plump man, with cherubic features and curly locks that tumbled to his shoulders. He wore a purple velvet coat, knee breeches, and silk stockings. In his right hand he carried a single lily, which somehow compounded the effect of his costume. He stopped behind the lectern, gazing raptly a moment at the lily, and finally looked up. The audience twittered with laughter and gave him a modest round of applause.

"Just between us, lover," Lola whispered in Starbuck's ear, "he ought to trade that lily for a pansy."

"You think so?"

"I'll lay odds he's queer as a three-dollar bill!"

"No bet!" Starbuck chortled. "I got a hunch I'd lose."

Billed as the Apostle of Aestheticism, Wilde was currently in the midst of a grand tour of America. His career as a poet-playwright had already brought him much fame in Ireland and England, and he'd been treated as a dignitary by the eastern press. In one interview, he had stated that the purpose of his tour was to bring culture to the "colonists." Tonight his reception was something less than overwhelming. Westerners apparently weren't ready for culture or the finer points of aesthetic expression. His lecture on interior

decorating played to stifled yawns and impromptu
bursts of laughter. Even the *grandes dames* of Denver
society were hard pressed to stay awake. He cut the
lecture short and marched offstage in a towering snit.
The performance drew scattered applause, and a rush
for the doors.

Starbuck and Lola traded smiles and said nothing.
Stepping aside, they waited while Rothacker and his
wife made their way to the aisle. Rothacker's mutton-
chop whiskers were split wide in a wry grin. He motioned toward the stage.

"Would you like to meet the illustrious Mr.
Wilde?"

"Who?" Starbuck croaked dumbly. "Me?"

"Why not?" Rothacker laughed. "We plan to interview him tomorrow, before his second lecture. That
should be good for an introduction."

"I—"

"We'd love it!" Lola interrupted with a mischie-
vous smile. "Wouldn't we, Luke?"

Starbuck gave her a hard look. "You really want
to?"

"Ooo pleeze!" Her eyes sparkled with suppressed
mirth. "Just for me!"

"Well—"

"It's settled, then," Rothacker said quickly. "Come
along, Luke! A little culture never hurt anybody."

The publisher led the way backstage. The door to
Wilde's dressing room was open, and four women,
gushing compliments, were just leaving. The poet
looked a little frazzled and somewhat sour around the
mouth. His smile was forced.

Rothacker simply walked in and began talking. A seasoned newshound, he employed flattery with the subtle touch of a diplomat. Wilde, who was a creature of his own vanity, responded immediately. By the time introductions were completed, he was once more in character, pompous and wholly self-centered. Yet he seemed taken with Starbuck. There was a twinkle in his eye, and, to Lola's delight, he ignored everyone else. He put a chubby finger to his lips, contemplative.

"Starbuck." He repeated the name slowly. "Ah, but of course! You're the detective fellow, aren't you?"

Starbuck looked uncomfortable. "How'd you know that?"

"Why, dear man!" Wilde trilled breezily. "I read about you while I was in New York. One of those publications peculiar to America. The *Police Gazette*, I believe it was called. But a splendid article nonetheless! Indeed it was."

Starbuck smiled without warmth. "I guess I missed that issue."

"Then more's the pity!" Wilde said cheerily. "A truly gripping account it was! All about that poor sod you laid to rest in Deadwood."

A pained expression came over Starbuck's face. "I wouldn't exactly call him a poor sod."

"Well, no matter!" Wilde laughed, and his voice went up a couple of octaves. "You put the bugger out of his misery! And didn't I say to myself what a grand name for it? Deadwood! So apropos, and imagery at its purest. Now, don't you agree?"

Starbuck stifled the impulse to say what he was really thinking. "I'll take your word for it."

"Pathos, dear fellow!" Wilde made an effeminate gesture and laid his hand on Starbuck's arm. "Poets love tragedy, and a tragic figure even more. We're all very sensitive, you know?"

Lola smiled and took a possessive grip on Starbuck's other arm. "I've told Luke that very thing, Mr. Wilde! You see, I'm an artiste myself . . . a singer."

"How nice." Wilde gave her a withering look, then turned swiftly to Rothacker. "Now, about the interview you requested. I regret to say a second lecture in Denver appears fruitless. I've an engagement in Leadville, and I believe I'll travel there tomorrow."

"That's a shame," Rothacker said affably. "You might have drawn a better audience tomorrow night."

"I think not." Wilde shook his head with a condescending air. "Aestheticism does require a certain sophistication."

Rothacker grunted, smothering a laugh. "I wish you luck, then. Leadville's one of our rougher mining camps."

"Indeed!" Wilde arched one eyebrow and looked down his nose. "Well, now, I've great rapport with the working class. I wouldn't wonder they'll embrace the message with open arms!"

The conversation ended there. Wilde saw them to the door and closed it firmly. Outside, Rothacker pantomimed a limp-wristed gesture and rolled his eyes at Starbuck. Waving him off, Starbuck lagged back and took Lola by the elbow. His voice was sardonic.

"You've got some sense of humor."

Lola mimicked his dour expression. "Whatever do you mean?"

"Don't play coy!" Starbuck muttered. "You jumped at the chance to get me and Wilde together. You all but sicced the bastard on me!"

"Why, Luke Starbuck!" Lola batted her china-blue eyes. "Would I do a thing like that?"

"You not only would—you did!"

"Honestly, lover!" Her eyes seemed to glint with secret amusement. "I saved you from a fate worse than death! Your face went white when he latched on to your arm."

Starbuck's mouth suddenly split in a lopsided grin. "One thing's for sure! That little sweet pea probably won't make it out of Leadville alive. They'll stick his aesthetics where the sun don't shine!"

Lola's throaty laughter floated out over the opera house. A few moments later, on the street, Starbuck declined Rothacker's invitation to a late supper. Then he flagged a hansom cab and assisted Lola inside. They drove straight to the Brown Palace Hotel, where he'd maintained a suite for the past several years. Only recently had Lola become a permanent fixture in his life and the sole partner in his bed. He took her there now, and neither of them spoke a word. Their sense of urgency was mutual, somehow heightened by the evening.

Within minutes, naked and disheveled, they were locked together.

Starbuck kissed the vee between her breasts. Then he rolled away and sprawled exhausted on the bed. She wiggled into the crook of his arm and pillowed her head on his shoulder. For a while, time lost measure and meaning. She lay still and sated, far beyond the limits of her most vivid fantasies. She felt fulfilled and wanted.

Yet deep within she knew she possessed only a part of him. She was his woman, but he was still his own man. He shared his secrets with her and confided in her as he would in no other human. There was implicit trust in that sharing, for at root he was a man of privacy and ingrained cynicism. She accepted those things, careful never to smother him or demand more than he could give. She understood him with a wisdom that was both intuitive and practical. Only by allowing him to go free was she assured he would return. She was content with the arrangement, secure in the knowledge that he needed her. He would never give all of himself, but the bond between them was the single bond in his life. She asked no more.

Presently Starbuck stirred. He pulled her close and held her quietly for a moment. Then he nuzzled her unbound hair, his voice muted and curiously gentle.

"I leave day after tomorrow."

"You—you've taken another case?"

Starbuck bobbed his head. "Wells Fargo and another stageline hired me. They've got a little problem with a gang of robbers. Nothing too serious."

"I'll bet!" She tweaked the hair on his chest. "You're not fooling anybody, lover-man. If it wasn't serious, they wouldn't come to you!"

"All in a day's work," Starbuck said easily. "Wouldn't be any fun if it wasn't sticky."

"Where are they sending you?"

"Virginia City," Starbuck told her. "The one in Montana."

Lola sat bolt upright. Her breasts shimmered in the glow of lamplight spilling through the parlor door. She stared down at him with an expression of mild wonder.

"I was offered a job in Virginia City!"

"Yeah?" Starbuck asked idly. "Who by?"

Her brow furrowed in concentration. "Stinson? No, wait a minute. It was Stimson. Omar Stimson! He owns the Gem Theater there."

"How come he contacted you?"

"Thanks a lot!" Lola gave him a pouty look. "Whether you know it or not, I've made a name for myself, too. All kinds of people have tried to hire me away from Jack Brady! It just so happens I like the Alcazar and I like Denver."

Starbuck chuckled softly. "I guess folks know a good thing when they see it."

"They certainly do!" She tossed her head. "Stimson offered me a thousand dollars for *one week* in Virginia City!"

"Jesus!" Starbuck was impressed. "He must've meant business!"

"Of course he did," Lola replied airily. "In case you haven't noticed, I do tend to draw a crowd."

"You've got a way with men, all right. I reckon I'd be the first to admit it."

Lola fell silent a moment. A strange look came over her face, and she seemed to stare straight through him. Then she suddenly giggled and squirmed around like soft wax.

"Holy Hannah!" she squealed. "I just had a brain-storm!"

"Since you're gonna tell me anyway, go ahead."

"Just suppose—" She hesitated, her eyes bright as berries. "Now, hear me out before you say any-thing. Just suppose I took the job in Virginia City. I could—"

"No!" Starbuck cut her short. "Thumbs down, and that's final!"

"Just listen, for God's sake!" She scooted closer and went on in a rush. "I could be your ears and your eyes. You'd be amazed what a girl picks up around men! Not to mention what I could worm out of Stim-son himself. He probably knows everybody who's anybody in Virginia City!"

"I said no, and that's that."

"Aww c'mon, lover!" she cooed. "How many chances will we have to work together? It's made to order, once in a lifetime!"

"You're wasting your breath," Starbuck said ston-ily. "I don't need any help, and on top of that, it's too dangerous. The people I'm after are cutthroats and murderers! One slip and you'd wind up with your neck on the chopping block."

"Oh, don't be silly!" she said, lifting her chin. "I've been twisting men around my little finger all my life. Do you really think I couldn't do it in Virginia City? Do you?"

"I didn't say that," Starbuck mumbled. "I just said it's too dangerous."

"Have a heart, Luke." Her voice dropped to a whisper. "I want to do it. And I'd be good at it! You know I would."

"I still say no," Starbuck murmured uneasily. "Besides, you can't quit your job at the Alcazar. There's no sense to it."

"Forget Jack Brady!" she hooted. "If I want a week off, he'll grin and bear it. Believe me, he will! He wouldn't *dare* risk losing me to another joint in Denver."

Starbuck was tempted. Her logic was indisputable, and the danger was far less than he'd claimed. No one would suspect a famous variety star of being an undercover operative. There was, moreover, the lack of hard intelligence about the gang. An extra set of eyes and ears would be a tremendous asset in Virginia City. At length, still not fully convinced, he took a deep breath and exhaled slowly. His tone was tentative.

"I'll think about it."

"Hotdamn!" She laughed and clapped her hands like an exuberant child. "I'll wire Stimson first thing in the morning."

"Hold your horses!" Starbuck barked gruffly. "I said I'll *think* about it. That's all, nothing more!"

"Anything you say, lover."

Lola let it drop there. He held out his arms, and she lowered herself into his embrace. She nestled close against him, warm and cuddly and submissive. Yet her eyes danced merrily, and inside she was jubilant.

She knew she had won.

Late the next afternoon Starbuck and Lola entered a
shop on Blake Street. He still had grave misgivings
about their plan, and his mood was somber. But she'd
cajoled and wheedled, and an hour ago the last obsta-
cle had been removed. Omar Stimson, owner of the
Gem Theater, had replied to her wire. She was booked
for a one-week engagement in Virginia City.

Inside the shop, they were greeted by Daniel Cameron. He was a master gunsmith and Starbuck's personal armorer. Unknown to anyone but themselves,
he had developed an advanced .45 cartridge that was
a deadly manstopper. He advised Starbuck on weapon
selection and kept the detective's guns in superb
working order. Wizened and gray-haired, he was considered the dean of western gunsmiths.

Starbuck trusted no man completely. A careless
word, however inadvertent, might very well jeopardize the assignment. So he told Cameron only the salient details, omitting any mention of Virginia City.
Cameron was momentarily stunned by what he heard.
He knew the manhunter to be a loner; the idea of an
assistant seemed somehow foreign. All the more so
since the assistant was a woman, and one greatly admired by Cameron. He glanced at Lola a couple of
times but kept his own qualms about the arrangement
to himself. When Starbuck finished talking, Cameron
nodded sagely and spread his hands on the showcase
counter.

"How can I help you, Luke?"

"She'll need a gun," Starbuck said quietly. "A hideout of some sort, just in case she gets in a tight fix."

Cameron sometimes joined them for a drink at the Alcazar. He was on a first-name basis with the girl, and he turned to her now with a frank stare. "The truth, Lola. How familiar are you with firearms?"

"No big mystery!" Lola cocked her thumb and forefinger. "All you do is point and pull the trigger!"

"In other words," Starbuck said in a resigned voice, "she doesn't know beans. So the simpler the better— something foolproof!"

"A tall order," Cameron observed. "But if we're talking about a tight fix, then it would probably be at point-blank range."

Opening the showcase, he took out a Colt New Line Pocket Revolver. Some six inches long, it was single-action, chambered for .41 caliber, and held five rounds. He laid the Colt on the counter and next brought out an over/under-barreled Remington Derringer. A stubby weapon, roughly half the size of the Colt, the derringer was .41 caliber and held two shots. He tapped one, then the other, with his finger.

"Both are effective at close range," he noted. "The Colt has the advantage of five shots. Otherwise, there's little to choose between."

"You forgot something, Daniel." Starbuck looked Lola up and down. "Her stage clothes don't leave much room for concealment. Leastways, they don't conceal a helluva lot of *her*."

"Very funny!" Lola gave him a sassy grin. "I don't recall any complaints before!"

"No, Luke's right," Cameron agreed. "The Colt

would never do. It's much too large, and your costumes are much too . . . revealing."

Starbuck inspected her with a clinical eye. "How about that garter you always wear? The big wide one, just above your knee. Any chance you could pull it up higher?"

"How high?"

"High enough so it wouldn't show when you flash your legs."

"I don't see why not."

"Here." Starbuck handed her the derringer. "Stick that in your garter, and you're all set. It goes where you go, and nobody the wiser."

Lola hefted the stubby pistol. "I only see one problem."

"What's that?"

"Hidden way up *there*"—a devilish smile played at the corners of her mouth—"it'll sure slow down my draw!"

"Well, if it comes down to it," Starbuck deadpanned, "you could always fake 'em out. Nobody'd expect you to show 'em a gun—up there."

Lola blushed, and Cameron suppressed a laugh. Then, still chuckling to himself, Starbuck took the derringer and demonstrated how it worked. Thumbing the tiny hammer back, he pressed the trigger; repeating the process emptied both barrels in quick succession. He next explained the loading mechanism and the method of gingerly lowering the hammer once the gun was loaded. Lola got the knack of it in short order and was soon handling the derringer with practiced ease. Satisfied, Starbuck finally allowed her to load it and stuff it into her purse. Cameron threw in a box of shells on the deal, and after Starbuck paid him, he walked them to the door. There the two men shook hands and Lola gave the gunsmith a peck on the cheek.

Outside, arm in arm, Starbuck and the girl strolled off toward the center of town. Cameron paused in the doorway, watching until they rounded the corner. He had no idea where they were headed or what their assignment entailed. Nor was he interested in learning the particulars. Certain things about the manhunter were best left unknown. Yet one thing was uppermost in his mind. A new thought that brought with it a sly, wrinkled grin.

Starbuck and Lola Montana made the perfect team. A mix of nerve and spunk, with an added dash of deadliness. A tough act.

Chapter Three

Starbuck crossed into Montana a week later. From Denver to Salt Lake City, he had taken an overnight train. There he'd switched to the narrow-gauge Utah Northern, which was the only line north through the mountains. He was traveling in disguise, and his cover name was Lee Hall.

The Utah Northern crossed the Continental Divide at Monida Pass. The elevation was almost seven thousand feet, and the tracks then dropped sharply into the Beaverhead Valley of Montana. West of the valley, the Bitterroot Range rose majestically into the clouds. To the east, the battlements of the Rocky Mountains towered skyward. The terrain was rugged, with thick pine forests and sheer canyons, all interlaced with a dizzying network of streams and rivers. It was a land of bitter winters and short summers, at once inhospitable and alluring. Yet no man went there without feeling the pull of something elemental. A sense of having stepped backward in time.

The town of Dillon was a mountain way station. Crude and windswept, it consisted primarily of warehouses and freight outfits. There the goods and supplies hauled in by the railroad were off-loaded;

lumbering Studebaker wagons then completed delivery to the mining camps and settlements of southwestern Montana. For those traveling to the hinterlands, Dillon was also the rail terminus. While the Utah Northern continued on to Butte, outlying areas were accessible only by stagecoach. The Gilmer & Salisbury line was the principal carrier.

The train arrived in Dillon shortly before noon. Starbuck stepped down from the lead coach, carrying a battered warbag. He wore rough clothing—woolen jacket and linsey shirt—and his pants were stuffed into mule-eared boots. His face was covered with whiskery stubble, and he smelled as rank as a billy goat. A handlebar mustache, one of many theatrical props he employed, was glued to his upper lip with spirit gum. His overall appearance was that of a toughnut, someone who managed a livelihood without actually working. He might have been a grifter or a thimblerigger or a robber. He looked vaguely predatory and dangerous.

Operating undercover demanded a certain gift for subterfuge. Early on in his career, Starbuck had discovered in himself something of the actor. That trait, combined with a flair for disguise, allowed him to assume a variety of roles. Over the years, his ability to transform himself into someone else had played a vital part in his survival. Articles in national publications—which invariably carried his photo—had robbed him of anonymity. His face was known and his reputation as a mankiller was widely circulated. So the characters he portrayed were crafted with an eye to outward appearance. Then he worked out a cover story, added a few quirks and mannerisms, and Luke Starbuck simply ceased to exist. His life rested solely on the skill of his performance.

Walking away from the train depot, his thoughts centered on guile and subterfuge. Lola had preceded him to Virginia City by one day. She would be playing herself, the visiting celebrity and headliner at the Gem Theater. Yet a worm of doubt still gnawed at him regarding her performance offstage. How well she handled herself, and how subtly she asked questions, would prove the critical factors. Then, too, her manner toward him would require a performance in itself. He'd told her that he would make the initial contact; whether openly or in secret would depend on the situation. For all his coaching, she was nonetheless a tyro, inexperienced at undercover work. A smile, even a familiar look, might easily tip their game. There was no margin for error, and no second chance in the event something went wrong. He worried about that a lot.

The noon stage was about to depart when he arrived at the station. He purchased a ticket, casually inquiring about the route. The agent informed him Virginia City was some thirty miles east of Dillon and there was one stop along the way. Barring the unforeseen, the stage would pull into Virginia City before sundown. Outside again, he tossed his warbag to the driver and climbed aboard the coach. Then he pulled his hat down over his eyes and settled back in the seat.

His thoughts immediately returned to Lola.

· · ·

Alder Gulch wound through hillsides choked with pine and quaking aspen. Daylight Creek coursed down the gulch in an easterly direction and eventually emptied into the Madison River. A short distance up the gulch lay one of the great gold bonanzas of the western frontier. It was called Virginia City.

Wallace Street, the town's central thoroughfare, was a seething anthill. Some fifteen thousand men were working claims along the gulch, and more were arriving daily. Knots of miners crowded every corner, and the boardwalks were a shoulder-to-shoulder jostling match. The general hubbub of shouts and drunken laughter was deafening and constant. Above it all rose the strident chords of rinky-dink pianos mixed with the wail of fiddles and the sprightly twang of banjos. The rowdy throngs and the discordant sounds were somehow reminiscent of a circus gone wild.

The street itself was little more than a hurdy-gurdy collection of saloons, gambling dives, and dance halls. There were hotels and cafés, along with a couple of banks and an assortment of business establishments. But the town's commerce was devoted largely to separating the miners from their gold dust. Sin was for sale, and every joint, from the rawest busthead saloon to the dollar-a-dance palace, had a bevy of rouge-cheeked charmers. The girls were decked out in spangles and short skirts, and their faces were painted brighter than a carnival Kewpie doll. Their one mission in life was to beguile the customers with sweet talk and snakehead whiskey. Anything extra was negotiable.

Darkness had fallen over Virginia City when Starbuck pushed through the doors of the Gem Theater. The crowd inside was a mixed bag, mainly teamsters and miners. Men were standing three deep at the bar, and every table in the place was occupied. The gambling layouts—everything from faro to chuck-a-luck—were ranged along the wall opposite the bar. Toward the rear of the room there was a small orchestra pit, directly below the footlights of a wide stage. No musicians were in sight, and the stage curtain was drawn.

Starbuck shouldered through the mob at the bar. He ordered whiskey and paid the barkeep. Then he turned one elbow hooked over the counter, and inspected the room. The evening had only begun, and he assumed it was still too early for the night's opening stage show. Yet the place was already jammed, with more men crowding through the door every minute. All the signs indicated that Lola Montana would be playing to standing room only. In the meantime, while the men waited for the show, there was no scarcity of entertainment. An ivory-tickler was pounding an upright piano near the end of the bar. A small dance floor was packed with miners and house girls, whooping and stomping in a wild swirl. It looked curiously like a wrestling match set to music.

Looking past the dancers, Starbuck suddenly spotted Lola. She was seated at a table down front, close to the orchestra pit. Beside her was a barrel-gutted giant of a man. He was wide and tall, and despite his girth he appeared solid as a rock. His face was pitted with deep pockmarks, and he had flat, muddy eyes. He was talking with expansive gestures and staring at Lola with a wolfish smile. On the table was an ice bucket and a bottle of champagne, and their glasses were full. The man paused to quaff a drink, then went on talking. Lola merely sipped, listening attentively.

On impulse, Starbuck decided to take a chance. His plan, loosely formulated, was to establish himself as a hardcase and somehow infiltrate the gang of stagecoach robbers. Before then, however, he needed to make contact with Lola and determine what she'd learned thus far. But it had to be done without arousing suspicion, and the moment at hand appeared made to order. He thought he might easily bring down two birds with one stone.

Starbuck chugged his whiskey and placed the glass on the bar. Then he walked straight to the table where Lola and the man were seated. She looked up, genuinely surprised and somewhat startled. Still, she kept her wits, and no sign of recognition passed between them. Starbuck ignored the man.

"How about it, little lady?" He grinned broadly. "Wanna take a twirl around the dance floor?"

"Shove off!" the man rumbled. "Miss Montana don't dance with strangers."

"Lee Hall's the name." Starbuck's grin widened to a smirk. "I take it you're Mister Montana?"

"You take it wrong!" The man glowered at him through slitted eyes. "The name's Pete Johnson, and you'd better mark it down. Around here, I'm better know as bull o' the woods."

"Well, don't that take the cake!" Starbuck laughed,

spread his hands. "Folks generally allow I'm cock of the walk."

"Lemme tell you something, sonny." Johnson hitched his chair back and stood. He jabbed Starbuck in the chest with a thorny finger. "Close your flytrap and make tracks, or I'm gonna stunt your growth!"

Starbuck hit him without warning. Johnson went down like a poled ox, blood seeping out of his mouth. Yet he was clearly a scrapper of some experience, and uncommonly agile for all his bulk. He rolled away, scattering tables and chairs as he came to his feet. Then he advanced on Starbuck, snarling a murderous oath.

Coldly, with the look of a man who was enjoying himself, Starbuck waited. Johnson launched a hay-maker, and he easily slipped inside the blow. Shifting slightly, his shoulder dipped and he sank his fist in the big man's underbelly. A whoosh of air burst out of Johnson, and he doubled over, clutching himself with a breathless woofing sound. Starbuck exploded two splintering punches on his chin.

Johnson reeled backward into the orchestra pit and sat down heavily. He shook his head, groggy from the punishment he'd absorbed but not yet done for. He planted one arm on the floor and started to lever himself upright. Starbuck took a couple of steps forward and methodically kicked him in the head. The impact collapsed him, and his skull bounced off the floor like a ripe melon. Then a shudder swept through his massive frame and he settled onto his back. He was out cold.

Starbuck dusted his hands and turned toward the

table. He saw three housemen headed in his direction, all of them carrying bungstarters. Lola idly waved them off and beckoned to him. A nervous ripple of laughter went through the crowd as the bruisers veered around him and approached the orchestra pit. He waited until they'd dragged Johnson away, then walked to the table. He doffed his hat in an elaborate bow.

"Little lady," he said in a loud, cheery voice, "I shorely hope I haven't caused you any trouble."

"Perish the thought!" Lola graced him with a dazzling smile. "Would you care for a glass of champagne, Mr. Hall?"

"Why, thank you, ma'am!" Starbuck seated himself and tilted his hat at a rakish angle. "Don't mind if I do."

"To the victor!" Lola lifted her glass in a toast. "A man as good as his brag—cock of the walk!"

Starbuck let go a great bellywhopper of a laugh. He filled Johnson's empty glass and drank to her toast. The crowd slowly lost interest, and people at nearby tables went back to their own affairs. The ivory-tickler struck up a lively tune and the wrestling match on the dance floor once more resumed. Lola leaned forward, still smiling a devastating smile. Her voice was low and conspiratorial.

"That was some entrance you made, lover!"

"Worked out pretty good." Starbuck sipped champagne, watching her over the rim of his glass. "Got us together and let everybody know Lee Hall's in town. You just keep acting like I've charmed you out of your drawers. That way we can have a drink every night and swap information."

"No problem," Lola said brightly. "The joker you whipped really was bull o' the woods! Nobody will come anywhere near me—not when you're around."

"What's the story on Johnson?"

"I know everyone is scared witless of him! Even Stimson—the owner of this joint—caters to him. He asked me as a special favor to have a drink with the big gorilla. We were just getting acquainted when you showed up."

"How're things otherwise?"

"Christ!" Lola spat in a sibilant tone. "It's no wonder Stimson offered me a thousand a week. To put it charitably, the boys in Virginia City are a little uncouth. You ought to hear what they shout when I'm onstage!"

Starbuck smiled. "Never saw a miner yet with any class. Course, as I recall, you asked to come here. Nobody twisted your arm."

"You're all heart!" Lola said sweetly. "Maybe I shouldn't tell you what I've learned by keeping my eyes open!"

"No more wisecracks," Starbuck promised. "What'd you find out?"

"Well, for one thing," Lola said in a hushed voice, "there's something funny about Stimson. I noticed it today, when I was rehearsing with the band. He's got an office upstairs, and there was a regular parade through there all afternoon." She paused, toying with her champagne glass. "From the looks of them, they're all part of the sporting crowd. I've been around enough to recognize the type."

Starbuck was thoughtful a moment. "Hard to say what it means. Offhand, though, I'd doubt it has anything to do with the gang."

"That's the other thing!" Lola's eyes got big and round. "So far as I can tell—there's no gang!"

"No gang?" Starbuck looked at her seriously. "How'd you come by that?"

"I got the musicians talking. We were taking a break, and I just casually mentioned I'd heard about the stagecoach robbers. Told them I was scared to death the whole trip over here from Dillon."

"What was their reaction?"

"Oh, the robbers are real enough! Nobody denies that. But everyone believes it's several gangs, all operating on their own. Not a single word—not even a rumor—about *one* gang leader!"

"I hope to hell they're wrong," Starbuck said, troubled. "Otherwise we're here on a wild-goose chase."

"Speak of the devil!"

Starbuck glanced around and saw the musicians drifting into the orchestra pit. He turned back to Lola. "Time for the first show?"

"Almost." She pulled a face. "Will you wait till I'm through?"

"Not tonight. We don't want to give anyone ideas."

"I'm staying at the Virginia Hotel—room two-oh-four—in case you get any ideas."

"We'll see," Starbuck said evasively. "However it works out, let me contact you. Don't make any moves on your own."

"Anything you say, lover." Lola rose and gave him a brilliant smile. Her voice was gay and pitched loud enough to be heard over the drone from nearby tables. "I do want to thank you for a lovely conversation, Mr. Hall. Drop around anytime! You're always welcome."

"I shorely will, Miss Montana! That's a puredee promise!"

Lola nodded and walked toward a door leading backstage. Starbuck lit a cigarette and poured himself another glass of champagne. He decided to stay for the show and then move on to another joint. While he hadn't mentioned it, he was registered at the Virginia Hotel, and he thought he might look in on her later. He was abruptly jerked back to the present when a man halted beside the table.

"Evening."

"Hullo." Starbuck looked at him through a wreath of smoke. "Help you with something?"

"I'd like to talk with you a minute. Mind if I have a chair?"

"All depends on who's asking."

"Omar Stimson. I own the place."

Starbuck shrugged and waved his hand. "Take a load off your feet."

"Thanks."

Stimson was short and heavyset, paunchy around the middle. His face was moonlike and his nose was veined red from an intimate acquaintance with liquor. A long black cigar jutted from his mouth. He lowered himself into a chair.

"You're pretty handy with your fists."

"I get by," Starbuck allowed. "That fellow a friend of yours?"

"Johnson?" Stimson shook his head. "No, he's just one of the regulars. Asked me to introduce him to Miss Montana, and I did the honors."

"Way he acted, anybody would've thought he had a bill of sale on the lady."

"Johnson's used to doing the pushing, not vice versa."

"The bigger they are," Starbuck said stolidly, "the harder they fall."

Stimson munched his cigar, nodded wisely. "If you don't mind my asking, what's your name?"

Starbuck gave him a wooden look. "Lee Hall."

"Uh-huh." Stimson's expression was one of veiled disbelief. "Where do you call home, Mr. Hall?"

"Texas." Starbuck took a slow drag, exhaled smoke. "New Mexico. I drift around."

"What's your line of work?"

"Little of this and a little of that."

"Jack-of-all-trades, huh?"

"You ask a lot of questions."

"No offense," Stimson said quickly. "I was just impressed by the way you manhandled Johnson. I'm always on the lookout for a good bouncer."

Starbuck grinned ferociously. "I don't hire out. You might say I'm self-employed."

"Of course." Stimson chuckled a fat man's chuckle. "A little of this and a little of that."

"Beats working for a living."

"I suspect it does." Stimson heaved himself to his

feet. "Well, enjoy your stay in Virginia City, Mr. Hall."

"I intend to, Mr. Stimson. I shorely do."

Stimson nodded pleasantly and walked away. Starbuck laughed to himself, inwardly delighted with the evening's work. He thought things had gone even better than he'd planned. Lola would continue to ferret out choice tidbits on the local grapevine. Word of the drubbing he'd given Johnson would spread rapidly. Omar Stimson would doubtless let it drop he was using an alias and was a mite touchy about questions. All of which, lumped together, would fuel the impression he wanted circulated throughout Virginia City.

Lee Hall was a man slightly windward of the law.

Chapter Four

Starbuck spent the next three days prowling around town. Every mining camp, much like a river at flood tide, had hidden undercurrents. He meant to determine the order of things in Virginia City.

Starting uptown, he leisurely reconnoitered the camp. His job was made easier by virtue of the brawl with Pete Johnson. The sporting crowd evidenced a strong dislike for Johnson, and not without reason. A bullyboy, overbearing and obnoxious, he was noted for throwing his weight around. According to Lola, the rumor was he'd been put out of commission for a week, perhaps longer. His jaw was broken and his gonads were swollen the size of gourds. The upshot was that Starbuck, in the guise of Lee Hall, had become the talk of Virginia City. The sporting crowd treated him with deference and applauded the neat job he'd made of Pete Johnson. He was welcome wherever he went.

The dives along Wallace Street proved to be a lode of information. Starbuck was a good listener and versed in the techniques of subtle interrogation. He concentrated on saloons and gaming dens, for these were the principal gossip mills of any boomtown. He talked with gamblers and pimps, bartenders and grifters, and what seemed a legion of ordinary miners. Once they were engaged in conversation, he guilefully prompted them along with rapt interest and a few leading questions. Upon parting, he knew virtually everything they knew, and no one the wiser. He slowly pieced together the story of those hidden undercurrents.

John Duggan, president of the Virginia City Mining Association, was not altogether the civic partisan he pretended. Nor was his concern over vigilantes wholly altruistic. There was, instead, bad blood between Duggan and Wilbur X. Lott, the man behind the vigilante movement. The problem stemmed from economic conflict and opposing interests. Duggan was the stalking horse for financiers and businessmen, the growing cadre of mine owners. Lott, who worked his own claim on Daylight Creek, was the self-appointed champion of the independent miners. The collision was all but ordained, one that sooner or later touched every mining camp. Virginia City was merely the latest battleground.

All gold bonanzas, in the beginning, were strictly surface operations. The gold was discovered above ground, generally along creeks or rivers. The most common method of extracting dust and nuggets from loose earth was known as placer mining. The dirt was shoveled into a rocker, which was nothing more than a crude sluice box. The whole affair was rocked back and forth while water moved the material down a series of flumes. Since gold was heavier than dirt, it dropped to the bottom and was trapped there. A placer miner needed little more than a strong back and some ordinary tools. His claim was his ticket to independence. He worked it himself, and *all* the dust went into his poke.

Quartz mining, on the other hand, was the search for gold below ground. A tunnel was sunk in the earth, or burrowed into a mountain, and followed the vein wherever it traveled. The tunnel was shored with wooden beams, and the quartz was dislodged from the earth with blasting powder. Then the loose quartz was run through an ore crusher to separate the gold. The process required stamp mills and heavy equipment, and men to work the mines. Which in turn required enormous amounts of capital, and investors. There was, moreover, the need to acquire surrounding claims; only in that manner could the vein be followed and the investment protected. Complicated and costly, it was a game that attracted wealthy businessmen and moneyed entrepreneurs. Once quartz mining began, it generally tolled the death knell for placer miners. There was no room for small operators when the stakes were boosted sky-high.

So the lines were now drawn. On one side stood John Duggan and the members of the mining association. On the other stood Wilbur X. Lott and the independent miners. The two sides were at loggerheads, and there would be no compromise. The robbers, in effect, were being used as the catalyst in a power struggle. The real issue was control of Virginia City and untold millions in gold. The vigilante movement was merely an outgrowth of that conflict. A fight be-

tween the little dog and the big dog over a bone. A
golden bone.

Starbuck was hardly surprised. Always the cynic,
he knew that men's motives were seldom what they
appeared. Ambition and greed were often cloaked in
the pious rhetoric of do-gooders. Yet his curiosity
about the vigilantes had led quite naturally to questions about the robbers, and there he was surprised.
All he'd heard tended to confirm what Lola had told
him. No one gang was thought to be responsible for
the robberies. Nor was there the slightest hint of a he-
wolf gang leader. The general consensus was that cutthroats and robbers infested the countryside. It was
considered to be a murderous form of free enterprise,
with devil take the hindmost.

The thought occurred that he was somehow being
used by John Duggan and the mining association.
Then, upon reflection, he concluded it was unlikely.
Horace Griffin, the Wells Fargo superintendent, was
not easily hoodwinked. Nor was Munro Salisbury, the
stageline owner, a man given to jumping at shadows.
In their opinion, one gang was responsible for the
express-shipment holdups. That in no way discounted
the possibility that other robbers were preying on lone
miners. Their belief, quite simply, was that the number of stage holdups almost certainly indicated an organized gang and a Judas. For all he'd heard to the
contrary, Starbuck still agreed with their argument.
Some inner voice told him it was so.

One other point seemed beyond dispute. Sheriff
Henry Palmer was apparently a hell-on-wheels lawman. Apart from the robbers he'd captured—and han-

ged—he had personally killed four outlaws in gunfights. The common wisdom, expressed by miners as well as the sporting crowd, tagged him a resourceful and dedicated peace officer. At the same time, everyone thought he was faced by staggering odds. His war on the criminal element, despite a full complement of deputies, was hampered by the mountainous terrain and the sheer number of outlaws. While it was an uphill battle, his efforts had brought accolades from as far away as the territorial capital. The attorney general of Montana had nominated him for the post of U.S. marshal. The honor had boosted his reputation yet another notch in Virginia City.

Starbuck briefly considered contacting the sheriff. Then, on second thought, he rejected the idea. When working undercover, he seldom revealed himself to local peace officers. Some were resentful and jealous of outsiders, and others were simply more hindrance than help. There were exceptions, but those were lawmen Starbuck knew personally. They belonged to a loose confederation of peace officers he corresponded with regularly, and all of them had contributed in some fashion to his rogues' gallery. Even with them, however, he exercised great caution. Too many men liked to hear themselves talk, and a slip of the lip might very well imperil his life. So he was doubly cautious about Henry Palmer. There were too many factions at work in Virginia City, and the sheriff was still an unknown quantity. All in all, a lone hand seemed the wiser option.

By his third day in town, Starbuck was forced to admit he was stymied. He had unearthed a great deal of interesting, and sometimes intriguing, information. But none of it was especially germane to his investigation. Nothing he'd uncovered thus far shed any light on either the gang or the gang leader. In fact, everything he had learned tended to obscure an already murky situation. He decided to let it rest for a couple of days. He was by now a familiar figure around the camp, and he'd managed to get thick with the sporting crowd. Sooner or later someone would say something worth hearing, and his years as a manhunter had taught him a vital lesson. Only the killing was done swiftly. The stalk should never be rushed.

Every evening he made it a practice to drop by the Gem Theater. He stayed only for one show, and he never attempted to monopolize Lola's time. She joined him at his table, and for appearance's sake he always ordered a bottle of champagne. They laughed and flirted, and so far as anyone could tell, he was simply one of her many admirers. She related whatever she'd learned during the day, and once the champagne was finished it was generally time for the second show. He then tried his hand at faro or went on to another dive. Thus far, he had steered clear of her hotel room, restricting all contact to the theater. He was still leery of arousing suspicion.

Tonight, as was his habit, Starbuck drifted into the Gem as the first show got under way. Stimson greeted him jovially and ushered him to a ringside table. A waiter quickly materalized with a bottle of champagne and two glasses. Starbuck lit a smoke and settled back to enjoy the show. Lola sang a couple of sultry ballads, all alone onstage, the house gone quiet as a church. Then a chorus line pranced out of the wings, and she led them in a rollicking, sometimes bawdy, dance number. The crowd gave her a thunderous ovation, and she disappeared with one last flash of her magnificent legs. The next act, a team of acrobats, romped out to mild indifference. The Gem's clientele wasn't much on gymnastic feats.

A short while later Lola appeared from backstage. She wandered through the audience, pausing here and there to chat a moment and accept congratulations. Then, fending off a drunken miner, she made her way to Starbuck's table. He rose with a courtly bow and held out her chair. She favored him with a beguiling smile.

"Good evening, Mr. Hall."

"Miss Lola." Starbuck seated himself and poured champagne. "You sure wowed 'em tonight! Yessir, that was some show."

"Aren't you sweet!"

"Compliments come easy where you're concerned, Miss Lola."

"You sly rogue!" Her voice suddenly dropped. "God, I couldn't wait to get out here! I'm onto something, lover. Something important!"

"Stay cool!" Starbuck cautioned. "Half the people in this joint are still eyeballing you."

Lola laughed as though he'd said something marvelously amusing. "I've been bringing the musicians along slow and easy. They're all boozers and the biggest gossips in the world. Just before the show, one of them got me aside on the q.t. and gave me an earful. I mean the lowdown!"

"Let's hear it."

"Have you ever heard of Doc Carver?"

"Not that I recollect."

"Well, hold on to your hat, lover! You won't forget him after tonight."

"Is he a local man?"

"No," Lola said softly. "He's a sharpshooter. You know, one of those trick-shot artists. Stimson brought him here early this summer for a limited engagement. But his act was so popular he was held over almost two months."

"So what's that got to do with anything?"

"Only this," Lola replied, her tone low and urgent. "His daughter was murdered."

"Daughter?" Starbuck looked confused. "You just lost me."

"She was part of the act! Carver shot cigarettes out of her mouth and all those other routines sharpshooters do. From what I gather, she was a real beauty. Gave the act a touch of class!"

"Why was she murdered?"

"Now it gets interesting!" Lola's face was animated, eyes flashing. "My musician friend says she got in over her head. She learned something she wasn't supposed to know, and it got her killed."

"What was it she learned?"

"Nobody knows." Lola collected herself, casually took a sip of champagne. "Here's the topper, though! The rumor's all over town it had something to do with the stage robberies."

"Any names?" Starbuck demanded. "Some idea as to who killed her?"

"Not a peep," Lola said ruefully. "There was talk that she was having an affair—"

"Wait a minute!" Starbuck broke in. "You mean she was sleeping with somebody?"

"So everyone thought! But no one had any inkling of who, or where she met him, or anything else. She was a very secretive little lady!"

"When was she killed?"

"Not quite a month ago."

"What happened to her father?"

Lola's eyes danced merrily. "He took off like a ruptured goose! Everyone thinks he knew who did it and why—and skipped town to save his own neck!"

"If he knew so much, then why wasn't he killed?"

"Search me, lover! I'm just telling you what I was told."

Starbuck mulled it over a moment. "Any idea where he skipped to?"

"Believe it or not—" Lola laughed. "He joined Buffalo Bill's Stage Show!"

"Bill Cody?"

"The one and only!" Lola bobbed her head. "There was an item in the paper. He went straight as a bumblebee from here to North Platte, Nebraska. Cody's theatrical troupe headquarters there."

"I'll be go to hell!"

"Will it help? Does it give you a lead of any kind—a clue?"

"I don't know," Starbuck said slowly. "I'll have to think on it."

"Well, I've got another show to do. Will you wait

on me? I damn sure don't want to be kept in suspense until tomorrow night!"

"Tell you what." Starbuck hoisted his glass, pretended to toast her. "You go on to the hotel after the show. I'll meet you in your room."

"Goody, goody! Looks like my lucky night!"

Lola downed her champagne and hurried backstage. Starbuck sat like a dreamy vulture, staring off into space. After a while, he rose from his chair and dropped a double eagle on the table. His expression was still bemused.

He walked from the theater as the band thumped to life.

Lola entered the hotel shortly after midnight. One of the Gem's bouncers had escorted her from the theater. His presence ensured that she would not be bothered by late-night drunks and rowdies on the street. He saw her into the lobby, then bid her good night. She waved to the desk clerk and swiftly mounted the stairs.

On the second floor, she proceeded along the hallway to her room. She unlocked the door and stepped inside. A match flared in the darkness, and she uttered a sharp gasp. Chuckling softly, Starbuck lit a table lamp, trimmed the wick low. She locked the door and turned to face him. Her voice was shaky.

"You scared the living bejesus out of me!"

"Sorry." Starbuck dropped into one of the chairs beside the table. "I wanted to avoid being seen. Figured the odds were better if I let myself in before you arrived."

"So you picked the lock?"

"One of my minor talents." Starbuck motioned to the other chair. "Come sit down. We've got some talking to do."

Lola tossed her cape on the bed and crossed to the chair. She studied his dour expression a moment. "Why do I get the feeling it's bad news?"

"Not bad, exactly," Starbuck remarked. "But there's been a change of plans. I have to go to North Platte."

"Omigawd!" Lola yelped. "You're going after Doc Carver!"

"Got no choice." Starbuck's square features creased with worry. "I've thought it through, and it's the only way. Unless I got lucky, I could hang around here till doomsday before I turned up a lead. A talk with Carver might do the trick *muy pronto*."

"Then you believe it—about him and his daughter?"

"I believe she was murdered. Whether or not it had anything to do with the robbers—" Starbuck lifted his hands in a shrug. "I reckon I'll have to let Carver tell me that."

"Why else would he have run?"

"That's got me puzzled." Starbuck massaged his jaw. "Apparently it's pretty common knowledge he joined Cody's show. So if somebody was afraid he'd spill the beans, why not go to North Platte and kill him? He's just as much a threat there as he was here."

"Maybe the robbers—the gang leader—didn't read the paper."

"Maybe," Starbuck conceded. "Guess I won't know till I ask."

Lola cocked her head to one side. "What makes you think he'll talk? After all, his daughter was murdered and he hasn't spoken up yet. He might tell you to take a hike!"

Starbuck smiled. "I'll reason with him."

"God help him!" Lola said with feigned horror. "When do you leave?"

"The end of the week," Starbuck told her. "We'll leave right after you finish your engagement at the Gem. That way, I'll know you got out of here safe and sound."

"Oh, for—"

"No argument!" Starbuck halted her protest with an upraised palm. "You're not staying here alone. I've already made up my mind, and the discussion's closed!"

"You're a worrywart! I'm perfectly capable of looking after myself!"

"Only one trouble." Starbuck was deadly earnest. "You've got a taste for undercover work and you're good at it. If I left you here, you'd keep on digging. I won't take that chance."

"Don't be too sure!" Lola's lips curved in a teasing smile. "I didn't have time to tell you everything tonight. You might want me to stick around . . . when you hear about Stimson."

"Stimson?" Starbuck returned her gaze steadily. "What about him?"

"He's a crook!" Lola announced. "You remember the musician who told me about Doc Carver? Well, he also told me that Stimson controls the vice in Virginia City. The gambling dives, the whorehouses, everything! They all pay a percentage off the top, or else they don't operate. Stimson's word is law, and he runs things with an iron fist!"

"Your musician friend?" Starbuck said wonderingly. "How come he blabs everybody's secrets to you? That's the part I'd like to hear."

"Oh, call it a woman's wiles!" Lola gave him a sexy wink. "I told you I have a way with men. And, sweetie, it sure makes undercover work easier. God, does it ever!"

"All the more reason to get you out of here! You're liable to put the whammy on the wrong man and wind up in hot water."

"What about Stimson?" Lola implored. "I'm positive he'd extend my engagement another week! Let me stay, and I'll bet anything I get the goods on him. I just know it!"

"No soap," Starbuck said stubbornly. "You leave on the same stage with me."

"Spoilsport!" Lola stuck out her bottom lip. "You're passing up the chance to blow this town wide open. And I'm the girl who could do it!"

"You're forgetting one thing."

"What's that?"

"I wasn't hired to get Stimson. I'm after a gang of robbers . . . not some sleazy vice boss."

"Well—" Lola replied with a charming little shrug. "It would have been fun, anyway. And besides, he's such an oily bastard he deserves to get caught!"

"Got you hooked, doesn't it?"

"Hooked?"

"Undercover work," Starbuck observed dryly. "You act like a kid turned loose in a candy store."

Lola stood and languidly moved to his chair. She sat down in his lap, encircled his neck with her arms. Her voice was furry velvet and she put her mouth to his ear.

"Luke?"

"Um-hum?"

"Would you let me work with you again . . . on another case?"

"I might."

"Promise?" she purred. "Cross your heart?"

"Think it'd be worth my while?"

"Why don't I give you a sample and let's see?"

"Sounds fair to me."

Lola extinguished the lamp. She kissed him and her tongue darted inside his mouth. She squirmed her bottom into his groin and felt his manhood harden. Her hand drifted like a tingling snowflake down his chest, then went lower still. She slowly unbuttoned his pants.

Starbuck suddenly rose and carried her to bed.

Chapter Five

Starbuck pulled into North Platte on the afternoon train. The Union Pacific depot was large and sprawling, constructed of brick. A two-story hotel abutted the rear of the station house, with a wing extending eastward. He went inside and took a room for the night.

The trip from Virginia City had consumed the better part of a week. By stage and train, he and Lola had made their way to Denver. There he'd laid over a night and then caught the northbound for Wyoming. At Laramie, he had switched to the Union Pacific and continued on to Nebraska. The roundabout route was tedious and wearing. Yet, for all the inconveniences, it had relieved him of a major worry. Lola's brief stint as an undercover operative had ended with her engagement at the Gem Theater. She was once more safely in Denver.

No longer in disguise, Starbuck registered at the hotel under his own name. He was pressed for time, and he thought it would speed things along if he approached Carver openly. After dropping his warbag in the room, he returned to the lobby. His inquiry about Buffalo Bill's theatrical headquarters was apparently routine stuff in North Platte. The desk clerk simply pointed him in the right direction, noting it was a short walk. Outside, he turned west on Front Street.

The town's main thoroughfare bordered the railroad tracks. Once a frontier outpost, the settlement had expanded along the banks of the South Platte River. A cavalry cantonment, Fort McPherson, was the hub of the community. The business district was centered on the fort, and behind it, toward the river, was a growing residential area. Stores and shops lined Front Street, but North Platte was still very much a small town. A brisk walk in any direction ended on open prairie.

Some distance past the fort, Starbuck stopped before a modest frame house. To the rear was a large barn and a log corral. A group of men, dressed in range clothes and vaquero costumes, was standing outside the barn. Several Indians were squatting in a patch of shade near the corral. Their faces were smeared with war paint, and their manner of dress pegged them as Pawnees. All of them looked like actors in a traveling stock company.

Starbuck circled the house and walked toward the barn. The loafers standing outside gave him a quick once-over, then went back to talking. He entered through the wide double doors and found himself in what appeared to be an office. The front of the barn had been partitioned off, and two men were busily at work. One was seated behind a table littered with correspondence and ledgers. The other sat at a rolltop desk, scribbling furiously with pen and paper. The wall behind them was emblazoned with show posters. Among the more eye-catching were advertisements for *The King of Border Men* and *The Scouts of the Plains*. All of them depicted Buffalo Bill in epic proportions.

The man behind the table glanced up. "Do something for you?"

Starbuck approached and halted. "I'd like to see Doc Carver."

"He's out."

"How about Bill Cody?"

"He's busy."

"Tell him it's important."

"I handle important matters for Colonel Cody."

"Who are you?"

"John Burke, manager of the company."

"Then you won't do." Starbuck's tone was flat and hard. "Suppose you just tell Cody I'm here."

"Now—" Burke hesitated, looked deeper into the pale stare. "What's the name?"

"Luke Starbuck."

"He doesn't like interruptions . . . but I'll try."

"You do that."

Burke stood and moved to a door at the end of the room. He rapped once and entered. The other man turned from his desk, watching Starbuck a moment. Then he dropped his pen and rose, walking forward.

"Are you *the* Luke Starbuck—the detective?"

"Usually," Starbuck acknowledged. "You've got the advantage on me."

"Oh!" The man smiled sheepishly. "I'm Prentiss

Ingraham, Mr. Starbuck. I write all of Bill's adventure stories."

Starbuck was familiar with the product, if not the man. It was common knowledge that one or more ghostwriters churned out the dime novels about Buffalo Bill. The stories were pure invention, written in a florid style, and pandered to the public's taste for hair-raising derring-do. The plots generally subjected Buffalo Bill to capture by savage Indians or desperados; by some ingenious trick he always managed to foil the villains and emerge victorious. A great many people accepted the stories as literal truth.

Around Denver, where Cody's stage show had appeared several times, he was known as See Me Bill. The nickname derived from his flamboyant style of dress and his passion for telling big windies about himself. His official autobiography, published not quite two years ago, merely served to reinforce the point. Westerners were now of the opinion that he was no longer able to distinguish between the dime-novel yarns and the reality of his years on the Plains. Starbuck, for his part, saw it as a sad commentary. He knew that Cody had served as chief of scouts for several cavalry regiments and had been awarded the Medal of Honor for bravery in action. He thought the truth far more compelling than the fiction.

"I've read a couple of your stories," Starbuck remarked, nodding toward the desk. "You writing a new one?"

"No, not a novel," Ingraham explained. "I'm working on a new play. We open in Chicago week after next, and from there we tour the East. Bill always insists on something fresh—original—to kick off the season."

"How do you keep coming up with ideas?"

Ingraham grinned and tapped his head. "All a product of the imagination! Our audiences like them wild and woolly!"

Starbuck couldn't argue the point. For the past decade, the Buffalo Bill Combination had toured America. The stage shows were a mix of vaudeville and melodrama. The shooting exhibitions and roping acts were generally a prelude. The feature attraction was a play starring Bill Cody, some farfetched tale involving danger and damsels in distress. The show was booked solid every year, and every performance played to a full house. Buffalo Bill was by now an institution, almost a household word. Theater owners considered his show money in the bank.

"What we do," Ingraham went on, "doesn't compare with your work, Mr. Starbuck. I've followed your cases in the newspapers, and I must admit I'm fascinated by the detective business. Have you ever considered doing an autobiography?"

"If I do," Starbuck said with a note of irony, "I'll look you up, Mr. Ingraham. You did a helluva job for Cody."

"Oh, no, you're mistaken! Bill wrote that himself!"

"In here, Mr. Starbuck." Burke reappeared in the doorway. "Colonel Cody will see you now."

Starbuck smiled at Ingraham and turned away. He crossed the room, moving past Burke, and stepped into an inner office. The walls were decorated with Indian regalia and all manner of weapons, and several overstuffed chairs were grouped around a long table. As Starbuck entered, two men rose from their chairs. One of them he immediately identified as Bill Cody.

Buffalo Bill looked the part of a hero. He was easily six feet tall, with broad shoulders and the straight-arrow carriage of a soldier. He wore a goatee and mustache, and his hair hung in ringlets over his shoulders. He was attired in fringed buckskins and knee boots, and a brace of ivory-handled pistols were strapped around his waist. He grinned broadly and extended his hand.

"Welcome, Mr. Starbuck!"

"I appreciate your time, Mr. Cody."

Starbuck sensed he was somewhat ossified. Cody's eyes were slightly glazed and his breath smelled of liquor. All of which seemed to confirm his reputation as a boozer. Still, he was in dazzling good humor and clearly delighted by the interruption. He shook Starbuck's hand vigorously.

"I don't mind saying it's a pleasure to meet you, Mr. Starbuck! You are the premier detective of our fabled West! God strike me dead if you're not!"

Starbuck brushed aside the compliment. "Every cripple does his own dance."

"You're too modest!" Cody motioned the other man forward. "Let me introduce you to someone who chronicles the deeds of men such as ourselves. Luke Starbuck, meet Edward Judson. Otherwise known as Ned Buntline!"

"Mr. Starbuck." Buntline pumped his arm. "I've been an admirer of yours for years."

Starbuck was mildly surprised. A writer by trade,

Buntline was perhaps the best-known dime novelist of the day. There were many people who credited him as well with Bill Cody's success. Some years ago they had teamed up to produce the original stage show and several Buffalo Bill dime novels. Then, by all accounts, Cody had severed the partnership and sent Buntline packing. The writer's presence today made for interesting speculation.

"Don't stand on formality!" Cody trumpeted. "You boys grab a chair!"

"I wonder—" Starbuck stopped him with a gesture. "Would it be possible to speak with you in private? I don't mean to intrude, but it's important."

"You're not intruding!" Cody assured him. "We were just sitting around chewing the fat. Weren't we, Ned?"

Buntline got the hint. "Why don't I check with you later, Bill? That will give you time to think things over."

"Capital idea!" Cody agreed. "I'll sleep on it overnight."

"Tomorrow, then." Buntline glanced at Starbuck. "Hope to see you again, Mr. Starbuck."

Cody ushered him to the door with an arm around his shoulders. Buntline paused, talking quietly a moment, then went out. Cody firmly closed the door and turned back into the room.

"You showed up just in the nick of time, Mr. Starbuck."

"Oh?" Starbuck inquired. "How so?"

"That sorry bastard come all the way out here from New York! Since we busted up, his luck turned sour and he's looking for a meal ticket. He's got some damnfool notion I'll take him back."

"And you won't?"

"Never!" Cody struck a dramatic pose. "Nothing personal, you understand. We had what might be termed an artistic difference of opinion. Ned always ignored the facts of my life on the Plains! He chose to write plays that presented me as some godlike creature. Absolute tommyrot!"

"Whereas you wanted to tell it the way it happened?"

"Exactly!" Cody said in an orotund voice. "I believe in realism, Mr. Starbuck. I want the public to experience it as though they were there. I have a reputation to maintain!"

For Starbuck, any lingering doubts were dispelled. Cody had clearly fooled himself, lost touch with reality. He genuinely believed that Bill Cody the scout and Buffalo Bill the legend were one and the same. He saw himself as that intrepid hero depicted in the dime novels. It was self-deception at its worst, and almost laughable. The man standing before him was no longer Bill Cody. He was, instead, an illusion. The product of some hack writer's dizzy fantasies.

"I see your point," Starbuck said with a straight face. "Too bad Buntline lives in a dreamworld."

"Well, enough of my problems! Sit yourself down—can I call you Luke?—I never was much on ceremony."

"Sure thing, Bill." Starbuck smiled to himself, took a chair. "So far as I'm concerned, *Mister* was something folks called my dad."

"My sentiments exactly!" Cody said, seating himself. "Now, what can I do for you. Luke? I'd guess you're not here on a social visit."

"Your manager—Burke—didn't he tell you?"

"God, no! Burke wouldn't say 'boo' in front of Buntline. No love lost between those two!"

"Tell you the truth, I didn't want to say too much in front of Burke. What brought me here's a little delicate . . . confidential."

"I respect a confidence," Cody intoned. "Anything you say goes no further!"

"Figured as much," Starbuck said equably. "Just between us—I need to have a talk with Doc Carver."

"By jingo!" Cody's brow furrowed. "Is Carver in trouble with the law?"

"Nothing like that." Starbuck dismissed the idea with a wave of his hand. "When I asked outside, Burke told me Carver's not here. So I thought you could put me in touch."

"I'm afraid Burke misled you. Carver's not here—not on the property—but he's in North Platte. He has a suite at the hotel."

"The hotel?" Starbuck repeated. "Well, that takes a load off my mind. I started to think he'd flown the coop."

"Flown—" Cody stopped, frowning heavily. "Then he is in trouble!"

"What makes you say that?"

"I was a lawman myself once! Guess I've still got a nose for it when something smells fishy."

"I'll be dipped!" Starbuck prompted him. "So you actually wore a star?"

"U.S. deputy marshal!" Cody said proudly. "That was back in Kansas, the spring of '68. Some soldier boys deserted and stole a bunch of horses from the army. Bill Hickok and me tracked 'em all the way to Colorado and nabbed the whole gang. Killed three and brought back eleven prisoners!"

"You mean to say you worked with Wild Bill himself?"

"Other way around," Cody corrected him. "Hickok worked with me! I asked the army to deputize him and send him along as my assistant. That's how he got his start as a peace officer."

"Think of that!" Starbuck marveled. "You and Wild Bill!"

Cody preened like a peacock. "A good man and a stout friend! I taught him everything I knew, and he went on to become one of the great marshals of the West. Yessir, we made quite a team in the old days!"

Starbuck suspected it was all a windy tale. Yet Cody's garrulous bragging abruptly resolved another question in his mind. He'd been stalling, wondering how much he should reveal about Doc Carver. Now he decided the less said the better. No secret was safe with Buffalo Bill Cody.

"That's a mighty interesting story, Bill. Wish I had more time to jawbone, but time's awasting. I reckon I'd best be on my way."

"Hold on!" Cody said quickly. "I got myself sidetracked, and you never told me about Carver."

"Now that you mention it," Starbuck countered, "a minute ago you said you smelled something fishy. What'd you mean?"

"Oh, call it a hunch," Cody said with a shrug. "Carver's been off his feed lately. I just figured it had something to do with Virginia City."

"Virginia City?" Starbuck's look betrayed nothing. "I don't follow you."

Cody spread his hands in a bland gesture. "Carver finished an engagement there last month. I jumped to the conclusion he'd got himself in Dutch with the law."

"Couldn't prove it by me," Starbuck said, rising to his feet. "I'm here to get a deposition in a civil suit. Course, I'm not at liberty to disclose the details. You'll have to ask Carver about that."

"Maybe I will," Cody said absently. "I only asked because I wanted to make damn sure he'll be available next summer."

"What happens next summer?"

"Great thundering cannonballs!" Cody boomed jovially. "You haven't heard, have you? That's when the world gets a gander at my new Wild West Show!"

Starbuck appeared confounded. "What's a Wild West Show?"

"I'm quitting the stage!" Cody beamed. "P. T. Barnum has shown me the light! Last year he merged with James Bailey, and they're calling their circus the Greatest Show on Earth. Their first engagement was Madison Square Garden—and it was a sellout!"

"Yeah?" Starbuck was still bemused. "So what's that got to do with the West?"

"Spectacle!" Cody thundered gleefully. "The public wants spectacle and pageantry! That's exactly what I plan to give them. After this season, we're through with theaters. We'll play in outdoor arenas and circus tents, anywhere masses of people can be brought together. We'll make Barnum and his goddamn midget look like hayseeds!"

"Are you talking about a western circus?"

"Not bad, Luke!" Cody was caught up in a tempest of imagination. "Only it'll be more on the order of the old Roman circus. We'll have wild animals and trick-shot artists and all these new rodeo events. We'll have savage redskins and cavalry charges, and pitched battles on horseback. I tell you, it will revolutionize the show business!"

"A Wild West Show?" Starbuck shook his head, considering. "Yeah, I suppose something like that would go over big with easterners."

"It damn sure better!" Cody said with a rolling laugh. "Otherwise, I'll be scratching a poor man's ass. I've hocked my soul to put this show on the road!"

"Well, I wish you luck, Bill."

"I'm obliged, Luke. Good wishes from a man of your caliber means a lot! Wherever we're playing, you'll always be welcome. Buffalo Bill's personal guest!"

Starbuck thought it unlikely. He'd never had much use for showoffs and braggarts, men who forever sought the limelight. Their ways were foreign to him, and beneath their bravado he'd always detected something of the phony. Yet he found himself curiously ambivalent about Bill Cody. A scout who had won the Medal of Honor was no counterfeit hero.

Upon reflection, Starbuck decided the theatrics and the tall tales were a pardonable offense. He supposed there was room in the world for one See Me Bill.

And a Wild West Show.

Chapter Six

On the way uptown Starbuck scarcely noticed passersby. His thoughts turned from Cody to Doc Carver. He mentally reviewed all he knew about the sharpshooter.

William Carver was an easterner and a former physician. Some years earlier he had abandoned his medical practice for a more lucrative career in show business. Shooting exhibitions were all the rage, and Carver possessed a natural gift with firearms. In 1878, using a rifle, he had captured the coveted title World's Champion Marksman. Glass balls were thrown into the air, and he'd broken 5,500 out of 6,211 tries. From there, he had gone on to exhibitions throughout America and Europe. He billed himself as the Evil Spirit of the Plains, trading on the world's fascination with the West. While he claimed to have fought in the Minnesota Sioux uprising, he had never fired a gun in anger. He was a sawbones turned showman.

Apart from those details, Starbuck possessed little in the way of hard intelligence. He knew Carver's daughter had been murdered, and he knew Carver had hastily departed Virginia City. The rumors surrounding those events were unsubstantiated and therefore of limited value. Few men broke under interrogation unless confronted with cold facts. So today's game of wits would rely largely on bluff. A liberal amount of conjecture flavored with a dab of truth.

At the hotel, Starbuck inquired Carver's room number. The desk clerk informed him it was a suite and pointed him upstairs. On the second floor, he turned left and walked to the end of the hall. He rapped on the door marked 230 and waited. Then he rapped harder.

Some moments passed before the door opened. The man facing him was slim and lithely built, with a brushy mustache. His eyes were steady and phlegmatic, and his features were hawklike. He looked anything but the coward.

"May I help you?"

"Dr. W. F. Carver?"

"Yes."

"I'm Luke Starbuck." Starbuck smiled genially. "Bill Cody said you might be able to spare me a few minutes."

"For what purpose?"

"A private matter."

"I see." Carver hesitated a beat, then swung open the door. "Come in."

"Thank you."

The suite was large and comfortably furnished. On other side of the parlor there were doors leading to separate bedrooms. A bay window provided a southern exposure, overlooking the river. The parlor was well appointed, with a sofa and three easy chairs.

Vases filled with wild prairie flowers were scattered around the room.

Carver closed the door and turned into the parlor. He motioned Starbuck to a chair. "What business do you have with Cody?"

"None." Starbuck placed his hat on a table, sat down. "I'm a private detective."

"Starbuck?" Carver took a seat on the sofa, suddenly nodded. "Why, of course! You're the investigator from Denver. I've read about you in the *Police Gazette*."

"Don't believe a word of it," Starbuck said affably. "Their reporters seldom bother to check the facts."

Carver chuckled politely, crossed his legs. "Well now, what brings you to see me, Mr. Starbuck?"

"Virginia City." Starbuck let him hang a moment. "I'm investigating a series of murders."

"I—" Carver paused, his expression guarded. "I don't believe I understand."

"Are you familiar with Mr. Wilbur X. Lott?"

"Anyone who's been to Virginia City has heard of Wilbur Lott."

"Then you know several miners have been murdered there recently. He hired me to look into the matter."

"I understood Lott was the moving force behind the vigilante movement. Why would he hire a private detective?"

"He needs proof," Starbuck lied, deadpan. "Before he hangs anybody, he wants the evidence to back his play."

"I find that rather astounding . . . to say the least."

"Why so?"

"Lott's a scoundrel!" Carver informed him stiffly. "Nothing more than a demagogue with political ambitions!"

"You seem well informed about Virginia City."

"A man like Wilbur Lott attracts attention. In fact, he takes great pains to keep himself in the public eye."

"I never judge a client," Starbuck observed neutrally. "I just do the job I was hired to do."

"In that case"—Carver's eyebrows drew together in a frown—"why have you come to me?"

"Your daughter was murdered there last month."

Carver blinked, licked his lips. "I fail to see the connection."

"Lott thinks the murders and the stage holdups are the work of one gang."

"What has that to do with my . . . daughter?"

"Everything," Starbuck said pointedly. "There's talk around Virginia City that your daughter got herself mixed up with the stage robbers."

"That's preposterous!" Carver laughed, but it didn't ring true. "The most absurd thing I've ever heard!"

"Some folks say your daughter was murdered because she learned too much for her own good."

"Idle gossip and speculation, nothing more!"

"It gets worse." Starbuck fixed him with a piercing look. "I don't know how to say it tactfully, Dr. Carver. Your daughter was having an affair with somebody—"

"A lie! A damnable lie!"

"—and that somebody was responsible for her death."

"How dare you!" Carver shouted. "Nothing of the sort ever happened. Never!"

"No?" Starbuck's tone turned curt and inquisitorial. "Then how come you took off running?"

"What?"

"You almost set your pants on fire getting out of Virginia City! Who scared you off?"

"Nobody!" Carver shook his head wildly. "Nobody scared me off!"

"You're lying!" Starbuck said roughly. "Somebody killed your daughter, and you hauled ass before he could kill you."

Carver went ghastly pale. "You don't know what you're talking about."

"Come off it!" Starbuck pressed him. "Don't you want your daughter's murderer caught and hung?"

"I refuse to listen any longer! I want you to leave, Mr. Starbuck. Now!"

Starbuck gave him a jaundiced stare. "You'll listen till I'm done talking, Carver. If you're not concerned about your daughter, then maybe you ought to worry about yourself. You're living on borrowed time."

Carver regarded him with profound shock. "What do you mean?"

"Stop and think about it!" Starbuck's voice was harsh, insistent. "Wherever you are, you're still a threat to the killer. Distance doesn't mean a damn thing! One of these days he'll wake up to the fact that you could still identify him and put his head in a noose. That's the day he'll track you down and kill you."

"You're wrong." Carver averted his gaze. "That will never happen."

"Stop kidding yourself!" Starbuck persisted. "You've only got one hope—and that's me!"

"You?" Carver made an empty gesture with his hands. "How can you help?"

"Tell me his name," Starbuck said grimly. "I'll find him and kill him. That way, you're off the hook for good."

A shadow of anxiety clouded Carver's features. He passed a hand across his eyes and swallowed hard. He opened his mouth to say something, then appeared to change his mind. Finally he took a deep breath and exhaled slowly.

"There's a lawyer in Virginia City."

"What's his name?"

"George Hoyt."

"He killed your daughter?"

"No," Carver said hesitantly. "But he can tell you things . . . names."

"Whose names?" Starbuck asked. "Your daughter's killer? The stage robbers?"

"I won't say any more, Mr. Starbuck. I've already said too much. Go back to Virginia City and talk to George Hoyt. He knows everything . . . all of it."

"You're talking in riddles!"

"I'm sorry." Carver screwed up his features in a tight knot. "I won't involve myself any further. That's all I have to say."

Silence thickened between them. After long deliberation, Starbuck's face took on a sudden hard cast. His tone was offhand, almost matter-of-fact.

"One last thing."

"Yes?"

"Don't shoot off a wire to anybody in Virginia City."

"Why would I do that?"

"Who knows?" Starbuck said coldly. "But if you warn anybody about our little talk . . . you're a dead man."

"You have no need to threaten me, Mr. Starbuck."

"Let's just call it a word to the wise."

The hallway door opened. A young girl stepped into the parlor, her arms laden with packages. As she turned to place the bundles on a nearby table Carver bounded off the sofa and hurried across the room. His expression was instantly jocular and his voice light-hearted.

"There you are, my dear!" He kissed her soundly on the cheek. "How was your shopping?"

"Oh, fine, considering the selection—"

"We have a visitor!" Carver took her elbow and steered her forward. "One of the West's most respected private investigators. Permit me to introduce Mr. Luke Starbuck."

Starbuck stood. "Pleasure to meet you, ma'am."

The girl was in her early twenties. She was slender and quite attractive, with hazel eyes and glossy auburn hair. Though built along dainty lines, she carried herself erect and proud. Her smile was like a cameo come to life. She met Starbuck's gaze with a charming nod.

"Luke, this is Sally Devlin." Carver put his arm around the girl's waist and gave her a hug. "She's my new assistant. Joined the act after I returned from Virginia City."

"I'd say you did your act proud, Doc."

"Quite a bundle, huh?" Carver laughed and squeezed her tighter. "Don't know what I'd do without Sally! A pretty girl makes all the difference—in lots of ways!"

The girl blushed and dropped her eyes. Starbuck noted Carver's possessive attitude and thought it a cozy arrangement. She was easily half the sharpshooter's age, and he wondered how they'd got together. Then, just as quickly, he dismissed it from mind. Saloons and whorehouses were overrun with girls looking for escape. Sally Devlin wouldn't be the first to find it with an older man.

"Guess I'll be on my way, Doc."

"Luke, it's been a rare treat! Glad you could stop by."

Carver's jolly manner seemed wholly for the benefit of the girl. He walked Starbuck to the door and warmly shook hands. Then, at the last moment, he lowered his voice.

"Thanks for going along. I wouldn't want Sally to know anything about our talk. Might upset my love nest!"

"You just make sure you don't forget my word to the wise."

"I'm no fool, Luke. I heard you the first time."

Starbuck let go his hand and moved into the hall. Walking toward the stairs, his thoughts swiftly turned to Virginia City. And a lawyer named George Hoyt.

• • •

From the lobby, Starbuck headed for the hotel bar-room. He'd already decided to catch the morning westbound, and he reminded himself to check departure schedules. Yet he was still brooding on his conversation with Doc Carver. Something nagged at him, something he had overlooked.

Hard-won experience had taught him a vital lesson. Detective work was not altogether a matter of analytical reasoning. There was an element of instinct involved, and a man learned never to ignore those swift-felt impulses. His instinct told him he'd missed some critical lead while interrogating Carver. He couldn't put his thumb on it, and he was disturbed by the oversight. He thought a drink might wash away the cobwebs. A shot of popskull was known for its restorative effects.

The barroom was dim and pleasantly cool. The hour was early, and few of the tables were occupied. Only one man stood at the polished mahogany bar. Starbuck looked closer and saw that it was Ned Buntline. Too late, he tried to reverse course without being seen. Buntline spotted him and waved.

"Starbuck!" he called out. "Join me for a drink. I'm buying!"

Buntline was short and stocky, with bags under his eyes and sagging jowls. There was something baroque about him, even though his fingernails were gnawed to the quick and he had a nervous habit of twisting his mustache. The inveterate hustler, he was glib and clever, forever playing the angle. He was also a man with a checkered past.

Some years ago he had been caught bare-assed with another man's wife. He killed the husband in a duel and narrowly escaped being lynched by a mob. Later, following an altercation in New York's theater district, he had incited a riot. After being tried and convicted, he had spent a year in prison. Then, during the Civil War, he'd proved himself such a malcontent and troublemaker that he was eventually cashiered out of the Union Army. Upon returning to New York, he had at last found his true calling in life. He turned to purple prose and the printed page, where lies and chicanery were the accepted norm. He became a dime novelist.

Starbuck was aware of the details. Buntline's unsavory past had in turn been chronicled by the *Police Gazette* and several western newspapers. He wanted nothing to do with the writer, but he saw no way to avoid it. To decline a man's invitation was the worst of insults, and never done lightly. He agreed to one drink.

Buntline immediately launched into a tirade directed at Bill Cody. His tone was vituperative and his eyes blazed with resentment.

"Bastard!" he cursed sullenly. "After all I've done for him, you'd think he'd have a little gratitude!"

"Has he turned you down?"

"Not yet," Buntline said, his voice raw with bitterness. "But I see the handwriting on the wall. Tomorrow he'll give me the fast shuffle—so long and goodbye!"

Starbuck raised an uncertain eyebrow. "You figure he owes you something, that it?"

"He owes me everything!" Buntline replied angrily. "I *invented* Buffalo Bill Cody!"

"What do you mean . . . invented?"

Buntline laughed a tinny sound. "Before I took him underwing, he was just another dime-a-dozen army scout. I literally yanked him out of obscurity with the books and plays I wrote. I *sold* him to the public! I took a nobody and convinced America he was the white knight of the frontier. I made him famous—a legend!"

"Maybe so," Starbuck ventured. "Course, you had something to work with. A Medal of Honor winner isn't exactly a 'nobody.' "

"You think not?" Buntline said with wry contempt. "The true Scout of the Plains was a man named Frank North. The summer of '69, I came west to sign him up for a series of books. He turned me down cold, wouldn't touch it! So I looked around, and lo and behold, there stood Cody." He paused with a sourly amused look on his face. "Today Frank North's a nobody and Buffalo Bill's a national institution. You still think I didn't invent him?"

"If you did," Starbuck remarked succinctly, "then you should've stuck to the truth. These dime novels read like a kid's fairy tale. Nothing personal, but it's pure bullshit!"

"All history is bullshit," Buntline said, not in the least offended. "Whoever chronicles an event does so with an eye on posterity. Why should I be any different? I'm in the process of creating America's my-

thology! The fact that it's bullshit—based on false
heroes—means nothing. A hundred years from now
what I've written will be accepted as gospel truth.
All mythology—Greek, Norse, Anglo-Saxon—was
created the same way. Like it or not, legends aren't
born . . . they're invented."

"Cody will be sorry to hear it."

"No, not Cody!" Buntline scoffed. "Most of the
time he's so drunk he couldn't ride a hobbyhorse.
He'll die believing his own press clippings!"

"Well, like you said," Starbuck commented, "you
sold him to the public. I guess he's got to live up to
his reputation."

A crafty look came over Buntline's face. "I could
sell you twice as easy and twice as fast. Your reputation's the real article—documented fact!"

Starbuck squinted at him. "Are you offering to
make me part of your mythology?"

"Why not?" Buntline's eyes crinkled with a smile.
"In your case, there's no need for bullshit. You're a
legend waiting to be born!"

"Thanks all the same." Starbuck wagged his head.
"I reckon I'll have to pass."

"Stop and think!" Buntline admonished him. "Your
autobiography alone would make a fortune! Add dime
novels and stage appearances, and you'd end up ten
times as famous as Cody. Don't you understand? You
would *eclipse* Buffalo Bill!"

Starbuck tossed off his drink. "You ever tried to
poke hot butter in a wildcat's ear?"

"I don't get your point."

"You write so much as a word about me and you'll get the point goddamn quick. Savvy?"

"Your loss, not mine." Buntline shrugged, sipped at his whiskey. "By the way, I meant to ask earlier. What brought you to North Platte?"

"Well, I got wind you were here. So I came all the way from Denver to give Cody a message."

"Oh?" Buntline eyed him warily. "What message was that?"

"You've heard about his Wild West Show?"

"Yes?"

"I told him there's no room in it for a butthole named Buntline."

Starbuck compounded the insult. He fished a cartwheel dollar out of his pocket and dropped it on the counter. Then he turned and walked from the barroom.

His smile was jack-o'-lantern wide.

Chapter Seven

The Virginia City stage rolled to a halt outside the express office. One of the passengers on top of the coach was a ragtag, down-at-the-heels miner. His features were hidden by a floppy slouch hat and a wild, matted beard. He looked like a cocklebur with eyes.

Starbuck climbed down off the stage. To all appearances, he was another in the horde of miners flocking to Alder Gulch. He wore an oversize mackinaw and he moved with the stoop-shouldered gait of someone broken by hard times. The phony beard, which was a customized theatrical prop, completed his disguise. He collected a worn carpetbag from the luggage boot and shuffled toward the boardwalk. He was all but invisible in the crowds thronging the street.

The disguise was essential to the plan he'd formulated. His interrogation of Doc Carver had confirmed a chain of events in the case. He had established a tenuous link between the Carver girl's murderer and the stage robbers. He had also uncovered the name of a potential informant, George Hoyt. The next step was to grill the lawyer and add still another link to the chain. Yet there was no certainty that Hoyt could be trusted. So the approach would be made in the guise of a scruffy miner. Afterward, Starbuck would resurrect the hardcase and drifter, Lee Hall. The switch in disguises would provide him freedom of movement wherever the case might lead. No one, including Hoyt, would be the wiser.

Starbuck prudently avoided the Gem Theater. He bypassed as well the Virginia Hotel, where he'd stayed while Lola was in town. Instead, he checked into a sleazy fleabag near the red-light district. He requested a room to himself and paid in advance. Upstairs, he sprawled out on the bed and caught a nap. The trip from North Platte had been long and tiring, and he wanted his wits about him tonight. Toward sundown, he rose and inspected his disguise in the washstand mirror. Then he went in search of George Hoyt.

The lawyer's office was on Van Buren Street. Starbuck found it by checking along side streets as he wandered through the heart of town. A wooden sign hung over the door and a shaft of lamplight spilled through the window. He walked past and saw a lone man seated at a desk. After checking the street in both directions, he felt reasonably confident he'd gone unobserved. He turned and retraced his steps. He went through the door without knocking.

The man looked up from a desk littered with paperwork and open law books. He was tall and gangling and wore wire-rimmed glasses. His eyes were magnified through thick lenses, and his features were somehow ascetic in appearance. He smiled pleasantly.

"May I help you?"

"Are you George Hoyt?"

"Yes, I am."

Starbuck locked the door and pulled the blind on the window. Then he moved forward and took a chair in front of the desk. Hoyt's eyes were large and wide behind the glasses, as though seen through the wrong end of a telescope. His expression was one of mild befuddlement.

"Why did you lock the door?"

"We need to have a talk . . . in private."

"Who are you?"

"What's in a name?" Starbuck watched him, alert to the slightest reaction. "I was sent here by Doc Carver."

All the blood leached out of Hoyt's face. His lips worked silently, and an odd furtiveness settled over his features. When at last he spoke, there was a faint catch in his voice.

"What do you want?"

"For openers"—Starbuck fixed him with a steady, inquiring gaze—"tell me about the Carver girl's murder."

Hoyt's mouth popped open. "If Carver really sent you, then why didn't he tell you himself?"

"I heard his version," Starbuck said gruffly. "Now I want to hear yours."

"Until you've identified yourself, I can't see why I owe you an explanation."

"Humor me." Starbuck studied him with icy detachment. "Otherwise, I'm liable to get mad and break your glasses."

Hoyt blinked, swallowed hard. Then he very gingerly nodded his head. "I was escorting Alice back to her hotel one night. It was quite late, and the street was empty. Someone fired from the shadows and missed me. Alice was killed . . . by mistake."

"Why would somebody want to murder you?"

"In addition to my law practice, I serve as the county prosecutor. I've sent several men to the gallows and made a great many enemies. Apparently one of them tried to assassinate me."

"The men you prosecuted," Starbuck asked, "were those the outlaws caught by Sheriff Palmer?"

"Yes."

"And you figure one of their friends tried to even the score?"

"It would appear so."

"Where had you been the night Alice Carver was killed?"

Hoyt looked acutely uncomfortable. "At my home."

"You said it was late . . . how late?"

"A little after three in the morning."

Starbuck played a hunch. "You were having an affair with her, weren't you?"

"I loved her," Hoyt confessed. "I still do. What happened between us is none of your business."

"Maybe." Starbuck eyed him in silence a moment. "Let's go back to the killer. How was he tied in with robbers?"

"I didn't say he was."

"We both know different, don't we?"

"You're putting words in my mouth!"

"Like hell!" Starbuck said curtly. "What was his name?"

"I have no idea."

"Doc Carver says you do."

"Thats impossible!" Hoyt blurted. "It was dark and I never saw anyone. Carver knows that!"

"He's changed his mind. He thinks it was somebody connected with the robbers."

"Thinking doesn't make it so!"

"Don't spar with me!" Starbuck's jawline tightened. "Carver's convinced the killer was one of the gang. Maybe even the gang leader himself."

"Gang leader?" Hoyt's forehead blistered with sweat. "Carver's crazy! I know nothing of any gang!"

Starbuck was gripped by a strange feeling. Some complex of instinct and experience told him the lawyer wasn't lying. Yet there was an underthought struggling to take shape in his mind. He tried to focus on it, quickly give it form and meaning, but he drew a blank. He put it aside and returned to the interrogation.

"How come Carver believes there's a gang?"

"I'm afraid you'd have to ask him."

"I'm asking you!" Starbuck regarded him dourly. "And I want an answer . . . now."

Hoyt avoided his gaze. "I can't tell you what I don't know."

Starbuck examined his downcast face. "All right, let's try another tack. You said you're the county prosecutor?"

"That's correct."

"So you have considerable dealings with Sheriff Palmer?"

"Yes, I do."

"What's his opinion?" Starbuck demanded. "Does he think there's a gang?"

"Not one gang," Hoyt said lamely. "I seriously doubt anyone in town believes that."

"How about the stagecoach robberies?" Starbuck inquired skeptically. "Has Palmer ever indicated—even hinted—that he thought they were the work of one gang?"

"No," Hoyt replied vaguely. "Not to my knowledge."

"So Alice Carver's death was a mistake? Somebody was after you and got her instead. That's your story?"

An indirection came into Hoyt's eyes. "Yes, that's exactly how it happened. A tragic accident."

"And the gang wasn't involved?"

"Who are you?" Hoyt said, his voice clogged. "Why are you trying to make me admit something that never happened?"

"Doc Carver hired me." Starbuck paused, gave him a narrow look. "Whatever his reasons are, he decided your story's a load of hogwash. He sent me here to kill whoever murdered his daughter."

Hoyt stared at him, aghast. "I don't believe you! Carver's not that big a fool!"

"You're the fool," Starbuck countered. "You're holding out on me, and that could buy you a world of grief."

"I've told you the truth!"

"Not the whole truth," Starbuck pointed out. "Somebody killed Carver's daughter and threatened his life. That's why he hightailed it out of town. I think you know that somebody's name."

Hoyt pursed his lips as if his teeth hurt. "You will never make me believe you're working for Doc Carver. It just doesn't make sense!"

"Believe what you want," Starbuck said, getting up. "Only keep it to yourself. I wouldn't want anybody to know we had ourselves a chat."

"No one would listen even if I told them."

Starbuck walked to the door, then turned back. "I'll be around awhile. Don't let your lip slip, or you're liable to see me again."

"Very well," Hoyt said hollowly. "You have my word on it."

The door opened and closed, and Starbuck was gone. George Hoyt pulled out a handkerchief and mopped his forehead. Then he seemed to wilt, staring blankly at the door.

His eyes were rimmed with fear.

The Gem Theater was packed. The barroom was doing a brisk business, and large crowds were gathered around the gaming tables. Onstage, a juggler played to an indifferent audience.

Starbuck stood at the bar. Earlier, he'd returned to his seedy hotel room and performed a change in character. The miner's outfit, along with the phony beard, had gone into his carpetbag. Then he'd donned his old garb and plastered the handlebar mustache in place with spirit gum. Waiting until the desk clerk was busy, he had slipped out of the hotel unobserved. The carpetbag had been consigned to an alley trash heap, and he'd made his way to the Gem. He was now in the guise of Lee Hall.

Watching the show, he was aware of the looks from those around him. The fight with Pete Johnson was still remembered, and word would quickly spread that he was back in town. His purpose was to make himself visible and put the grapevine to work. Whatever he'd hoped to learn from George Hoyt, the grilling had proved a washout. He was convinced the lawyer had lied, but he was reluctant to push too hard too fast. He planned to wait a couple of days, allowing the pressure to build, and then try again. In the meantime, he would take another stab at his original scheme. He would let it be known that Lee Hall, the toughnut and drifter, was available. If there actually was a gang, the message would be passed along soon enough. All he could do was dangle the bait and await a nibble.

Omar Stimson, the Gem's owner, stopped by and bought him a drink. Starbuck played it mysterious about his absence from town. His response to Stimson's questions was a cryptic smile mixed with vague doubletalk. He left the impression he'd been involved in something slightly windward of the law.

While they were chatting, Pete Johnson walked through the door. He spotted Starbuck at the bar and halted in his tracks. Starbuck returned his glowering look with a wooden expression. The staring contest ended when Johnson blinked first. He turned on his heel and marched out the door with a stiff-legged stride. Starbuck chuckled softly.

"Guess he recollects our last go-round."

"Watch yourself," Stimson warned. "Johnson's a sore loser. He's been known to carry a grudge."

"That's his problem," Starbuck said lightly. "I don't look for trouble, but I'm always willing to oblige."

"Just thought I'd mention it."

"I appreciate the advice."

Stimson wandered off into the crowd. Starbuck had another drink, pleased by the incident. The vice boss of Virginia City apparently held him in some esteem. It was the sort of thing that would draw attention and thereby peg his reputation a notch higher. After finishing his drink, he decided to make the rounds. The more dives he visited, the faster the word would spread. And perhaps, with a little luck, he would get a nibble.

Outside the theater, he eased through a knot of miners ganged around the entrance. Then he stepped off the boardwalk and angled toward a gaming den on the far corner. He was almost to the middle of the street when a slug nicked the shoulder of his coat. A split second later the report of a gun sounded directly behind him. All thought suspended, he acted on reflex alone. He dodged sideways, pulling his Colt as a second bullet whistled past. Then he hit the ground in a rolling dive, dimly aware of men stampeding in every direction. On the third roll he spun himself about, flat on his belly. He thumbed the hammer and brought the sixgun to bear.

A third shot kicked dust in his face. He saw Pete Johnson standing in an alleyway, pistol extended at arm's length. Starbuck's finger feathered the trigger, and the Colt spat a sheet of flame. Then, with no more than a pulsebeat between shots, he emptied the gun. Johnson was driven backward as though struck by lightning. His arms windmilled crazily and the impact of the slugs sent him reeling in a strange, nerveless dance. He slammed into the wall of the theater; then his knees collapsed and he dropped his pistol. He pitched raglike to the ground. An eerie stillness settled over the street.

Starbuck pushed to his feet and began shucking empty shells. He reloaded as he walked to the alley. There he stopped and stood for a moment looking down at the body. All five shots were in the chest, less than a handspan apart. He grunted to himself and holstered the Colt. Then he caught a flicker of movement out of the corner of his eye. Omar Stimson stepped off the boardwalk and halted beside him.

"Looks like Johnson was feeling lucky."

"Sorry bastard!" Starbuck cursed savagely. "He tried to backshoot me!"

Stimson slowly inspected the blood-spattered corpse. He shook his head, whistled softly under his breath. "You're even better with a gun than you are with your fists."

"I generally get by." Starbuck paused, looked at him. "Guess I should've listened a little closer. You shore called the turn."

"You want some more advice?"

"Hell, why not?"

"Sheriff Palmer frowns on gunplay. Do yourself a favor and talk polite when he questions you."

"God a'mighty damn! It was self-defense, pure and simple!"

Stimson shrugged. "I'm just offering you a pearl of wisdom. Take it for what it's worth."

"You talk like he's some tough lawdog!"

"You will, too . . . when he's done with you."

Henry Palmer was a man with hard eyes and steel in his voice. He was trimly built, with dark wavy hair and a determined jaw. His bearing was monolithic, and he possessed a strong animal magnetism. He looked like someone accustomed to having his own way.

Starbuck was seated opposite him. On the sheriff's desk lay the Colt used to kill Pete Johnson. So far the questions had been general, almost conversational in tone. But now Palmer hefted the sixgun and studied it critically. The gutta-percha handles and lustrous blue finish gave it a distinctive appearance. He deftly unloaded the Colt and closed the loading gate. Then he eased the hammer to full cock and lightly touched the trigger. The hammer instantly dropped. He nodded and looked up.

"A hair trigger," he said quietly. "I would venture to say everything inside this pistol has been over-hauled by a very competent gunsmith. Would I be wrong?"

"Search me," Starbuck said with a guileless smile. "I won it in a poker game."

"Who was your opponent . . . Doc Holliday?"

"You've got me all wrong, Sheriff!"

"No, Mr. Hall." Palmer's gaze bored into him. "Your shooting tags you for precisely what you are. You're a professional gunman!"

Starbuck rocked his hand, fingers splayed. "There's no law against a man protecting himself."

"In Virginia City"—Palmer's eyes were angry, commanding—"I am the law! A few weeks ago you whipped Johnson in a brawl, and tonight you killed him. That makes you a troublemaker in my book!"

"Johnson started it both times."

"So I've been told," Palmer said shortly. "Except for that, I'd have you under lock and key right now."

"I'm a mite confused, Sheriff." Starbuck's square face was very earnest. "Why'd you take my gun and haul me over here if you don't aim to arrest me?"

"Your habits interest me."

"Habits?" Starbuck repeated. "I don't get you."

"You were here for a week; then you disappeared for almost two weeks." Palmer paused with a speculative stare. "Now you're back . . . and nobody saw you arrive."

Starbuck gave him a walleyed look of amazement. "How'd you know all that?"

"I make it my business to know," Palmer said without inflection. "What I don't know is where you went—and what you did—when you left here."

"Any law says I gotta tell you?"

"No." Palmer's face grew overcast. "But there's a law you haven't heard about. I put it into effect and I enforce it."

"What law's that?"

"Everybody is entitled to one mistake. You made

yours by being too handy with a gun. Cause any more trouble, and I'll post you out of town."

"Oh?" Starbuck smiled crookedly. "Suppose you posted me and I took a notion to stay. What then?"

Palmer regarded him with clinical interest. "Then I'll kill you."

Starbuck let it drop there. His Colt was returned and he was allowed to leave. On the street, he paused and lit a cigarette, highly pleased with himself. He'd killed a man and he had put himself crosswise of Virginia City's badass sheriff. All in one night.

The word would spread like wildfire.

Chapter Eight

Starbuck awakened shortly before noon. He hadn't slept well, and his head felt groggy. He threw off the covers, sat for a moment on the edge of the bed. He dully recalled he was in the Virginia Hotel.

Last night, he'd gone straight from the sheriff's office back to the Gem Theater. His reception was even better than he had anticipated. Omar Stimson greeted him like a celebrity and insisted on buying several rounds of drinks. Killing a man—particularly Pete Johnson—had boosted his stock in Virginia City. The details were told and retold by those who had witnessed the shooting. He modestly allowed them to embroider on the truth.

From the Gem, Starbuck had made a tour of the dives along the street. The sporting crowd treated him something like a conquering hero. Strangers stood in line to shake his hand, and drinks were on the house. Before long, he'd consumed enough liquor to act the part of a drunken loudmouth. He began by bragging about the shootout; then he went on to relate the highlights of his standoff with the sheriff. By the end of the night, he had told the story no fewer than a dozen times. He finally called it quits, acting only slightly drunker than he actually was, and checked into the hotel. He was thoroughly satisfied with his performance. Lee Hall was the talk of the town.

Today, with a bright noontime sun streaming through the window, his thoughts turned to other matters. As he shaved, it occurred to him that he was somewhat impressed by Sheriff Henry Palmer. The lawman was tough and resourceful, and he ran a tight town. His credentials were in no way diminished by the robberies and murders; his record of ten outlaws hanged and four killed was noteworthy by any standard. He was, moreover, a deadly mankiller. Starbuck recognized the breed on sight, for the quality was one shared by all boomtown peace officers. The warning issued by Palmer last night was no idle threat. Any man posted out of Virginia City would be wise to depart without delay. The alternative was to face the sheriff—and be killed.

One thought led to another. Starbuck's ruminations about the sheriff brought him once more to the matter of George Hoyt. The lawyer's story was entirely plausible; it was reasonable to assume the outlaws would seek revenge against the county prosecutor. Yet, by that yardstick, it was equally safe to assume the outlaws would have attempted to assassinate the sheriff. And that wasn't the case. So Starbuck knew his instinct hadn't played him false. Hoyt had lied, and there was no logical explanation to justify the lie. Despite his devious manner, the lawyer clearly wasn't in league with the robbers. But if that was true, then the lie seemed all the more unfathomable. Only one answer presented itself. Someone else, not the robbers, had murdered the Carver girl. All of which led to a still greater riddle.

Who was George Hoyt protecting . . . and why?

Starbuck pondered the question as he dressed. Doc Carver was lying and George Hoyt was lying, and none of it made sense. He glued the mustache onto his upper lip, all the while searching for some rhyme or reason. At last, completely buffaloed, he walked to the bed and retrieved his pistol from beneath the pillow. He checked the loads and lowered the hammer on an empty chamber.

A knock sounded at the door. Starbuck crossed the room, his thumb hooked over the Colt's hammer. He stopped beside the doorjamb.

"Who's there?"

"I got a message for Lee Hall."

"Who from?"

"Lemme in and I'll tell you."

Starbuck twisted the key and backed to the center of the room. He leveled his sixgun on the door.

"C'mon in . . . slow and easy!"

The door creaked open. A tall, lantern-jawed man stepped into the room. He was grizzled and lean, with cold eyes and a tight-lipped expression. He looked like an undertaker at a funeral service, sober but not really sad. He closed the door and kept his hands in plain sight.

"I come in peace," he said solemnly. "You don't need no gun."

"Who're you and what's your business?"

"The name's Frank Yeager."

"I'm still listening."

"I got a proposition for you."

"What sort of proposition?"

"I don't talk so good lookin' down a gun barrel."

Starbuck wagged the pistol. "Take a seat on the bed. Put your hands on your knees and don't try anything sudden."

"Sudden ain't my game."

Starbuck waited until the man was seated. Then he pulled up a straight chair for himself and straddled it backward. He let the Colt dangle loosely in his hand.

"Awright, Mr. Yeager," he said churlishly. "What is your game . . . just exactly?"

"You killed Pete Johnson last night."

"So?"

"Johnson worked for me." Yeager's brow puckered with a frown. "Somebody's gotta fill his boots. I figgered you might be the man."

Starbuck was instantly attentive. "How do I know you're not trying to get even for Johnson? Sounds the least bit like a setup."

"If I wanted to kill you," Yeager observed, squinting querulously, "I'd just wait and bushwhack you some dark night. Why bother to rig a setup?"

"Guess you got a point," Starbuck conceded. "Course, it doesn't change things one way or the other. I got my own game and I play a lone hand."

"Yeah, I know." Yeager's eyes narrowed, and a smirk appeared at the corner of his mouth. "Word's around you snuck off and pulled a job last week."

Starbuck gave him the fisheye. "Where'd you hear that?"

"Little bird told me." Yeager laughed without humor. "I hear you're from Texas and you got no use for the law, and it's short odds your name ain't Lee Hall. I hear lots about you."

"Maybe too much," Starbuck bristled. "I never cared much for a man with a long nose."

"Don't get bent out of shape! Folks talk and I listen. No harm done!"

"Why all the interest in me?"

"You got guts!" Yeager grunted sharply. "And you damn sure ain't no tyro with a gun! Anybody that puts Pete Johnson away knows his business. So I figgered I'd sound you out."

"Since you don't hear so good, try watching my lips. I'm not for hire."

Yeager barked a short, harsh laugh. "You might change your tune when you hear the wages!"

"Try me and see."

"Anywheres from five to ten thousand a crack."

"Dollars?"

"Gold dust or dollars, it all spends the same."

Starbuck regarded him with a long, slow look. "What line of work are you in?"

"I rob stagecoaches."

There was a long pause of weighing and appraisal as the two men examined one another. At length, Starbuck fixed him with a corrosive stare. "Ten thousand? You wouldn't be pulling my leg, would you?"

"One way to find out," Yeager said simply. "Come along on a job and see for yourself."

"When did you have in mind?"

"You got a horse?"

"I could buy one easy enough."

"Not without everybody knowin' it." Yeager considered briefly, then nodded. "One of my men will come get you tomorrow night. He'll bring an extra horse."

"Where're we headed?"

"You'll see"—Yeager's eyes veiled with caution—"when we get there."

A fleeting look of puzzlement crossed Starbuck's face. "How'd you know I'd go for the deal? I could've turned you in to the sheriff and collected myself a reward."

"Four of my boys are waitin' outside the hotel."

"So what?"

"Unless they get the high sign from me, you'd be cold meat the minute you hit the street."

"You don't play for chalkies, do you?"

Yeager's mouth set in an ugly grin. "I only bet on sure things. You'll see what I mean the first trip out."

"Yeah, I reckon I will at that!"

"Okay if I get up now?"

"Jesus!" Starbuck stood with a foolish smile and quickly holstered his pistol. "I clean forgot I had you covered!"

"Well, don't forget tomorrow night. Somebody'll rap on your door right about dark."

"Frank, if you want a sure thing—bet on that!"

Starbuck walked him to the door and they shook hands. When Yeager was gone, he turned back into the room with a jubilant grin. The bait had been taken, hook and all! He'd got the invite he needed, and it had come from the gang leader himself. Which left only one question.

Who the hell was Frank Yeager?

An early September frost touched the land. In the valleys, where cottonwoods lined the creeks, a blaze of yellow foretold oncoming autumn. On the hillsides, columns of silver birch were flecked through with orange and gold. The air was sharp and crisp, and the mountains marched westward to the horizon. A brilliant sunrise lighted the pale sky.

The terrain got rougher as the men climbed steadily higher into the mountains. They followed the corduroy road that connected Virginia City with the railhead at Dillon. The steep grade was a series of hairpin curves and sudden switchbacks, twisting upward through the countryside. Frank Yeager led the way, and strung out behind him were five riders. The men wore mackinaws, and their horses puffed clouds of smoke in the frosty air. No one spoke.

Starbuck was the third rider in line. The other men were a coarse lot, hard and tough, still somewhat standoffish. He understood he was the new recruit, as yet untested. All the others were veteran highwaymen, old hands at robbery and murder. He'd been assigned the middle spot in the column, and it took no mental genius to figure the reason. He would be observed closely and entrusted with only the most menial chores. His every action would be noted, and his performance would determine his future with the gang. Today was a baptism into their ranks, and very much a test. It was his first job.

Four nights past, one of the gang had appeared at the hotel. His name was Charley Reeves, and he was

there at Yeager's order. He led Starbuck to the edge
of town, where two horses were hidden in a stand of
trees. They rode westward along a rutted wagon road,
and Reeves maintained an aloof silence the entire
way. Sometime after midnight, they forded a creek
and turned into the yard of a log house. Frank Yeager
greeted them at the door.

Over a jug of whiskey, Starbuck had been briefed
on the layout. Yeager operated a small cattle outfit,
located on Rattlesnake Creek. He supplied beef to
butcher shops in Virginia City, and he'd built a reputation as an honest rancher. In truth, the ranch was
nothing more than a clever front. The gang assembled
there before a robbery, and only then were they told
the details of the job. After the holdup, the loot was
split and the gang immediately dispersed. Since they
never returned to the ranch, there was no way to track
them from the scene of the robbery. None of them
were known outlaws, and no one suspected their in-
volvement. The operation, for all practical purposes,
was foolproof.

Subsequently, Starbuck discovered that Yeager had
not been entirely forthcoming. Over the next two
days, while they waited for the gang to assemble, he
listened more than he talked. From snatches of conversation between Yeager and Reeves, he slowly became aware that the operation was both complex and
skillfully organized. Altogether, there were apparently
a dozen or more gang members. Some lived in town
and others worked claims along Alder Gulch. Yet they
were rotated from job to job, and only five or six men
took part in any one holdup. As a result, their periodic

absences went unnoticed, and thereby the risk of exposure was reduced. The same men were never used on two jobs running.

The greater revelation, however, had to do with the upcoming holdup. In discussions of the job, it became abundantly clear that Yeager had inside information. He already knew the value of the express shipment, and he was certain it would depart Virginia City on the morning stage. The clincher came when he told them the strongbox would be secreted beneath the floorboards of the coach. While he made no mention of an informant, the conclusion was all too obvious. There was a Judas working for the stageline.

The gang members themselves were no great surprise. To a man, they were cold and callous, and placed little or no value on human life. They joked openly about express guards who had put up a fight and died in the effort. Yet, for all their grisly humor, they treated Starbuck with grudging respect. The story of his shootout with Pete Johnson had made the rounds, and none of them doubted his coolness under fire. Still, he was an unknown quantity as a robber, which caused them to reserve judgment. His test would come on the stage road to Dillon.

Starbuck was under no illusions. Today, as they rode higher into the mountains, he knew he would have but one chance to prove himself. Steady nerves and teamwork were attributes demanded of every member of the gang. A new recruit who appeared shaky—or too much of a lone wolf—was a risk no one could afford; his first job would be his last. Starbuck understood the danger and accepted it without qualms. He had every intention of pulling his own weight.

The holdup went off without a hitch. Yeager selected a sharp switchback on an uphill grade. Then he posted two men on either side of the road, with himself to the front and Reeves to the rear. An hour or so later, the stagecoach slowly rounded the curve. On the grade, the driver was forced to hold his horses to a walk, with no chance for a sudden burst of speed. Yeager simply stepped into the road while the others rose from hiding and covered the stage. All of them were masked, brandishing their weapons in a threatening manner, and Yeager's commands were obeyed without hesitation. The express guard dropped his shotgun, and the passengers obligingly tore up the floorboards and tossed out the strongbox. From start to finish, the robbery took less than ten minutes. Then the stage was allowed to proceed on its way.

The strongbox was carried into the woods. There Yeager blew off the lock with his pistol. The contents were an equal mix of bullion, gold dust, and bags of coins. The value, listed on an enclosed manifest, was fifty-six thousand dollars. While the men laughed and clowned, Yeager divvied the loot into separate piles. Reeves brought his own horse and Yeager's horse forward, and one pile went into their saddlebags. The other pile, amounting to some five thousand dollars per man, was divided among the gang members. Then they mounted and scattered to the winds.

Yeager asked Starbuck to wait behind. He left Reeves loading the saddlebags and walked Starbuck back to the road. His face was twisted in a possum grin.

"Well, what d'you think? Was I lyin' or not?"

"Hell, no!" Starbuck laughed. "Easiest money I ever made in my life."

"Figgered you wouldn't have no complaint."

"No complaint," Starbuck agreed. "But I got a question."

"What's on your mind?"

"How come you take half?" Starbuck inquired easily. "You never told me it worked that way."

Yeager gave him a dirty look. "It don't pay to get greedy."

"A man's entitled to ask."

"I plan the job and it's me that takes most of the risks! On top of that, I guarantee every time you ride you'll get a payday. Which ain't exactly nothin' to sniff at! So let's just say it all evens out in the end."

"I wasn't bellyachin' . . . just curious."

"Now you know." Yeager studied the ground a moment, then glanced up. "You handled yourself real good, Lee. Keep your nose clean and stay out of trouble. I'll be in touch before long."

"Any idea how long?"

"Don't get antsy," Yeager ordered. "When I've got a payday lined up, you'll hear about it. Understand?"

"Whatever you say, Frank."

Starbuck waved and swung aboard his horse. He reined about and rode toward Virginia City. The thought occurred that he could have killed Yeager just now and reported the case closed. Yet he knew that would have been only a half-truth. Frank Yeager was not the man he'd been hired to kill.

Over the last four days Starbuck had studied the gang leader closely. Yeager possessed a certain cunning, and he was an excellent tactician when it came to pulling a holdup. But he was no mental giant, hardly a thinker. Nor had he displayed the flair for organization and planning that were the hallmarks of the operation. He was a field commander, nothing more.

Simple deduction led to an obvious conclusion. Somehow, in a way not yet revealed, the entire operation was directed by a mastermind. The robbers themselves were little more than puppets; someone in the background pulled the strings. One intriguing possibility was that the Judas and the mastermind might be the same man. Only time and deeper investigation would tell. But of one thing there was no longer a shred of doubt. Frank Yeager was merely the gang leader. He was not the ringleader.

And that was the man Starbuck had been hired to kill.

Chapter Nine

Outside Virginia City, Starbuck turned north. He skirted the town until he hit the rutted wagon trail. Then he rode west toward Rattlesnake Creek.

Earlier, upon parting company with Yeager, he'd been undecided as to his next move. He was convinced Yeager took orders from whoever masterminded the robberies. There was also reason to believe that inside information was being passed along to the gang. It followed, then, that there was a pipeline into either the express office or the stageline company. The Judas was someone with access to confidential shipment schedules, highly restricted information. All of which put a whole new complexion on the problem.

Starbuck could no longer afford to trust anyone. Topping the list were the men who had hired him. Munro Salisbury, president of the stageline, had direct knowledge of the express shipments. John Duggan, who headed the mining association, was also privy to inside matters. It seemed unlikely that either man was directly implicated in the holdups. Yet, however improbable, it was nonetheless a factor that merited consideration. The greater likelihood was that the Judas enjoyed the confidence of one or both of the men. So anything they knew was very probably known by the Judas. That being the case, the option of contacting either Salisbury or Duggan was foreclosed. To do so would risk blowing his cover.

Still, Starbuck desperately needed a lead. His suspicions were valueless without hard evidence. He somehow had to unearth the identity of the mastermind and ringleader, not to mention the Judas. But he couldn't confide in Salisbury or Duggan, nor could he question them as to likely suspects. By process of elimination, that left only Frank Yeager.

Several things were apparent. Foremost was that Yeager's half of the loot would somehow be split with the ringleader. Unless Starbuck missed his guess, the division would occur fairly rapidly. There was little honor among thieves, and Yeager would not be entrusted with the haul for any length of time. The premise seemed solid, and from it evolved two very distinct possibilities. The ringleader would appear at Yeager's ranch and collect his share of the spoils. Or, barring that, Yeager would deliver the split to someone in Virginia City. One way or the other, an exchange was inevitable.

In Starbuck's view, it boiled down to a matter of risk. The ringleader would place himself in greater jeopardy by traveling to Yeager's ranch. Aside from the risk of being seen, it would immediately establish a connection. The wiser choice would be to effect the exchange in Virginia City. For one thing, Yeager's appearance in town would draw little attention. For another, the teeming crowds and street activity offered a better chance of secrecy. Yeager could move about at will and pick his time. No one would suspect he was there to make a payoff.

For all that, Starbuck was still determined to hedge his bet. He'd learned long ago that trying to outguess a crook was a sticky proposition. The only certainty was that the exchange would take place at night. Anyone cunning enough to organize the robberies would not hazard a payoff in broad daylight. Whether at Yeager's ranch or in Virginia City, the meeting would occur under the cloak of darkness. So there was only one logical spot to set up a surveillance. And that spot was Rattlesnake Creek.

Late that afternoon, Starbuck dismounted in a grove of trees. To the west, the sun was dipping lower behind the mountains. He tied his horse and walked forward to the creek. Yeager's house was some distance beyond the far bank, but easily visible. He took a position screened by the treeline and lit a cigarette. Then he settled down to wait.

Everything appeared in order. Yeager and Reeves, much as he'd expected, had taken a shortcut through the mountains. Their horses were unsaddled and standing hipshot in the corral. By rough estimate, he calculated they had ridden into the ranch some two hours ago. A tendril of smoke drifted from the chimney, and he caught the scent of coffee on an upwind breeze. He imagined they were eating supper about now, and his stomach rumbled in protest. The detective business, he told himself wryly, was a tough way to make a living. Outlaws had all the best of it . . . till the end.

Starbuck's wait ended three cigarettes later. As dusk settled over the land Yeager emerged from the house. His saddlebags were thrown over his shoulder, and the weight was sufficient to make him list. There seemed little doubt the pockets were stuffed with bullion and gold dust. He walked swiftly to the corral and draped the saddlebags over the top rail. Then he caught up his horse and snubbed him near the gate. He began saddling.

Easing away from the creek, Starbuck hurried through the trees. His hunch had panned out; Yeager was headed for Virginia City and a payoff. Yet Starbuck knew an even larger gamble was about to commence. To trail Yeager into town—in the dark—would require that he stick too close for comfort. Even if Yeager didn't spot him, the sound of hoofbeats from behind would betray his presence. Either way, it would alert Yeager and spoil the game. So he had no choice but to ride ahead and take up watch on the outskirts of town. He was betting Yeager would stick to the wagon road.

He mounted and galloped hell-for-leather toward Virginia City.

The night was dark as pitch. Starbuck stood in the shadows of a whorehouse at the west end of Wallace Street. The red-light district was swarming with miners, every crib and bagnio turning them away at the doors. No one even glanced in his direction.

Starbuck judged it to be somewhere around eleven o'clock. He'd been waiting nearly two hours, and still no sign of Yeager. While he'd pushed his horse, he hadn't thought Yeager would poke along. Unless the gang leader showed soon, it would mean he had circled and entered town somewhere else. Or worse, that his destination was not Virginia City after all. A sinking feeling crept over Starbuck as he considered the thought.

Then, suddenly, he stiffened and edged deeper into the shadows. Yeager rode past at a walk, slumped slouch-shouldered in the saddle. Starbuck tugged his hat low and joined the stream of miners on the boardwalk. He stayed a good twenty paces behind, following slowly as Yeager moved toward the center of town. At the next corner, Yeager turned south on Van Buren. Starbuck kept to the north side of Wallace and stopped at the corner. He saw Yeager rein into an alleyway.

Crossing the street, Starbuck hurried to the alley. He eased his head around the corner of a building and watched as Yeager rode halfway down the block. There the gang leader halted at the intersection of an alleyway which ran in the opposite direction. He took a long look around, then dismounted and moved across the intersection on foot. He hitched his horse to the banister of a stair landing and quickly unfastened his saddle bags. With the saddlebags thrown over his shoulder, he climbed the stairs to a second-floor landing. He stopped before a door and knocked. Several moments passed before the door opened in a flood of light. He stepped inside.

Starbuck's pulse skipped a beat. The distant alley was the one in which he'd killed Pete Johnson. It

flanked the Gem Theater and emerged onto Wallace
Street, the town's main thoroughfare. More to the
point, Lola had told him that Omar Stimson, the theater owner, had an office on the second floor. Frank
Yeager had just climbed the stairs to the Gem's rear
entrance.

Whirling around, Starbuck sprinted back to the corner. He turned onto Wallace Street and rushed along
the boardwalk. He bulled through the throngs of miners, roughly shoving and jostling as he moved down
the block. When he pulled up outside the Gem, no
more than thirty seconds had passed since he'd observed Yeager mount the stairs. He pushed through
the bat-wing doors and halted.

The barroom was packed with a boisterous crowd.
His gaze swept the room, then abruptly stopped. He
saw Omar Stimson standing behind several miners at
one of the faro layouts. The play was heavy, and the
Gem's owner seemed to have his eye on the dealer.
As Starbuck watched, a bouncer threaded his way
through the men ganged around the table. Tapping
Stimson on the shoulder, he whispered something under his breath and jerked a thumb upstairs. Stimson
asked a question, and the bouncer bobbed his head.
After a moment, one eye still on the faro game, Stimson turned away. The bouncer swiftly cleared a path.

Starbuck held his place by the door. He lit a cigarette, gazing over the flare of the match. Stimson,
preceded by the bouncer, crossed the room and went
up the stairs to the second floor. On the upper landing,
they entered a hallway and walked toward the rear of

the building. Starbuck snuffed the match and took a long, thoughtful drag.

All of it fitted and everything he'd seen made sense. Yet he was struck by a sudden doubt. Some visceral instinct told him things were not as they appeared.

Omar Stimson wasn't the man he'd been hired to kill.

Starbuck sat concealed behind a trash heap. Across from him was Yeager's horse and the stairway leading to the Gem's rear entrance. Some fifteen minutes had elapsed since he'd walked from the theater and found himself a vantage point in the alley. He waited with the patience of a hunter stalking dangerous game.

His conviction was stronger now. What began as a swift-felt impulse had been buttressed by hard-won experience. After seven years as a detective, he had gained considerable insight into the mentality of criminals. One of the prime lessons he'd learned had to do with the inner workings of the underworld. There was a certain code which governed any criminal enterprise. The more complex the operation, the more rigid the system became; where big money was involved, the rules were all but carved in stone. The code was formulated by the underworld hierarchy, and it was enforced with ruthless savagery. No one broke the rules and lived.

So far, the chain of command had followed a standard pattern. Frank Yeager recruited men into the gang and led them in the actual holdups. Yet he operated under the sanction of someone at a higher level, and he was accountable for every job. Clearly, the man he reported to was Omar Stimson, the vice czar of Virginia City. In turn, Stimson answered to someone still higher. A percentage of all criminal activity—whether vice or stage robbery—was funneled to a man at the top. An overlord whose word was law in any underworld enterprise. A man with political clout.

In Starbuck's experience, vice and politics were inseparable. Without political protection, no vice czar could exert control over the diverse elements within the underworld. He'd found it to be true in other mining camps, such as Tombstone and Deadwood. On another assignment, which took him to San Francisco, the trail had led from train robbers to a vice boss to a political kingpin. Even in Denver, his own town, a thug named Lou Blomger controlled vice and crime through dominance of the political apparatus. Never before had he encountered an exception. Wherever he traveled, he found politics and vice to be the original strange bedfellows. Virginia City would prove no different.

Hidden behind the trash heap, Starbuck considered the knotty question of how to proceed. Frank Yeager was plainly an underling, low man on the totem pole. He could easily be captured and made to talk. Charged with robbery and murder, he would gladly spill his guts to avoid the hangman's noose. That would implicate Stimson and thereby place him on the road to the gallows. Still, there was a vast difference between the two men. A stage robber was expendable, merely a pawn to be sacrificed. A vice czar was virtually immune to prosecution.

Stimson was a dominant force in the underworld. By extension, that made him a key member of the local power structure. Should he decide to name names, he could implicate the man—or men—who ruled Virginia City. Therefore, even if he were taken into custody, he would not talk. Whoever he reported to would grant him immunity in exchange for silence. No indictment would be handed down and he would not stand trial. He would, instead, walk away free.

Accordingly, Starbuck saw nothing to be gained by hasty action. The smarter move was to lie low and play a waiting game. Yeager had led him to Stimson, and that was by no means the end of the trail. Nor was it the last of the payoffs. The haul from the robbery would be split once again, and this time Stimson would make the delivery. Perhaps tonight, maybe not until tomorrow. But Starbuck thought it would be done without undue delay. He planned to follow wherever Stimson led.

Shortly before midnight Yeager emerged from the upstairs office. His saddlebags were empty, and he came down the stairs like a man relieved of a burden. Then he mounted his horse and rode off. Starbuck simply hid and watched. He was resigned to a long wait.

Not ten minutes later the door again opened. The bouncer stepped onto the upstairs landing and peered around the alley. He was a bruiser, heavily muscled, with a thick neck and powerful shoulders. A bulge underneath his suit jacket indicated he had a pistol stuffed in the waistband of his trousers. At length, he turned and signaled the all clear. Omar Stimson moved through the door and followed him down the stairway. The vice czar was carrying a leather satchel.

Starbuck suddenly felt vindicated. The bouncer was clearly riding shotgun on the contents of the satchel. Which meant everyone involved knew the robbery had taken place and they were expecting to be paid off tonight. He waited until Stimson and the goon reached the end of the alley. When they rounded the corner onto Van Buren Street, he quit the trash heap. He tailed them at a discreet distance.

Stimson's route was an exercise in stealth. With the bouncer at his elbow, he crossed Wallace and proceeded north on Van Buren. Halfway down the block he turned sharply into an unlighted alley. From there he walked eastward and emerged on Jackson Street. Then he again swung north, moving past several darkened business establishments. Near the corner, he stopped and rapped on a door. A few moments later the door opened in a shaft of light. Stimson and the bruiser stepped inside, and the door closed behind them.

Starbuck hesitated at the mouth of the alley. Streetlamps flickered at both ends of the block, and he was wary of being spotted. Finally, satisfied there was no one about, he crossed to the east side of Jackson Street, Hugging the shadows, he darted from doorway to doorway, working his way toward the far corner. Some distance down the block, he ducked into the doorway of a hardware store and flattened himself against the wall. Almost directly opposite him was the building Stimson and the bouncer had entered. The blind was drawn, but the glow of a lamp shone from inside. On the plate-glass window was a sign done in fancy gold scrollwork. The lettering was dimly illuminated by the corner streetlight:

ALDER GULCH ASSAY COMPANY
Cyrus Skinner
President

The name meant nothing. Yet the connection, however tenuous, was immediately apparent to Starbuck. An assayer was actively involved in the gold-mining business and privy to all sorts of privileged information. Which tended to raise more questions than it answered. Was Skinner the ringleader or the Judas or the political kingpin? Or was he all three rolled into one? Then, again, perhaps he was none of those things. It was entirely possible that Stimson used him to dispose of the stolen bullion and gold dust. Still, whatever else he was, the assayer was definitely another link in the chain. A bit of investigation might very well prove him to be the last link. The Virginia City overlord.

Across the street, the door of the assay office abruptly opened. Stimson's bouncer stepped outside and swung the door shut. Starbuck had only a moment to wonder why Stimson had remained behind. Then he realized he was in an exposed position, perfectly visible. The bouncer glanced in his direction and froze.

There was nothing for it. The options were to kill

the man on the spot or attempt to run a bluff. Starbuck hastily unbuttoned his pants and pulled out his pud. For a moment his bladder seemed paralyzed, and he thought it was a lost cause. Then he gritted his teeth and strained and finally got the waterworks into operation. He doused the hardware store door with a steamy spray that sounded wetly in the still night. A puddle formed around his boots, and he shook his pud once for good measure. Finished, he tucked himself away and pretended to fumble with the buttons on his pants.

The bouncer was watching him intently. Yet Starbuck thought his chances were improving by the moment. He was wearing a common mackinaw, and his features were somewhat obscured in the silty glow of the streetlamp. By acting the part, he might still pass himself off as a drunken miner. He wobbled out of the doorway, careful to keep his head ducked low. Staggering along, he lurched and swayed with the rubbery-legged gait of a man crocked to the gills. At the corner, he walked straight into the lamppost and rebounded with a muttered curse. A quick glance confirmed that the bouncer was watchful but apparently not alarmed. Starbuck rounded the corner and went weaving down the street.

The immediate danger had passed. Whether or not he'd fooled the bouncer completely remained to be seen. Tomorrow he would put it to the test and find out. But for now he had a more pressing problem. A question that still echoed through his mind.

Who—and what—was Cyrus Skinner?

Chapter Ten

Starbuck went about his usual routine the next day. He thought it important that everything appear normal. Another unremarkable day in the life of Lee Hall.

Yet his nerves were raw with tension. When he awakened, he felt oddly unsure about what lay ahead. He mentally reviewed the events of last night while he shaved. There was every chance he would be asked questions; his answers would have to be both believable and convincing. Otherwise, today might be his last day in the guise of Lee Hall.

His concern centered on two seemingly unrelated matters. The first had to do with his horse. Upon arriving in town the previous evening, he'd gone straightaway to the livery stable near Chinatown. He had ridden hard, and he figured he was at least a half hour ahead of Frank Yeager. At the livery, he had rented a stall and insisted on looking after the horse himself. That gave him an opportunity to ditch the sacks of gold dust and coins stowed in his saddlebags. He scooped away straw and manure and dug a hole in the floor of the stall. Then he buried the gold, certain that no one would poke around beneath a pile of horse apples. After tending to the horse, he'd crossed town and taken up his post outside the whorehouse. There was only one flaw in his actions to that point. Anyone who cared to check could easily establish the time he'd arrived in town. He would have to be prepared for questions.

His second concern was by far the more troublesome. The close call last night with Stimson's bouncer still weighed heavily. He thought he'd pulled it off; the drunken-miner act was one of his more memorable performances. But he'd learned long ago never to take anything for granted. It was entirely possible the bouncer had recognized him. Apparently, after delivering the satchel, Stimson had dismissed the man and stayed behind for a private talk with Cyrus Skinner. Whether or not the bouncer had returned and informed Stimpson of the incident was the key question. In retrospect, Starbuck concluded he must assume it had happened in just that manner. False confidence, particularly at this juncture, was a pitfall he could ill afford. Better to put it to the test and determine where he stood. Tonight he would beard Stimson at the theater watchful for any telltale signs of hostility. A bold front might very well turn the trick.

In the meantime, there was the matter of Cyrus Skinner. Starbuck was somewhat at a loss as to where he should start. The assayer was a complete cipher, an unknown quantity. His association with Stimson appeared anything but legitimate; their clandestine meeting directly linked him to the stage holdups. Yet his overall role presented a whole grab bag of possibilities. He might be anything from a fence for the stolen gold to the political kingpin of Virginia City.

An investigation, however, would prove a tricky proposition. Overt snooping would pose the hazard of alarming both Stimson and Skinner. So the questions would have to be framed in a casual manner and directed to people who had no dealings with either man. That greatly limited the scope of the investigation and bothered Starbuck more than he cared to admit. Still, he saw no alternative to discreet inquiry. He was too close to risk blowing the case.

Starbuck emerged from the hotel at noontime. As was his custom, he went directly to a café across the street. There he wolfed down a breakfast of beefsteak and eggs and sourdough biscuits. He topped off the meal with a cup of coffee strong enough to grow hair and left a four-bit tip. Outside, with a toothpick stuck in his mouth, he stood for a while basking in the sun. Then he strolled upstreet at a leisurely pace.

The afternoon was spent drifting from saloon to saloon. Starbuck shot a few games of pool and let himself be conned into a small-stakes poker game. The sporting crowd was out and about, and they greeted him as one of the fraternity. Everywhere he went he bought drinks for others, while he himself nursed a schooner of beer. His conviviality, along with the free drinks, assured him of company at every stop. He talked with bartenders and gamblers, thimbleriggers and shills, and a seemingly endless parade of saloon girls. One way or another, he steered the conversation onto gold and the looming prospect of quartz mining. From there, he worked the talk around to promising claims and the latest assay reports. A leading question sometimes brought the name of Cyrus Skinner into the discussion. Then he listened a lot, pretending off-hand interest and bored curiosity. By the end of the day, he'd pumped the sporting crowd for all they knew. It wasn't much.

Cyrus Skinner was an old-timer in Virginia City. He'd opened a one-man assay office shortly after gold was discovered along Alder Gulch. As the camp mushroomed into a boomtown his business had prospered and grown, until now he pretty much had a corner on the assay market. He was a mainstay in the local Democratic party, though he'd never held office or achieved prominence in the political arena. Widely respected, he was known as a man of character and scrupulous honesty. He took an occasional drink but shunned the gambling dens and apparently steered clear of the town's parlor houses. According to the sporting crowd, he was a rabid civic booster and a man with no known vices. Which made him square as a cube.

Starbuck retired to his hotel room shortly after sundown. He sprawled out on the bed and slowly digested all he'd learned. While none of it was revealing, the sum and substance sparked his cynicism. Any man with no known vices was, in his view, automatically suspect. A veneer of morality all too often masked oddments of an unwholesome nature. Based on what he had seen last night, that seemed very much the case with Cyrus Skinner. But he still had no cold, hard facts, no proof. Nor had he the slightest notion of where to look.

With the onset of darkness, he rose and lighted a lamp. Tomorrow, even though it was a risk he preferred to avoid, he would kick over one last stone. He had only a vague hope that it would uncover anything new and startling about the mysterious assayer. Tonight he would tackle another, and equally unsettling, problem. The matter of Omar Stimson and his eagle-eyed bouncer.

Starbuck began washing up for supper. As he soaped his hands his gaze was attracted to his warbag. He always left it on the floor beside the washstand, and he always left the clasps unfastened. He saw now that the clasps were fastened and the warbag itself had been moved slightly. The discovery at once angered him and sent a chill along his backbone. He knew exactly what it meant.

Someone had searched his room.

Whatever he'd expected, Starbuck's reception at the Gem was something of a shock. He no sooner bellied up to the bar than Omar Stimson appeared at his elbow. The theater owner greeted him warmly and ordered a drink on the house.

"Been out of town?" Stimson inquired genially. "I missed you the last few days."

Starbuck thought it a crafty ploy. The question revealed nothing and it still opened up a can of worms. He had no idea where it would lead, but he decided to play along.

"I'm surprised you even knew I was gone."

"You're a regular now, Lee! I always look after a good customer."

"Well, like I told you before—" Starbuck paused

and sipped his drink. "I got business that takes me here and there."

"Oh, I remember!" Stimson laughed. "A little of this and a little of that. Wasn't that it?"

Starbuck smiled. "I don't gather much moss."

"Some folks are wondering about that very thing."

"What d'you mean?"

"I hear Sheriff Palmer has been asking around about you."

"Why so?"

"Big excitement yesterday." Stimson fixed him with a sly look. "The morning stage to Dillon was robbed. Or hadn't you heard?"

"Somebody mentioned it," Starbuck said vaguely. "Are you trying to tell me the sheriff thinks I had a hand in that holdup?"

"You be the judge," Stimson replied with a shrug. "There's a rumor to the effect he searched your hotel room this afternoon."

"The hell you say!" Starbuck appeared dumbfounded. "Why would he do a thing like that?"

"I imagine he was looking for stolen gold."

"Kiss my dusty butt!" Starbuck said hotly. "Wonder where he got such a damnfool notion?"

"Word's around you got yourself a horse."

"How'd you know that?"

"People talk," Stimson said with a bland gesture. "Someone at the livery stable mentioned you'd rented a stall. When Palmer got wind of it, he went over and checked out the horse."

"What in tarnation for?"

"Evidently the sheriff has got you pegged as a bad

character. If the stage driver could identify your horse, then you'd be up a creek. See what I mean?"

"Not a chance!" Starbuck crowed. "Goddamn horse's own mother wouldn't recognize him!"

"Glad to hear it." Stimson was silent a moment, thoughtful. "One other thing you ought to consider."

"Oh?"

"The hostler said you brought your horse in a little before nine last night. In case you're asked, you better be able to account for your whereabouts."

"Simplest thing on earth!" Starbuck said boldly. "I rode in yesterday afternoon and stopped at one of the cathouses. Always take my time when I go to get my log sapped. So it was late before I made it down to the livery."

"Looks like you're in the clear, then."

"You bet your boots I am!"

Stimson chatted awhile longer, then wandered off. Starbuck wasn't quite sure what to make of the conversation. On the surface it seemed Stimson merely wanted to warn him about the sheriff. Then, again, there was an undertone of suspicion to the questions. Almost a sense of interrogation. Either way, Starbuck decided on an abrupt change of plans. Tomorrow night very well might be too late.

Tonight was the time to kick over that last stone.

A few minutes before seven, Starbuck slipped out of the Gem. He walked to the corner and crossed the street to his hotel. He went straight through the lobby and out the back door. A narrow passageway between buildings led to Jackson Street, and there he paused. He slowly inspected the street in both directions.

The town's main intersection, which he'd crossed only moments before, was clogged with the usual nighttime crowd. Jackson Street itself was dimly lighted and appeared empty. At length, satisfied he hadn't been followed, he stepped from the passageway. He hurriedly moved to the opposite side of the street and cut into the alley. A quick walk brought him to Van Buren, and there he turned north. George Hoyt's office was a few doors up the block.

On his previous visit Starbuck had found the lawyer working late. He was banking on that being the case tonight. Otherwise, he would have to ask directions to Hoyt's home, and that would compound an already dicey situation. His luck held. A beam of light filtered through the plate-glass window. He strode rapidly to the door and ducked inside.

George Hoyt looked up from his desk. His expression was one of surprise and mild curiosity. Then, still silent, he watched Starbuck lock the door and pull the blind. The disguise was different, but Starbuck's furtive manner triggered a memory of their last meeting. Hoyt suddenly made the connection, and his face went slack with fear.

"You!"

"Nobody else." Starbuck moved forward and took a chair. "Figured it was time we had ourselves another talk!"

"But I—" Hoyt stammered. "I kept my word! I spoke to no one about you or our conversation!"

"Never doubted it," Starbuck assured him. "That's not why I'm here."

"What do you want, then?"

"We're going to make a swap. You come clean and provide me with certain information. In return, I'll keep you out of prison."

"Prison!" Hoyt shook his head dumbly. "What are you talking about?"

"Cyrus Skinner."

Hoyt's mouth popped open and he sat transfixed. His face went chalky, and behind the wire-rimmed glasses a pinpoint of terror surfaced in his eyes. When at last he spoke, his voice had an unusual timbre.

"I have nothing to say . . . nothing."

"Yeah, you do," Starbuck said tightly. "I'll spell it out for you. Frank Yeager and Omar Stimson are going to hang for murder. Skinner will probably get a life sentence. You're just small fry, but you're still an accessory before the fact. So you're looking at twenty, maybe thirty years."

"Who are you?"

"U.S. deputy marshal," Starbuck said without expression. "I was sent here to get the stage robbers. One thing led to another, and I kept turning up more names. All I need to make a case are a few more details, and that's your way out. You come clean, and I guarantee you won't serve a day."

"I don't believe you," Hoyt said, his face careworn. "If you know so much, why do you need me?"

"Corroboration." Starbuck smiled crookedly. "I infiltrated Yeager's gang and helped him rob the stage yesterday. Then I trailed him to Stimson, and Stimson led me to Skinner. You turn state's evidence—corroborate my story—and you're off the hook. Otherwise, you win yourself a striped suit."

There was a stretch of deadened silence. Hoyt seemed caught up in a moment of indecision, and his eyes drifted away. Then he pursed his lips in a forlorn expression.

"What do you want to know?"

"Tell me about Skinner." Starbuck regarded him evenly. "I've already got the goods on Yeager and Stimson."

"Cyrus Skinner," Hoyt said hollowly, "controls the county political machine. He purposely stays out of the limelight, but he's the power behind the throne. No one gets into public office without his stamp of approval."

"Which includes you?"

"Yes." Hoyt was unable to meet his gaze. "Skinner handpicked me for county prosecutor. As an added inducement, he promised to back me for the legislature in next year's election. I agreed to turn a blind eye to the robberies and other irregularities."

"Such as?"

"Graft and corruption. Skinner uses Omar Stimson as a front man. All the vice operations pay protection money, and it ends up in Skinner's pocket."

"How about Sheriff Palmer?" Starbuck persisted. "Is he Skinner's man, too?"

"Palmer's the exception," Hoyt said softly. "He's a political maverick, an independent. He campaigned on his own ticket and beat Skinner's candidate three to one."

"Why hasn't he gone after Skinner?"

"Why would he?" Hoyt responded. "Very few people even know that Skinner's the kingpin. He operates through others and keeps himself insulated from the dirty work."

"What about the robbers Palmer caught? The ones you tried and hanged. Were they part of Yeager's gang?"

Hoyt gave him a dull stare. "Those men were just garden-variety bandits. So far as I know, Palmer doesn't suspect an organized gang. He certainly doesn't suspect Yeager! No one does."

"Palmer's no dimdot," Starbuck said doubtfully. "Are you saying he doesn't suspect there's a Judas working for the stage company?"

"Judas?"

"An inside man," Starbuck elaborated. "Someone who supplies advance information on the gold shipments."

"Good Lord!" Hoyt's mouth froze in a silent oval. "I always wondered how Yeager picked the right stages!"

"You mean nobody ever said anything to you about an inside man?"

"Not a word," Hoyt said with a hangdog look. "But then, of course, I never asked. I didn't want to know the details, especially beforehand. Too many express guards were being killed."

Starbuck read no guile in his face. "All right, we'll let that pass. What about Doc Carver? How'd he get involved?"

"He wasn't involved," Hoyt remarked. "He was just an innocent bystander."

"Then how come he took off running?"

"He had no choice," Hoyt said miserably. "His daughter—Alice—learned something she wasn't supposed to know."

"What was that . . . just exactly?"

"I have no idea." Hoyt swallowed and his Adam's apple bobbed. "Skinner refused to discuss it with me."

"Did Skinner know you were sweet on the Carver girl?"

"Oh, yes." A look of anguish came into Hoyt's eyes. "He knew how I felt. He knew it all along."

"Was Skinner the one who murdered her?"

"She—" Hoyt faltered, his voice barely audible. "Alice wasn't killed."

"She's alive!" Starbuck was genuinely astounded. "The Carver girl's alive?"

"Alice and her father—"

The window exploded and a trash can struck the floor in a shower of glass. Starbuck reacted on sheer instinct and threw himself backward in his chair. He crashed into the wall, pulling his Colt as the chair collapsed and he toppled to the floor. Hoyt jackknifed to his feet and gaped at two men dimly visible through the shattered window. Then the men opened fire with sawed-off shotguns; three quick blasts hammered Hoyt into the rear wall. The fourth blast ripped away the top of his head, and his knees buckled. He slumped forward beneath a mist of brains and gore.

Starbuck levered himself up on one arm before the men could reload. He sighted on the shadowy figures and thumbed off a hurried snap shot. One of the men screamed and dropped his scattergun. Starbuck triggered another shot and then realized he was firing at an empty window. The men were gone, and in the sudden stillness he heard pounding footsteps on the boardwalk. He stood, moved swiftly to the window, and took a cautious look outside. He saw the men turn the corner of a building and disappear into the alley. Muttering to himself, he cursed the darkness and his own shooting. The man he'd hit wasn't wounded seriously, for they were both running at top speed. He sensed there was nothing to be gained by chasing after them.

A look around confirmed what he already knew. George Hoyt was dead, and with him had died any hope of a quick break in the case. Worse, the killing meant that Stimson had not been fooled. Someone had shadowed Starbuck tonight and trailed him to the lawyer's office. The masquerade was over, and he no longer needed a disguise.

His cover was blown.

Chapter Eleven

Starbuck waited near the door. A crowd of morbid onlookers was gathered outside the shattered window. To the rear of the office, Sheriff Palmer and a deputy were inspecting the corpse. Their features were grim, their voices a low murmur.

In the aftermath of the shooting, several miners had collected on the boardwalk. Gunfire tended to draw spectators, and word of the killing quickly spread uptown. Starbuck had sent a man to fetch the sheriff and then kept the crowd at a distance. The shotgun and a splotch of blood on the boardwalk were his alibi. He'd thought it prudent to preserve the evidence.

Henry Palmer had arrived shortly thereafter. Starbuck, still in the guise of Lee Hall, had related the details of the killing. But he had refused to explain his presence in the lawyer's office. Only in private, he insisted, would he elaborate further. A quick look around convinced the sheriff that Starbuck had not participated in the murder. The fresh blood trail outside, along with the shotgun, indicated Starbuck had wounded one of the assassins. The condition of the deceased, riddled with four loads of buckshot, verified that two men had taken part in the shooting. Palmer had agreed to withhold judgment, pending a full explanation.

Under other circumstances, Starbuck would have taken matters into his own hands. Cyrus Skinner was clearly the man he'd been hired to kill. Yet he realized that any attempt to call Skinner out would accomplish nothing. There was no hard evidence, and the assayer would simply refuse to fight. No assassin, Starbuck could hardly kill Skinner in cold blood. He always gave a hunted man a chance, however slight. The fact that he'd blown his cover further complicated the situation. So the alternative, at least for the moment, was to work through the law. He saw it as the only way to build a solid case.

Palmer's examination took less than a half hour. He dispatched someone with a message for the undertaker and left his deputy to guard the murder scene. Once the body was removed, he ordered that the window be boarded up and the door locked. Then, motioning to Starbuck, he led the way outside. The crowd parted, and they walked toward Wallace Street. Neither man spoke.

All the way across town Starbuck weighed various options. He wondered how little he could tell Palmer and still obtain the lawman's cooperation. The fly in the ointment was Cyrus Skinner. He had only circumstantial evidence, and he needed hard-and-fast proof before he could act. Then there was the additional factor of the Judas. He still had no positive identification, and he'd lost all chance of operating undercover. So it was vital that the sheriff commence an immediate investigation. In the end, he decided to tell Palmer everything.

A short while later they entered the sheriff's office. The furnishings were sparse, with a single battered desk and several wooden armchairs. Off the main room, several barred cells were visible along a corridor. To all appearances, there were no prisoners in the lockup and they had the place to themselves. Palmer hooked his hat on a wall peg and circled around the desk. He waved Starbuck to a chair.

"Let's get down to cases." He dropped into a swivel chair, elbows on the desk. "What was your business with George Hoyt?"

Starbuck lit a cigarette, exhaled smoke. "It's a long story, and no need to cover the same ground twice. Why don't I start at the beginning?"

"Start anywhere you please."

"Well, first off, I'm not Lee Hall. The name's Luke Starbuck. I'm a private detective, operating out of Denver."

"I assume you can prove that?"

"Check with Munro Salisbury and John Duggan. They hired me, and they'll vouch for the fact that I've been working undercover."

"If you are Starbuck"—Palmer fixed him with a stern look—"you've got a rep as a mankiller. Were you sent here to put somebody away?"

"I was hired to bust up a gang of stage robbers."

"That doesn't answer my question."

Starbuck hesitated, chose his words with care. "I've never killed a man unless he was trying to kill me."

"All right, skip it for now." Palmer's frown deepened. "What's this about a gang of robbers?"

Starbuck briefly recounted the details of his assignment. He covered the salient points leading to his infiltration of Yeager's gang. Then he went on to relate how he'd tied both Stimson and Skinner to the robbery ring. He finished by repeating everything George Hoyt had told him.

"That's pretty much the story," he concluded. "Hoyt's confession nailed it down tight."

Palmer merely listened, coldly silent, eyeing him with a mixture of dismay and surprise. He drummed the desktop with his fingers, digesting what he'd heard. Then he leaned back in the creaky swivel chair.

"If it's true, that would mean Skinner rigged Alice Carver's death. What was the purpose?"

"Hoyt was just about to tell me when the shooting started. So I never found out."

"What would it have to do with the stage robberies?"

"Good question," Starbuck admitted. "I frankly don't know."

"Maybe Hoyt was feeding you a line."

"How so?"

"Somebody with a score to settle was out to get him. They tried once before and got the Carver girl instead. Sounds to me like he was trying to mislead you—throw you off the track."

"Why would he invent a story about the girl?"

"Beats me." Palmer massaged his jaw, considering. "But there's one thing I can tell you for a fact—Alice Carver is dead!"

"What makes you so certain?"

"I saw it myself! Hoyt sent for me the night she was killed. Her dress was covered with blood and she was cold as a mackerel. No maybe about it!"

"Did you feel her pulse?"

"Hell, no!" Palmer said sharply. "I know a corpse when I see one!"

"Hoyt told me it happened late at night. In the dark, it'd be easy to fake something like that . . . wouldn't it?"

A strange light came into Palmer's eyes. "I still don't buy it. We buried her the very next day! I was standing right there when they put her in the grave."

"Where was her father?"

"He vamoosed sometime during the night."

"Gets curiouser and curiouser, don't it?"

Palmer was silent for a time. At last, as though to underscore the question, he looked Starback squarely in the eye. "What are you after? Let's quit beating around the bush and get to it."

Starbuck flicked an ash off his cigarette. "I want to exhume the Carver girl's coffin."

"Dig her up?" Palmer's expression turned to blank astonishment. "Why, for Chrissake?"

"A couple of reasons," Starbuck said with dungeon calm. "If the coffin's empty—or there's someone else in it—that means Hoyt was telling the truth. In other words, somebody went to a lot of trouble to make the girl's death believable. I intend to find out why."

"What's the other reason?"

"If the murder was a fake, then it substantiates everything Hoyt told me about Skinner. Wouldn't you agree?"

"Not necessarily." Palmer steepled his fingers, peered across the desk. "We'd still have only Hoyt's word that Skinner was behind it. And a dead man's word—especially secondhand—isn't admissible in court."

Starbuck's mouth curled. "You seem to forget the daisy chain I mentioned. Yeager to Stimson to Skinner. All in one night—the night of the robbery."

"Still inadmissible," Palmer growled. "You're just guessing what Stimson had in that satchel. You couldn't swear to it under oath."

"You surprise me, Sheriff." Starbuck looked at him questioningly. "Hoyt led me to believe there's no love lost between you and Skinner. Maybe I heard him wrong."

Palmer brushed away the thought with a quick, impatient gesture. "We're in opposite political camps, but that's neither here nor there. So far as I know, Cyrus Skinner just dabbles in politics. He's no kingfish or power behind the throne! And I'll eat your hat if he's involved in these robberies. He's just too god-blessed straight!"

"That's the whole point," Starbuck noted. "He wears a starchy collar and acts holier than thou. Nobody would ever suspect he's behind the robbers and the vice payoffs. Not to mention the political shenanigans."

"Hard to swallow." Palmer lowered his head, tight-lipped. "Stimson's a different ball of wax. I wouldn't put anything past him! But I'll lay odds Skinner's no part of it."

"Why would Hoyt accuse an innocent man?"

"Who knows?" Palmer paused, jawline set in a scowl. "Maybe him and Stimson were splitting the vice payoffs. For that matter, they might've had you pegged as an undercover man from the start. Maybe the whole idea was to lead you to Skinner—put you on a blind trail."

"It won't wash." Starbuck's voice was firm. "I had them fooled down the line. It was business as usual—and nobody gave me a tumble."

"If you had them fooled"—Palmer's eyes burned with intensity—"then how come George Hoyt's dead? You slipped up somewhere, and probably more than once. Otherwise, he wouldn't have a quart of buckshot up his gizzard."

Their eyes locked. Starbuck gave him a straight, hard look, challenging him, and there was an awkward silence. He marked again that the sheriff was a cool customer, but nonetheless susceptible to spite and petty intolerance. At last, his expression stoic, he broke the impasse.

"What's your problem?" he asked bluntly. "Are you pissed off because I worked my own game in your bailiwick?"

"Wouldn't you be?" Palmer said with a flare of annoyance. "Even the Pinkertons make it standard practice to work with local law officers."

"Maybe that's why the Pinks lose so many men. I operate on a real simple principle, Sheriff. The fewer people who know about me, the longer I'll live."

"Say what you mean!" Palmer said crossly. "You didn't trust me enough to take me into your confidence. That's it in a nutshell, isn't it?"

"Nothing personal," Starbuck observed. "Until tonight, I had to play it close to the vest. All that changed after my talk with Hoyt."

"What's Hoyt got to do with me?"

"He gave you a clean bill of health . . . told me you're not involved with Skinner."

"How come you put so much faith in what a jackleg lawyer has to say?"

Starbuck dropped his cigarette on the floor, crushed it underfoot. "I had him by the short hairs, and Hoyt was no dummy. He saw a way to make a deal and save his own hide. So there was no reason for him to lie to me about Skinner. The truth was his only way out."

"I suppose it's possible," Palmer said without conviction. "But I'm still not entirely sold. Cyrus Skinner just don't seem like the type."

"Would you stake your reputation on it?"

"No," Palmer said grudgingly. "I wouldn't go that far."

"Then I take it you've got no objection to starting an investigation—do you?"

"You talking about Skinner?"

"And Stimson," Starbuck added. "I wounded one of his men tonight. I'd hazard a guess it was one of the bouncers at the Gem. Find the man and squeeze him, and he'll spill the beans on Stimson."

"Where does that get us?"

"It'll get Stimson indicted for the murder of the county prosecutor. That's one charge nobody will get quashed, not even Cyrus Skinner. Once Stimson's indicted, then you offer him a deal."

"Talk or hang!" Palmer nodded solemnly. "That what you had in mind?"

"On the button," Starbuck acknowledged. "I'll wager Stimson knows all there is to know about Skinner. Graft and political corruption, the vice payoffs and the stage holdups. You get him to turn songbird and it's all over but the shouting. He'll put a noose around Skinner's neck."

"How about Frank Yeager?"

"Hold off till you've got Stimson's balls in a nutcracker. Then you can suit yourself about Yeager. Let him hang or use him as a corroborating witness . . . whichever seems best."

Palmer looked on the verge of saying something but apparently changed his mind. He eyed Starbuck skeptically. "What are you planning to do?"

"I'll tell you in about an hour."

"An hour?"

"After we've dug up Alice Carver."

The Virginia City cemetery was on a hillside west of town. The graves were marked with wooden crosses and crude headstones. A sickle moon bathed the landscape in a pale, ghostly light.

Starbuck and Palmer were in shirtsleeves, their coats tossed on the ground. The night was chilly, and despite a brisk northwesterly wind their foreheads glistened with sweat. They dug silently, standing at opposite ends of the grave, already knee-deep in an open hole. Their shovels rose and fell with a methodical rhythm, flashing dully in the moonlight. A mound of earth was heaped at one side of the grave.

Some while earlier, they had left the sheriff's office by the back door. Palmer had expressed the opinion that the job would be easier done in daylight. Starbuck agreed, but he'd stressed the need for secrecy. He was determined that there be no leak of their visit to the graveyard. Whatever they found, if word of the exhumation got out it would immediately alert Cyrus Skinner. Thus far, only Palmer was aware of the disclosures made by George Hoyt, the murdered lawyer. That provided an edge they desperately needed. One that might well make or break the investigation.

Palmer grouched and complained, still not wholly convinced. But in the end, Starbuck's view had prevailed. A couple of shovels were collected from the jail toolshed, and they trudged off toward the cemetery. No one saw them leave town.

An hour or so had passed, and they were now hip-deep in the grave. Starbuck's shovel suddenly struck something solid, and they both paused. Then he jabbed lightly with the shovel, and a wooden *clunk* echoed from the hole. Gingerly, they began scooping out the last few inches of dirt. The top of a pine coffin slowly became visible in the dim light. After widening the hole around the sides, they stopped and leaned on their shovels. Starbuck ducked his chin at the coffin.

"Who does the honors?"

"Be my guest."

Palmer scambled out to level ground. He dusted himself off, then went to one knee beside the grave. Starbuck found footholds on either side of the hole and set himself with his back to the headstone. Then he wedged his shovel under the coffin lid and pried upward. The rusty nails protested, loosening with the screech of metal embedded deeply into wood. He worked the tip of the shovel all the way around, levering with the handle until he'd sprung the last of the nails. The lid popped free of the coffin.

Stooping down, Starbuck grasped the lid and swung it aside. He fished a match out of his vest pocket and struck it, cupping the flame in both hands. Palmer leaned into the grave as he opened his hands in a flare of light. The coffin was empty.

Starbuck doused the match and hoisted himself out of the hole. Palmer was slack-jawed, still on one knee, staring downward with stunned disbelief. A moment passed, then he stood and glanced at Starbuck with a baffled look. His face was pinched in an oxlike expression.

"I guess that makes me the prize sucker of all time."

"Forget it," Starbuck said with grim satisfaction. "I wasn't sure myself till I struck that match."

"Dirty bastards!" Palmer cursed furiously. "Half the town must have been in on it!"

"I'd tend to doubt it," Starbuck said quietly. "Outside of Skinner and his bunch, all they needed was the undertaker. Somebody probably put a gun in his ear and gave him the word. So long as it wasn't his own funeral, why should he care?"

"He'll damn sure care when I get through with him!"

"Don't go off half-cocked," Starbuck cautioned.

"Before you kick up too much dust, there's one last thing I want you to look into."

"What's that?"

"The Judas," Starbuck replied levelly. "Find him and you'll have an even stronger case against Skinner."

Palmer uttered a noncommittal grunt. "Tell you the truth, all this Judas business sounds like a pipe dream to me."

"No," Starbuck corrected him, "there's got to be an inside man. The holdups are too slick for it to work any other way. The case won't be closed till we nail him to the wall."

"Easy for you to say," Palmer grumbled. "Where would you suggest I look?"

"Omar Stimson," Starbuck advised. "Once he turns canary, he'll whistle any tune you name. Ask him about our Judas."

"Any more instructions?"

"I reckon that ought to do it."

"Then I've got a question of my own."

"Shoot."

"Now that you've looked in the coffin, what's next? You had something in mind, or we wouldn't be out robbing graves in the middle of the night."

A wintry smile lighted Starbuck's eyes. "While you're handling things here, I figured I'd tie off a loose end."

Palmer's gaze sharpened. He stared at Starbuck with the beady look of a stuffed owl. "What loose end?"

"A little lady by the name of Alice Carver."

Chapter Twelve

Starbuck traveled by stage from Virginia City. He took a roundabout route, switching from stage to train. At a whistle stop outside Butte, he finally boarded the Union Pacific eastbound. His destination was Chicago.

Once burned, Starbuck was now twice as careful. He assumed he was being watched night and day by Stimson's men. In turn, his every movement would be reported to Cyrus Skinner. He therefore took inordinate measures to guarantee he wasn't tailed. On guard constantly, he at last assured himself no one shadowed his backtrail. Only then did he discard the guise of Lee Hall and assume his own identity. He boarded the eastbound train confident his destination was unknown.

Four nights later he arrived in Chicago. Once inside the depot, he bought a newspaper and turned to the theatrical advertisements. The Buffalo Bill Combination was currently playing at Sprague's Olympic Theater. He checked his watch against the show schedule and saw that he still had time to catch the evening performance. Outside Union Station he stepped into a hansom cab and told the driver not to spare the whip.

He was anxious now for what seemed a long-overdue meeting with Alice Carver.

The ride to the Loop district was a treat in itself. Starbuck was widely traveled, but St. Louis was the largest city he'd previously visited. Framed against a full moon, the skyline of downtown Chicago was a staggering sight. The tall buildings dwarfed anything he had seen before and made Denver look like a quaint hamlet. He was particularly impressed by the brick and stone architecture, the absence of buildings constructed of wood. Then he recalled the Great Fire of '71, a holocaust that had razed three square miles and left a hundred thousand people homeless. Wood was subsequently banned as a building material in the downtown area. A new Chicago rose from the ashes, and within a year the restoration was complete. Starbuck, never easily impressed, was taken with the Windy City.

On Randolph Street, the hansom dropped him outside the theater. Show posters announced William F. Cody's appearance in an original play entitled *Buffalo Bill's Pledge*. Starbuck inquired at the box office and was directed to the stage entrance. He proceeded down a passageway between buildings and talked his way past a watchman at the rear door. Backstage was a tableau of pandemonium in motion. Frontiersmen in makeup and Indians tricked out in war paint were rushing about in a general atmosphere of confusion. A donkey, which apparently had some role in the melodrama, was braying loudly and kicking at anyone within range. To an outsider, the show business had the look of disorganized chaos.

Starbuck spotted Cody standing in the wings. The scout was attired in fringed buckskins, bleached a snowy white, and the ivory-handled Peacemakers were strapped around his waist. From beneath a broad sombrero his hair flowed over his shoulders in hot-curled waves. He turned as Starbuck spoke his name. He smelled of rosewater lotion and rye whiskey.

"Well, bless my soul!" he cackled. "Where'd you drop from, Luke?"

"Points west," Starbuck said evasively. "Just pulled in a little while ago."

"Don't tell me you came all that way to see the show!"

"Not exactly," Starbuck commented. "I'm looking for Doc Carver."

"Look no further!" Cody flung his arm in a grand gesture. "There's your man!"

Starbuck moved closer and gazed past the drawn curtains. Carver was onstage, standing near the foot-lights, with his face to the audience. He had a rifle balanced over his shoulder and he was aligning the sights through a small hand mirror. His assistant, Sally Devlin, was upstage, hands clasped behind her back and her profile turned toward him. A lighted cigarette, trailing wisps of smoke, protruded from her lips. Below the footlights, a snare drum rolled ominously from the orchestra pit. Carver let the tension build a moment longer, then fired over his shoulder. The cigarette exploded in a shower of sparks and tobacco, and the girl immediately held the shredded stub high overhead. The audience broke out in a cheering, spontaneous ovation.

Carver shamelessly milked the applause. Then, ever the consummate showman, he swiftly moved on to the next trick shot. Starbuck watched only a short time before turning back to Cody. He motioned toward the stage.

"How long does the act last?"

"Three more shots." Cody adopted a lordly stance, thumbs hooked in his gunbelt. "Doc's a great crowd pleaser! He gets them warmed up before we do the play. Always helps to have an audience in the proper mood."

"He's good, all right." Starbuck's tone was matter-of-fact. "Course, his daughter's not bad, either. Takes spunk to let yourself be shot at."

"Alice is a trouper!" Cody said effusively. "Born to the show business—a natural performer!"

"She's easy on the eyes, too."

"Very easy!" Cody lowered one eyelid in a burlesque leer. "I sometimes regret that I'm a happily married man."

"I suppose she has lots of gentlemen admirers?"

"Their number is legion, Luke! So many she has to fight them off with a switch!"

"You don't say?" Starbuck mused out loud. "The only stage women I've known were sort of fast and loose. Guess she's not that way, huh?"

"Oh—" Cody hesitated, cocked his head in a shrewd look. "All of a sudden, I detect a detective at work. Why so much interest in Alice? I thought you were here to see Doc."

"Curiosity." Starbuck spread his hands, shrugged. "Last time around, Doc introduced her to me as Sally

Devlin. I reckon it got me to wondering."

"That's just her stage name . . ." Cody's voice trailed off and he suddenly looked upset. "God-almighty! I recollect you told me Doc was involved in a civil suit. That wasn't so, was it? It's a divorce action, involving Alice! She's been named as a co-respondent, hasn't she?"

"Why?" Starbuck inquired calmly. "Does she play around with married men?"

"I warned Doc!" Cody fumed. "She's a wonderful girl and bright as a penny. But she's got the morals of a heathen squaw!"

"So she does play—"

Starbuck glanced past him and abruptly stopped. The stage door had opened and two men paused at the watchman's desk. One of them was Omar Stimson's bouncer, the hooligan who had spotted him on the street in Virginia City. He was vaguely aware of applause and the blare of the orchestra from the theater. He sensed the trick-shot act was ending and the Carvers would walk offstage at any moment. His gaze shifted quickly to Cody.

"Are those Peacemakers loaded?"

"Only with blanks." Cody read his expression, tensed. "What's wrong, Luke?"

"Don't look around!" Starbuck ordered. "A couple of hardcases just came through the back door. I've got reason to believe they're here to kill Alice Carver."

"Judas Priest!" Cody croaked. "What are we—"

"Shut up and listen!" Starbuck interrupted. "Do exactly what I say! Get out on that stage and stop the

Carver girl. Don't let her come back here! Understand?"

Cody paled. "She's already coming offstage! Her and Doc!"

"Then move—now!"

Starbuck walked toward the rear door. Behind him, he heard a muffled conversation as Cody tried to stall the Carvers. Directly ahead, the two men were moving slowly in his direction. Neither of them recognized him, for he was no longer in the guise of Lee Hall. Their eyes went instead to the wings, and Alice Carver. He halted several paces away, blocking their path.

"You boys should've stayed in Virginia City."

Too late, the men reacted to the words. Starbuck's hand was in motion even as he spoke. The Colt appeared from beneath his suit jacket and leveled at arm's length. A beat behind, the men clawed at the pistols inside their coats. Starbuck fired two rapid shots, one report blending with the other. The first slug drilled through the bouncer's breastbone and the second struck him below the left nipple. He collapsed as though his legs had been chopped off and fell spread-eagle on the floor. His sphincter voided and a bulldog pistol slipped from his hand.

The other man got off one shot. The bullet nicked Starbuck's sleeve and thudded into a stage set across the way. Starbuck brought the Colt to bear and emptied it in a blinding roar. His shots were deliberate and spaced no more than a pulsebeat apart. The heavy slugs stitched three red dots straight up the man's sternum to the base of his throat. His mouth opened in a

silent scream and he vomited a hogshead of blood
down his shirtfront. Then the light went out in his
eyes and his knees folded like an accordion. He
slumped to the floor without a sound.

Still watchful, Starbuck shucked empties and reloaded the Colt. He moved forward and checked both
men, satisfying himself that they were dead. All
around him the troupe of actors, frontiersmen and Indians alike, were gawking at him with looks of pop-
eyed wonder. At last, turning away from the bodies,
he directed his gaze to the stage wings. He breathed
an inward sigh of relief.

Doc Carver was pressed flat against the wall. Buffalo Bill Cody had thrown the girl to the floor and
covered her with his own body. She was alive and
unhurt, no worse for the experience.

Starbuck promised himself she would talk.

Some hours later the backstage area had been restored
to order. The police had come and gone, ruling the
killings justifiable homicide. The bodies had been removed to the city morgue, and Bill Cody had led a
gaggle of reporters to a nearby saloon. His recounting
of the shootout had lost nothing in the telling.

On Starbuck's orders, Doc Carver and his daughter
had been sequestered in the sharpshooter's dressing
room. No mention of their role in the killings had
been made to the police. So far as the authorities
knew, the dead men had followed Starbuck to Chicago with the express purpose of assassinating him.
There was no hint of the underlying scandal and the

magnitude of the investigation. The police had been fobbed off with a story of stage robbers and unsolved murders.

Starbuck was now in the midst of his own inter-rogation. Seated across from him were Alice Carver and her father. The girl appeared in shock, and Carver's expression was somehow crestfallen. The atmosphere in the dressing room was oppressive, charged with tension.

"No more lies!" Starbuck eyed father and daughter with a steady, uncompromising gaze. "I want the truth, and I want it now. So don't try dancing me around. Talk straight and talk fast!"

Carver flushed and bobbed his head. "How did you find out . . . about Alice?"

"George Hoyt told me," Starbuck said impassively. "Just before he was murdered."

The girl began to weep, snuffling and whimpering like a hurt puppy. She pulled out a dainty handker-chief and buried her face in her hands. Carver soothed her with a shushing sound and patted her gently on the shoulder. Then he turned back to Starbuck.

"I couldn't level with you in North Platte. Surely you can understand—I had to protect Alice—at all costs! The only out I saw was to send you to Hoyt."

A stony look settled over Starbuck's features. "You and your daughter have gotten several people killed. Tonight you almost bought the farm yourselves."

"Nonsense," Carver said, a bit too quickly. "You told the police those men were after you."

"Don't play dumb!" Starbuck flared. "Skinner sent them here to kill both of you. Unless you cooperate, he'll try again. You know too much for him to let you live."

"No!" Alice protested with a sudden cry. "I don't believe it! Cyrus would never harm me!"

"Think not?" Starbuck's gaze narrowed. "Then who sent them? Suppose you tell me that."

"I have no idea," Alice murmured, sobbing into her hanky. "I only know it wasn't Cyrus."

"You're lying!" Starbuck said abrasively. "You sleep around, and your affairs end up with dead men all over the place. So cut the crocodile tears and dry your eyes! I don't buy your act anymore."

"Hold on, now!" Carver interjected. "I won't allow you to talk to my daughter that way!"

"Button your lip," Starbuck warned him. "Your daughter's virtue doesn't interest me. I'm only interested in *who* she's slept with! So stay the hell out of it and let her speak for herself."

Starbuck disliked the cruel sound of his voice. Yet the girl's confession was essential to the case, and he was determined to make her talk. He looked at her now with a cold stare.

A strained stillness fell over the dressing room. Alice Carver's face drained of color and she blinked, as though somewhere within herself a festering conflict had at last been resolved. Then she dabbed at her tears and took hold of herself. She sat straighter, lifted her chin defiantly, and the transformation was startling. She gave Starbuck a look that could have drawn blood.

"Very well," she said stiffly, her lips white. "Ask your questions."

"Tell me about Skinner," Starbuck prompted. "How did you get involved with him?"

"Through George Hoyt." Her eyes shuttled away. "George and I began keeping company soon after our act opened in Virginia City. He was considerate and lots of fun, and we had good times together. Then one night he introduced me to Cyrus."

"So you dropped Hoyt?" Starbuck goaded her. "Even though you knew he was stuck on you?"

"Yes, I did!" she snapped. "I never made any promises! Besides, I have a perfect right to choose who I—"

"We know what you do," Starbuck said caustically. "I take it Skinner was smitten by your charms and vice versa?"

"What of it?" Her cheeks burned with a blush. "Cyrus Skinner is a very attractive man . . . very kind."

"Save it for your diary!" Starbuck's face toughened and he squinted at her. "How long before you found out Skinner was involved in stage holdups and dirty politics?"

"I was never certain." Her look belied her words. "Not until that last night."

"The night Skinner ordered Hoyt to fake your murder?"

"Yes." Her voice was unnaturally grave, subdued. "Omar Stimson came to Cyrus's home—"

"Where were you?"

A pulse throbbed in her neck. "In the bedroom."

"What happened next?"

"Stimson was raving." Her lips trembled slightly. "He started shouting about vice collections and robberies, and how he was being cheated on the split. Before Cyrus could stop him, he mentioned something about the boss—"

"Wait a minute!" Starbuck was suddenly very quiet, eyes boring into her. "What boss? Who was he talking about?"

"I don't know." She squirmed uncomfortably in her chair. "He was just threatening to go see the 'boss.' Apparently it's someone Cyrus reports to on their . . . business affairs."

"All right, go on with what you were saying."

"Cyrus slapped him and told him someone else was in the house. They argued a little while, and then Stimson stormed out in a rage. Afterward, Cyrus was very upset, concerned for me. He said we couldn't trust Stimson to keep quiet."

"He thought Stimson might go to the 'boss' and tell him you'd overheard the conversation?"

"Something like that." She smiled wanly, remembering. "Of course, Stimson never actually saw me. But Cyrus was afraid to take the chance. He said if Stimson talked, then I would never leave Virginia City alive."

Starbuck let out his breath in a low whistle. "Now it all ties together. Skinner rigged it with Hoyt to fake your death. Then Hoyt spread the story that it was the work of outlaws trying to murder him. So that got you off the hook and it left Omar Stimson with nothing to tell the 'boss.' Isn't that about the gist of it?"

Alice Carver's hand darted to her hair like a dying bird. "Cyrus loved me very much. He jeopardized himself for my sake . . . and what we'd shared."

"No question about it," Doc Carver added hastily. "Skinner arranged the whole thing and got us out of town that same night. His only condition was that we were never to tell anyone—and stay away from Virginia City."

Starbuck heaved himself to his feet. "Doc, your secret's safe with me. You and Alice just keep quiet, and don't worry about a thing. I'll see to it you're never bothered again."

"What about Skinner?" Carver asked gloomily. "Will you have to . . ."

"I'll do my damnedest to take him alive. That's the best I can promise."

Starbuck departed on that note. Outside the dressing room, he walked toward the stage entrance. His mind turned to train schedules and the journey ahead. He figured tonight's killings had bought him a week's grace, no more. Once the news hit Virginia City, all bets were off. He would have lost the element of surprise, and the edge.

The night watchman nodded as Starbuck opened the door and stepped into the chill night air. He ran full tilt into Bill Cody. The scout stumbled and almost lost his balance. He was glassy-eyed and clearly feeling no pain. He gave Starbuck a tipsy grin.

"You're all set, Luke! I let those reporters have an earful!"

"Wish I could've been there to hear it, Bill."

"Ol' Deadeye Starbuck!" Cody laughed uproariously. "You're gonna have yourself one helluva write-up in tomorrow's papers. Course, it won't do my show any harm, either. I took a modest share of the credit—knowing you wouldn't mind."

"Don't mind a bit," Starbuck said earnestly. "You showed plenty of guts tonight, Bill. I couldn't have done it without you."

Cody's chest swelled and he stood a little straighter. "Guess I didn't do so bad at that. I've been shooting blanks so long I almost forgot what real gunpowder smells like."

"An old war-horse like you never forgets."

"Well, it's damn white of you to say so, Luke! Why don't I buy you a drink and we'll swap a few windies?"

"Another time, maybe. I've got a train to catch."

"Where the devil you off to now?"

"Headed west," Starbuck said with an odd smile. "Look me up whenever you're in Denver."

Cody wrung his hand and smote him across the shoulder. Then Starbuck turned and hurried toward the street. As he walked away it occurred to him that he had played into luck with Buffalo Bill's Combination. Tonight's backstage drama had positively identified the man he'd been hired to kill. Only one man knew about Alice Carver's empty coffin. Therefore, only one man could have sent the killers to Chicago. A man who was called boss by Virginia City's underworld leaders.

His name was Henry Palmer.

Chapter Thirteen

The east end of Wallace Street was blocked by a shoulder-to-shoulder horde of miners. The crowd choked the intersection, and the roofs of several business establishments were packed with men. Their attention was riveted on the sheriff's office.

Farther upstreet, the noon stage slowly ground to a halt. Starbuck stepped from the coach, and his gaze was immediately drawn to the commotion. He'd departed Chicago six days ago, and he looked somewhat the worse for wear. His eyes were bloodshot from too little sleep and his features were etched with fatigue. He stared at the massed throng with a fuzzy expression, thoroughly bewildered. After collecting his warbag, he stopped a miner hurrying past. The man responded to his inquiry with a shout and a huge grin.

"Hanging! Frank Yeager's gonna swing!"

The reply jolted Starbuck out of his funk. A surge of adrenalin pumped through him and he was suddenly galvanized with energy. He ducked into the hotel and left his warbag with the desk clerk. Then he crossed to the south side of the street and rushed along the boardwalk. Halfway down the block the crowd grew denser, with miners packed into a solid wedge.

He pushed and shoved, bulling through their ranks, and finally fought his way to the intersection. The sheriff's office and the jail were on the opposite corner. To the rear of the building, on an open plot of ground, stood a timbered scaffold. Several armed deputies held the crowd at a distance.

A hush fell over the miners as Starbuck edged around the corner. He stopped, staring intently across the street. Frank Yeager, arms strapped to his sides, was positioned over the gallows trapdoor. Apparently the death warrant had been read and the condemned man had already spoken his last words. As Starbuck watched, the sheriff loosened a hangman's noose dangling from the crossbeam. Palmer then slipped the noose over Yeager's head and cinched the knot tight behind the left ear. Yeager's eyes glistened and his labored breathing was audible in the eerie quiet. He looked like a bayed animal, paralyzed and desperate.

Palmer walked to the rear of the gallows and halted beside a long wooden lever. His expression was phlegmatic, no trace of emotion. He seemed to hesitate for an interminable length of time, though only a few seconds elapsed. Then he took hold of the wooden lever and yanked it hard. The trapdoor popped open and Frank Yeager shot through the hole. A split second later he hit the end of the rope with a suddenness that jarred the scaffold. His neck snapped and his head crooked over his shoulder at a grotesque angle. His body hung on a plumb line, swaying gently to the creak of the rope. A dark stain spread over the crotch of his trousers.

Somewhere in the crowd a man loosed a yipping

cheer. The assemblage took up the cry, and within moments the voices of a thousand or more miners were raised in a thunderous bloodroar. On the scaffold, Palmer seemed wholly oblivious to the bedlam on the street. He knelt at the edge of the trapdoor and felt for a pulsebeat on Yeager's neck. Then he stood, motioning to a couple of the deputies, who hurried beneath the scaffold and lifted the dead man into the air. Palmer removed the noose, and the body was lowered to the ground. The crowd began chanting his name as he descended the gallows steps. The sheriff waved and disappeared through the back door of the jail.

A chill settled over Starbuck. Something was all wrong here, and he had no ready explanation. Frank Yeager should not have gone quietly to his death. He should have accused, instead, the man who'd hanged him. The boss of Virginia City, Henry Palmer. Yet it was clear that Yeager had suspected nothing. Nor was there any evidence of hostility among the miners and townspeople. The crowd had actually cheered the sheriff.

Starbuck turned and walked away. A prickly uneasiness pervaded his thoughts, and he felt curiously disoriented. The case had taken a queer and totally unexpected twist while he was in Chicago. He needed information, details and hard facts. Only then could he sort things out and decide on his next move. He drifted along as the crowd quickly dispersed to saloons and gaming dens upstreet. A hanging was always good for business.

By the time he entered the hotel, Starbuck had regained his composure. His features were a mask of bonhomie and jolly good humor. He approached the front desk, where he'd left his warbag, with a confident stride. He nodded pleasantly to the desk clerk.

"You missed a helluva show!"

"Just my luck!" the desk clerk grouched. "Biggest thing that's happened around here since Heck was a pup!"

Starbuck thought there was little chance he would be recognized. On previous stopovers at the hotel, he'd been operating under the guise of Lee Hall; today he was himself. The desk clerk seemed the talkative sort, and the lobby was empty. He figured it was as good a place as any to start asking questions. He leaned on the counter, his expression quizzical.

"Who was the jaybird they hung?"

"Frank Yeager!" the desk clerk said importantly. "Only the top dog of a gang of stage robbers and murderers!"

"No joke?" Starbuck marveled. "How'd he get himself caught?"

"Sheriff Palmer captured him and brought him to trial. He confessed, and the jury sentenced him to hang."

"Confessed?" Starbuck repeated, genuinely astonished. "Why would he do a thing like that?"

The desk clerk chortled. "There's a rumor the sheriff put a gun to his head. Anyway, Yeager wrote it out and signed it, and he named names. Set the whole town back on its ear!"

"You talking about gang members?"

"Well, that was only part of it. Turns out a couple

of big muckamucks here in town were involved. One was Omar Stimson, owned the Gem Theater. The other was Cyrus Skinner—and that really blew the lid!"

Starbuck took a tight grip on himself. "What's so important about Skinner?"

"Everybody thought he was the pillar of the community! But Yeager accused him of being the mastermind behind the robberies *and* the political kingfish of Virginia City. Appears he was right, too! Skinner lit out and he hasn't been heard from since."

"What happened to the other one . . . Stimson?"

"Dead and buried! Sheriff Palmer cornered him in his office, over at the Gem. The damn fool resisted arrest—pulled a gun—and the sheriff shot him down on the spot. Guess he figured he'd hang anyway, so what the hell!"

"How about the gang?"

"Now there's a story!"

The desk clerk gleefully recounted events of the past twenty-four hours. A news story had appeared yesterday regarding a private detective and a shootout in Chicago. The story implied that the stageline had little faith in the sheriff; thus an undercover agent had been assigned to the case. Adding to the controversy was the fact that the sheriff had captured Yeager but none of the gang. The vigilantes had mobilized, with their leader, Wilbur X. Lott, issuing a call for citizen justice. Late yesterday three gang members had been run to earth and summarily hanged. Earlier today two more robbers had been taken prisoner, and they were scheduled to hang before sundown. It was both an object lesson to outlaws and a direct challenge to the sheriff. The vigilantes planned to hold a public necktie party on the edge of town. Their act, in effect, would place them above the law.

"The town's divided," the desk clerk concluded. "Some support the sheriff and some support the vigilantes. God knows where it'll end!"

Starbuck thought it an appropriate comment. He signed the register and collected his warbag. Then he climbed the stairs and moved along the hallway to his room. His carefree manner vanished the moment the door closed. He was now thoroughly confounded.

Standing at the window, he stared out across the mining camp. He mentally catalogued all he'd learned in Chicago. The Carver girl's story, added to the backstage shootout, led inexorably to one conclusion. Sheriff Henry Palmer was the shadowy "boss" of Virginia City.

Yet that certitude had now gone by the boards. Palmer's actions over the past week or so were those of a dedicated lawman. He had wrung a confession out of Yeager and brought the gang leader to trial in open court. At the same time, he had exposed the town's vice lord and killed him in a gunfight. Finally, he'd put Cyrus Skinner to flight and thereby scuttled the entire conspiracy. All of which would have proved suicidal—if Palmer actually was the "boss."

Any of the men involved, particularly Stimson and Skinner, could have turned the tables. By identifying Palmer, they could have saved themselves and gained revenge in one stroke. But none of them had pointed an accusing finger and no allegations had been directed at the sheriff. Events, it appeared, were at variance with everything unearthed in Chicago. Nothing jibed, and for all practical purposes there was no case. The theory about Henry Palmer had been scotched.

Starbuck found himself in a quandary. There was no doubt whatever that a conspiracy existed. Alice Carver's story, in that respect at least, had been borne out by what he'd uncovered on his own. Yet the principal suspect—until an hour ago the only suspect—was seemingly absolved of guilt. Which raised the specter of still another imponderable.

Who was the phantom "boss" of Virginia City?

Late that afternoon the sun slowly retreated toward the mountains. The creek was molten with sunlight and the road through Alder Gulch was jammed with miners. Their destination was a clearing on the outskirts of town.

Starbuck was lost in the crowd. He estimated there were easily twice as many men as had attended Frank Yeager's hanging. More were arriving by the minute, with a greater number from claims upstream along the gulch. The turnout indicated the vigilantes had mustered strong support.

From his vantage point, Starbuck had what amounted to a ringside seat. He stood on a small knoll which directly overlooked the clearing. A large alder tree, with massive branches sweeping outward, dominated the scene. He thought it ironic that the alder had already been dubbed the Judas Tree. The Judas he sought, who was still unidentified, no doubt appreciated the joke even more. Understandably, the vigilantes had selected the name solely for its biblical symbolism. All who robbed and murdered their fellow men were by definition the worst of traitors. Or so the vigilantes claimed.

Strangely, Starbuck was not an advocate of vigilante justice. He hunted down outlaws and killed them, which was a form of summary execution. Yet he operated within the framework of the law, and he considered it contemptible to kill in cold blood. By his code, a mob was never to be trusted. There was no reason in their ugliness, no temperance in their rage.

Some years ago, on his first job as a range detective, he'd witnessed the madness of mob action. Hired by a group of ranchers, he had trailed a gang of horse thieves to No Man's Land. Following a gun battle, the ranchers had hanged the surviving gang members in a frenzy of bloodlust. With no power to intervene, he had gone along, even participated in the lynching. But he'd thought less of himself in the aftermath, and he hadn't slept well for some months. Since then, he had avoided vigilantes like a virulent disease.

Today he was reminded of that long-ago incident. In the clearing below, a group of some twenty vigilantes were gathered around the alder tree. Wilbur X. Lott, their leader, was busily orchestrating the proceedings. A cadaverous man, with a hooked nose and a downturned mouth, he was attired in a hammertail coat and a high-crowned black hat. His voice was loud and astringent, like that of a schoolteacher instructing unruly children. Which was not too far from the truth. He was teaching the rudiments of slow and painful death.

The men waiting to be hanged were apparently resigned to the ordeal. Their hands were tied behind their backs and their expressions were vacant, almost bovine. One of the robbers was Yeager's lieutenant, Charley Reeves. The other man was a hapless gang member whose name meant nothing to anyone. With seeming indifference, they allowed themselves to be positioned beneath a stout tree limb. Then ropes were tossed over the limb and crude nooses were fitted around their necks. Several vigilantes stepped forward and took hold of the slack ropes. Oddly, they looked like teams about to engage in a tug-of-war.

On Lott's command, the vigilantes hauled back on the ropes. The robbers, dancing frantically on empty space, were hoisted off the ground. Their eyes bulged and seemed to burst from the sockets with engorged blood vessels. Their gyrations spun them kicking and thrashing, while their features purpled, then turned darker. Their mouths popped open and their swollen tongues gradually changed from blackish amber to deep onyx in color. They vainly fought the ropes until the last gasp of air was gone, and even then their frenzied struggles lessened only by degrees. Several minutes passed while they slowly strangled to death.

Starbuck eased through the crowd and made his way back to the road. As he walked toward town it occurred to him that Wilbur X. Lott was either a rank amateur or an inhuman sadist. He tended to think it was the latter. Lott had staged a gruesome spectacle with only one thought in mind. After today, the vigilante leader would be known as a fearsome avenger, the champion of honest men. It was a reputation that would serve him well when he threw his hat into the political arena. The hanging of the stagecoach robbers was strictly incidental. A sideshow to beguile the mob and win support.

On the edge of town, Starbuck spotted Henry Palmer. The sheriff was standing outside a whorehouse on the fringe of the red-light district. From there, he had observed the mass gathering of miners and the hangings. That he hadn't attended—or attempted to interfere—was a gauge of the mood in Virginia City. His expression was somber as he watched Starbuck approach.

"Hello, Luke." He nodded stiffly. "Heard you'd checked into the hotel."

"I got back in time to see Frank Yeager take the drop."

"Why didn't you come by the office?"

Starbuck ignored the question. "That was a nifty piece of work with Yeager. From what I hear, you got him to squeal like a stuck hog."

"Nothing to brag about," Palmer said, no timbre in his voice. "I should've followed your advice—gone after Stimson's bouncer."

"What stopped you?"

"Figured I'd make Yeager talk and build a stronger case. It worked fine till things went haywire."

Starbuck eyed him keenly. "Stimson's bouncer wasn't around, anyway. He trailed me to Chicago."

"I read about it." Palmer shook his head ruefully.

"Guess we outfoxed ourselves. Stimson must've had a tail on you the whole time."

"Appears that way."

"How'd you do with Alice Carver?"

"Blind alley." Starbuck opened hs hands, shrugged. "She wasn't with her father, and all my other leads fizzled out. I suppose she'll turn up someday."

"Yeah, probably so." Palmer hawked and spat, eyes rimmed with disgust. "Seems like tough breaks always come in bunches."

Starbuck looked down and studied the ground a moment. "What're you doing about Skinner?"

"I've put out feelers." Palmer's face twisted in a grimace. "If he's still in Montana, I'll hear about it."

"You really think he'd stick around?"

"No," Palmer said with a sour look. "I'd say he's far away and still running."

"Wouldn't surprise me." Starbuck arched one eyebrow. "How'd Stimson come to pull a gun on you?"

"Your guess on that's as good as mine. I thought he'd go along peaceable, and instead he made a fight of it. I was lucky to get him before he got me."

"Too bad," Starbuck remarked. "He would've made a better witness than Yeager."

"Too bad and too late," Palmer added without humor. "By the time I got to Skinner's office, the news was already out. He skipped town one step ahead of me."

"Word travels fast," Starbuck said evenly. "What about the Judas . . . anything turn up?"

"No hard proof." Palmer seemed to look through him. "But I'd bet my bottom dollar it was Skinner.

His assay business gave him all sorts of inside information. Course, the way things sit, we'll probably never know."

"I reckon not." Starbuck nodded absently. "How do you figure to stop the vigilantes?"

"I don't." Palmer regarded him with great calmness. "I couldn't deputize enough men to stop them. Besides, it'll eventually run its course anyhow. Wilbur Lott won't be able to hold them together."

"He seems to be doing a pretty fair job so far."

"A couple of days don't mean a thing. A week from now it'll all be ancient history."

"Hope you're right." Starbuck gave him a sideways look. "If you're not, it's liable to get ugly. Vigilantes generally wind up lynching innocent people before they're through."

"I almost wish they would!" Palmer said fiercely. "Then I'd have an excuse to stretch Wilbur Lott's skinny neck!"

"Write me and let me how how it turns out."

Palmer looked surprised. "That sounds like you're calling it quits?"

"No reason to stay." Starbuck's smile was cryptic. "Skinner's the only one left alive, and he's long gone. I reckon I'll just close the file on this one. I've got other fish to fry."

"Another case?"

"Sheriff, there's always another case!"

Starbuck pumped hs hand vigorously and walked off toward town. He wondered if Palmer realized he'd lied not once but several times during the conversation. Then, with a sardonic chuckle, he put it from mind. He had a fish to fry that wouldn't wait.

A sucker fish otherwise known as Cyrus Skinner.

Chapter Fourteen

The night was cold and dark. Starbuck stood in the alley behind the Alder Gulch Assay Company. With the butt of his Colt, he broke an upper pane of glass in the rear window. He listened intently for a moment before holstering the pistol. Then he slipped his hand through the broken pane and unlocked the window catch.

A burlap bag lay at his feet. Inside were various tools he'd purchased earlier at a hardware store. After raising the window, he pushed the bag through and lowered it to the floor. He climbed over the sill, then closed the window and drew the blind. The door to the room was shut, and a quick look around convinced him he was in Cyrus Skinner's private office. He pulled a candle from his pocket and lit it with a match. Directly opposite him was a squat floor safe, positioned against the wall. Grunting with satisfaction, he dripped hot wax on the edge of a nearby desk and sealed the candle in place. Then he opened the bag of tools and went to work.

The break-in had been prompted by several factors. A remark by Henry Palmer during their conversation that afternoon had provided the key. The sheriff, immediately after killing Stimson, had gone from the theater to Skinner's office. But word of the shooting had preceded him, and he found Skinner had already skipped town. Which meant Skinner had been caught unprepared, with no time to organize his escape. He'd taken flight on the spur of the moment.

Starbuck understood the criminal mentality. Over the years, he'd developed the knack of stepping into the other man's boots and viewing a situation from the crook's perspective. Everything he had learned to date indicated Cyrus Skinner was a careful man, a methodical planner. So it was reasonable to assume Skinner would have prepared—in advance—for any eventuality. In particular, he would have taken steps to secure his financial position. He would not have fled into poverty.

Yet an assay business was hardly a conduit for large amounts of gold. It followed, then, that Skinner would have developed a method for disposing of the stolen bullion. Starbuck was less interested in the method than in where the gold had gone. He felt confident that when he found the gold he would find Skinner. Since there had been no time to destroy records, Skinner had very probably left behind a paper trail. A file, or perhaps a ledger, that would lead ultimately to a bank. From there, it would be only a matter of legwork to locate Skinner himself. A thief and his money were seldom far apart.

Starbuck's plan was simple. Tonight's job would appear the work of a common yeggman. No one would suspect he'd looted the office, and there would be nothing to indicate the actual purpose of the robbery. He attacked the safe with a drill punch and a four-foot crowbar. Within ten minutes, he had peeled the safe door and was pawing through the contents. He found more than he'd expected.

The stolen gold was on deposit at a bank in Salt Lake City. There was a ledger indicating the dates of deposit and a current balance in excess of one hundred thousand dollars. Stuck inside the ledger was a dossier on one Robert Dempsey. Documented therein was evidence that Dempsey had murdered his former partner in a mining venture; the spot where the body had been buried was clearly marked on an enclosed map. On the map as well were directions to a spot identified simply as Dempsey's Cabin. Some twenty miles south of Virginia City, the cabin was located on Stinking-water Creek.

Starbuck puzzled on it for several minutes. Then, suddenly, he grasped the significance of the dossier and map. The man named Robert Dempsey was Skinner's conduit for the stolen gold. The bullion was somehow transferred to Dempsey, and he in turn arranged to deposit it with the bank in Salt Lake City. But Skinner was apparently a cautious man and operated on the principle that there was no honor among thieves. He'd gathered evidence of the old murder and used it as an instrument of blackmail against Dempsey. He thereby ensured that the gold would arrive safely in Salt Lake City. At the same time, he had guaranteed Dempsey's silence.

Cyrus Skinner's vanishing act was no longer a mystery. Whether or not he'd gone on to Salt Lake

City was a moot point. His first stop was pinpointed precisely on the map.

A cabin on Stinkingwater Creek.

The sun was at its zenith. A narrow ribbon of water snaked through a boulder-strewn canyon. On one side of the creek, the shoreline was sheltered by trees. On the other, a crude log cabin was silhouetted against distant mountains. Smoke drifted lazily from the chimney.

Starbuck lay concealed in the trees. By the angle of the sun, he judged he'd been watching the cabin for nearly an hour. No one had appeared during that time, even though the cabin was clearly occupied. He took heart from the fact that there were two horses standing hipshot in a split-log corral. One man rarely had need of an extra mount.

The wait was slowly beginning to wear on his nerves. He'd ridden through the night, following the road south from Virginia City. Early that morning he had hit Stinkingwater Creek and left his horse tied in a grove of trees. On foot, he had then made his way upstream, pausing frequently to check the map. After spotting the cabin, he'd bellied down and wormed the last hundred yards. He was now bone-tired and on edge, and toying with the idea of rushing the cabin. He decided to give it another five minutes.

The cabin door abruptly opened and a man stepped outside. Starbuck watched as he walked toward the creek with a bucket. He was large and burly, and in no way fitted the description of Cyrus Skinner. Which pretty well pegged him as Skinner's secret accomplice, Robert Dempsey. A pistol was strapped on his hip, and the holster shifted higher as he stooped down at the creek. He dipped the bucket into the water.

"Don't move!"

Starbuck's command was rapped out in a hard voice. Dempsey froze for an instant; then he dropped the bucket and dodged sideways. He moved uncommonly fast for a big man, and the pistol appeared in his hand before he'd taken a full step. He suddenly stopped in his tracks, whirling and crouching, and fired blindly at the treeline. Starbuck shot him twice, centering both shots within a handspan of his shirt pocket. The slugs jarred him backward and his bootheel caught on a rock. Then the gun fell from his hand and he spraddled out on the creek bank. He lay perfectly still.

On his belly, Starbuck squirmed a few yards upstream and took cover behind another tree. He watched the cabin for several moments and thought he saw a shadow of movement behind the window. He cupped one hand to his mouth and yelled.

"Skinner!" He waited a beat. "I know you're in there. Let's talk!"

A long moment slipped past. Then, his voice muffled from within the cabin, Skinner called out. "Who are you?"

"Luke Starbuck! I'm a private detective—the stage-line hired me!"

"How do I know you won't kill me?"

"Doc Carver asked me to take you alive! I promised I'd try!"

"Carver?" Skinner sounded doubtful. "What's it to him?"

"His daughter's still sweet on you! Besides, he figures they owe you one for getting them out of town!"

"Why should I believe you?"

"You've got no choice!" Starbuck replied. "You can come out and live. Or I'll burn you out and kill you. Take your pick!"

Skinner hesitated only briefly. "All right, you win! I'm throwing my gun out. Don't shoot!"

The cabin door opened and Skinner tossed his revolver on the ground. Then he took a tentative step outside and halted, hands raised overhead. He stared apprehensively at the treeline.

Starbuck scrambled to his feet. He kept Skinner covered and cautiously forded the creek. As he moved closer he saw why Alice Carver had lost her head. Skinner was an unusually handsome man. His features had a chiseled look, with a cleft in his chin and piercing dark eyes. His hair was raven black and wavy, and he was built along lithe, muscular lines. He was a ladies' man who looked the part.

"How did you find me?" Skinner asked nervously. "I never told anyone about Dempsey."

"Tricks of the trade," Starbuck said with a tired smile. "You might say I followed a paper trail."

Skinner appeared bemused. "Alice couldn't have told you—she didn't know!"

"She told me lots of other things."

"Such as?"

"The whole setup," Starbuck said matter-of-factly. "How do you think I got onto your game?"

"What game?"

"The stage holdups," Starbuck observed. "Your political connections. You and Stimson and Yeager. . . . everything."

"I don't believe you!" Skinner said in an aggrieved tone. "It wasn't Alice! You got to me through Yeager."

Starbuck shrugged, watching his eyes. "When did you learn I was on the case?"

"The night—" Skinner stopped, shook his head. "Good try! I never heard your name before today."

"Believe it or not," Starbuck countered, "I'm trying to pull your fat out of the fire. Alice also told me about your boss."

Skinner gave him a blank stare. "What boss?"

"You sure loused it up," Starbuck went on with a mirthless grin. "He must've been some ticked off when he found out you'd faked the Carver girl's death."

"I don't know what you're talking about."

"You've got one chance." Starbuck's voice dropped. "Tell me his name—turn state's evidence—and let me go after him. Otherwise, you'll wind up in the bone-yard."

"Oh?" Skinner blustered. "What makes you think so?"

"You're the last witness!" Starbuck said urgently. "The only one who knows the full story. He means to kill you and he'll do it—unless I stop him."

Skinner glanced away and stared for a long while at nothing. He was quiet so long Starbuck began to think he wouldn't answer. But finally he sighed and spread his hands wide. His face was stricken with a look of dread and uncertainty.

"All right," he conceded glumly. "I'll make a deal with you. Deliver me to the territorial capital and put me in the custody of the attorney general. Then I'll tell you anything you want to know."

Starbuck examined the notion. "Helena's a long way off. Why not tell me now?"

"I want insurance." Skinner grinned weakly. "You get me there alive and I'll talk! Not before."

A moment elapsed while they stared at one another. Then Starbuck nodded. "You've got yourself a deal. We'll spend the night in Virginia City and catch the morning stage. That ought to put us into Helena day after tomorrow."

"No!" Skinner's eyes froze to pinpoints of darkness. "I won't go back to Virginia City!"

"Don't worry," Starbuck said with a clenched smile. "I won't let him get you."

"I refuse!" Skinner's voice was choked with terror. "I'm as good as dead the minute I set foot in town!"

"Quit squawking!" Starbuck silenced him with a frown. "You're my prisoner, and nobody will harm you while you're in my custody."

"He'll try," Skinner whispered desperately. "You know he'll try!"

"I know he's dead if he does."

Starbuck considered it a no-lose proposition. By returning to Virginia City, he might end the case quickly and permanently. Helena would delay things a few days, but time was now on his side. Either way, he'd gained the edge at last.

He went along to the corral while Skinner saddled a horse.

Dusk was settling over Virginia City. Starbuck and Skinner rode into town as the last rays of light were leached from the sky. Their arrival was timed perfectly with the supper hour and onrushing darkness. The streets were virtually empty.

Starbuck thought it wiser to bypass the livery stable. The sooner he got Skinner undercover, the better. Then, if an assassination attempt was made, it would be made on ground of his own choosing. He led Skinner to the hotel and they dismounted out front. As they moved to the hitch rack, he heard a coarse shout from across the street. He looked around, and his blood went cold.

Wilbur X. Lott and a group of vigilantes had just emerged from a café. With hardly a break in stride, they stepped off the boardwalk and hurried toward the hotel. Their eyes were fastened on Skinner, and the look on their faces was the look of death. A cone of silence enveloped them as they approached in a tight phalanx.

Too late, Starbuck realized his mistake. The focus of his concentration had been on one man, a lone killer. He'd forgotten that a pack of killers now roamed the streets of Virginia City. A lynch-crazed pack, sworn to hang Cyrus Skinner. He felt slow and stupid, and he silently cursed himself. In his rush to get one man, he'd overlooked the greater danger. The mob.

Lott halted directly in front of him. The vigilantes spread out and slowly surrounded the hitch rack. Skinner's features turned ashen and he unwittingly moved closer to Starbuck. Lott uttered a dry laugh that sounded like a death rattle.

"Well, now, Mr. Starbuck! You are a detective, aren't you?"

"Skinner's my prisoner." Starbuck's eyes went steely. "I won't turn him over, Lott. So call off your dogs."

"Why should we fight?" Lott's face was a mask of righteous propriety. "A man in your profession understands the need for summary justice. Our goals are the same, Mr. Starbuck."

"Shove it!" Starbuck's voice was alive with contempt. "I work my own game, and it's not done yet. I've still got need of Skinner."

"That's unfortunate," Lott replied with cold hauteur. "You see, we want to ask him a few questions ourselves. I suggest you stand aside."

Starbuck's mouth clamped in a bloodless line. "Why don't you try moving me aside?"

"Come now!" Lott scoffed. "You're in a hopeless position, Mr. Starbuck. Unless, of course, you're willing to die just to make a point."

The snout of a pistol jabbed into Starbuck's spine. He stared at Lott, his look dark and vengeful. Then, with an effort of will, he forced himself to nod, signifying he'd lost. Lott laughed and motioned to his men with a brusque gesture.

"Bring them both along," he ordered. "I think Mr. Starbuck might learn something."

Lott walked off upstreet. The vigilantes crowded around Starbuck and Skinner, and they fell in behind. Several minutes later they entered the clearing on the outskirts of town. The Judas Tree stood bathed in a spectral glow of starlight. The ropes from yesterday's hangings still dangled over the limb, and there was a ghoulish aspect to the scene. A man was assigned to watch Starbuck, and others hustled Skinner beneath the tree. After a noose was slipped around his neck, several vigilantes took hold of the rope. Then Lott stepped forward and faced him.

"Cyrus, you're going to die." He spoke the words with a kind of smothered wrath. "How you die depends on whether or not you cooperate."

Skinner stood numb with shock. "I—I've done nothing."

Lott glanced past him and gestured. The rope snapped taut and Skinner was snatched off the ground. He clawed wildly at the noose, which cut deeper into his throat as the weight of his body pulled the loop ever tighter. His eyes were maddened and bulging, vivid with pain. He kicked and jerked, dancing on thin air, and his face turned a dark shade of purple. Then, at a signal from Lott, the vigilantes abruptly released the rope. Skinner dropped on the ground and fell to his knees. He tore the noose free and sucked wind into his starved lungs. He gagged, clutching at his throat, and coughed raggedly. His breathing was a labored wheeze in the still night.

"Cyrus, that's only a sample," Lott warned with cold menace. "You'll die by inches unless you give me a full confession."

"No more!" Skinner pleaded hoarsely. "I'll talk—I swear it!"

"A wise decision," Lott intoned. "I have only one question, so pay very close attention. Tell me about Henry Palmer."

"He's the boss! He fed me the information about the express shipments, and I passed it along to Stimson and Yeager. He controlled everything ... all of us!"

"Where did he get the information?"

"The express company," Skinner babbled. "He's the sheriff ... they never suspected anything ... he was hanging robbers ... they let him see the shipment schedules ... so he could catch more robbers."

"These robbers he hung?" Lott demanded. "Were they part of the gang?"

"Only a con game ... make everybody think there wasn't a gang!"

"Why didn't Yeager spill all that during his trial?"

"Yeager didn't know! No one but Stimson and me knew about Palmer. That's why he killed Stimson ... resisting arrest ... would've killed me, too. But I fooled him, got away!"

"How about politics?" Lott persisted. "Who controlled the county machine?"

"Palmer!" Skinner rasped. "It was always Palmer! I was only his front man. He organized it ... pulled the strings ... through me!"

"Thank you, Cyrus." Lott grinned an evil grin. "You've confirmed everything I suspected right along. Now, for the record, I have one final question. Do you swear before almighty God that you've told the whole truth?"

"Yes!" Skinner's eyes filled with panic. "With Christ as my witness—I do!"

"Good," Lott said viciously. "Hang him!"

Skinner threw up a hand, palm outward. His mouth opened in protest and then clicked shut in a strangled gasp. The vigilantes heaved on the rope and jerked him off his knees. Another tug lifted him into the air, his arms and legs flapping in a spastic struggle. A rictus of agony crossed his features and he wet his pants. His hands dug insanely at the noose.

The man guarding Starbuck edged closer. His eyes were bright with fascination, and Skinner's death struggles seemed to compel him forward. He took another step and another, transfixed by the sight. Then, all else forgotten, he stood staring upward, spellbound.

Starbuck turned and vanished into the darkness.

Chapter Fifteen

A single lamp lighted the sheriff's office. Starbuck angled across the street and gingerly stepped onto the boardwalk. He pulled the Colt, thumbing the hammer to full cock. Then he catfooted toward the door.

Outside, he paused and flattened himself against the wall. One ear cocked to the door, he listened for several seconds. There was no sound from within, and the silence sparked a vague feeling of unease. He took a firm grip on the doorknob and braced himself. The door creaked as he threw it open and extended the Colt to arm's length. The office was empty.

Still wary, he moved through the doorway and stopped just inside. He slammed the door shut and stood for a moment, scanning the room. The desk was littered with paperwork, and a potbellied stove crackled with warmth. Everything appeared normal, and yet a curious sense of desolation pervaded the office. He collected the lamp from the desk and walked swiftly to the door of the lockup. All the cells were empty; the barred doors along the corridor yawned open. He returned to the office and slowly holstered the Colt. His expression was troubled.

Some inner voice told Starbuck the worst had hap-

pened. There were no deputies around and the jail-
house was deserted. All the signs indicated the office
had been vacated hurriedly, sometime within the last
hour. He thought it entirely probable that the sheriff
had gotten word of Skinner's capture. Further, with
Skinner in the hands of the vigilantes, it would be
logical to assume that the last link in the conspiracy
had been revealed. Cyrus Skinner, in an attempt to
save himself, would spill his guts about the "boss" of
Virginia City. Which meant Henry Palmer would
have been under no illusions about his own fate. He
was the next candidate for the Judas Tree.

Starbuck was gripped by a sense of time running
ahead of him. His eyes felt scratchy and burnt out,
and he wearily massaged them as he considered his
options. The smart move, on Palmer's part, would
have been to depart town hastily. Only by vanishing
into the night would he outdistance the hangman's
rope and certain death. In that event, Starbuck had no
choice but to pick up the trail and give chase. Yet
there loomed before him the question of where to
start. He abruptly realized that he knew virtually nothing of a personal nature about Henry Palmer. Wife
and family aside, he had no idea as to where the sheriff lived. A man's home, most assuredly, was the first
place to look. Where to ask directions, however,
posed a problem. He couldn't afford loose talk and
speculation, not with the vigilantes on the prowl. He
somehow had to cover his own tracks.

Once more outside, he turned toward the center of
town. He figured the hotel was perhaps the best place
to inquire. A gold piece, backed by a subtle threat,

would ensure the night clerk's silence. As he walked, his mind drifted unwittingly to the vigilantes. There was an inescapable note of irony, not to mention a certain rancor, in his attitude. On general principles, he detested mob justice and the element of anarchy underlying any vigilance movement. On a personal level, he burned with a quiet, steel fury toward Wilbur X. Lott. The vigilante leader had taken his prisoner at gunpoint and compounded the insult by threatening his life. He allowed no man that liberty, and sooner or later Lott would be made to pay the piper. All the more so since Starbuck considered Lott a malevolent force, no less evil than the outlaws themselves. An ambitious man was too often a sinister man, and therefore the most dangerous of all.

Still, in the end, it boiled down to a matter of priorities. Wilbur X. Lott was strictly personal business, and settling his hash would wait. In the meantime, there was a more pressing problem, one that topped Starbuck's list. He was determined that the vigilantes wouldn't beat him to Henry Palmer.

Later, looking back on the moment, Starbuck would be struck by the blend of timing and coincidence. As he approached the main intersection a group of miners emerged from the café on the corner. Their raucous laughter attracted his attention, and he stopped dead in his tracks. Through the fly-specked window he saw Palmer seated at a table inside the café. The sheriff was sopping stew gravy from his plate with a piece of bread. Even as Starbuck watched he popped the bread into his mouth and began chewing. His demeanor was that of a man without a trouble in the world.

Starbuck was immobilized by the sight. He briefly wondered if Palmer somehow hadn't heard about Skinner. Then, upon second thought, he discarded the notion. The odds dictated that Palmer had learned of Skinner's capture within minutes after it happened. Yet there he sat, calmy eating his supper. It beggared the imagination.

The supper hour was drawing to a close. All up and down the street the boardwalks were jammed with men out to see the elephant. With the exception of Palmer, only three diners still lingered in the café. Starbuck debated whether to make his play inside or risk a showdown on the crowded street. Then he saw a waitress approach the table and refill the sheriff's coffee mug. He again experienced the sensation of fleeting time. To delay might very well cut his slight lead over the vigilantes. He decided to wait no longer.

Palmer was seated at a window table, facing the door. Starbuck entered quickly and halted just inside the café. His hand was underneath his suit jacket, gripping the butt of the Colt. His gaze bored into Palmer, inviting a move. A moment passed while the two men stared at each other. Then the sheriff carefully wrapped both hands around his coffee mug. A token act, it signified he chose not to fight.

Alert to trickery, Starbuck slowly approached the table. He saw, upon moving closer, that there was a strangeness about Palmer. The sheriff's eyes were oddly vacant and his features were fixed. He had a faraway look, as though the focus of his concentration were centered on something dimly visible in the distance. He nodded to Starbuck.

"Have a chair."

"You're a regular sackful of surprises."

"How so?"

"I figured you'd fight the minute I showed."

"I don't want to kill you, Luke."

"You'll have to try"—Starbuck's tone was impersonal—"if you intend to walk out of here."

"No, I won't." Palmer paused, met his gaze with an amused expression. "There's no way you can force me to draw . . . not just yet."

Starbuck seated himself across the table. He lit a cigarette, all the while watching Palmer's hands. Then he snuffed the match and exhaled a cloud of smoke.

"What's your game?"

Palmer's smile was bleak. "You tell me your secrets and I'll tell you mine."

"Go ahead," Starbuck agreed. "Ask away."

"Have Lott and his bunch hung Skinner?"

"He was on his way up the last time I saw him."

"Did they make him talk?"

"Oh, he talked!" Starbuck took a long draw on his cigarette. "He'd still be talking if he hadn't run out of things to say."

"I suppose the questions were about me?"

"Nobody else." Starbuck spoke the words in little spurts of smoke. "Skinner identified you as the boss of Virginia City. Vice, politics, and stage holdups . . . the whole can of worms."

"I'm not surprised," Palmer said equably. "Cyrus always was short on guts."

"Why shouldn't he talk? He knew you meant to kill him the same way you killed Stimson."

"A double-crosser deserves what he gets."

Starbuck eyed him, thoughtful. "You're talking about the Carver girl, aren't you?"

"Am I?"

"Skinner tricked you," Starbuck said, not asking a question. "You thought she was dead till the night we opened the coffin."

Palmer seemed to wrestle with himself a moment. He turned the coffee mug in his hands, examining it like some curious artifact. Finally, with a great shrug of resignation, he glanced up.

"You're right." His voice was at once reasonable and tinged with anger. "Skinner played me for a sucker. The way he rigged her death—and that phony funeral—was a big mistake. He was thinking with his balls instead of his brains."

"So what?" Starbuck asked. "There was no real harm done. She never actually knew who you were."

"She knew I existed! After we dug up her coffin, I got the full story out of Stimson. Maybe she didn't know my name, but she knew too much. That's why Skinner got her out of town."

"What was the alternative?"

"He should've come to me!" Palmer replied. "What she overheard wasn't his fault. I wouldn't have held it against him."

"Probably not." Starbuck tapped an ash off his cigarette. "But you would've killed Alice Carver."

"That was Skinner's second mistake. By letting her live, he put everybody's tail in a crack."

"I'll give you credit," Starbuck said with a lightning frown. "It was a mistake you damn sure tried to correct."

"You mean that fiasco in Chicago?"

"I wouldn't exactly call it a fiasco. Another minute, and those boys would've got the girl and me *and* Doc Carver. It almost worked."

"Too little too late," Palmer said morosely. "Strictly a last-ditch effort. By then, things were unraveling so fast I was always a step behind. I lay it to George Hoyt's death."

"You didn't order him killed?"

Palmer grunted, shook his head. "Stimson took it upon himself. He got wise to you, and then his boys trailed you to Hoyt's office. He figured to wipe the slate clean—kill you both."

"So you were still in the dark at that point. You didn't know who I was till I told you myself?"

"Unfortunate, but true," Palmer affirmed. "And that's when I made my big mistake. I should've killed you out at the graveyard and buried you in that empty coffin."

"Why didn't you?"

"Tell you the truth—" Palmer paused and stared at him a long moment. "I was so goddamn mad at Skinner I wasn't thinking straight. By the time I quit seeing red, you were already on your way to Chicago."

"One thing puzzles me," Starbuck said, watching him inquisitively. "How'd you get Stimson to send his boys after me?"

"Carrot and the stick." Palmer's mouth lifted in a tight grin. "I let him think he could square himself by getting rid of you and the Carver girl. He swallowed it, bait and all."

"Meanwhile—" Starbuck gave him a short look. "You were rigging a double-cross of your own. Yeager didn't know the score, so you charged him with robbery and murder. Then you killed Stimson for resisting arrest. If you'd got Skinner, that was the game. Nobody would've been left alive to identify you."

"Almost pulled it off, too! I just never figured Skinner to run that fast. Guess he saw the handwriting on the wall."

"He wasn't in any doubt that you meant to put him under."

"How'd you find him?" Palmer said, genuinely curious. "That was a slick piece of detective work."

"It's a long story," Starbuck said flatly. "Let's stick with you for the moment. Tell me how you got the inside dope on those gold shipments."

"Wasn't all that hard," Palmer noted. "The boys over at the express office never suspected the law was behind it. I generally managed to get a peek at the shipment schedules."

"What about your deputies?" Starbuck remarked. "Were they involved?"

"No," Palmer said briskly. "I kept them busy chasing small-timers. It was good whitewash and it had everybody fooled down the line. Leastways till you showed up."

"One last question." Starbuck stubbed out his cigarette in an ashtray. "Why are you admitting all this so openly?"

There was a prolonged silence. Palmer's stare revealed nothing, and he might have been deaf for all the change in his expression. He studied Starbuck at length before answering.

"Correct me if I'm wrong," he said coolly. "You're thinking this will end one of two ways. Either Lott and his thugs hang me, or you'll do the honors. Would that be a fair statement?"

"Close enough to count."

A smile shadowed Palmer's lips. "Wilbur Lott will never hang me."

"That a fact?" Starbuck regarded him with a level gaze. "What makes you think so?"

"I'm the law!" Palmer said forcefully. "It's Cyrus Skinner's word against mine, and that's no contest. All I have to do is bluff and stick to it—and they wouldn't dare hang me!"

"So you're betting it all on one turn of the cards?"

"Why not?" Palmer said grimly. "If I run, you'd be right behind me. I'm better off to take my chances here . . . tonight."

"And if Lott doesn't hang you?"

"Then it's between us," Palmer said pointedly, "and I'll have to kill you. That's why I said you couldn't force me to draw . . . not just yet."

"In other words," Starbuck commented, "there's no need to kill me if they do end up hanging you?"

Palmer nodded gravely. "I don't kill for sport. Unless your death serves some purpose, why bother?"

"That's real charitable of you." Starbuck's gaze was very pale and direct. "For the sake of argument, let's suppose you don't hang. What makes you think

I wouldn't kill you—instead of the other way around?"

Palmer shrugged off the question. "You kill men but you don't murder them. I've never imposed such rules on myself."

"You're saying you'd backshoot me?"

"Something like that," Palmer said without irony. "Better you than me, Luke."

Not for the first time, Starbuck's admiration was stirred. The man seated opposite him was a cold-blooded cutthroat, with all the conscience of an aroused scorpion. Yet Palmer possessed icy nerves and bold cunning, the very attributes a lawman prized most. Under different circumstances they might have been allies, if not friends. Tonight, Starbuck could offer him nothing more than a quick death.

"You won't stand the chance of a snowball in hell with the vigilantes."

"I disagree," Palmer said firmly. "I've lived by my wits all my life. It won't be any chore to outfox Wilbur Lott."

"If you're wrong, it's not a pleasant way to die. He's a strangler, not a hangman."

"What's your point?"

"Draw now." Starbuck looked him square in the eye. "You'll never know what hit you."

Palmer deliberated a moment. His expression was abstracted and he seemed to be weighing the proposal. Then he slowly wagged his head.

"No soap," he said with assurance. "I'll worry about you after I've dealt with Lott."

"It's your funeral."

"What the hell!" Palmer laughed. "A high roller always plays for table stakes."

"Only one trouble."

"What's that?"

"You're playing into a cold deck."

Palmer suddenly stiffened. His eyes shifted to the window and he stared upstreet. In the erratic flicker of lamplight, he saw Lott and the vigilantes marching toward the intersection. A man in the lead rank carried a coiled rope, and one end was knotted in a hangman's noose. All along the street miners stopped and gawked as the vigilantes strode past.

"Well, Luke . . ." Palmer rose from his chair. "Time to play out the hand. Wish me luck."

"A dead man needs more than luck."

Palmer grinned and crossed the room with a determined stride. At the door he paused, squaring his shoulders; then he threw it open and stepped outside. He moved directly toward the vigilantes.

Starbuck stood and walked from the café.

Chapter Sixteen

The boardwalk outside the café was jammed with miners. Pushing through the crowd, Starbuck noted that all four corners of Wallace and Jackson were packed with ghoulish onlookers. He shouldered past the men at the front and took a position beside the lamppost. Then his attention was drawn to the street.

Henry Palmer halted in the middle of the intersection. He planted himself as though he'd taken root, legs spread wide. The shiny star pinned on his vest gleamed brightly in the lamplight. His expression was stolid and his stance was that of a monolith, somehow immovable. He threw up an arm, palm outward.

"That's far enough!" he called brassily. "You boys are through for the night!"

The vigilantes stopped several paces away. Their features registered surprise and momentary confusion. A moment of stark silence ensued while they stood immobilized by Palmer's glowering stare. On the boardwalk, the spectators appeared spellbound, watching with trancelike awe. Then Wilbur X. Lott took a step forward.

"No, by God!" Lott shouted. "We're not through! We've only just started!"

Palmer fixed him with a baleful look. "I'm ordering you to disband—now!"

"Order and be damned!" Lott said fiercely. "It's you we want, Palmer."

"On what charge?"

"Murder! Highway robbery! Contempt for the laws of man and sacrilege against a higher law—the law of God!"

"Wilbur, are you preaching a sermon?" Palmer's tone was laced with mockery. "Or maybe you're play-acting for the crowd? You always did have a flair for the dramatic."

"Save your ridicule!" Lott yelled. "It won't work! We've got the goods on you and your gang of road agents!"

"Are you asking me to believe you have proof?"

"I'm not asking!" Lott thundered. "I'm telling you! Cyrus Skinner confessed not ten minutes ago. He named you as the leader—the mastermind!"

"For the benefit of everyone here"—Palmer gestured around with a sardonic smile—"how did you extract that confession?"

"With a rope! We let him dangle till he decided to come clean!"

"Come off it, Wilbur! You put the words in his mouth and choked him until he told you what you wanted to hear. Isn't that how it happened?"

"He told us the truth! The whole truth! How you organized the gang and used him as a mouthpiece. He named you as the man responsible for the holdups and killings. The boss!"

"It won't hold water," Palmer informed him. "A

confession obtained under duress isn't admissible in court."

"We're not debating technicalities. Skinner identified you! That's all the proof we need."

"Proof?" Palmer repeated scornfully. "You hung your witness, Wilbur! All we have is your version of what you strangled out of him. And as everybody knows—you're a confirmed liar!"

Someone in the crowd laughed, followed by low snickering and several open catcalls. Lott flushed and his eyes went garnet with rage. His voice rose suddenly.

"You have been condemned to hang, Henry Palmer! By the Lord God Jehovah, we will not be denied!"

Palmer's smile seemed frozen. "Up until tonight, the men you've hung would have been convicted in a fair trial and duly executed. So I haven't interfered, even though you're operating outside the law. But it stops here, Wilbur! I order you—for the last time— to disband or face the consequences."

"Consequences, hell!" Lott crowed. "You can't hide behind that badge anymore!"

"Wrong again," Palmer countered. "I am the law, the *only* law! You have no authority in Virginia City."

"These men and that rope"—Lott flung his arm at the man holding the noose—"are all the authority I need!"

"Since you brought it up . . ." Palmer paused and appeared to tick off numbers. "I count only twenty men, maybe less. That wouldn't qualify as a quorum, not to mention a majority."

Lott brushed aside the objection with a broad wave. "We represent the town, the workingmen! If it's a majority you want, then we'll put it to a vote. Let the people decide!"

A ripple of approval swept through the crowd. Lott nodded and looked around with vinegary satisfaction. Then Palmer stilled the onlookers with upraised hands.

"Hear me out!" he said in a loud, commanding voice. "Where the mob rules, even innocent men fear for their lives. So I'm going to suggest a compromise that will restore order. At the same time, it will allow us to get at the truth once and for all!"

"Compromise?" Lott echoed suspiciously. "What've you got up your sleeve now?"

"Law and order!" Palmer announced in a ringing tone. "You disband your vigilantes and I'll surrender myself into the custody of Attorney General Blackthorn."

"Your political crony!" Lott hooted. "Don't make me laugh! Blackthorn's the one who put your name up for U.S. marshal. You'd walk away free as a bird!"

"On the contrary," Palmer said reasonably. "I would be charged and returned to Virginia City for trial. The issue would be settled in a court of law— by a jury of my peers."

The spectators were divided. All eyes were trained on the two men, and the miners listened raptly as their voices were pitted in counterpoint. Until now, it appeared a standoff, with neither man assured of carrying the argument. Then, abruptly, Wilbur X. Lott spread his arms and appealed directly to the crowd.

"Don't listen to him!" Lott bellowed. "He's trying to run a sandy! You let him surrender to his political pals, and he'll be long gone forever. Either we hang him tonight or we've lost. He'll escape justice—the people's justice!"

"Use your heads!" Palmer retorted. "I am a duly elected peace officer. Hang me, and the attorney general will issue a blanket murder warrant. And your name will head the list, Wilbur Lott!"

"Well, you won't be around to see it! Your term of office is about to expire . . . at the end of a rope!"

"There's the real issue here tonight!" Palmer said explosively. "You want my job! You'd crawl in bed with the devil and sell your soul for the chance to be sheriff. Say it's not so and brand yourself for the hypocrite you are!"

For a moment, Starbuck thought Palmer had won. It was a telling argument, all the more persuasive because it was true. Not a man in the crowd doubted that Wilbur X. Lott would indeed sell his soul to wear a tin star. Yet no voice was raised in Palmer's defense. Instead, a gruff buzz of murmuring broke out among the onlookers. The sound swelled and took on an ugly, guttural tone.

Lott sensed the ominous change in mood. He shook his fist in the air and cried out violently. "To the Judas Tree!"

A spate of jubilant shouts erupted from the crowd. There was a sudden milling and a mixed chorus of countermanding orders. Bloodlust transformed them on the instant into a mob.

"Get some torches!"

"No! Why take the time?"

"Do it now!"

"Where?"

"The hotel balcony!"

The miners surged off the boardwalk and engulfed Henry Palmer. He was disarmed and dragged bodily to the hotel veranda. The rope whistled over the railing of the upstairs balcony and dropped beside his head. Someone slipped the noose around his neck and cinched the knot tight. Eager hands grabbed the tail end of the rope, and the men set themselves to pull. Then Lott stayed them with a sharp command. He mounted the veranda steps and looked up at Palmer.

"Before you meet your Maker," he asked unctuously, "do you have any last words?"

"Only for you!" Palmer's eyes blazed. "I'll reserve a spot for you in hell. Don't keep me waiting too—"

"Hang him!"

The slack went out of the rope and Palmer was jerked aloft. His legs thrashed vainly at the air and his hands dug madly at the noose. His windpipe constricted and his features took on a ghastly look of terror. Then, like a thunderbolt, a gunshot split the night. A bright pearl of blood mushroomed beneath his badge and an expression of amazement crossed his face. His struggles ceased and the light in his eyes blinked out. He slumped dead.

The instant of tomblike stillness that followed was suddenly shattered. Someone yelled and pointed, and the crowd turned to look. Starbuck stood on the opposite corner, the Colt extended at shoulder level. A wisp of smoke curled out of the gun barrel, slowly drifted away. He lowered his arm.

Wilbur Lott muttered an unintelligible oath. He leaped off the veranda steps and charged across the street. The crowd parted before him, opening a corridor to the lamppost outside the café. He hauled to a stop a couple of paces from the boardwalk and grasped the lapels of his swallowtail coat. His face was ocherous.

"You've just signed your own death warrant, Mr. Detective!"

"Oh?" Starbuck's expression was sphinxlike. "How's that?"

"You killed Palmer!" Lott snarled. "You undermined the work of the Vigilance Committee!"

Starbuck gave him a dark smile. "I put a dead man out of his misery. You'll have a helluva time charging me with murder."

"I charge you with obstruction of justice!"

"Whose justice?" Starbuck laughed in his face. "Christ, you're enough to make a buzzard puke! You get your kicks watching men strangle to death, don't you?"

Lott stabbed out with a bony finger. "You'll know very shortly whether or not that's true. I impose on you the sentence of death!"

"How do you figure to make it stick?"

"Quite easily," Lott intoned. "I intend to escort you across the street and order my men to hang you. Now, hand over that gun!"

Starbuck leveled the Colt and thumbed the hammer. His voice was suddenly edged. "Why don't you take it from me?"

"Look around you," Lott said, motioning at the crowd. "Your gun won't save you from all these men! One word from me and they'll tear you to shreds."

Starbuck's eyes hooded. "One word from you and you're a dead man."

"You're bluffing!"

"Try me," Starbuck said softly. "Only take a deep breath before you do. It'll have to last a long time."

Lott seemed turned to stone. He suddenly realized a wrong word would speed him into eternity. His gaze riveted on the snout of the pistol and a vein pulsed in his forehead. A leaden moment slipped past before he glanced up at Starbuck. He swallowed nervously.

"We appear to be at a stalemate, Mr. Starbuck."

"Here's the way we'll play it, Lott. I'm leaving town tomorrow on the noon stage. You call your dogs off—give me your oath we've got a truce—and I'll let you walk away. Otherwise, your vigilante days are over."

Lott squinted at him in baffled fury. "You have my word."

"Swear it"—Starbuck wiggled the barrel of the Colt—"by your Lord God Jehovah."

"I swear it," Lott grated out. "But make sure you're on the noon stage. Our truce ends there!"

"That's the third time you've threatened my life. I generally don't allow it to happen more than once. So listen close and believe what you hear."

"A pronouncement from on high, Mr. Starbuck?"

"No, just damn good advice," Starbuck said coldly.

"Get down on your knees tonight and pray to your God that we never meet again."

"And if we do?" Lott bristled. "What then?"

Starbuck smiled. "I'll punch your ticket to the Promised Land."

"Anything more?"

"You've heard all I've got to say."

"And you have until noon tomorrow—no longer!"

Lott turned on his heel and walked away. He rejoined the vigilantes and ordered Palmer's body strung up from the hotel balcony. Then, staring straight ahead, he led his men to a nearby saloon. The crowd slowly dispersed to the dives and gaming dens along the street. Within minutes, a ghostly silence descended over the town.

Starbuck crossed to the hotel. He glanced up at the body as he mounted the stairs and entered the door. His assignment was ended in Virginia City, and nothing he'd done gave him cause for regret. Nor was he touched by remorse for Henry Palmer.

A man played the cards he was dealt.

Late the next morning Starbuck called on John Duggan. He'd had no contact with the mining association president since their initial meeting in Denver. The purpose of the call was to deliver his report, which could then be passed on to Munro Salisbury, owner of the stageline. There was also the matter of his fee.

Duggan looked like a man who had spent a sleepless night. His jowls sagged and his eyes were circled with dark rings, the lines etched deep. He greeted

Starbuck with a sallow smile and escorted him into a cramped, utilitarian office. The room was dominated by a scarred mahogany desk, with sectional maps of Alder Gulch pinned to the walls and a large filing cabinet wedged into one corner. He waved Starbuck to a wooden armchair.

"Have a seat, Luke." He dropped into a swivel chair behind the desk. "I had a feeling you'd be around today."

"I'm catching the noon stage," Starbuck said, lighting a cigarette. "Figured I'd bring you up to date before I left."

"Have you read the morning newspaper?"

"No." Starbuck exhaled a cotton wad of smoke. "A reporter tried to buttonhole me at the hotel last night. I told him 'no comment' and gave him the fast shuffle. What'd he write?"

Duggan unfolded a newspaper and pushed it across the desk. "You tell me . . . fact or fiction?"

Starbuck scanned the front page, smoking quietly. The story was emblazoned with bold headlines and fairly simmered with purple prose. Centered on the page was a photograph of the Judas Tree, with a limp body dangling from a rope. His own name was prominently featured throughout the text, and he found the details surprisingly accurate. Several direct quotes from Wilbur X. Lott were somewhat at variance with the facts. At last, he folded the newspaper and tossed it on the desk. He looked across at Duggan and shrugged.

"It's pretty close to the mark. They're a little confused about the Carver girl and how I tracked down

Skinner. But there's not a whole lot I'd add. Probably couldn't have written a better report myself."

"How do you think the reporter found out we hired you?"

"Beats me," Starbuck admitted. "I guess that's why they're called newshounds. What makes you ask?"

"Wilbur Lott," Duggan said, tapping the newspaper. "You'll note he's trying to take a major share of the credit. We feel that's not in our best interests."

"When you say 'our,' I take it you mean the mining association?"

"I do indeed," Duggan acknowledged. "We hired you—along with the stage company—and we want the credit. Lott had no part in breaking the case!"

"Call a news conference," Starbuck suggested. "Let the facts speak for themselves."

"Would you agree to a joint interview?"

"Nope," Starbuck said shortly. "I try to steer clear of reporters. You don't need me, anyway. All you have to do is point out one simple fact. Lott hasn't done anything but hang a bunch of people."

"Unfortunately, he'll claim otherwise, and the public has a tendency to believe what it reads in print."

Duggan launched into a long-winded dissertation on the politics of Virginia City. Starbuck listened with only half an ear. He subscribed to no particular ideology and he'd always considered politics a dirty word. To him, it was a matter of supreme indifference which faction controlled the political apparatus. By whatever name, the party in power was no less corrupt than its opponents. He stubbed out his cigarette as the civics lesson drew to a close. Duggan concluded by once more asking him to submit to a newspaper interview.

"Sorry," Starbuck replied with a poker face. "You hired me to kill a gang leader. By my count, you got your money's worth several times over. Let's just leave it there."

Duggan studied him with a reproachful frown. "Doesn't it bother you that Lott might end up running Virginia City?"

"I'm not my brother's keeper." Starbuck cracked a smile. "It's a job better suited to preachers and politicians."

"Suppose I told you Lott and his vigilantes hanged an innocent man this morning?"

"Anyone I know?"

"His name was Jack Slade."

"Are you saying he had nothing to do with the robbers?"

"Nothing whatsoever!" Duggan looked worried. "He was a saloon tough and a general troublemaker."

"Why'd Lott hang him?"

"Slade picked a fight with one of the vigilantes last night. Lott ordered him out of town by sunup and he refused to leave. So now he's decorating the Judas Tree."

Starbuck's jawline hardened. "I reckon that means it's started."

"What's started?" The worry lines on Duggan's forehead deepened. "I don't follow you."

"Sooner or later vigilantes get around to hanging all the badmen and desperados. But it's a goddamn hard habit to break! So some unlucky stiff winds up being lynched before things get back to normal. With Lott, that might take a while . . . and a few more unlucky stiffs."

"Now that you mention it," Duggan said uneasily, "I understand Lott threatened to string you up."

"Yeah, he had some such notion."

"Then all the more reason to grant the press an interview. You could do Virginia City a favor and settle a personal score—all in one stroke!"

Starbuck deliberated a moment. "I reckon not. One way or another, the grave always straightens out hunchbacks."

"Hunchbacks?" Duggan stared at him. "What's that got to do with Lott?"

A slow smile spread across Starbuck's face. "It's an old saying. Some men spend their lives trying to get themselves killed. Wilbur Lott fits the mold."

Duggan hesitated, considering. "I also heard you threatened to kill him."

"Nooo," Starbuck said slowly. "It was more on the order of a promise."

"Hmmm." Duggan eyed him with a scrutinizing look. "You wouldn't have a crystal ball, would you, Luke?"

"I'm a detective, not a swami."

"Sometimes there's only a fine line separating promise and prophecy."

"Let's just say"—Starbuck smiled cryptically— "Wilbur Lott's a hunchback with one foot in the grave."

"Hallelujah!" Duggan laughed. "I've got an idea

Virginia City will be in your debt for a long time to come."

"That reminds me," Starbuck said without expression. "Our deal was half down and half on delivery. I delivered last night."

Still chortling, Duggan opened his desk drawer and pulled out a signed check. "Like I said, I thought you might drop around today. I believe the balance due was five thousand."

"On the nose." Starbuck inspected the check and tucked it into his shirt pocket. "Much obliged."

"Quite the contrary," Duggan said gratefully. "We're the ones who are obligated. You did a whiz-bang of a job, Luke."

"All in a day's work."

"Amen to that!"

Duggan walked him to the door. There he thrust out his hand and warmly pumped Starbuck's arm. With a wave, Starbuck stepped outside and strolled off in the direction of the hotel. He was whistling tunelessly under his breath.

Some while later Starbuck emerged from the stage-line office. He handed the driver his ticket and waited until his warbag was stowed securely in the luggage boot. Then he climbed aboard the coach and took a window seat. On impulse, he fished out his pocket watch and checked the time. He saw it was twelve-o-nine, and his eyes immediately swept the street. Wilbur Lott and the vigilantes were nowhere in sight.

The twelve o'clock deadline had come and gone.

Yet Lott had apparently weighed the wisdom of revoking their truce. Starbuck thought it a damn shame.

High noon seemed an appropriate death hour . . . for a hunchback.

Chapter Seventeen

The Alcazar Variety Theater was mobbed. Scarcely a table remained vacant, and the barroom was crowded to capacity. With the first show still a half hour away, it was already standing room only. Lola Montana, as usual, would play to a packed house.

Jack Brady, proprietor of the Alcazar, stood near the door. His thumbs were hooked in his vest and a cigar jutted from his mouth like a burnt tusk. The turnout seldom failed to put him in an expansive mood, and tonight he looked enormously pleased with himself. The star of his show was the toast of the town, the single greatest drawing card in Denver. Only today he'd boosted her salary to a level that none of his competitors would dare match. He was congratulating himself on his foresight when a commotion at the door attracted his attention.

Starbuck was trapped just inside the entranceway. Voices were raised in congratulations and well-wishers ganged around for a quick handshake. Brady and a couple of bouncers rescued him from the crowd. The housemen charged into the melee and roughly cleared the well-wishers away. Then, their arms spread wide, they formed a protective cordon. The theater owner greeted Starbuck with an ebullient grin.

"Welcome back, Luke!"

"Thanks," Starbuck mumbled, eyeing the crowd. "I feel like I just stepped into a goldfish bowl."

"The price of fame!" Brady laughed. "You'd better get used to it."

"I'd sooner have a little privacy."

"No more!" Brady crowed. "That's a thing of the past, Luke. You're a public figure now!"

"Who says?"

"Everybody and his brother!" Brady said gleefully. "Don't you read the papers?"

"Not lately," Starbuck grouched. "I've been on a train for the last couple of days."

Starbuck had pulled into town earlier that evening. He'd gone directly to his hotel suite, where he treated himself to a long soak in a hot bath. Afterward, he had ordered supper from room service and penned two messages to be delivered by a bellboy. One went to Lola, and the other went to Horace Griffin, division superintendent of Wells Fargo. Then he'd dressed and caught a hansom cab to the Alcazar. He hadn't read a newspaper since departing Virginia City.

"Take my word for it!" Brady assured him. "Half the goddamn world knows who you are tonight. You're big news—headline news!"

"Worse luck," Starbuck said with a pained expression. "Got a table for me, Jack?"

"The best in the house—reserved and waiting!"

The bouncers led the way. A path opened before them, and Brady escorted him to a table near the orchestra pit. Starbuck felt somewhat like a clown in a

parade. All eyes were on him and a buzz of excitement swept through the theater. He was no sooner
seated than a waiter appeared with a bucket of iced
champagne. Brady fussed around longer than necessary, clearly delighted with the sideshow atmosphere.
Finally, Starbuck was alone at the table. He lit a cigarette and tried to ignore the stares.

A short while later Horace Griffin arrived. Brady
again made a production of escorting the Wells Fargo
superintendent to the table. Griffin seemed amused by
the attention and put on a show of wringing Starbuck's hand. The waiter materialized with another
glass and deftly poured champagne. Then, at last, the
activity around the table slacked off.

"Happy days!" Griffin hoisted his glass in a toast.
"Looks like you're the man of the hour, Luke."

"Don't rub it in," Starbuck said gruffly. "Jack
Brady already beat the drum till my ears are ringing."

"I thought it was a celebration! Isn't that why you
invited me to join you?"

"Not exactly," Starbuck informed him. "We've still
got some unfinished business."

"What sort of business?"

"How would you like to recover part of the stolen
gold?"

"From the Virginia City holdups?"

"That's the idea."

Griffin was openly surprised. "I'd like that a lot,
Luke. Needless to say, it would be a feather in both
our caps. The home office might even come through
with a bonus."

Starbuck grinned. "I never turn down money."

"What's involved in recovering the gold?"

"A lawyer and a shovel."

"I beg your pardon?"

Starbuck pulled a small ledger from his pocket. He briefly explained that the ledger itemized Cyrus Skinner's gold deposits in a Salt Lake City bank. He suggested that Wells Fargo institute a court suit—with the ledger as prima facie evidence—against Skinner's estate. Then he produced a piece of paper, with a hand-drawn diagram of the Virginia City livery stable. He recounted the story of the stagecoach robbery—in league with Frank Yeager and the gang—and how he'd later hidden his share of the loot. A bold X on the diagram marked the correct stall. He told Griffin the gold was buried a foot or so down, not counting manure. A shovel and a few minutes' digging would do the trick.

"With Skinner's estate," he concluded, "and what you find in the stall, it'll nudge a hundred and ten thousand dollars. Not exactly what you'd call chicken feed."

"How true!" Griffin took a thoughtful sip of champagne. "I can't help but wonder about the others . . . Yeager and Stimson and Henry Palmer."

"What about them?"

"Well, it's possible their share of the robberies might be recovered. Would you be interested in looking into it—for a percentage?"

Starbuck wagged his head back and forth. "I was hired to get them . . . not their bankrolls."

"You're perfectly right!" Griffin agreed quickly. "We'll put a lawyer to work on it."

"Have him contact me," Starbuck offered. "I could point him in the right direction."

"I will indeed!" Griffin once more lifted his glass. "Here's to you! Wells Fargo won't forget the job you've done."

Starbuck's grin widened. "I'll depend on it, Horace."

"Good evening, Luke!"

Ned Buntline approached the table. He halted with a fraudulent smile and an outstretched hand. Starbuck studiously declined the handshake. He looked the writer up and down.

"Where'd you drop from, Buntline?"

"New York," Buntline replied, lowering his arm. "I came in on the evening train."

"What brings you to Denver?"

"You do!" Buntline gave Griffin a perfuntory nod and seated himself. "I'm here to make you a millionaire, Luke!"

Starbuck regarded him with impassive curiosity. "I thought we already had this discussion."

"That was before!"

"Before what?"

"Before Virginia City!" Buntline said with cheery vigor. "Before you routed a gang of robbers and singlehandedly faced down a vigilante mob!"

"How'd you hear about that?"

"You're too modest!" Buntline's smirk turned to a smug grin. "The newspapers have all but made your name a household word. You're a sensation back east!"

"So?"

"So you're famous!" Buntline cackled. "You killed five men—including a renegade sheriff—all in a matter of weeks!"

Starbuck looked annoyed. "I shot Palmer the way you would a crippled horse. I don't take any pride in it."

"A trifle!" Buntline said confidently. "Only one point has significance. You are the foremost lawman on the western frontier!"

"I'm not a lawman," Starbuck corrected him. "I'm a private detective."

"Whatever you are"—Buntline's eyes took on a tinsel glitter—"you're the deadliest mankiller extant. You've overshadowed Wild Bill Hickok and Wes Hardin and all the others. You stand alone at the apex of your profession!"

Starbuck's eyebrows drew together in a frown. "I don't travel in the company of gunmen. I told you once and I'll tell you again—I'm a detective."

Buntline appraised him with a crafty look. "By any name, you've captured the public's imagination. Virginia City was an epic struggle—good versus evil—and you're now something more than a nameless man-hunter. You are on the verge of greatness!"

"Forget it," Starbuck said shortly. "Go peddle your snake oil somewhere else."

"Confound it, Luke!" Buntline objected. "Listen to reason! You'll make a fortune off of dime novels and stage appearances. Within a year, you'll be rich as Midas!"

Starbuck hesitated just long enough to lend emphasis to his words. "Get the wax out of your ears and pay real close attention. I don't want any part of you or your schemes—and that's final!"

"Stop and think!" Buntline persisted. "It's not just the money we're talking about! I'm offering you something few men ever attain. Sign with me, and I'll make you part of our mythology . . . *one of the immortals!*"

"You've overstayed your welcome." Starbuck jerked a thumb toward the street. "Hit the bricks, and be damn quick about it!"

"You're passing up the opportunity of—"

Starbuck stood and moved swiftly around the table. He snatched Buntline out of his chair and spun him around. One hand took hold of the writer's coat collar and the other grabbed him by the seat of his pants. Then Starbuck danced him up on tiptoe and marched off at a fast clip.

"Gangway! We're comin' through!"

The crowd split as though cleaved apart. Starbuck hustled Buntline out of the theater and through the barroom. One of the housemen obligingly opened the door and stepped aside. Halting at the last moment, Starbuck lifted the writer bodily and gave him the bum's rush. Buntline landed on his rump and bounced across the sidewalk. His hat went flying and he rolled face down in the gutter.

Grinning broadly, Starbuck dusted his hands and walked back to the theater. All around him men cheered and applauded and pressed forward to slap him on the shoulder. As he approached his table the orchestra thumped to life and the curtain swished open. A chorus line, led by Lola Montana, cavorted out of the wings. Their legs flashed and they bounded onstage in a swirl of skirts. Then the tempo of the music quickened and they went into a high-stepping dance routine.

Lola stared past the footlights and her eyes fastened on him. She pranced downstage, her bloomers revealed in a showy cakewalk, and gave him a dazzling smile. The chorus girls squealed and kicked higher, and Lola dimpled her lips in a beestung pucker. Her hand touched her mouth and she blew him a kiss.

Starbuck sat down to a thunderous ovation.

Late that night, Starbuck unlocked the door to his hotel suite. Lola preceded him through the foyer and tossed her cape on a chair. Then she turned and stepped into his arms. She kissed him long and passionately.

"Ummm!" She groaned and lightly caressed his cheek. "That's sweeter than sugar and twice as nice!"

"Careful what you wish for," Starbuck joked, tightening his embrace. "It's liable to come true."

"Not so fast!" Lola slipped from his arms. "I want to change into something more comfortable, and I want a drink." She lowered one eyelid in a bawdy wink. "Then I want you—all night!"

Starbuck watched her disappear into the bedroom. He chuckled, amused by her antics, and crossed to the liquor cabinet. There, he collected a couple of glasses and a brandy decanter, and moved to the sofa. After placing everything on the coffee table, he shrugged out of his suit jacket and loosened his tie. He filled both glasses and left them standing. Then he lounged back on the sofa and lit a cigarette.

A time passed before Lola returned. She wore a sheer cambric peignoir and high-heeled slippers. Her breasts were visible through the gauzy fabric, and a bare leg showed as she crossed the room. She smelled faintly of lilac.

Starbuck extinguished his cigarette. She sat down beside him, and he handed her a snifter of brandy. Without a word, they clinked glasses and sipped. Their eyes met and held, and something unspoken passed between them. She ran her tongue over her lips and smiled.

"Welcome home, lover."

"I'll second the motion."

"Did you miss me?"

"What do you think?"

"I think maybe you did . . . a little bit."

"Now you're fishing for compliments."

"Well, a girl does like to hear sweet talk!"

"Talk's cheap." Starbuck nodded to a jewel box on the coffee table. "How about something more permanent?"

"A present!" Lola's eyes got big and round. "For me?"

"Open it and see."

The jewel box was large and wide, covered with plush velvet. Lola opened it slowly and then suddenly caught her breath in a sharp gasp. Inside was a diamond and sapphire pendant, mounted on a necklace of interlocked diamond rosettes. The stones sparkled richly in the lamplight, and she seemed mesmerized by the interplay of colors. Then she snapped the lid closed and clutched the box to her breast. Her eyes filled with tears.

"Oh, Luke!" She blinked, and a teardrop rolled down her cheek. "It's beautiful!"

"Hell, don't cry!" Starbuck's grin was so wide it was almost a laugh. "You're supposed to be happy!"

"You dope!" Lola sniffed and clutched the box tighter. "Why do you think I'm crying?"

"Yeah—" Starbuck looked embarrassed. "I just never saw you cry before, that's all."

"Some presents are worth crying over! God, it must have cost a fortune, Luke!"

"Only a small fortune," Starbuck said with a waggish grin. "I wanted you to have a memento of Virginia City. I couldn't have done it without you."

"Honestly?" Lola wiped the tears away. "You're not just saying that?"

"Cross my heart." Starbuck stitched a cross over his shirt pocket. "Without you, I would've never got wind of Alice Carver. And without her, I'd have never broken the case. So I owe it all to you."

Lola took another quick peek at the pendant. Then her eyes cleared and she fixed him with a sly look. "You're a terrible liar, Luke Starbuck."

"I wouldn't lie about a thing like that!"

"Yes, you would!" Lola's laugh was low and infectious. "You paid more for this pendant than you earned on the case. How do you explain that?"

"Nothing simpler." Starbuck gave her a jolly wink. "You were due a present long before Virginia City."

"Why?" Lola asked, a devilish glint in her eye. "I want to hear you tell me."

A smile tugged at the corner of Starbuck's mouth. "I reckon I just did."

Lola knew better than to push him too far. In his own way, he had indeed told her what she wanted to hear. He was an emotional nomad; therefore, his choice of words was always oblique. Yet, however roundabout, it was enough for Lola. She adroitly switched to another topic.

"How long will I have the pleasure of your company?"

"How long you figure you could stand me?"

"Don't play cat and mouse!" Lola shook a rougish finger at him. "You checked your mail before you came to the theater—didn't you?"

"So what?"

"So tell me!" Lola mocked his grumpy expression. "How long until your next case?"

"Whoa, now!" Starbuck protested. "Don't get any harebrained ideas!"

"Why, whatever are you talking about?"

"You know damn well!" Starbuck said sternly. "You got a taste of undercover work and you like it. Just don't expect to tag along on every case!"

Lola let the remark pass. "Something in your mail must have been very interesting!"

"Goddamn, aren't a man's secrets safe anymore?"

"Not from me," Lola cooed, batting her lashes. "You're an open book, lover!"

Starbuck sat there with a funny look in his eye. After a moment he chuckled softly. "A fellow from

Santa Fe wants to see me. His letter sounded the least bit urgent."

"Outlaws in Santa Fe?"

"High-class outlaws," Starbuck confided. "I got the impression he wants to talk about the Santa Fe Ring."

"Omigawd!" Lola yelped. "Weren't they the ones behind the Lincoln County war?"

"Nobody's proved it . . . yet."

"When would you leave?"

"All depends," Starbuck said with a shrug. "I wired the fellow and told him to hop the next train to Denver."

"In that case, we shouldn't waste any time."

"What'd you have in mind?"

"Something naughty and wild!"

"Got any samples?"

Lola laughed a sultry, deep-throated laugh. She scooted across the sofa and snuggled close. Her arms went around his neck and she pulled his head down. Then she kissed him with fierce abandon, her tongue darting his mouth. When at last they separated, her voice was warm and husky.

"Ooo how I want you! Take me to bed, lover!"

Starbuck took her.

Epilogue

El Paso
September 22, 1883

Starbuck stepped onto the veranda of the Parker House Hotel. Beyond the mountains, the last rays of sunset streaked the sky like dull fire. A bluish dusk slowly settled over El Paso.

The hotel was situated on the east side of San Jacinto Plaza. From the veranda Starbuck had a commanding view of the broad square and the uptown business district. He walked forward and took a seat in a cane-bottomed rocker. He lit a cigarette and loosened the Colt in its crossdraw holster. Then he set the rocker into motion.

A patient hunter, Starbuck let his mind wander while he waited. He recalled hearing that the conquistadores had originally named the town El Paso del Norte. Surrounded by mountains, it lay nestled in the Tularosa Basin and provided a natural pass to the north over the Franklin range. To the southwest, across the Rio Grande, lay the Sierra Madre range. The mountains formed a backdrop for El Paso's counterpart on the Mexican shoreline, Paso del Norte. Yesterday, on the train, he'd heard that Paso del Norte was a place where gringo lawmen seldom ventured. He thought it a revealing comment, all part and parcel of a widely accepted belief. El Paso itself was considered the toughest border town on the frontier.

Formerly a wilderness crossroads, El Paso had been little more than a stopover to somewhere else. The trail from Sante Fe to Mexico City ran directly through the plaza, while the stage route connecting San Antonio with the Pacific Coast meandered off in the opposite direction. Only two years ago, with the arrival of the Southern Pacific Railroad, the sleepy village had undergone a startling transformation. The daily trains from east Texas had disgorged a horde of saloon-keepers and cardsharps, whores and gunmen, and the usual assortment of hardcases. There were fortunes to be made in a boomtime bordertown, and El Paso welcomed harlot and outlaw alike with open arms. The town mushroomed under an uneasy alliance of commerce and vice.

The danger to lawmen was in no way exaggerated. El Paso's first marshal had lasted only a few months. His replacement, a former Texas Ranger, was Dallas Stoudenmire. Within a week of taking office, Stoudenmire had killed three men and established himself as a fighting marshal. Only last year, after running afoul of the sporting crowd, Stoudenmire had been removed from office. Some months later he'd been killed in a shootout with the Manning brothers, who allegedly controlled much of the vice district. The message was clear to men who wore a badge. El Paso was an open town, with no great pretense of law and order. A peace officer who believed otherwise risked his life on a daily basis.

Staring out across the plaza, Starbuck thought it a point worth remembering. He had arrived by train only last night, and he was under no illusions about his own safety. In the event he was recognized, there were any number of men in El Paso who would gladly gun him down from behind. Not the least among them was the man he sought. Still, he had opted to work openly rather than operate undercover. He'd come here to kill Wilbur X. Lott.

Hardly to his surprise, Starbuck's prediction regarding the Virginia City vigilantes had proved correct. Some six weeks past, Lott and his band of stranglers had lynched a man mistakenly identified as a horse thief. Lott, who had failed in his bid for political office, was already at odds with the authorities. The hanging of yet another innocent man merely quickened his downfall. He was charged with murder and promptly fled Virginia City. A fugitive warrant was issued and the territorial governor posted a reward of a thousand dollars. He was wanted dead or alive.

The reward was a matter of no consequence to Starbuck. He had a personal score to settle, and the law had provided the legal means. While he couldn't spare the time for an investigation, he had no intention of allowing Lott to escape justice. After reflecting on it, he'd decided to approach the problem in a roundabout manner. Through Jack Murphy, his chief informant in the Denver underworld, he had put out feelers across the West. Among thieves and desperados, the moccasin telegraph was the principal source of information. Over a month passed before word drifted back to Starbuck via the grapevine. Wilbur X. Lott was holed up in Paso del Norte.

According to Starbuck's informant, Lott spent most of his time on the Mexican side of the Rio Grande. Paso del Norte was a sanctuary for gringo badmen, immune to the laws of extradition and the long arm of American peace officers. Lott lived across the border and apparently visited El Paso only after dark. He was known to prefer the company of gringa women, and his favorite hangout was the White Elephant Saloon, on the west side of the plaza. He was operating under the alias William Latham, and these days he sported a beard. He had no known associates in El Paso.

Last night, upon arriving in town, Starbuck had checked into the hotel. Except for meals, he'd kept to his room throughout the day. His plan was simple and direct. He would stay out of sight during the day and thereby avoid the risk of alerting Lott. At sundown, he would take up a post on the hotel veranda and maintain a watch on the White Elephant. Sooner or later, his quarry would show. Then he would walk across the plaza and perform the job by the most expedient means. Tonight's stakeout was the first of what might very well prove to be a marathon. Yet, however long it took, he had no qualms or reservations. He was prepared to wait for the chance to kill Wilbur Lott.

Starbuck's vigil paid off on his third cigarette. He

saw Lott appear from Main Street, which angled off in the direction of the bridge connecting El Paso with Paso del Norte. The streetlamps were lighted and the former vigilante was easily recognizable. The beard he'd grown had altered his appearance, but his cadaverous frame and hooklike nose were impossible to disguise. He crossed to the west side of the plaza with the air of a man whose troubles are few and far behind. A moment later he disappeared through the doors of the White Elephant.

No great believer in luck, Starbuck nonetheless took it as a good omen. To locate Lott on the first night seemed at the very least providential. He stood and ground his cigarette underfoot. Tugging his suit jacket over the Colt, he moved directly to the veranda stairs. The prospect of killing a man worked on him like some mystical anodyne. At such times, his heartbeat slowed, and his nerves, as though cauterized, simply ceased to function. He operated solely on instinct and reflex, some atavistic sense tuned not so much to survival as the need to kill swiftly. He crossed the plaza with no thought of personal danger. His whole attitude was zeroed on the task ahead.

The White Elephant was a cut above most bordertown watering holes. A long mahogany bar dominated one side of the room. Behind the counter a massive French mirror, flanked by nude paintings, adorned the wall. Opposite the bar was a row of gaming tables, and toward the rear of the room was a small dance floor. A piano player and a fiddler provided the entertainment, while a bevy of saloon girls ministered to those with a taste for companionship. The crowd was boisterous and loud, the atmosphere congenial. No one paid Starbuck the slightest attention.

Wilbur Lott stood with his elbows hooked over the bar and one foot firmly planted on the brass rail. He had a drink in one hand and a bosomy redhead attached to his arm. His mode of dress was still somewhat funereal, with a swallowtail coat topped off by a broad-brimmed hat. Beneath the coat, a bulge on his right hip betrayed the presence of a holstered pistol. His expression was that of a man with lechery on his mind. He looked as if he were swapping dirty ideas with the redhead.

Starbuck wedged in beside him. Lott's concentration was on the girl, and several moments passed without incident. Then, after a wayward glance in the backbar mirror, Lott suddenly stiffened. His eyes went wide with fright and he pushed off the counter. Starbuck nodded with a wry grin.

"How's tricks, Wilbur?"

"I—" Lott faltered, his face ashen. "What do you want?"

"Dumb question," Starbuck needled him. "You're a fugitive from justice."

"You have no authority in Texas!"

"Why stand on formalities?" Starbuck quipped. "Kiss your lady friend goodbye and we'll be on our way."

Lott glowered at him through slitted eyes. "I'm not going anywhere with you!"

"Yeah, you are," Starbuck said evenly. "Way it works out, you've got a choice. Come along peaceable, and I'll take you back to Montana. Otherwise, you and the undertaker are set for a one-way ride."

"No!" Lott said with sudden resolve. "I won't fight and you won't kill me in cold blood!"

"Wanna bet?" Starbuck let go a ferocious laugh. "The reward dodger says dead or alive. Open season on Wilbur X. Lott."

The redhead believed him. She gently disengaged her hand from Lott's arm and eased away from the bar. For all his bravado, Lott too sensed his life was in imminent peril. He saw in Starbuck's gaze a look of predatory eagerness. His attitude underwent an abrupt turnaround.

"Listen to me, Starbuck!" His voice was heavy, stark. "I grant you we hung the wrong man. But we didn't know that at the time. It was a mistake—an accident!"

"How do you accidentally lynch somebody?"

"He was on a stolen horse! We didn't find out till later he'd bought it off the real thief. By then, it was too late!"

"Pretty flimsy," Starbuck said with a sardonic look. "The law don't issue a dead-or-alive warrant on accidental homicide. Sounds like you hung one too many men, Wilbur."

"It wasn't that!" Lott muttered vehemently. "I made too many political enemies, and they were out to get me. Any excuse would've done!"

"Tit for tat," Starbuck observed. "You hung a whole slew of men over nothing but politics. Why shouldn't somebody hang you for the same reason?"

"For God's sake!" Lott implored. "It was an accident—I swear it!"

"Tell you what," Starbuck said in a musing tone. "I never was one to cause a man undue suffering. So I'll give you the same break I gave Henry Palmer."

"Palmer!" Lott blanched. "You shot him!"

"Square through the heart," Starbuck nodded sagely. "Quick and painless, and it don't spoil the looks of the corpse."

Sweat popped out on Lott's forehead. "I don't care much for that idea."

"Well, like I told you," Starbuck said matter-of-factly. "You've got a choice between me and Montana. Course, if I was you, I wouldn't let nobody strangle me to death. That's a goddamn hard way to cash out."

A vivid image of the Judas Tree flashed through Lott's mind. His throat constricted and his face turned pasty white. "I guess I'll have to chance it."

"Suit yourself."

Starbuck deliberately turned his head sideways. He signaled the barkeep, seemingly unconcerned about Lott. Yet, alert to any movement, he watched the large mirror out of the corner of his eye. The barkeep bustled forward.

"Yessir!"

"Who's your town marshal?"

"Jim Gillett!"

"Send somebody to fetch him—on the double!"

"What's the problem?"

"Get him over here and you'll find out."

Lott listened to the exchange with mounting dread. His expression became immobile and dark, and the muscles in his jaw knotted. Then, suddenly, he de-

cided to risk it all on one play. His eyes flashed with
a formidable glitter and his arm swept the swallowtail
coat aside. His hand closed over the butt of his pistol.

Starbuck seemed to move not at all. The Colt appeared out of nowhere and in the same instant his
head swiveled around. Lott's eyes were marblelike
with shock, and he somehow looked betrayed. As his
pistol cleared leather Starbuck feathered the trigger
and the Colt belched flame. Lott stood perfectly still,
a great splotch of red covering his breastbone. Then
the pistol slipped from his fingers and his legs buckled. He slowly slumped to the floor.

Holstering the Colt, Starbuck knelt beside the fallen
man. Lott lay with his head propped up against the
brass rail, his hat tilted askew. A trickle of blood
seeped out of the corner of his mouth and his
breathing was ragged. He stared at Starbuck with a
glassy expression.

"You tricked me."

"You tricked yourself, Wilbur."

"Dirty . . . pool . . ."

The words ended in a gurgled cough and Lott's
eyes rolled back in his head. Starbuck studied the face
a moment, almost a clinical examination. Then he
leaned forward and closed the eyelids with his fin-
gertips. He stood and nodded to the barkeep.

"Tell the marshal he'll find me over at the hotel."

"Yessir, cap'n! I shorely will!"

Outside, Starbuck crossed the plaza at a measured
stride. He heard again the last words of Wilbur X.
Lott. The thought occurred that what he'd done was
indeed dirty pool. But, then, there were no rules on

the killing ground. He smiled, not in the least troubled he'd sent a strangler to the grave. In the end, for those who held themselves above the law, only one code prevailed.

Some men deserved to die.

America's Authentic Voice of the Western Frontier

Matt Braun

Bestselling author of *Bloody Hand*

HICKOK & CODY

In the wind-swept campsite of the Fifth Cavalry Regiment, along Red Willow Creek, Russia's Grand Duke Alexis has arrived to experience the thrill of the buffalo hunt. His guides are: Wild Bill Hickok and Buffalo Bill Cody—two heroic dead-shots with a natural flair for showmanship, a hunger for adventure, and the fervent desire to keep the myths of the Old West alive. But what approached from the East was a journey that crossed the line into dangerous territory. It would offer Alexis a front row seat to history, and would set Hickok and Cody on a path to glory.

"Braun tackles the big men, the complex personalities of those brave few who were pivotal figures in the settling of an untamed frontier."
—Jory Sherman, author of *Grass Kingdom*

"Matt Braun has a genius for taking real characters out of the Old West and giving them flesh-and-blood immediacy."
—Dee Brown, author of
Bury My Heart at Wounded Knee

AVAILABLE WHEREVER BOOKS ARE SOLD
FROM ST. MARTIN'S PAPERBACKS

HC 8/02

READ THESE MASTERFUL WESTERNS BY MATT BRAUN

"Matt Braun is a master storyteller of frontier history."
—Elmer Kelton

THE KINCAIDS

Golden Spur Award-winner THE KINCAIDS tells the classic saga of America at its most adventurous through the eyes of three generations who made laws, broke laws, and became legends in their time.

GENTLEMAN ROGUE

Hell's Half Acre is Fort Worth's violent ghetto of whorehouses, gaming dives and whisky wells. And for shootist and gambler Luke Short, it's a place to make a stand. But he'll have to stake his claim from behind the barrel of a loaded gun . . .

RIO GRANDE

Tom Stuart, a hard-drinking, fast-talking steamboat captain, has a dream of building a shipping empire that will span the Gulf of Mexico to New Orleans. Now, Stuart is plunged into the fight of a lifetime—and to the winner will go the mighty Rio Grande . . .

THE BRANNOCKS

The three Brannock brothers were reunited in a boomtown called Denver. And on a frontier brimming with opportunity and exploding with danger, vicious enemies would test their courage—and three beautiful women would claim their love . . .

**AVAILABLE WHEREVER BOOKS ARE SOLD
FROM ST. MARTIN'S PAPERBACKS**

**Before the legend,
there was the man . . .**

And a powerful destiny to fulfill.

On October 26, 1881, three outlaws lay dead in
a dusty vacant lot in Tombstone, Arizona.
Standing over them—Colts smoking—were
Wyatt Earp, his two brothers Morgan and
Virgil, and a gun-slinging gambler named
Doc Holliday. The shootout at the O.K. Corral
was over—but for Earp, the fight had just
begun . . .

WYATT EARP

**MATT
BRAUN**

**AVAILABLE WHEREVER BOOKS ARE SOLD
FROM ST. MARTIN'S PAPERBACKS**

THE LAST
STAND

MATT BRAUN

St. Martin's Paperbacks

THE JUDAS TREE / THE LAST STAND

The Judas Tree copyright © 1982 by Matt Braun. Published by arrangement with Signet, an imprint of New American Library, a division of Penguin Books USA Inc.
The Last Stand copyright © 1998 by Winchester Productions, Ltd.

Cover photo © Comstock Images.

ISBN: 0-312-94605-8
EAN: 978-0-312-94605-0

Printed in the United States of America

The Judas Tree first Signet paperback edition / June 1992
St. Martin's Paperbacks edition / October 2003

The Last Stand St. Martin's Paperbacks edition / June 1998

St. Martin's Paperbacks are published by St. Martin's Press, 175 Fifth Avenue, New York, NY 10010.

10 9 8 7 6 5 4 3 2 1

**TO
THE TWINS
DAN AND TOM BIRKBECK
TWO OF A KIND AND BOTH ACES HIGH!**

Author's Note

The Last Stand is written as an allegory: a story in which people, things, and events have a symbolic meaning. The symbolism of this story relates to the long and sordid history of broken land treaties between the United States government and virtually all Indian tribes. There were many last stands in the westward expansion, from sea to shining sea.

Though based on actual events, *The Last Stand* is ten percent fact and ninety percent fiction. In 1909, there was a resistance to land allotments within the Five Civilized Tribes, and a National Guard unit was activated to quell the problem. Oklahoma was briefly in panic, with banner headlines in the newspapers, and men were killed. All else in this story is fiction.

Chitto Starr, the central figure in the story, represents those who fought—and died—for land granted in treaties "as long as grass shall grow and water shall run." He might have been Cheyenne or Sioux, Comanche or Apache, Seminole or Choctaw. Or any one of the warrior leaders who fought to the last stand. I chose to make him Cherokee.

What remains is a storyteller at work.

One

A bright October sun flooded the countryside. The air was crisp and clean, and trees fluttered with leaves gone red and gold. High overhead a vee of geese winged their way southward.

The men rode into town late that afternoon. Frank Starr and Tom Tenkiller entered by the farm road from the north. Jim Colbert, Redbird Smith, and Charley Foster appeared on the road south of town. Jack Fox and Henry Brandon rode along a side street from an easterly direction. Their horses were held to a walk.

The town was located in the old Creek Nation. Since statehood, and the influx of whites into Oklahoma, the town's population had swelled to more than a thousand. Hardly a center of commerce, it was nonetheless a thriving hamlet built on the trade of the area's farmers. The community was small but prosperous.

Preston, like most farm towns, was bisected by a main thoroughfare. The business district consisted of several stores, a feed mill, one bank, and a blacksmith who now tinkered on automobiles. There were few people about and little activity on a Monday afternoon. Typically the slowest part of the week, it accounted in part for the seven strangers on horseback. Their business was better conducted without crowds.

"What're you thinkin', Frank?"

Starr grinned. "I think we're gonna make a payday."

"Funny, ain't it?" Tenkiller shook his head. "Damn white people don't never believe anybody would rob their banks."

"Button your lip! Even *aniyonega* have ears."

Starr quickly scanned the street. He and Tenkiller were full-blood Cherokee, and the scattering of people on the sidewalks stared as they rode past. A couple of Indians, even though they wore white men's clothing and were mounted on good horses, still attracted idle curiosity. But no one appeared to have overheard Tenkiller's remark about banks.

A week past, Starr had assigned Charley Foster to scout the town. Foster, a half-breed who sometimes passed for white, had returned with a crudely sketched map. He reported that the bank was manned only by the president and two tellers. Law enforcement consisted of a town marshal, who operated without regular deputies and rarely patrolled the streets. The townspeople, apart from shopping and the usual errands, were seldom about on weekdays. All in all, Preston looked like easy pickings.

Starr had selected the town for just that reason. He robbed banks for a living, and he practiced prudence over greed. There was less money from a holdup in a small town, but there was far less chance of being caught. For two years, since the fall of 1907, when Oklahoma Territory and Indian Territory were joined in statehood, he had preyed on banks owned by white men. The pay was good, the hours were short, and he liked to think of it as retribution against those who had stolen Indian lands. There was a price on his head, and he was notorious as a gang leader who ran circles around the law. He hadn't yet seen the inside of a jail.

Downstreet, a Ford Model T pulled away from the local hardware store. The car backfired as the driver hooked into second gear and rattled past in a haze of dust. Tenkiller's horse shied away, spooked by the noisy contraption, and he fought to control the reins. Starr cursed roundly under his breath, glaring at the Ford as it rolled north out of town. He loathed the sight of automobiles, all the more so the clattering racket and the oily, foreign smell. He thought of them as a white man's invention, one more intrusion on a once-peaceful land. He sometimes worried that the days of a horseback outlaw were numbered.

The owner of the hardware store, standing in the doorway, watched as Starr and Tenkiller approached. Indians were no novelty in Preston, for members of the Creek tribe still owned nearby parcels of land, and worked as farmers. At first, he gave the riders scant notice, though he was struck by the fact that they were mounted on fine horses, built for endurance and speed. But then, glancing eastward, he saw two riders enter town from a sidestreet, both of them equally well-mounted. One was a half-breed and the other was clearly a full-blood, darker by a shade. A moment later he saw three more riders, full-bloods on good mounts approach from the south along Main Street. He wondered why seven Indians were riding into town at the same time, from different directions. Somehow, it seemed more than coincidence.

The storekeeper moved out of the doorway. He retreated inside, hidden from sight by the dim interior, and peered through the front window. He watched as the riders converged on the bank, directly across the street, their horses still held to a walk. Outside the bank, two men wheeled to the left and halted before the hitch rack along the sidewalk. Downstreet, the three men approaching from the south stopped in front of a mercantile store. A few doors north of the bank, the last two men reined in on the same side of the street.

There was a military precision to their movements. The riders on either side of the bank dismounted and took positions to cover the street in both directions. Some checked their saddle rigging, others dusted themselves off and, to a man, their eyes checked nearby buildings. One of the men outside the bank paused a moment and subjected the whole of the business district to a slow, careful scrutiny. Then, followed by a second man, he turned and crossed the sidewalk. They sauntered into the bank.

The hardware store owner was rooted a moment in shock. Any lingering doubt was quickly dispelled, and recovering his wits, he bolted for the rear door. In the alley, he turned south, hurrying next door to the barbershop, and burst through the back entrance. He startled the proprietor, who sat sound asleep in the high-backed barber's chair. His voice was strident.

"Wake up, Amos!" he yelled. "Injuns are robbin' the bank."

"Injuns?" the barber echoed dumbly. "Red Injuns?"

"Get the wax out of your ears. What the hell else color would they be? See there!"

The storekeeper pointed out the window. Still groggy, the barber swiveled out of the chair, following the direction of his finger. They stared at the horsemen across the street, and after a few seconds, the barber collected himself. "Injuns, all right," he allowed. "You sure they're robbin' the bank?"

"Goddamn right I'm sure! You think they're makin' a deposit?"

"I didn't say that, Harley."

"Bastards are fixin' to steal our money. You got a gun?"

"I keep a pistol in the drawer. Why?"

" 'Cause I want you to watch 'em like a hawk. I'm gonna run down and warn the marshal."

"What if they try to ride off?"

"Hell's bells and little fishes! You cut loose and shoot their asses off, Amos. What d'you think?"

"I think you'd better hurry up and fetch the marshal."

Harley Meecham rushed out the back door. Amos Ledbetter moved past the barber chair and opened a drawer beneath the wall mirror. He took out a Smith & Wesson Double Action revolver that hadn't been fired in ten years, and hastily checked the loads. Then, as he turned toward the window, he had a sobering thought. Those men really were Indians!

He wondered if it was Frank Starr's gang.

Inside the bank, Starr halted as Tom Tenkiller shut the door. The cashier's window was to the rear, and beyond that stood a massive safe, the steel doors closed. To his immediate left, seated behind a desk, the bank president was engaged in conversation with a man dressed as a farmer. One teller stood at the cashier's window while the other worked on an accounting ledger.

"Don't nobody move!" Starr announced. "This is a holdup."

There was an instant of leaden silence. At the desk, the president stared at him with disbelief, and the farmer swiveled around in his chair. The cashier froze, watching him intently, and the other teller paused with his

pen dipped in an inkwell. Tenkiller positioned himself
to cover everyone in the room.

"You folks be sensible, now," he said jovially. "No
need anybody gettin' hurt over money."

Starr walked to the cashier's window. He casually
wagged the snout of his pistol, nodding to the teller.
"Forget your cash drawer. Let's have a look in the
safe."

"I—" The teller swallowed. "I don't know the combination."

"You mean to say it's locked?"

"Yessir."

"Well ain't that a helluva note."

Starr turned from the counter. His gaze fixed on the
man seated behind the desk. "You the head of this here
concern?"

"I am."

"What's your name?"

The man was stout, with florid features and heavy
jowls. He glared back with a tight-lipped scowl. "I am
Horace Kendall."

"C'mon, Mr. Kendall," Starr said pleasantly. "Let's
talk a little business."

Kendall stood, still glowering, and moved forward.
Starr motioned him to a gate at the side of the cashier's
cage, and walked him to the safe. With a sardonic smile,
Starr rapped on the steel door.

"I'm here to take out a loan. Open 'er up."

"I can't do that," Kendall said firmly. "We were
about to close for the day. I have it set on a time lock."

"What's a time lock?"

"The latest thing, a timing mechanism. There's no
way to open it until nine tomorrow morning."

Starr searched his eyes, then grinned. "You're a poor

liar, Horace. Besides which, you ain't got till tomorrow morning.''

''I don't understand.''

''Why, sure you do.'' Starr thumbed the hammer on his pistol, placed the barrel to the banker's head. ''You got ten seconds to get 'er open. Otherwise your wife's a widow.''

Horace Kendall paled, his forehead beaded with sweat. He hesitated a moment, then spun the combination knob on the safe. After three rotations, he turned the handles and swung open the doors. A shelf on the inside was piled high with stacks of cash.

''Looky what we got here!'' Starr pulled a folded gunnysack from inside his coat and thrust it at the banker. ''Just the big bills, Horace. Forget the chicken feed.''

Kendall grunted sourly, began stuffing bills into the gunnysack. When he was finished, Starr had him tie the top of the sack in a knot and hand it over. ''Thank you kindly,'' Starr said, backing away. ''You'll make it home for supper after all, Horace.''

The banker waited until Starr turned toward the gate at the cashier's cage. Then his hand dipped into a recess inside the safe and reappeared with a stubby bulldog revolver. As he brought the gun to bear, Tom Tenkiller fired from the front of the room. The slug struck Kendall below the sternum, and a rosette of blood brightened his somber vest. He collapsed at the knees, slowly slumped to the floor.

''Goddammit!'' Starr howled, looking from Tenkiller to the body. ''Why'd he do a fool thing like that?''

''Don't ask me,'' Tenkiller said, somewhat amazed himself. ''Sonovabitch tried to shoot you in the back.''

''You can just bet your butt that put the town on notice. Let's get the hell outta here.''

A roar of gunfire—several shots in rapid succession—suddenly sounded from outside. Starr glanced through the front window and saw gang members popping shots at merchants who had appeared in doorways along the street. Across the way, the town marshal and Harley Meecham stood on the sidewalk, blasting away with pistols. Another volley erupted and the lawman's right leg buckled under the impact of a slug. He went down on his rump.

Starr hefted the gunnysack in one hand, his pistol in the other. The gunfire swelled in intensity as he and Tenkiller rushed outside and moved toward the hitch rack. On either side of them, the men posted as guards were trading shots with merchants up and down the street. A pistol barked from the doorway of the barbershop, and Charley Foster, the half-breed, staggered sideways in a shuffling dance. He crashed through the window of the mercantile store.

Firing on the move, Starr and Tenkiller stepped off the sidewalk. Their horses were wall-eyed with fright as the men pulled the reins loose and bounded into the saddle. A bullet opened a bloody gash on Starr's left forearm, and the gunnysack filled with cash fell from his hand. He whirled his horse and fired, dropping Amos Ledbetter in the door of the barbershop. From upstreet, a rifle cracked, and Tenkiller windmilled out of the saddle, hitting the ground hard. He tried to rise, then pitched facedown in the dirt.

Starr leaned out of his saddle to grab the gunnysack. Dust spurted inches from his hand as a rifle ball pocked the earth, and he hauled himself upright by the saddlehorn. Across the street, the town marshal rose unsteadily to his feet and triggered three quick shots. One of the slugs sizzled past Starr's ear and he wheeled about, fighting to control his horse, and ripped off two shots in return. The lawman slammed backward, stumbling haywire into the wall of a building, his shirtfront splotched with blood. He fell dead on the sidewalk.

All along the street storekeepers were firing from windows and doorways. The other gang members hastily mounted, their pistols belching flame in a steady roar. Upstreet a merchant bellowed in pain, dropping his rifle. In the opposite direction, the blacksmith tumbled to the ground beside the fender of a flatbed Reo truck. Then, with Starr in the lead, the gang reined their horses around and spurred for the edge of town. Their one thought now was escape, to survive the hailstorm of gunfire. They thundered north along the farm road.

Behind them, the townspeople peppered their retreat with a barrage of lead. Harley Meecham got off one last shot as the outlaws gigged their horses in headlong flight. After a moment, lowering his pistol, he stared around at the carnage with a stunned expression. The marshal lay dead at his feet, and a few doors away, the barber lay puddled in blood. Outside the bank, one of the robbers was sprawled in the street, and another hung limp in the shattered window of the mercantile store. He thought it looked like a slaughterhouse.

The pistol dropped from his hand and his legs suddenly went rubbery. Townspeople appeared all along the street as he sat down beside the body of the marshal. He wiped his face with a trembling hand, still deafened by gunfire. His eyes glazed over with shock.

The sickly-sweet stench of death brought bile to his throat.

Two

The intersection of Harrison and Second was the hub of downtown Guthrie. Offices for federal agencies occupied the upper story of the International Building, which was located on the southeast corner. Across the street was the Palace Hotel, where the politicians made their home when the legislature was in session. A few blocks away, the state capitol stood like a monolith at the east end of Oklahoma Avenue.

On any given night Harrison and Second was a beehive of activity. There businessmen and politicians, and the usual coterie of lobbyists, came together in pursuit of the good life. All the gambling dives and saloons were gone, abolished by law on the eve of statehood. But fine restaurants, not to mention wine and whiskey, were still to be found where men of influence gathered. Some men, especially in Guthrie, were more equal before the law than others.

Owen McLain sat alone at a table in the Bluebell Café, around the corner on Harrison. The fare was meatloaf and spuds rather than prime rib and imported

French wine. Still, it was near the office, within walking distance of his rooming house, and a ringside seat for the nightly gatherings of Guthrie's elite. From the window, he watched as a state senator and a high-roller lobbyist stepped out of a Cadillac Touring Car and entered the hotel. He reckoned their meal tonight would wipe out his month's salary.

From relative poverty, McLain had risen to the bright lights of the capital. His parents, who homesteaded a farm in Lincoln County, had been killed in a tornado when he was eighteen, the summer of 1898. After selling the farm, he'd served a hitch in the army and then caught on as a deputy sheriff. The work suited him, for his boyhood heroes had been marshals like Bill Tilghman and Heck Thomas, the scourge of outlaws in Old Oklahoma Territory. Three years ago he had landed a job as a deputy U.S. Marshal, operating out of the Guthrie office. A month ago, at age twenty-nine, he had been promoted to Chief Deputy.

Surprisingly, none of the other deputy marshals resented his promotion. Though most of them were older, they all agreed he had earned the spot. In three years, he'd apprehended more train robbers and whiskey smugglers than any man on the job. Then, too, there was the attendant publicity from having killed four men in the line of duty. Some people thought he was cut from the mold of the old gunfighter marshals, men like Tilghman and Thomas. He regretted every killing, but not the comparison. He took it as the highest accolade.

McLain's reputation was known and respected throughout all of Oklahoma. A man of intelligence and quick wits, he had discovered early on that a peace officer survived to a large extent on sharp reflexes and flawless instincts. He was a solid six-footer, lithe and broad through the shoulders, with light chestnut hair and a brushy mustache. His size, and the hard cast to his steely-blue eyes, were generally enough to dissuade lawbreakers from pressing their luck. For those who opted to fight, he was as quick with his fists as he was with a gun.

Finished with his meal, he pulled out the makings and began building a smoke. He still preferred roll-your-owns to tailor-made cigarettes, a holdover from his days in the army. After creasing the paper, he sprinkled tobacco into the fold, deftly rolled it with one hand, and sealed the flap with a lick. He returned the Bull Durham bag to his pocket and popped a match on his thumbnail. As he lit up, Bob Newton, the deputy on night duty, stopped at his table. He snuffed the match.

"Why do I get the feeling you're lookin' for me, Bob?"

" 'Cause I'm here," Newton said with an amiable shrug. "The boss sent me to find you."

McLain stood. "What's he want?"

"Hell, Owen, you know him better'n that. He's big on orders but short on the why."

"Well, let's go find out."

McLain followed him out of the café. On the street, they turned toward the corner, where a group of politicians were glad-handing one another outside the hotel. For the most part, McLain had no use for politicians and the legion of bureaucrats who inhabited the statehouse. The legislature seemed to him little more than a nest of thieves, controlled by shadowy business interests, and he thought there was truth to the adage that power corrupts. But he nonetheless liked Guthrie, and the excitement of being around the capital. The whole town seemed to have leaped into the twentieth century.

Guthrie was forever in the midst of change. Every home in town had electric lights, and horse-drawn streetcars had long since been replaced with electric trolley cars. Dusty washboard streets gave way to broad thoroughfares paved with brick, all the better to accommodate automobiles of the modern era. A thriving economy centered around the state capitol, buttressed by all manner of industrial and business concerns. Even the high wires hummed, with the advance of Alexander Graham Bell's marvelous invention, and Guthrie became the first community in Oklahoma to install a telephone exchange. Civic boosters were justifiably proud of the town's progress.

McLain shared their pride, with one exception. As he and Newton crossed the street, a massive Pierce-Arrow, tricked out with brass fittings and a tonneau upholstered in morocco leather, roared around the corner. The driver let out a loud squawk on the horn, and they hopped across the trolley-car tracks to avoid being run down. Having served in the cavalry, McLain was no great advocate of the automobile. Whether his opinion was outdated, or a sign of backward thinking, was a matter of little concern. He still thought a horse was the best way to get from here to there.

On the opposite corner, they entered the International Building and made their way upstairs. The main room was crowded with desks for deputy marshals, and at the rear, there was a private office for the U.S. Marshal. McLain rapped on the door and found Fred Gilmore seated behind a mahogany desk, puffing furiously on a cigar. A political appointee, Gilmore was in his early forties, grown heavy around the middle, with thinning hair and an easygoing disposition. Tonight he looked worried.

"Have a chair, Owen." He motioned with his cigar. "A telephone call came in an hour or so ago, and Newton called me at home. I thought we'd better talk."

McLain seated himself. "Way you look, it's serious."

"That hardly covers it. Frank Starr and his gang robbed the bank in Preston this afternoon. They killed the bank president, the town marshal and a couple of merchants. Two of Starr's men were killed as well."

"Jesus," McLain muttered. "Sounds like a blood-bath."

"Indeed." Gilmore clamped the cigar in his mouth. "The call was from the Okmulgee County sheriff. He and his posse lost the trail a few miles east of Preston. He thinks Starr is headed for Cherokee country."

"No surprise there. Starr knows he's safe with the Cherokees. His big brother sees to that."

"You're referring to Chitto Starr."

"One and the same."

"What do you know about him?"

"I always suspected he provided hideouts for Frank. Trouble was, I could never prove it."

McLain considered Frank Starr his one setback as a deputy marshal. For two years he had crisscrossed the state in pursuit of Oklahoma's most infamous bank rob-ber. At every turn, he'd been outfoxed or outrun, frus-trated by a will-o'-the-wisp who simply vanished into the wilds of Cherokee country. He laid a good deal of the blame on Starr's brother.

Gilmore puffed a wad of smoke. "Have you ever met Chitto Starr?"

"Nooo," McLain said slowly. "Never had the plea-sure."

"From what I read in the newspaper, he's quite the renegade. He and his followers have played Holy Han-nah with the land allotments. Even the leaders of the Cherokee tribe have turned on him."

"Well, at least he doesn't rob banks. That's more than you can say for his brother."

"Perhaps." Gilmore was silent a moment. "I think

it's time you made the acquaintance of Chitto Starr. I want you to bring in his brother—dead or alive.''

McLain sat straighter. ''I'd welcome the chance. But I never had much luck huntin' Starr. I'll understand if you send someone else.''

''Nobody else has caught Starr, either. You're the best man for the job, and we both know it, Owen. Let's leave it at that.''

''I'll head out first thing in the morning.''

''Good.'' Gilmore tapped an ash off his cigar. ''Contact the sheriff when you get to Tahlequah. His name slips my mind.''

''Ed Prather,'' McLain said with a frown. ''You'd best send him a wire to make it official. Otherwise, he'll drag his feet.''

''Why is that?''

''Prather likes to run his own show. He's not partial to federal marshals in general, and me in particular. We've butted heads before.''

Gilmore nodded thoughtfully. ''I'll see to it that he gets the message. You're in charge, and he can like it or lump it.''

''I just imagine he'll lump it.''

''And, Owen . . .''

''Yeah?''

''Starr killed four men today. I would prefer that he not be brought back for trial. Do we understand one another?''

McLain understood perfectly. A trial was oftentimes prolonged, and the outcome never certain. Summary justice, on the other hand, was swift—and final.

He'd just been handed a death warrant on Frank Starr.

The Markham house was in the uptown residential district. There the wealthier families of Guthrie congregated in an enclave of imposing homes. McLain knocked on the door not quite an hour later.

Amy Markham opened the door. "Owen!" she said gaily. "What a pleasant surprise."

"Hope it's not too late," McLain said, doffing his hat. "Am I disturbing anything?"

"Don't be silly."

Amy pulled him into the foyer. She was vibrant and vivacious, with enormous hazel eyes and exquisite features. A month ago, shortly after his promotion, she had accepted his proposal of marriage, and the wedding was planned for the following June. She took his arm and walked him into the parlor.

"Look who's here," she said brightly. "Owen came to call."

John Markham, her father, was seated in an easy chair, reading the Guthrie *Statesman*. His wife, Alice, was perched on the sofa, crocheting a bedspread. Markham was a lawyer, one of the original settlers of Guthrie, and none too pleased by his daughter's betrothal. He thought the prospects for the wife of a peace officer were bleak at best.

"Good evening," he said, folding his newspaper. "Won't you have a seat?"

"Yes, do," Alice Markham added. "We so enjoy your visits, Owen."

"Thanks all the same," McLain begged off. "I just got an assignment and I'll be gone awhile. Thought I'd drop by to see Amy."

"A field assignment?" Markham said quizzically. "What with your promotion, I assumed your duties would be more of an administrative nature."

"The marshal wanted me to handle the case personal. Frank Starr robbed the bank in Preston today."

Markham rattled the newspaper. "I've just been reading about Chitto Starr. I'd say he and his brother are birds of a feather.''

"Some folks wouldn't agree," McLain said. "Frank robs banks and kills people. Chitto's fighting the land allotments and underhanded government. I've heard him called a man of principle.''

"I find that a strange comment for a federal marshal. After all, you do work for the government.''

"Maybe so, but I've got no love for shady politicians. Way I see it, we flat gypped the Indians out of their land.''

McLain was not alone in his view. For generations, the Five Civilized Tribes had been sovereign nations, reigning over what was now the eastern half of Oklahoma. But white immigrants had illegally settled in Indian Territory, which was rich in farmland, timber, and vast untapped pools of oil. Congress, under pressure from the settlers and white power brokers, abrogated ancient treaties and forced the Indians to accept individual land allotments. The tribes, by government edict, had lost ownership of millions of acres of land.

"You think we stole the land?" Markham asked stiffly. "Come now, Owen, we're talking about statehood—what was best for all.''

"I'm just saying fair's fair. If I was Indian, I'd probably think the same way as Chitto Starr.''

"Sentiment will always fall before the march of empire. That, young man, is an immutable law of history.''

McLain was stung by the curt tone. "Guess that all depends on whose ox gets gored, Mr. Markham. Yours or theirs.''

Amy moved swiftly to end the debate. "Honestly, get two men together and all they talk is politics. I simply won't have it! Come along, Owen.''

She again took McLain's arm and maneuvered him

into the foyer. After draping a shawl across her shoulders, she led him onto the front porch. The sky was clear, dotted with stars, and a cool autumn breeze drifted out of the north. She snuggled against his arm.

"You ought to be ashamed," she said lightly. "You know Daddy's an old stick-in-the-mud. He'll never change."

"Yeah, you're right," McLain agreed. "I shouldn't have sounded off. I sure as the devil didn't come here to talk politics."

"Oh?" She vamped him with a look. "Something else on your mind?"

McLain enfolded her into his arms. He kissed her full on the mouth and she hugged him fiercely around the neck. She moaned deeply in her throat, her breasts pressed firmly against his chest, and felt his manhood harden along her thigh. At last, breathing heavily, she broke free of his embrace. She tapped him playfully on the nose.

"Don't get too frisky, Mr. McLain. We're not married yet."

"Why the hell do we have to wait till next June?"

"A girl needs a proper engagement. Everyone expects it."

"I'm not feelin' very proper right now. Maybe I'll get my mind off you while I'm out chasing Frank Starr."

"Oh, I seriously doubt it."

She laughed a low, gloating laugh, and kissed him again.

Three

Three days later Frank Starr and his gang forded Park Hill Creek. The stream was located outside Park Hill, five miles south of Tahlequah, in the old Cherokee Nation. The men were disgruntled at having lost the bank loot, and sobered by the deaths of two of their own. Their one consolation was that they had again outfoxed the white lawmen.

Chitto Starr walked forward to meet them as they splashed through the stream. He was a man of medium height, in his early fifties, with prominent cheekbones and coarse black hair that hung to his shoulders. Frank, who was seven years younger, wore his hair cropped shorter and was built along leaner lines. But the resemblance was striking, their features remarkably similar, their eyes dark and piercing. No one would have doubted they were brothers as Frank stepped off his horse.

"You look older," Chitto said, clasping his hand in a firm grip. "I heard the raid went bad."

Frank nodded somberly. "The *aniyonega* were wait-

ing when we came out of the bank. They killed two of
my men.''

''But you killed four of theirs. I am told the white
newspapers are calling it a massacre.''

''Let them call it what they will. I care nothing for
what they say.''

The camp was situated along the north bank of the
stream. Crude log cabins had been erected to house
Chitto's followers, the Keetoowahs, Cherokee full-
bloods. There, with their wives and children, fourteen
men adhered to the old tribal ways. They watched now,
standing outside their cabins, certain that Frank would
not be turned away. No kinsman, even an outlaw, would
be denied shelter and refuge.

A widower, Chitto lived alone in the smallest of the
cabins. His son, Will Starr, stood watching beside a
wagon and team, apart from the others. Though he hon-
ored his father, Will refused to join the Nighthawks, the
name given to those who formed the resistance movement. He worked at a hardware store in Tahlequah, and
earlier he had made a delivery to the old tribal seminary
in Park Hill. He'd come to visit his father when his
uncle rode into camp.

Will walked forward to join the older men. He was
struck by the irony of being an outsider in his own family. With his mother dead, and his uncle never married,
the two men were his only kin. But he believed his
father was fighting a war that was already lost, won long
ago by the white men. He shared the Nighthawks' reverence of the land, worrying constantly about his father,
yet could not bring himself to enlist in a hopeless cause.
As for his uncle, he considered it a matter of living on
borrowed time. He thought Frank Starr was destined for
the gallows.

"Uncle Frank," he said, stopping beside his father. "I'm glad you made it back all right."

"Who says he did?" Chitto interjected. "I was just telling your uncle that he needs a new line of work. He's not much of an outlaw."

The remark was all part of a running disagreement between the brothers. Chitto neither approved nor condoned his kinsman's lawless way of life. He was quick to make his displeasure known.

Frank looked amused. "You are one to talk. Where is your respect for the law?"

Will, who was twenty-seven, had been taught deference toward his elders. But he could not let the remark pass. "There is a difference," he said tersely. "My father works to restore honor to the Cherokees. You rob banks."

Frank laughed. "Your father terrorizes our people and makes them submit to his will. Does that make him more honorable than me?"

"Enough!" Chitto said sharply. "I will not have you argue over me like hens in a barnyard. We will speak no more of this."

There was a prolonged moment of silence. Chitto was a commanding figure, exerting his will on others through sheer strength of character. He possessed those traits of leadership that caused men to listen and obey, just as the Nighthawks followed him without question. His brother and his son were no different.

Still, though it was difficult for him to admit, his brother's remarks bore an element of truth. On his orders, the Nighthawks routinely enforced what he proclaimed a return to tribal law. Throughout the old Cherokee Nation, warnings were posted ordering the people not to accept land allotments, or to lease land to white men. Those who ignored the warning were ha-

rassed and threatened by the Nighthawks, and the more
flagrant violators were subjected to the ancient tribal
punishment: tied to a tree and lashed with a whip. A
great many Cherokees, growing daily in number, were
persuaded to return their land certificates to the government.

The use of force and intimidation came only after
years of failed diplomacy. In 1893, the government and
white power brokers began a movement to join Indian
Territory and Oklahoma Territory into one state. Leaders of the Five Civilized Tribes, grown cynical with the
white man's guise of friendship, lodged fiery protests.
They feared the Oklahomans would monopolize government and politics, and, with some justification, they
suspected a conspiracy to steal their lands. The machi-
nations that followed soon proved their suspicions correct.

Oklahoma Territory and the politicians in Washington were in accord on the critical issue. Joint statehood
would be impossible until all Indian lands had been allotted in severalty and the tribal governments abolished.
Congress authorized the President to act, and shortly
afterward a commission was appointed, with instructions to negotiate with the Five Civilized Tribes and
bring an end to tribal title of their lands. The enticement
offered by the Commission was full citizenship within
the republic.

Not surprisingly, the tribes were reluctant to
exchange independence for the questionable privilege of
citizenship. Based on experience, considering a century
of broken treaties, they had every reason to doubt the
faith of the government. The language of their treaty,
made in 1832, deeded them the land for as long as grass
should grow and water should run. But the Commission
countered that the number of whites living within the

Nations exceeded Indians by a ratio of three to one. The inequities suffered by whites under the red man's rule could be corrected only by the abolition of tribal government.

Congress directed the Commission to make up rolls of every man, woman, and child in Indian Territory. Ostensibly a preparatory step to the allotment of lands in severalty, everyone recognized it as the first step in the dissolution of the Five Civilized Tribes. Solidarity ceased to exist when the Chickasaw, Choctaw, and Seminole Nations agreed to dismantle tribal government in 1906. The Creek and the Cherokee still held out, but twenty million acres were at stake in the Nations, and the campaign for statehood was gathering momentum. There was no longer any question that Oklahoma Territory and Indian Territory would enter the Union as a single state.

In the end, all of the diplomacy, the delegations to Washington, and the written resolutions presented to the Great White Father were an exercise in futility. The Cherokee and the Creek leaders, faced with the might and determination of the federal government, finally succumbed to the inevitable. Tribal members were allotted 160 acres apiece, with millions of acres opened to exploitation by whites, and Congress promptly passed the Enabling Act. Oklahoma, encompassing all the previous lands of Indian Territory, was granted statehood in 1907.

The Cherokee who accepted allotment slowly adapted to the new order. But Chitto and his followers, the Keetoowahs, withdrew from what seemed to them an alien society controlled by whites. They mourned the loss of their native lands, the mountains and rivers and thick forests, and they refused to accept allotment. Shortly after statehood, they formed the Nighthawks, and though their numbers were small, they organized a campaign of fear and intimidation directed at the people, as well as the leaders of the old Cherokee Nation. United by a sense of betrayal, they vowed to fight until tribal sovereignty was once more restored.

Today, standing between his brother and his son, Chitto wondered how it would end. His son, though loyal and sympathetic to the Nighthawks' cause, had elected to follow the white man's road. His brother rebelled by robbing banks and killing whites, and adopting a devil-may-care attitude toward tomorrow. Yet he could never deny either of them.

"You are welcome here," he said to Frank. "You and your men can stay in my cabin."

"Only for tonight," Frank replied. "We'll move on come morning. Trouble could still be dogging my trail."

"You think they will send more lawmen after you?"

"I have no doubt of that, brother. They want my head in a noose."

"That's the problem with killing whites," Chitto said, as though thinking out loud. "Maybe you should go to Doublehead Mountain. You would be safe there."

Frank shrugged. "I need a payday to keep my men in line. We'll probably start scouting another bank."

"You will rob one bank too many someday. I wish you—"

A rider on a spotted pinto pounded into the camp. Chitto looked around and saw Joseph Lynch, his lieutenant and second-in-command, jump down off the horse. Lynch's eyes darted from him to Frank, and back again. His bark-dark features were taut.

"I was up at Park Hill and saw the sheriff and four deputies headed this way. Didn't know why he was comin' here, but figured I'd warn you. Now that I see Frank—''

''Get mounted!'' Frank shouted to his men. He turned to Chitto. ''Sorry I brought the law to your doorstep. I'll see you around, brother.''

''Just ride and don't look back,'' Chitto replied. ''I'll keep Prather talking as long as possible.''

Frank stepped into the saddle. He gigged his horse and led the gang downstream at a hard lope. They disappeared into a stand of trees a short distance from camp. Chitto glanced around at his son.

''You go, too,'' he said. ''No need for the sheriff to find you here.''

''What's the difference?'' Will said stubbornly. ''I don't care what—''

''Leave!'' Chitto ordered. ''*Now*!''

Will walked away with a chastised look. He climbed aboard the wagon, popped the reins, and drove off along a rutted trail to the west. Chitto watched a moment, then motioned to Lynch. His voice was firm.

''Have someone bring my rifle. Get the men armed and position them outside the cabins. I want the women and children inside.''

''Do you expect trouble?''

''The sheriff thinks he will find Frank here. I will not allow him to search the cabins.''

Lynch grunted. ''Then there will be trouble.''

''Just do as I say, Joseph. Hurry.''

Some ten minutes later Sheriff Ed Prather and four deputies rode into camp. He found Chitto and Lynch, rifles cradled across their arms, standing in the clearing. The other Nighthawks were ranged along the front of the cabins, their rifles at the ready. He reined to a halt, and the deputies fanned out on line, two on either side of his horse. His gaze fixed on Chitto.

"Let's not get jumpy," he said. "I'm here on official business."

"What business is that, Sheriff?"

Prather was a large man, with a bold front and a ham-fisted manner of dispensing justice. He didn't like Indians in general, and he was especially affronted by those who greeted him with rifles. His mouth razored in a hard line.

"I have a warrant for your arrest, Mr. Starr. I'll thank you to lay down that rifle and come along peaceable."

Chitto was expecting questions about his brother, not himself. Yet his look betrayed nothing. "Why do you come here for me?"

"Two charges," Prather told him. "One, you threatened bodily harm to chief W. C. Rogers, headman of the Cherokees. And second—"

"I have not harmed Rogers. Come for me when I do."

"And second, you're charged with inciting to riot. You've badgered Indians to go on the warpath about these land allotments."

"That is not true."

"True or not doesn't matter," Prather said bluntly. "I've got a warrant and I intend to arrest you. We'll let a jury decide whether you're guilty."

"A white jury?" Chitto said without inflection. "I think I'm liable to be guilty."

"That's neither here nor there. Do like I told you and lay down that rifle."

"I will not go with you."

"Don't be a damn fool, Starr. You're under arrest and that's that."

Chitto stared at him. "I will not go."

A turgid silence fell over the camp. Prather snapped, goaded on by temper and arrogance. No Indian could be allowed to resist arrest, not in his county. He motioned his deputies forward.

"Somebody put the manacles on this red nigger. Hop to it!"

A deputy swung down out of the saddle. As he started forward, manacles in hand, Prather reached for his pistol. Joseph Lynch pivoted, raising the muzzle of his rifle, and fired a quick snap shot. The slug clipped Prather's coatsleeve and struck a mounted deputy off to one side. From near the cabins a rifle boomed, and the deputy with the manacles dropped dead on the ground. Another deputy got off one shot before the gunfire became general.

Prather abruptly lost his nerve. He wheeled his horse around, ducking low, as the Nighthawks loosed a ragged volley. The air was alive with the angry snarl of bullets, and still another deputy slumped forward in the saddle, clutching his side. A Nighthawk outside one of the cabins staggered, his shirt bright with blood, and fell spread-eagled on his back. Chitto fired at Prather, who was leading the retreat, but missed. The lawmen whipped their horses north out of camp.

The blast of gunfire trailed off into stilled quiet. Chitto watched after the lawmen a moment, his features stolid. Then he glanced at the fallen deputy and turned to stare as a woman threw herself on the mortally wounded Nighthawk. He shook his head.

"No good will come of today. We have taken a new road."

Lynch nodded. "The *aniyonega* will return. Should I get the men ready to ride?"

Chitto gazed into the distance. "I will not run just yet."

"What would you do?"

"Instruct them in our ways, old friend. Let us prepare."

Four

Owen McLain approached Tahlequah late the next afternoon. He rode a blaze-faced roan gelding, with his bedroll tied behind the cantle. Four days on the trail had restored a sense of vitality he felt only when working in the field. From his early days as a peace officer, the effect had always been the same. A manhunt honed his instincts to a finer edge.

The countryside of northeast Oklahoma was at once familiar and foreign. There were more white people than ever before, and there were more automobiles on the road. Yet he experienced the sensation of moving backward in time whenever he rode into the old Cherokee Nation. Oddly, though much of the land was now owned by whites, there was something immutable about the rolling hills and the shelterbelt of timbered forests. He still thought of it as Cherokee country.

Over the years McLain had come to admire the Cherokees. Tillers of the soil, they were a people who cultivated the land with something approaching reverence. Theirs was a thriving agrarian society that rivaled even the most prosperous Midwestern farm community. Long ago, before the Civil War, many Cherokees had operated plantations, slave owners as large as any in the South. But in the decades afterward, like their white counterparts, they had become a nation of farmers. They drew sustenance from the land.

For all that, the Cherokees were unlike white men in other ways. Before statehood, theirs was a sovereign nation, governed by their own laws. By treaty, their authority extended only to Cherokee citizens, and white men were exempt from all prosecution except that of a federal court. Yet there were no extradition laws, and federal marshals had to capture wanted men and return them to white jurisdiction. The problem was compounded by the fact that the Indians had little use for white man's law; the marshals were looked upon as intruders in Cherokee country. The tribal Light Horse Police refused assistance, and in time, the country became infested with fugitives. All too often the red men connived with the outlaws, offering them asylum.

Following statehood, McLain discovered that the problem had expanded to include red lawbreakers. The sanctuary formerly offered the white desperadoes was suddenly available to a Cherokee on the run; all the more so since he was now fleeing white lawmen. There were exceptions, but few Cherokees would assist a federal marshal in the apprehension of a fellow Cherokee. To some degree, McLain faulted the Cherokees themselves for his failure to capture Oklahoma's most notorious bank robber. But in larger degree, he gave credit where credit was due. Frank Starr was a master at eluding pursuit.

Upon entering Tahlequah, McLain was reminded again that the Cherokees, by any standard, were a remarkable people. The old capitol building, where a tribal council similar in structure to Congress had governed a nation, still dominated the town square. Across the way was the *Cherokee Advocate*, a newspaper printed in English and Cherokee, the two languages side by side. Of all the tribes, the Cherokees were the only ones with an alphabet, invented by Sequoyah nearly a century before. Their language could therefore be written, books and newspapers printed, all read by a literate people. No other tribe was able to preserve its culture in the ancient tongue.

Whenever he came here, McLain imagined how it once had been. In the days before statehood, Tahlequah was recognized as a symbol of progress throughout Indian Territory. Cherokee diplomats in swallowtail coats governed with no less dignity than their counterparts in Washington. White men were not allowed to own property except through intermarriage, and unlike western Plains Tribes, the Cherokees accepted no annuities or financial assistance from the government. A tribal chief acted as head of state, and the Cherokees were independent and free, virtually immune to white influence. All of that had changed with statehood, and McLain understood why so many of them were resentful of the white man's newfound dominance. He would have felt the same way.

On the far side of the square, the old supreme court building had been converted into offices for Cherokee County. The district court was on the second floor, with the tax assessor, the sheriff, and other county officials quartered on the ground floor. McLain reined to a halt on the street, and looped the reins of his gelding over the hitch rack. As he started up the walkway, he was struck again by the imposing brick structure, once the showpiece of the Cherokee Nation. He thought it ironic that most of the county officials were white, elected by a white majority at the polls. Few Cherokees, he told himself, would appreciate the irony.

A deputy ushered him into Ed Prather's office. His professional relationship with the sheriff was adversarial at best, and at worst, often antagonistic. Prather impressed him as an opportunist rather than a lawman, one who had sought and won public office as a base of power. On a personal note, he simply didn't like Prather, who was abrasive and disagreeably arrogant. The sheriff impressed him as a bully with a badge.

"Well, it's about time," Prather said, as he walked through the door. "Where the hell you been?"

McLain leaned against the doorjamb. He pulled out the makings and began rolling himself a smoke. "Last time I checked," he said in a flat voice, "I don't account to you for my whereabouts. What's your problem?"

"Don't you read the goddamned newspaper?"

"I've been on the road for four days. Why do you ask?"

"Oh, nothin' much," Prather said caustically. "Just that Chitto Starr shot the shit out of my boys. Killed Johnny Watkins, one of my best deputies, and wounded two more. How do you like them apples?"

McLain lit his cigarette. "Were you after Frank Starr?"

"No, I wasn't after Frank. He didn't rob any banks in my county."

"So what put you crosswise of Chitto?"

"What else?" Prather growled. "The sorry sonovabitch resisted arrest. Went to put the manacles on him and his pack of red niggers opened fire. Cold-blooded murder, that's what it was!"

"Sounds that way." McLain exhaled a plume of smoke. "How many of them did you get?"

''Who the hell knows? We was outgunned and caught with our asses in a shooting gallery. Lucky anybody got out alive.''

''Where was this?''

''Chitto's camp,'' Prather said. ''South of Park Hill.''

''And Frank wasn't there?''

''You don't listen too good. I know you're here lookin' for Frank. Gilmore wired me all about it a few days back. Don't you think I would've told you?''

''Had to ask,'' McLain said. ''Frank's at the top of my list.''

Prather cocked one eyebrow. ''Not anymore.''

''What's that mean?''

''That means you've got a new assignment. Gilmore took you off Frank and put you on Chitto.''

''You talked to Gilmore?''

''Late last night, on the telephone. Told me to tell you you've got new orders.''

''I'll have to hear that from Gilmore myself.''

Prather bridled. ''My word's not good enough?''

''Not a matter of your word.'' McLain stubbed out his cigarette in an ashtray. ''I like to hear things first-hand.''

''You got a way of rubbin' a man the wrong way. Anybody ever tell you that?''

''Nobody that ever mattered.''

''Here!'' Prather shoved the telephone across the desk. ''You don't believe me, call him yourself. He'll set you straight.''

McLain took a wooden armchair before the desk. He lifted the receiver, jiggled the hook, and a woman's voice came on the line. ''Operator, I want 2616 in Guthrie.'' He listened a moment, then nodded. ''Yes ma'am, thank you. I'll hold.''

There was a tinny buzz, then another, and a click on

the other end. "U.S. Marshal's office. Deputy Johnson speakin'."

"Wayne, this is Owen."

"Where you at?"

"Tahlequah."

"We figured you'd get there today. You wanna talk with the boss?"

"Yeah, I do."

"Hold on."

A moment later Gilmore came on the line. "Owen, I'm glad you called. Are you alone?"

"No," McLain said. "Not just exactly."

"Are you with Prather?"

"That's about the size of it."

"Then you listen and I'll talk. And try to keep a poker face, Owen. Don't let on what I'm telling you."

"I'm all ears."

"Prather called me last night," Gilmore said. "He tried to serve a warrant on Chitto Starr. Has he told you the charges?"

"Not yet."

"Inciting to riot. Claims Starr is agitating for a Cherokee uprising. You heard anything about that?"

McLain shook his head. "Not till just now."

"Neither have I. The second charge is threatening bodily harm against W. C. Rogers, the former Cherokee chief. Do you know him?"

"Only by name."

Gilmore sighed heavily. "The warrant was signed by Judge Ebersole, the district court judge. I've asked around, and I hear he's hell-on-wheels where Indians are concerned. Anything to it?"

"Yeah." McLain traded a sphinxlike look with the sheriff, who was watching him intently. "I'd say you hit the nail on the head."

"On the telephone, Prather sounds like some sort of demagogue. I got the distinct feeling he's trying to use the situation to make himself look good with white voters. You've dealt with him before. Do you think I'm right?"

"I'd lay money on it, and give you good odds."

"What about the charges? Is it possible Prather trumped up the whole thing and got Ebersole to sign the warrant? Are they that underhanded?"

McLain let go a sour laugh. "Do pigs eat slop?"

There was dead silence on the other end of the line. At length, Gilmore cleared his throat. "I'm caught in a touchy political situation here, Owen. Prather insists that the federal government is responsible for renegade Indians. He demands that we take over the case."

"You think that's the way to go?"

"I think Washington would agree. Whether the charges are false or not probably has no bearing at this point. Chitto Starr *appears* to be leading a rebellion. And appearances, right or wrong, are usually the reality in Washington."

The discussion was no longer about justice. Gilmore was a political appointee, and he couldn't *appear* to side with Indians over white lawmen. As he'd just admitted, perception rather than reality was the critical factor in Washington. McLain saw where it was headed.

"I'm still listening," he said. "How do you want it handled?"

"I want you to bring in Chitto Starr. Whatever the mitigating circumstances, he's now killed a peace officer. We have no choice but to take charge."

"What about Frank Starr?"

"A bank robber and an insurrectionist are horses of a different color. Keep in mind what I said about the appearance of things. Leave Frank Starr for another time."

"You're the boss," McLain said without conviction. "I'll take care of it."

"I'm sorry, Owen, but I hope you understand I've been put in a dubious position. Call me when you have Starr in custody."

"Anything else?"

"No, that's all."

"I'll be in touch."

McLain broke the connection. He looked across the desk at Prather. "Inciting to riot?" he scoffed. "Threatening bodily harm? How'd you get the judge to sign the warrant?"

Prather flushed, his color rising. "Them goddamn Nighthawks are a menace to the public. I won't have it in my county."

"Save it for election time. All the righteous indignation probably plays well with white voters."

"You're startin' to sound like an Indian lover, McLain. You gonna do your job or not?"

McLain fixed him with a hard stare. "Don't worry yourself about me. How do you know Chitto's still out there?"

"Couple of his women showed up just before dark yesterday. They brought me Johnny Watkins's body in a wagon."

"That doesn't mean Chitto's still there."

"Yeah, he's out there, all right. I questioned them women real good. They said he's not going nowhere."

"Why wouldn't he run? He must know he's wanted for murder."

"'Cause he's crazy as a loon! Hasn't got sense enough to run."

McLain studied on it a moment. "How many men does he have?"

"I never stopped to count," Prather said defensively. "Looked to be somewheres around a dozen, maybe more."

"Tell you what I want. You arrange to have twenty volunteers here three hours before sunrise. I'll deputize them then."

"Where the hell am I gonna get twenty men? This here's federal business now."

"You want me to clean up your mess, then you provide the men. Otherwise you can do your own dirty work."

"Awright, goddammit," Prather said in a surly tone. "You'll have your men. You satisfied?"

"I'll see you in the morning."

McLain walked out of the office. On the street he mounted his horse and rode to a livery stable a block west of the square. He arranged to stall the blaze-faced gelding, and paid extra for a ration of grain. The livery owner asked if he was staying just the one night, and he laughed despite himself. He told the man he would be gone long before the cock crowed.

Outside again, McLain walked toward a hotel on the south side of the square. He was carrying his Winchester carbine, with his saddlebags slung over his shoulder, and he looked like a man with a great deal on his mind. He was trying to figure out if he was madder at Ed Prather or Fred Gilmore. All in all, it seemed to be a toss-up.

Gilmore, he told himself, was a man who practiced expediency in the name of political survival. Prather, on the other hand, was a backwoods highbinder looking to grab the brass ring. To them, the end justified the means, and pragmatism was all part of the game. One was not better or worse than the other.

McLain saw the outcome all too clearly. Chitto Starr would be railroaded on trumped-up charges in the name of law and order. The alternative was that he would be killed fighting to restore a way of life that was lost to time. He was, in a sense, the last warrior.

A warrior who had outlived the old days, and the Cherokee Nation.

Five

Dawn broke with a smudge of light on the horizon. There was frost in the air and the horses snorted puffs of steamy smoke. The riders were strung out in single file, bundled in greatcoats and mackinaws against the cold, their mounts held to a measured walk. The sound of hooves on grass wet with dew carried faintly in the still air.

McLain rode in the lead. Directly behind him were Prather and two regular deputies, followed by a posse of eighteen men. Last night, in a series of rabble-rousing speeches around town, Prather had organized the band of volunteers. His appeal centered on the savage nature of the Cherokee renegades, the Nighthawks, and the danger they posed to white people throughout the county. The men who volunteered thought Indians should be kept in their place, and counted it an honor to ride against the upstart named Chitto Starr. All of them agreed to be deputized.

In the dusky overcast, they skirted west of Park Hill. The buildings stood like forlorn sentries, one more reminder of the faded glory of the Cherokee Nation. There, for decades before statehood, the seminaries educated Cherokee children in both their mother tongue and in English. The most promising students were later sent to universities in the East, where they were groomed for positions of responsibility and leadership. But in the end their training in business and law was no match for the floodtide of whites who coveted their land. The Cherokee Nation was no more.

McLain often thought the seminaries were a monument to what might have been. But today, he scarcely gave them a glance, his mind focused on the job ahead. From Prather, he had obtained a roughly sketched map of the terrain surrounding Chitto's camp, and of the camp itself. His plan was to approach from the west, through the heavy stand of trees bordering Park Hill Creek. He angled southwest from the seminaries and brought the men to a halt along the creekbank. He judged they were perhaps a half mile from the Nighthawks' camp.

From past manhunts, McLain knew that dawn was the best time for a raid. There was adequate light for shooting if a fight developed, and the early hour afforded the tactical element of surprise. Often as not, the wanted men were caught in their beds, taken unawares and without a fight. In the worst case, when they were somehow alerted, they were still groggy with sleep and unable to mount stiff resistance. Surprise gave a lawman the edge, and properly done, an insurmountable advantage. Sometimes it was the difference between life and death.

McLain had briefed the posse before leaving Tahlequah. He was thorough, detailing the plan on the map, explaining it step by step and how it would work to their advantage. He intended to overrun the camp, with five men assigned to storm each of the four log cabins, and take the Nighthawks while they were still asleep. His one concern was the women and children in the camp, and he issued a stern warning to the men. Anyone who harmed a woman or a child would answer to him.

The horses were left hitched to tree limbs. McLain and Prather took the lead, with the men trailing behind in single file. They ghosted through the silty light, the sound of their footsteps muffled by the rapid waters of the creek. Experience had taught McLain that the slow, silent approach was far less likely to alert the quarry, and spoil the surprise. He was particularly wary of dogs, concerned that an outbreak of barking would sound the alarm and alert the camp. A short distance from the clearing, he signaled a halt and motioned the men to the ground. Prather tagged along as he wormed his way to the edge of the treeline.

The cabins were situated some thirty yards across the clearing. There was no sign of movement, the camp wrapped in dawn stillness, no smoke drifting from the chimneys. McLain took that as a good sign, for the first chore on chilly mornings was to throw logs into the fireplace. Off to one side of the cabins, near the creek, horses stood bunched and hip-shot in a corral. To all appearances, the camp still slumbered in the quiet between dawn and sunrise. Yet there was something . . .

McLain stared out across the clearing. A visceral instinct, deep down in his gut, told him that all was not as it appeared. He slowly scanned the cabins, his gaze lingering here and there, looking for some telltale shadow behind windows, any sign of movement. He saw nothing, and though he listened intently, silence hung over the camp. Yet he couldn't shake the feeling that someone was out there, that he was being watched. He sensed something unseen in the murky dawn.

"What's wrong?" Prather whispered. "What're you lookin' at?"

"I don't know," McLain said. "I'll tell you when I find it."

"Looks quiet enough to me."

"Maybe too quiet."

"Well, hell, what'd you expect? The bastards are still asleep."

"Are they?"

"I don't see nobody. What's got you spooked?"

"Give it a good once-over. Anything different from the last time you were here?"

Prather slowly inspected the camp. His eyes moved from cabin to cabin, and then paused on the corral. He studied the horses for a time, finally shook his head. "Hard to tell," he said in a musing tone. "Everything happened so fast."

"You lost me," McLain said. "Hard to tell what?"

"Seems like there was more horses. But I wouldn't swear to it one way or another. I was mainly watchin' Chitto."

"How many more horses?"

"Just told you I don't recollect. I had my mind on other things."

McLain turned his gaze to the corral. He did a rough head count and came up with eighteen horses. That was more than enough mounts for twelve or fourteen men, particularly white men. But Indians prized horses above all else, and it was not unusual for a man to own a string of two or more. He wondered if there were horses missing from the corral. And if there were, where were they?

"This could be a washout," he said, almost to himself. "You remember tellin' me Chitto was crazy as a loon? Maybe he's crazy like a fox."

"What d'you mean?"

"Maybe he's already flown the coop."

"Huh?"

"Those women that brought your deputy's body into town? Suppose Chitto had them feed you a line of guff. Fooled you into believing he wouldn't take off. That would've bought him a long head start."

Prather winced. "You think he's run?"

"There's only one way to find out. Let's have a look in those cabins."

McLain climbed to his feet. But even as he stood up, the sensation of being watched flooded over him again. He hesitated, scanning the cabins, and saw nothing out of order. After a moment, he raised his arm and motioned forward. The men drifted out of the trees as the sky went from dusky gray to pale rose. He waited, Prather at his side, until the men spread out on a line. Then he signaled toward the cabins.

Like wraiths emerging into light, the men stepped clear of the treeline. McLain carried a Winchester Model 94, a stout carbine chambered for .30-.30, with the added punch provided by smokeless powder. Still, however modern his long gun, he continued to pack the old Colt .45 Peacemaker, with a 4¾-inch barrel. For close work, despite all the new technology, the pistol still had no equal as a manstopper. He hooked his thumb over the hammer of the carbine as the men moved into the clearing.

A scruffy dog, awakened with a start when the men appeared, leaped to its feet beside the nearest cabin. The mongrel advanced a few steps, hackles raised, and loosed a furious, snarling bark. Prather, who was armed with a Winchester pump shotgun, brought the weapon to his shoulder, sighted on the dog, and fired. The roar of the scattergun reverberated across the clearing, and the dog went down under a hail of buckshot. In the next instant, a pack of howling dogs sounded the warning from cabins around the camp. Prather racked another shell into the chamber.

"You goddamn fool!" McLain cursed. "Save it for something besides dogs!"

The element of surprise gone, McLain hurriedly motioned the men toward the camp. They spread out in squads, five men to a bunch, and rushed forward to raid their assigned cabins. Halfway across the clearing, a rifle cracked and Prather's hat went flying. For a moment McLain thought the shot had come from the cabins, to their front. But then, even as he cocked the hammer on his carbine, he realized the sound had come from the south, on their right flank. Disbelief was wiped away as comprehension flooded his mind.

They had walked into a trap!

The treeline on the south side of the creek erupted in a wall of gunfire. On the north side of the creek, the men rushing toward the cabins were caught in the middle of the clearing. The drumming roar from across the creek filled the quickening daylight with a hornets' nest of lead. One of the deputies flung out his arms, dropping his rifle, drilled through the chest, and pitched to the ground. Down the line, a volunteer screamed, blood pumping from a wound in his leg, and collapsed in a heap. A second volley ripped through the clearing.

McLain spun toward the creek, the carbine at his shoulder, and fired. He was vaguely aware of muzzle flashes along the opposite treeline, the buzz of slugs frying the air. Operating on reflex and nerve, he cranked the carbine's lever, hammering round after round at the dim figures hidden within the trees. Awareness registered in a corner of his mind, and he knew that he'd been lured into an ambush. Chitto and the Nighthawks, positioned to flank the posse, had waited until the men were out in the open before commencing fire. The element of surprise was turned back on the attackers.

Prather never got off a shot. He broke and ran, his features etched with panic, bullets dusting his heels. Here and there volunteers kept their wits and returned fire in a sporadic tattoo of gunshots. But as Prather sprinted for cover, another volunteer abruptly quit the fight, clutching a limp arm. The panic spread, moving through the ranks, and all along the line men began retreating toward the trees upstream. On the instant it became a wholesale rout, men dodging and weaving through a barrage of slugs. They ran for their lives.

The volunteer wounded in the leg still lay on the ground. Two men, summoning courage amidst another withering volley, grabbed him under the arms and dragged him toward safety. McLain covered their cumbersome retreat, firing the last round from his Winchester. He switched the carbine to his offhand, pulling the holstered Colt, and thumbed three quick shots at the Nighthawks. The chance that he'd hit anyone was remote, but he was buying time until the volunteers were out of danger. As he scrambled backward into the treeline, he emptied the Colt and rammed it in his holster. He began stuffing shells into the Winchester.

All around him men were taking cover in the timber. McLain fully expected the Nighthawks to come surging across the stream, turning a rout into a bloody pursuit. There was a fiendish brilliance behind the simplicity of the ambush, and he thought Chitto would press the advantage with a full-scale assault. But instead the gunfire abruptly ceased, and a deafening silence fell over the battleground. A wounded man moaned somewhere to his rear, and he heard someone thrash deeper into the brush. He kept his attention trained on the distant treeline.

The sun crested the horizon in a great flare of gold. Off to the east, beneath the trees across the creek, McLain saw riders moving downstream. The last thing he'd expected was for the Nighthawks to quit the field when they had so clearly won the engagement. In the glare of sunlight, he counted twelve, then fourteen riders, leading three packhorses and three spare mounts. Out of the corner of his eye he caught movement, and beyond the clearing, where the deputy sheriff lay dead, he saw women peering from the doorways of cabins, watching the riders. His gaze swung back to the mounted men, and he suddenly understood. The Nighthawks were conducting a planned withdrawal.

Some distance downstream Chitto Starr separated from the other riders. He rode to the edge of the creek, reining his horse to face the routed posse, and held his rifle overhead. His features were twisted in stark defiance.

"Do not follow me!" he shouted. "I will kill more of you!"

For a moment, McLain was too stunned to react. But then, certain beyond doubt that he was looking at Chitto Starr, he threw the carbine to his shoulder. He fired too quickly for the distance, missing the man and hitting the horse. Chitto swung out of the saddle, lithely stepping onto firm ground, as the horse fell dead at the water's edge. His voice carried through the morning with savage jubilance.

"You *cannot* kill me, white man!"

One of the Nighthawks galloped forward on a chocolate-spotted pinto. He was lean, with bark-dark skin, and he held out an arm as he neared the fallen horse. Chitto grabbed his arm, timing it with the grace of an acrobat, and bounded aboard behind him. The man whirled the pinto downstream and rode off, rejoining the Nighthawks. They disappeared into a copse of trees.

McLain stared after them for a long while. All too clearly he saw that Chitto Starr was no ordinary man. The Nighthawk leader had known the camp would be raided, and with considerable purpose, the ambush had been laid to drive home a message. There was no doubt that the message was at once a challenge and a warning. The words of a man who would stand and fight.

Do not follow me.

Six

All around the square people turned out to watch as the column pulled into Tahlequah. Under a bright forenoon sun, McLain and Prather led the mounted volunteers, followed by a wagon commandeered at the Nighthawks' camp. The volunteers were slumped in the saddle, their features downcast, unable to meet the gaze of those who crowded the square. They looked defeated.

The dead deputy, covered with a tattered blanket, was stretched out in the back of the wagon. Beside him, on a hastily rigged bed of pallets, were the two wounded volunteers. The wounded men, pale from the loss of blood, were carried into the office of Dr. Chester Rinehart. The wagon then continued on to the funeral parlor, where the deputy's body was unloaded by the undertaker. The townspeople watched in a dull state of shock.

Prather arranged for messengers to notify the families of the dead and wounded. Afterward, the volunteers were dismissed, and McLain followed the sheriff into the courthouse. Their mood was somber, and neither of them spoke as they entered the office. Earlier, at

Chitto's camp, McLain had questioned the women, only to be met by stony silence. He still had no idea as to where the Nighthawks were headed, though he was determined to resume the manhunt without delay. Prather seemed to have lost all interest in further pursuit.

McLain placed a telephone call to Guthrie. He was obliged to report, even though he was reluctant to admit having walked into a trap. A moment later Fred Gilmore came on the line. "Owen," he said, clearly anxious for good news. "Have you got Starr in custody?"

"Wish I did," McLain replied evenly. "He got away."

"Got away? You mean he was already gone?"

"No, he was still there. We got caught in an ambush."

"*Ambush*?" Gilmore echoed stridently. "Are you serious?"

"Dead serious," McLain said. "I underestimated Chitto, and no excuses for it. I take full responsibility."

McLain tersely related the details. He commented that Chitto Starr was a clever tactician, and a skilled fighter. "Just suckered me into it," he concluded. "Killed one deputy and wounded two others."

"Good God," Gilmore said with a heavy sigh. "How am I going to explain that to Washington?"

"Lay it off on me. Truth is, I got myself outgeneraled. Things went to hell in a hurry."

"But I understood he has only a small band of followers. Didn't you have him outnumbered?"

"Sometimes numbers don't tell the tale. Our side broke and ran."

Gilmore hesitated a moment. "Your voice sounds strange. Are you with Prather?"

"In the flesh."

"Are you trying to tell me Prather quit on you—caused the others to run?"

McLain glanced at the sheriff, who was staring out the window. "I think that'd be a fair statement."

"You're saying Ed Prather turned yellow?"

"No two ways about it."

"Christ," Gilmore groaned. "So what do we do now? Any brilliant ideas?"

"Not offhand," McLain said. "For openers, I'd like to get a line on Chitto. I don't want any more surprises."

"You're going after him, then? You still think there's a chance?"

"Never thought otherwise. Wherever he comes to roost, I'll find him."

"Don't let me down," Gilmore said in a worried tone. "Washington's looking over my shoulder, and I've already had a call from the governor. I need results this time."

"I'll do my damnedest and then some. You can count on it."

"Call me the instant you have any news."

The line went dead. McLain placed the receiver on the hook, trading a cool glance with the sheriff. He walked to a large map of Cherokee County, which was mounted on the wall. His eye traced a line east of Park Hill, the direction the Nighthawks had fled. He thumped the map with his finger.

"What's out here?"

"Nothing," Prather said shortly. "Lots of mountains and damn little else."

"Any idea why Chitto headed that way?"

"A man on the run couldn't find a better place to get lost. You're lookin' at hundreds of square miles of wilderness."

McLain studied the map. "Question is, where would he hide out? Anybody know him well enough to answer that?"

Prather shrugged. "Try his son, Will Starr. Works over at Grahm's Hardware, south side of the square. Not that he'll tell you anything."

"Why doesn't he ride with his father?"

"Will's one of our tame Injuns. He don't see eye-to-eye with his pa on this land allotment business. Leastways, where it comes to rough stuff with other Cherokees."

"Are they still thick? Would he know where Chitto's headed?"

"I'd say it's more likely than not."

"I'll start there," McLain said. "Anybody else come to mind?"

"Well—" Prather considered a moment. "There's Tom Tenkiller's wife. He was one of Frank Starr's gang. Got himself killed at that bank holdup—what's today, Saturday? Guess that would've been Monday."

"What's her name?"

"Jane Tenkiller," Prather said. "Lives three houses past the livery stable. Not that she'll tell you anything, either."

"How do you know?" McLain said. "Did you ever ask?"

"No, McLain, I never asked. That satisfy you?"

"What'll satisfy me is ten men, mounted and ready to ride tomorrow morning. I plan to go after Chitto."

"You're nuts!" Prather snorted. "Where am I gonna find ten men after what happened this morning?"

"Try putting a reward on Chitto. Thousand dollars ought to do it."

"Why would I do a thing like that?"

"Couple of reasons," McLain informed him. "You

started this mess with Chitto, and so far, it's got two of your deputies killed. That ought to justify a reward.''

"I'm still listenin'. What's the other reason?''

"That's even simpler. Get me the men or I'll tell everybody they've got a sheriff with a yellow streak a yard wide. Took off running at the first shot.''

"You're a goddamned—''

"Watch your mouth or I'll have to box your ears.''

Prather glowered at him. "You'll get your reward and be damned! But don't expect me to ride with you.''

"I wouldn't have it any other way, Sheriff.''

McLain walked out the door.

"Will Starr?''

"I've been expecting you, Marshal.''

Starr stood behind the counter of the hardware store. He glanced at Oscar Grahm, the owner, who was talking with a farmer about fence wire. Then his gaze shifted back to McLain. He had expected someone older.

"You're here about my father,'' he said without expression. "Everybody's heard what happened out at Park Hill.''

"Bad news travels,'' McLain observed. "Guess you know your father took off?''

"I heard that, too.''

"Any idea where he went?''

Starr folded his arms. "Even if I knew, why would I tell you? You're the law.''

"From what I'm told,'' McLain said, "you're a law-abiding man yourself. Otherwise you'd be with your father and the Nighthawks right now.''

"I do not agree with their methods. That's no secret.''

"Then help put a stop to it.''

Starr's eyes narrowed. "Would you betray your father?"

"Depends on the circumstances," McLain said, avoiding a direct answer. "Your father's killed two peace officers in the last two days. Doesn't that make a difference?"

"Maybe you don't understand something, Marshal. No matter what happens, my father will never surrender."

"You'd be surprised how many men say that. Most find a way to change their minds."

"Not this time." Starr unfolded his arms, spread his hands. "You will never capture my father; you will have to kill him. Would you ask me to help?"

McLain sensed that he'd been snookered. He tried another tack. "The longer this goes on, the more men will die. Do you want that on your conscience?"

"I think you do not know much about the Cherokees."

"How so?"

"We believe that every man is free to choose his own path. No man has the right to tell him otherwise."

"Even if that path gets people killed?"

Will Starr seemed to withdraw into himself. "I'm sorry," he said, in a distant voice. "I cannot help you."

McLain saw no reason to pursue it further. He'd thought it a long shot, and he wasn't surprised by the outcome. Still, as he left the store, he wondered if all Cherokees were as firm in their resolve. Freedom of choice seemed a dicey proposition when it put other men's lives at risk.

A short walk brought him to the home of Jane Tenkiller. The woman who answered the door was strikingly attractive, somewhere in her early twenties. Her dusky oval features were framed by hair with the jet-black brilliance of a raven's wing. When he introduced himself, she invited him inside and seated him on a worn sofa. He explained the purpose of his visit.

"I know little of Chitto," she said in reply. "Despite all this trouble, I still think he's a good man. I wouldn't say the same of his brother."

McLain nodded. "I understand Frank was responsible for your husband's death."

"Frank is a devil!" Her dark eyes flashed. "Tom would never listen to me, and now . . . he's gone. I wish somebody would kill Frank."

"Lots of people feel that way," McLain said, coaxing her on. "Trouble is, he goes to ground after he pulls a bank job. He's an awful hard man to catch."

"I despise him so much. He thinks he's smarter than anybody."

"Your husband ever say anything about Frank's hideout?"

She was on the verge of replying, and stopped. For a long moment, she searched his face. "You think that might be Chitto's hideout, too . . . don't you?"

McLain offered her a lame smile. "I have to admit the idea occurred to me. 'Course, it might be a case of two birds with one stone." He paused to underscore the point. "Brothers stick together."

"Do you intend to kill Chitto?"

"I'd prefer to bring him in alive, and that's the God's honest truth. I think he got a raw deal trying to make things right for the Cherokee."

She gave him a look of open assessment. Finally, after some deliberation, she shrugged. "Tom sometimes spoke of a stronghold in the mountains. He said they were safe there."

"Anything else?" McLain asked. "Did he say where in the mountains?"

''Frank swore him to secrecy, and he only talked of
it a few times. Mostly when he got drunk.''

''You remember anything that might give me a
clue?''

''No, nothing,'' she said. ''I would tell you if I
knew—just to spite Frank!''

McLain thought he'd heard the truth. She was an intelligent woman, young and attractive, embittered by the
loss of her husband. A woman with a score to settle.

He doubted Frank Starr would be safe in her company.

Later that afternoon McLain met with Major David
Lipe. A full-blood, Lipe was the former commander of
the Cherokee Light Horse Police. He retained the hon-
orary title, even though he was now a timber broker.
He greeted McLain in his office just off the town square.

Their discussion was at first strained. For a time they
had been adversaries, working different sides of the law.
Before statehood, Lipe had refused all cooperation of
the Light Horse with federal lawmen. But he was now
a convert, a supporter of statehood and land allotments,
and the free enterprise system so lucrative for timber
brokers. He was receptive when McLain spoke of Chitto
Starr.

''Damn both the Starrs!'' he said vehemently. ''One
a common outlaw and the other a turncoat who terrorizes his own people. How can I assist you?''

McLain considered the statement telling. Lipe was a
close associate of Chief W. C. Rogers, and he thought
they were probably behind the ''incite to riot'' charges
brought against Chitto. They were prospering under
statehood, and he silently wondered who was the patriot
and who was the turncoat? But he was looking for information, and not too particular where he found it.

"Got something on the grapevine," he said, unwilling to reveal his source. "Word's around that Chitto and Frank have a hideout in the mountains. Anything to it?"

"I've heard that myself," Lipe affirmed. "I regret to say it's a well-kept secret. No one seems to know the location."

"Maybe you could steer me in the right direction. Where's a good place to start?"

"I take it you are going after Chitto Starr."

"Bright and early tomorrow morning."

Lipe steepled his fingers. "Some people have gone into those mountains and never come out. You need a man who knows the land."

"A scout?" McLain said, nodding to himself. "That's not a bad idea, Major. Got anybody in mind?"

"Joe Blackbird."

Summoned from the rear of the building, Joe Blackbird entered the office a few minutes later. A full-blood, and a former sergeant in the Light Horse, he now worked for Lipe. He was tall and rawboned, with impenetrable eyes and angular features. He looked as though he'd long ago swallowed all emotion, and with it, any sense of fear. McLain pegged him as a dangerous man.

"Joe." Lipe addressed him with a tone of authority. "This is Deputy U.S. Marshal McLain. You may have heard he's looking for Chitto Starr."

"Yessir."

"The marshal has reason to believe Starr may have gone into the mountains. He needs a tracker and guide who is knowledgeable of the wilderness. I would like you to accept the assignment."

"Yessir."

"You will take orders from Marshal McLain, just as you would from me. Am I clear?"

"Yessir." Blackbird's gaze shifted to the lawman. "What are your instructions, Marshal?"

"We leave at first light," McLain said. "I'll have ten men deputized and ready to go, outside the courthouse. You can meet me there."

"Will I be deputized?"

"Would you like to be?"

"Yessir." Blackbird's mouth ticced in what might have been a smile. "A badge would be a good thing. 'Case I have to shoot somebody."

McLain saw nothing and everything in the curious smile. A smile he had seen before in a certain breed of men. Like the one standing before him now.

He'd just signed on a killer.

Seven

The sun dipped westward into deepening shadow. Across the vast stretch of mountains, trees painted vermilion and gold by autumn frost shimmered beneath fleeting light. Day slowly faded toward dusk.

A squirrel chattered as the men topped the crest of Jackson Mountain. They were fifteen miles southeast of Park Hill, their route through a latticework of rivers and streams densely forested by oaks and hickory. Chitto rode out front, winding beneath thick stands of pine trees at the higher elevation. Joseph Lynch, with the Nighthawks strung out in single file, followed close behind.

On the summit Chitto reined to a halt. He sat staring westward along their backtrail as the men and horses ascended the slope. A mountain brook rippled nearby, dropping steeply into the lowlands below, and a natural clearing lay in onrushing twilight on the reverse side of the crest. There was forage for the livestock, abundant water, and concealment within the trees. Hardly selected at random, it was a spot he remembered well from a lifetime spent roaming the mountains. He called a halt for the night.

Lynch reined up beside him. "Where do you want the camp?"

"In the clearing," Chitto said, gesturing to the back-slope. "Get everything unloaded and put the horses out to graze. We will have a fire tonight."

"Do we move on tomorrow?"

"Have the men cook enough food to last a day. I plan to welcome those who follow."

Lynch considered a moment. "Are you so certain they will come after us? We whipped them real bad at Park Hill."

"Yes, Joseph, I am certain," Chitto said softly. "White men are at their worst in defeat. Their pride drives them to seek another fight."

"What are your plans for tomorrow?"

"Let me think on it awhile. We will talk later."

"All right, I'll see to the camp."

"Joseph."

"Yes?"

"Tell the men we will make a stand here. Let them prepare themselves."

"Just as you wish. Should I take your horse?"

"Thank you, Joseph."

Chitto dismounted, and Lynch led his horse into the clearing. There, gathering the men, he began issuing instructions. He was respected as a fighter, clearheaded and calm in a tight situation, and the men readily accepted him as second-in-command. Some were assigned to tend the livestock, and others went about putting the camp in order. They worked with the seasoned economy of men accustomed to life in the wilderness.

Lynch worked alongside them. He helped unload the packhorses, securing the jumble of gear and provisions near the center of the camp. Then he moved on to supervise laying stones for a circular fire pit, and gathering wood to last the night. Before long, the horses were hobbled, let out to graze, and the men appointed as cooks began preparing supper. All the while Lynch's eyes were on the solitary figure standing at the summit. He wondered what Chitto planned for tomorrow.

For three years now, a year before statehood, Lynch had willingly walked in the older man's shadow. He had been the first to join when the Nighthawks were formed, convinced even then that resistance was the only path for Cherokee full-bloods. He recognized Chitto as a man of iron will and vision, a sage with the wisdom to outwit their enemies and the cunning to outsmart them when there was no resort but violence. The loyalty he felt was akin to that of ancient times, when the people swore allegiance to a leader who would not fail them in battle. He often thought of Chitto as the last warrior, a man anointed by the spirits in some mystical way. One who would yet rally all the Cherokees to their cause.

Lynch would have been surprised by Chitto's thoughts at that moment. Staring out into the embers of sunset, the Nighthawk leader was lost in ruminations of times past, and dishonor. Long ago, by ancient custom, the land was held in communal ownership by all the tribe. A man could farm as much land as he wanted, and tribal laws protected him in that right, for there was land enough for all the Cherokees. There was a spirit of collective enterprise, and the people were content under a system that allowed each man to prosper in his own way. But it was a system that seemed wasteful and sacrilegious to white men, who coveted private ownership, a deed with a man's name on it. So they destroyed what the Cherokees prized most, a land where all shared equally.

In the end, as a desperate last resort, Chitto joined with other tribal leaders in petitioning Congress for separate statehood. The Five Civilized Tribes adopted a resolution which detailed the terms of ancient treaties, the guarantee that red men would never be forced to surrender their sovereignty. Their petition requested that the new state be named Sequoyah, in honor of the fabled Cherokee wise man, and a delegation went to Washington to lobby for passage of the act. But Congress ignored them, moving ahead with joint statehood, and tribal leaders at last folded under the pressure, accepting land allotments as part of the new order. Chitto broke ranks with the Cherokee leaders, publicly damning them as weaklings who had brought dishonor to the tribe, and with it, the yoke of white oppression. He foreswore diplomacy and embraced the old tribal laws, a return to ancient ways. He chose the land allotments as a battleground.

But now, gazing into a smoldering sunset, he was reminded of the cardinal rule in any war. A battleground was forever fluid, shifting and changing with events, and the victors were those who took advantage of the unforeseen. He had been forced to spill white blood, and then, certain to be faced by superior numbers, he had been forced to retreat. Yet there was much to be said for guerrilla warfare, the hit-and-run tactics employed with devastating effect by such leaders as Geronimo and Jeb Stuart. There was much to be said as well for the role of the underdog, a small force with right on their side, persecuted by an oppressive government. All of which might be turned to still greater advantage on a fluid battleground. The opportunity to enlist others in the fight!

Lynch joined him on the summit. "We have the camp in good order. Supper should be ready by dark."

"That's fine," Chitto said, framed in the dying flare of sunset. "We want the men well-fed for tomorrow's work."

"What have you decided?"

"We will adopt the tactics of the spider."

"How do you mean?"

"A spider is the most patient of hunters, Joseph. He pounces only when his prey has been drawn into the web."

Lynch appeared bemused. "And where is our web?"

"There!" Chitto directed his gaze with an outthrust finger. "Nigger Jake Hollow."

Something more than a mile below the summit was a broad creek. Between the creek and the base of the mountain was a stretch of flatland, roughly a half mile wide and a mile long. Though it was not labeled on any map, the flatland was known among the Cherokees as Nigger Jake Hollow. Legend had it that before the Civil War, when aristocratic tribesmen owned slaves, a black man skilled with hunting dogs had been killed there in a monumental battle with a bear. The hollow was open ground, shaped somewhat like a horseshoe, heavily forested on three sides. The terrain surrounding the hollow rose steeply into rugged foothills.

"We will hit them there," Chitto went on. "I want a scout by the creek early tomorrow morning. He will warn us of their approach."

"You think they will move that fast?" Lynch asked. "From Tahlequah, they must cover almost twenty miles."

"White men pride themselves on a speedy hunt. Our tracks are easy to follow, and they will push their horses hard. I expect them here no later than noon."

"You have not been wrong about them yet. I sometimes think you read their minds."

"The *aniyonega* are not clever hunters, Joseph. They underestimate us and overestimate themselves. They are simple to trap."

"How will we attack them?"

"From three directions," Chitto said. "We wait until they have reached the upper end of the hollow. Our men will be placed on either side and to their direct front."

"Yes, I see it," Lynch said approvingly. "We will have them caught in a cross fire, on open ground. Unless . . ."

"Unless what?"

"Maybe they learned something from our ambush at Park Hill. What if they send a scout ahead?"

"Let them," Chitto said with an air of confidence. "Our tracks lead straight from the creek to the bottom of the mountain. Our men will be hidden in the trees. Think on it, Joseph. What would a scout see?"

"Most likely our tracks," Lynch said in a musing tone. "He will believe we crossed the mountain to the land beyond. That is how it looks."

"And why does it look that way?"

"Well, because our camp is on the back side of the mountain. Tomorrow, just as you ordered, there will be no cooking fire. What he sees will be obvious . . . but wrong."

"We are deceitful men." Chitto smiled, amused by the thought. "But deception twists the truth, makes the false appear real. That is how we will spring the trap."

Off to the west, a last ray of sunlight flickered on the horizon, then died. Dark settled quickly over the mountain, and the campfire shimmered like a beacon in the night. Lynch stared at it for a long moment, as though wrestling with a worrisome thought. He finally looked around.

"Chitto, there is something that bothers me. I would ask you a question."

"What troubles you, old friend?"

"We can fight here and draw blood. But the white men are many and we are few, and they have more blood to spill. Where will it end?"

Chitto grimaced. "Would you have us quit and run?"

"That is what I ask," Lynch said. "We could easily throw them off our trail and retreat to Doublehead Mountain. They would never find us."

"Joseph, you do not understand. I *want* them to find us."

"Yes, I know. You left a trail a blind man could see in the dark. What I'm asking is—why?"

"A man who does not fight cannot win. We have no choice but to fight."

"And you believe we can defeat the whites?"

"I know we can win," Chitto said firmly. "Come, let us have supper, Joseph. Then I will speak of this with you and the men."

They joined the men around the fire. Supper was stewed venison jerky, spiced with wild onions, and corn mush ladled out in tin plates. The men were famished, their last meal having been before dawn that morning, and they ate with ravenous gusto. When they were finished, they helped themselves to coffee, steaming in tin cups and laced heavily with sugar. Some of them stuffed pipes with rough-cut tobacco, and lit up with flaming branches from the fire. They waited to hear what was planned for tomorrow.

Chitto set his plate aside. His eyes shone in the reflection of the fire, and he looked from man to man. "Listen to me, brothers," he said in a prophet's voice. "I have had a vision."

A profound silence came upon the men. While they

were converts to Christianity, they nonetheless held to
old beliefs, passed along from generation to generation.
They knew there were spirits who spoke only to certain
people, and a vision was strong medicine. They waited
for Chitto's words.

"The Nighthawks have been called to lead!" His
eyes blazed with intensity. "We will fight the *aniyonega*
tomorrow, and we will win. We will fight them for a
hundred tomorrows—*and we will win.*"

Every man there was riveted by the power of his
voice.

"By our example," he said, "we will send a message
to the other tribes. The Choctaw, the Creek, the Chickasaw, and the Seminole. We will prove to them that the
white man can be defeated by those with the spirit to
win. They will see it is so, and they will join in our
fight."

Chitto paused, let the silence build. "And that is my
vision," he said, hammering the words. "The Nighthawks will unite all the tribes, lead them into rebellion!
We have been *chosen* to light the way."

No one moved, staring at him in awe. They were
mesmerized by his bearing, the impact of his words, the
sheer force of his vision. After a time, when they realized he was through speaking, they seemed to collect
themselves. Doak Threepersons, one of the first to join
the Nighthawks, finally found his voice. His expression
was that of an acolyte, a zealot.

"We hear you," he said in a dazed tone. "Your vision is strong, and all the tribes will know it as truth.
We will unite to overthrow the *aniyonega.*"

A murmur of approval swept through the men. As
though released from their silence by Threepersons,
they began talking among themselves, vowing to follow
the vision. Lynch was strangely quiet, perhaps struck

harder than any man seated around the fire. He knew now that the fight tomorrow would mark the Nighthawks for all time, a line drawn in the dirt. There was no turning back.

Chitto stared into the fire, his thoughts curiously inward. Unwittingly, the image that came to mind was the Great Seal of the State of Oklahoma. The outer part of the seal was a five-pointed star, with the emblem of each of the Five Civilized Tribes as one of the rays. The center of the seal depicted a pioneer and an Indian clasping hands, with the figure of justice, her scales balanced, standing between them. The hypocrisy of it seemed to Chitto an engraved symbol of arrogance.

Yet the hypocrisy extended even further. The white men, in a scrap thrown to the Indians, had named the state Oklahoma, a Choctaw expression meaning ''red people.'' Chitto took strength from his anger, and swore a private vow that he would never quit the fight. The Nighthawks would win, or the *aniyonega* would kill them. Himself included.

There was no longer any middle ground.

Eight

The sun was lodged in the sky like a brass dome. A northerly breeze pushed cottony clouds toward the peaks of distant mountains. Off to the east, in a thicket of trees along the riverbank, a flock of crows took wing. Their squalling cries were a strident sound in the morning silence.

McLain shaded his eyes with one hand. From the angle of the sun, he judged it to be somewhere around ten o'clock. Behind him, strung out in single file, were the ten volunteers he had deputized earlier. They were a mixed lot, laborers and workingmen, over half veterans of the Spanish-American War. The thousand dollars on Chitto Starr's head was more than any of them would earn in a year's time. They were already counting the money.

Just before dawn McLain had led them south from Tahlequah. They seemed more concerned with the reward than the danger, unfazed by the killings of the past few days. The last two men in line led packhorses, and they were provisioned for a week in the field. The war veterans were quick to brag that chasing Indians was a lark compared to following Teddy Roosevelt up San Juan Hill. They thought a couple of days would get the job done.

A hundred yards to their front Joe Blackbird rode with his eyes on the ground. The trail had led them east along Park Hill Creek and shortly after sunrise they had forded the Illinois River. There the tracks turned south and bordered the winding, serpentine river through mountainous terrain. The sign was plain to read, the earth churned dark beneath the hooves of horses, and Blackbird had set a fast pace. They were now some fifteen miles south of Tahlequah.

McLain was impressed with the scout. Blackbird was a man of few words, but clearly a tracker who knew his job. That morning McLain had noted that he carried a Winchester Model '86, chambered for .45-70 caliber, in his saddle scabbard. Though a potent round, McLain nonetheless preferred the flatter trajectory and improved accuracy of his .30-.30 carbine. Yet he was pleased to see that the scout packed a Colt .45 pistol, which still delivered the greatest punch of any sidearm. All in all, what he'd seen so far spoke well of Blackbird's service with the Light Horse Police.

Up ahead, Caney Creek flowed into the river from a northeasterly direction. The mountain overlooking the juncture was forested with hickory and oak, and the riverbank sloped some thirty yards downward from the treeline. Blackbird reined his bay gelding to a halt, and sat studying the ground for a long while. When the column closed the gap to within shouting distance and Blackbird still hadn't moved on, McLain signaled the men to a halt. He rode forward to meet the scout.

"What's wrong?"

Blackbird motioned away from the river. "They

turned off here onto that creek. I don't much like it.''

"That they turned off?'' McLain appeared puzzled. "Way it looks, they're headed deeper into the mountains. What's wrong with that?''

"Don't surprise me that they done that. I'm talking about their tracks.''

"What about them?''

"They're not trying to lose us,'' Blackbird said, staring upstream. "They could've taken to the river a ways back and kept to the water when they hit this creek. Sign's just too easy to follow.''

McLain looked down at the tracks. "You think they're laying a trail for us?''

"Got no better idea than you. But I don't like it.''

"Well, we've got no choice but to follow along.''

"Yeah, that's what bothers me.''

Blackbird rode off along the creek. McLain motioned the men forward, wondering if his scout had turned nervy. But then, on second thought, he discarded the notion.

Blackbird impressed him as a man who pissed ice water.

A red-tailed hawk veered into the wind beneath a noonday sun. Blackbird glanced up, distracted by the shadow, watching a moment as the hawk caught an updraft and floated away. He proceeded along the creek.

From their last stop, the posse had advanced some three miles through the lowland carved out by Caney Creek. There, on a tributary stream, the trail turned eastward and brought them roughly another three miles deeper into the mountains. There was still no sign that the Nighthawks were trying to cover their trail.

Blackbird had grown increasingly wary. He judged the tracks to have been made late yesterday afternoon, baked now to a crust by the morning sun. Apart from no effort to elude pursuit, what bothered him most was that the Nighthawks were clearly in no hurry. The sign indicated that fourteen riders had moved along at a steady pace, leading packhorses and spare mounts, without concern for their backtrail. They weren't loafing, but they weren't running either. That troubled him.

Eight years' service in the Light Horse had taught Blackbird to take nothing for granted. A veteran manhunter was ever alert to the unexpected, any deviation from how men reacted under stress. One of the cardinal rules was that fugitives tried to put as much distance between themselves and the law as fast as possible. All the more so when they were charged with the murder of peace officers, and faced swift justice at the end of a hangman's rope. Chitto Starr and his Nighthawks were too lackadaisical, almost careless. None of it made sense.

The tracks led south into Nigger Jake Hollow. Blackbird sat for a time inspecting the open ground, and the timbered foothills that bordered it on three sides. Finally, stepping out of the saddle, he broke open a pile of horse droppings with a stick. The dung was firm on the inside, and he scrutinized it like a philosopher contemplating some arcane puzzle. McLain left the men downstream and rode forward. He halted at the edge of the creek.

"What'd you find?"

"Way it looks—" Blackbird got to his feet. "They rode by here around dark yesterday."

McLain scanned the hollow. "You think they camped somewhere up ahead?"

"Yeah, it figures they would. They're not in any rush to get anywhere. That's Jackson Mountain you're lookin' at. They probably stopped on the other side."

"Are you worried they haven't broke camp yet? You think they're still around?"

"No way to tell," Blackbird said. "What worries me is crossin' that hollow. We'd be out in plain sight."

"What choice have we got?" McLain replied. "Thick as those woods are, it'd take us the rest of the day to circle around the mountain. We're already a day behind."

"Still don't like it."

"Do you see something out there that doesn't sit right?"

Blackbird slowly inspected the woods on either side of the hollow. His eyes moved on to the mountain in the distance, and lingered there a moment. He shook his head. "Don't see nothin' that's out of place. Just don't like it, that's all."

McLain trusted his own hunches. But he was faced now with another man's instincts, and no reasonable explanation for the caution. He briefly toyed with the thought of losing time thrashing through the woods, and just as quickly rejected the idea. Chitto and the Nighthawks were already too far ahead.

"Let's move on," he said. "We've still got lots of daylight."

Blackbird swung into the saddle. He pulled his Winchester from the boot and laid it across the pommel. His gaze drifted out over the hollow.

He still didn't like it.

Dappled sunlight filtered through the trees at the south end of the hollow. Chitto knelt behind the base of a hickory, flanked by Lynch and two of the Nighthawks. Five men were positioned in the woods east of the hollow, and the other five were hidden in the treeline to the west. Their orders were to wait until Chitto fired.

From behind the hickory, Chitto watched the two men conversing down by the creek. They were both known to him, the white man as well as the Cherokee, and he cursed beneath his breath. He collapsed the small brass telescope he usually carried in his saddlebags and stuffed it into his coat pocket. Off to the left, Lynch wormed through the underbrush and stopped a few feet away. He nodded toward the creek.

"Was Doak right?"

Early that morning Doak Threepersons had been posted downstream to watch the creek. Not quite an hour ago he had returned to the camp with disturbing news. "He was right," Chitto said grimly. "Their scout is Joe Blackbird."

"Damn traitor!" Lynch bristled. "One of our own people helps the *aniyonega* hunt us."

"Blackbird was never one of ours, Joseph. He belongs to Lipe and that crowd."

"Well, he would not be here except by Lipe's order. That makes Lipe a traitor, too."

"Lipe was always a traitor," Chitto observed. "He stood with the Council when they gave away our land."

"Who's the white man?" Lynch asked. "The one talking with Blackbird. Do you know him?"

"I remember him from the raid on our camp yesterday. I think he is probably a federal marshal."

"Whatever badge he wears, he doesn't scare too easy. Did you see anything of Prather?"

"No," Chitto said. "Prather has no stomach for this work. He likely stayed in Tahlequah."

"Where he belongs," Lynch added, "with the other cowards."

A silence fell between them. They watched as Blackbird rode deeper into the hollow, and a short distance behind, they counted eleven white lawmen. Chitto grunted with disgust.

"Blackbird suspects something," he said. "Why else would he have his rifle out?"

Lynch looked skeptical. "How would he know we're here?"

"You forget, he was the best of the Light Horse. His instincts kept him alive."

"Then we must correct that today. I will kill him myself."

"Wait for me to fire," Chitto admonished. "Blackbird must get close in order to bring the white men into our web. We want no one to escape."

"Let me have Blackbird," Lynch insisted. "Their leader is a good fighter, a man worth killing. Maybe you could shoot him."

"Yes, I think you are right, Joseph. He is worth killing."

Chitto watched Blackbird close the gap to within three hundred yards. The distance was not great, but he wanted them drawn into the interlocking fields of fire he'd laid out for his men. He waited, cautioning himself to patience, watching intently as Blackbird rode ever closer. Still kneeling he brought the rifle to his shoulder. His finger curled around the trigger.

He drew a bead on the white marshal.

The tracks led straight through the hollow. Blackbird was within a hundred yards of the treeline at the base of Jackson Mountain. His eyes flicked from the tracks to the trees, and a cold sensation settled in the pit of his stomach. The trail never deviated, and the sign indicated the Nighthawks had crossed over the mountain late yesterday. But some inner voice warned him not to accept what his eyes told him. He hooked his thumb over the hammer of his Winchester.

Up ahead, he caught a faint glint of light on metal. He reacted on sheer reflex, reining the bay to a stop and throwing the Winchester to his shoulder. At the edge of the woods, he saw the shadowy outline of a man with a rifle kneeling beside a tree. The Winchester recoiled with a flat bark, and the man in the treeline jerked erect, dropping his rifle. Despite the distance, Blackbird had a fleeting impression of the man he'd shot. Then a slug seared his ribs, followed by a puff of gun smoke from within the treeline. He wheeled his horse into a hard gallop.

McLain saw the scout fire. He pulled his carbine as Blackbird spun around, bent low in the saddle and rode toward him. In the next instant, his saddlehorn exploded under the impact of a bullet, and the trees bordering the hollow erupted with gunfire. The air suddenly came alive with the buzz of lead, and he spotted men to the direct front and on both flanks popping away with rifles. The realization flooded over him that he'd been drawn into another ambush, and he fired, dropping a man along the western treeline. He reined his horse sharply about as Blackbird rode past.

To the rear, several of the men were already in full retreat. But three of the army veterans were blasting away with their rifles, exchanging shots with the Nighthawks. One of the deputies flung his arms out, his chest splattered with blood, and dropped from the saddle. Blackbird fired at a headlong gallop, and a Nighthawk stumbled out of the trees, pitching to the ground. A slug struck another deputy's horse, dumping him from the saddle, and as he scrambled to his feet, his shirtfront blossomed with bright red dots. The last one reined about toward the creek.

McLain ducked as a bullet whistled past his ear. He felt a rush of shame that he'd again turned tail and run for his life. Still, caught out in the open, trapped within a withering cross fire, he knew it would be suicide to stand and fight. A volley from the Nighthawks punctuated the thought, and to his front, a deputy tumbled from the saddle and hit the ground in a dusty heap. Yet another one slumped forward, grabbing for his saddlehorn, drilled through the back a handspan above his belt. The survivors, trailed by the terrified packhorses, thundered along in a ragged line.

A last volley sped their retreat. They hit the creek in a wedge, reining their horses to the east, behind the cover of the trees on the shoreline. McLain began shouting commands, ordering them to dismount and bring their rifles. He had no idea if the Nighthawks would seize the advantage, pursue them through the wilderness in a running gun battle. But the risk was there, and he was gripped by an urgency to deploy his men in a defensive position. He got them spread out below the creek bank, watchful for any movement in the hollow. Only then did he start counting heads.

Three men lay dead where they had fallen during the ambush. The one shot through the back was slumped on the ground, his eyes wild with pain. Still another man, wounded in the leg, sat twisting a tourniquet around his thigh. McLain sent one of the able men to tend the wounded, ordering the others to keep a sharp watch. For a moment, he couldn't comprehend that he'd lost half his force. But the greater realization was that any of them had escaped alive. The snarl of bullets still buzzed in his head.

He told himself he should have listened to Joe Blackbird.

Nine

"**Y**ou are hurt bad."

"I have been shot before."

"Maybe so, but not this bad."

"See to the men, Joseph. I will live."

"That wound needs tending."

"Don't argue with me. Do as I say."

Chitto Starr lay beneath the canopy of trees. The left shoulder of his coat was matted with blood, and his arm hung limp at his side. Lynch started to press the argument, for he knew the Nighthawk leader was suffering. But he sensed it was an argument he could not win. Orders were orders, and he was not one to disobey. He turned away to look after the men.

The opening shot of the fight had struck Chitto in the shoulder. Even as he'd drawn a bead on the *aniyonega* marshal, Joe Blackbird had suddenly raised his rifle and fired. The impact of the slug had knocked Chitto off his feet, and he remembered wondering how Blackbird had spotted him. Yet his concern was not so much for the wound, but rather that his elaborate ambush had been spoiled. He felt oddly cheated.

Off in the distance, he heard Lynch's voice. He turned his head and saw the Nighthawks withdrawing from their positions along the sides of the hollow. They were moving through the trees, visible now and then in patches of sunlight; he couldn't tell if anyone had been wounded. For a moment, after he'd been hit, he seemed to have gone deaf, his ears roaring with the pain. But then, as though awakening, he had heard the drumming rattle of gunfire, too many shots to count. He waited now to hear the outcome.

Lynch watched the Nighthawks withdraw through the trees. A man appeared on the left flank, then two more, and finally another, carrying a body slung over his shoulder. A sharp misgiving came over Lynch as he moved forward and confirmed that the one being carried was dead. His concern deepened when he turned and saw the men positioned on the right flank emerge from the trees at the top of the hollow. Four were standing, and he had no need to ask about the fifth one, the one they were lugging by his arms and legs. He knew the man was dead.

The look on the men's faces was enough to curdle Lynch's blood. They placed the bodies on the ground with a tenderness that spoke of sorrow and grief and dazed disbelief. Like him, they were baffled as to how the plan had gone wrong, the abrupt and deadly turn-around. All in a split second, the ambush had disintegrated into a pitched gunfight, and two of their brothers were dead. Their expressions were a mix of incomprehension and aggrieved anger, and their dulled stares demanded an explanation. He had none to give.

But then, suddenly, their expressions changed. Their eyes went past him, to where their leader lay sprawled on the ground, soaked in blood. On the instant, their anger and confusion turned to riven fear. Lynch understood, for without Chitto they were nothing, a ragtag band of renegades unable to function on their own. Jerked back to the moment, he forgot the dead and the aborted ambush, and felt the contagion of their dread. His fear was no less than theirs, perhaps greater. He knew they were lost without Chitto.

The men gathered around as he knelt beside their leader. Chitto's forehead glistened with sweat; his eyes were glazed, vacant. Lynch took out his belt knife, inserting the blade beneath Chitto's shirt, and gingerly cut through the cloth, then the heavier fabric of the coat. With the wound exposed, he saw torn flesh where the bullet had plowed through the top of the shoulder and exited on the opposite side. But within the bloody pulp he also saw fragments of splintered bone, and his breath caught in his throat. The collarbone was shattered.

Lynch began issuing orders. He instructed eight men to take skirmisher positions in the trees, and keep a lookout on the white posse. Another man was dispatched to their camp on the back side of the mountain, to collect medicinal herbs, a clean shirt, and a rope. The last Nighthawk was sent to a creek at the east end of the mountain, to soak bandana handkerchiefs in water. When he returned, Lynch started sponging blood from the wound with wet cloth. Chitto gritted his teeth in pain.

"Aiieee," he muttered softly. "You will never be a nurse, Joseph."

"Sorry," Lynch apologized. "I must stop the bleeding before we can dress your wound. You are hurt worse than I thought."

"How bad is it?"

"The bullet went all the way through. So that does

not worry me too much. But your shoulder bone is broken.''

''Just broken?''

''No,'' Lynch said, hesitation in his voice. ''The bone is torn apart . . . in pieces.''

Chitto let out a slow breath. ''I thought I felt something grinding in there. I have no feeling in my arm.''

''You are lucky to be alive.''

''What of the men? Are they all right?''

''We lost two,'' Lynch said, holding a damp handkerchief to the wound. ''I fired on Joe Blackbird after he shot you, but I missed. He killed Eli Posey.''

''Eli,'' Chitto repeated in a whisper. ''Who else?''

''I think the white marshal shot Henry Ketch. Things happened so fast it was hard to tell. That's just the way it looked.''

''How many of the whites were killed?''

''Three.''

''Three!'' Chitto blinked with anger. ''We lost Eli and Henry and killed only three of them. How can that be?''

''Maybe we wounded a couple,'' Lynch said. ''There at the last, one almost fell off his horse.''

''But why so few? What happened?''

''Blackbird must have the eyes of an eagle. How else could he have spotted you? Everything went sour when he fired.''

''Tell me,'' Chitto said. ''All of it.''

''They scattered,'' Lynch replied. ''After Blackbird fired, they turned and kicked their horses into a gallop. Men riding that fast are not easy to shoot.''

''How could he have seen me? How?''

''You said it yourself, Chitto. He was the best of the Light Horse. His instincts kept him alive . . . even today.''

"I damn his soul to the white man's hell! We were betrayed by a Cherokee—a full-blood."

"They have betrayed us before. It will not be the last time."

Chitto nodded agreement. "I fear you are right, Joseph."

Noah Adair, the man sent back to the camp, returned with a cotton shirt, a length of rope, and a buckskin bag tied at the top with a drawstring. Lynch applied light pressure with the cold compress, then removed it, and saw that the wound had stopped bleeding. He opened the buckskin bag, which held several smaller bags, and rooted around until he found the one he wanted. The bag contained an ancient treatment for deep wounds, a mix of spider's web and several wild roots, pulverized into powdery flakes. He sprinkled the powder liberally over the wound.

Lynch next folded the shirt into a thick bandage, leaving the sleeves dangling loose. He placed the bandage over the wound, front and back, and used the sleeves to tie it off around Chitto's neck. To secure the shoulder as much as possible, and prevent further injury, he had to immobilize Chitto's left arm. With Adair's help, he raised the Nighthawk leader's upper torso a few inches off the ground. Working quickly, with Adair supporting from the rear, he encircled Chitto with the rope, from chest to hip, anchoring the useless arm to the body. He bound the rope with a slipknot, leaving the right arm free. They gently lowered Chitto to the ground.

Throughout the ordeal, Chitto's jaws were clamped tight. But as they eased him to the ground, his mouth parted in a wheezy, strangled groan. His face was beaded with sweat, and his eyes were glassy, bright with pain. He lay perfectly still for a time, then managed to take a deep breath, and his vision seemed to clear.

Lynch and Adair were hovering over him, and his glance went from one to the other. His mouth quirked in a faint smile.

"Do not worry," he said. "I am a hard man to kill."

"Maybe so," Lynch remarked. "But we have to get you out of here. This place will not be safe after dark."

"Are the *aniyonega* still at the creek?"

"Who knows what they will do? We cannot take the chance."

"Go check on them, Joseph. Use my spyglass."

Lynch took the telescope from Chitto's coat pocket. He left Adair to watch him and moved off through the woods. At the edge of the treeline, he went down on his belly and snaked forward beneath dappled sunlight. He extended the telescope and slowly glassed the stretch of timber east of the hollow. For a moment, he saw nothing; then he looked closer. There was movement.

Along the creek bank, he saw a man hidden behind a tree. Another man was moving from tree to tree, briefly visible in patches of sunlight. The distance was too great, but Lynch thought it was the white marshal. He scanned the wooded area thoroughly, and counted seven men, including one who looked like Joe Blackbird. From all appearances, they were in a defensive position, barricaded behind the creek bank. But their dead still littered the hollow, and he knew they weren't going anywhere. He collapsed the telescope.

A few moments later he knelt down beside Chitto. "They are still there," he said. "I think they are waiting until dark to collect their dead."

"You can never trust a white man to do the sensible thing. Leave a rear guard to cover our movement."

Lynch did a quick calculation. "I can only leave two men. Climbing the mountain will be a difficult job. We need four men to carry Eli and Henry." He paused, knowing he would get an argument. "And I want four men to carry you."

"No," Chitto said sternly. "Get me on my feet and I can walk. One man will be enough should I need support."

"Four men," Lynch countered, his gaze steady. "I will not have you die on me trying to climb that mountain. Do not argue with me, Chitto. The matter is settled."

Their eyes locked. Noah Adair looked from one to the other, amazed that Lynch would countermand an order. At length, with a grudging sigh, Chitto broke the staring contest. "You are probably right, Joseph. I don't feel much like a walk."

Lynch quickly got the withdrawal organized. He assigned Doak Threepersons and Ben Dewey to act as rear guard. Four men were picked to carry the bodies of the dead Nighthawks. The other four, including Adair, lifted Chitto off the ground, their rifles slung, and cradled him in their arms. Lynch assigned himself to bring up the rear and ordered them to move out. They began the arduous climb up the wooded slope.

There was no way to conceal their withdrawal from Nigger Jake Hollow. Burdened by the weight of the dead and wounded, the men were slowed in their climb, forced to take the simplest route up the mountainside. They avoided thick stands of trees altogether, and wherever possible, they chose the easier path across bald spots of open ground. Lynch was all too aware that their tortuous progress was visible to the white men from the distant creek. He still thought there was small likelihood they would attempt pursuit, not with dead of their own to tend. Yet he weighed on the side of caution, for Chitto's assessment was correct. White men rarely did the sensible thing.

The rear guard withdrew in their wake. Lynch occasionally paused to search the hollow with the telescope, and to assure himself that the whites were holding their position. As the grade steepened, the climb became even more grueling, and the men struggled under their loads. But by late afternoon, exhausted and parched from their labor, they finally topped the crest. Their camp on the backslope was as they had left it that morning, the horses secured to a picket line. Chitto was placed beneath a tree, and Lynch ordered the men to drink their fill and grab a cold meal. He planned to depart within the hour.

After releasing the men, Lynch filled a canteen with fresh water from the stream. He found Chitto weak and spent, his features drained of color from the punishing trek up the mountain. Kneeling down, he supported Chitto's head with one hand and held the canteen to his mouth with the other. Chitto greedily drank the water, and after several long swallows, he appeared somewhat refreshed, his color improved. He silently nodded his thanks.

"Listen to me," Lynch said. "You are hurt worse than you think, and you need a doctor. We can find one at Stilwell."

Stilwell was the nearest town, some ten miles to the northeast. Chitto shook his head. "After today, there will be a bounty on me. Even in Stilwell, I would be betrayed. I will not risk capture."

"That is a chance we must take. Without a doctor's care, you risk death itself."

"I would gladly die before I let the *aniyonega* take me prisoner."

"Don't be stubborn," Lynch said sharply. "Old-time herbs will not cure a smashed shoulder. You need an operation."

Chitto smiled. "You forget, Joseph. We have killed many white lawmen now. I will not be hung on a white man's gallows." His smile faded. "You and the men would be hung as well. I will not let that happen."

"Every man here would take that risk. They know how bad you are hurt."

"Do not question my orders, old friend. Lead us to Doublehead Mountain and we will bury our dead there. I will recover because the spirits will not let me die. Too much remains to be done."

Lynch had considerably less faith in the power of the spirits. But his loyalty would not permit him to ignore, or disobey, so direct an order. He instructed the men to break camp just as quickly as their meal was finished. Within minutes, the men got busy stowing gear in packs and saddling the horses. Threepersons and Dewey, the rear guard, entered camp as the dead Nighthawks were laid over their saddles and lashed in place. All that remained was to get Chitto mounted.

Not a man in the camp thought he could ride. While one of them held his horse, Lynch got his foot in the stirrup and Adair pushed on his rump. Threepersons took his right arm from the other side and they all hefted at once, lifting him into the saddle. Chitto grimaced, his features chalky with pain, and for a moment they thought he would fall. But he collected himself, his left arm strapped to his side, and took the reins in his right hand. For all his composure, he looked like a man being lanced with hot knives. He nodded to Lynch.

"Lead the way, Joseph. I am ready to travel."

Lynch appeared less than convinced. He swung aboard his horse and gave the column one last inspection. Then he motioned the Nighthawks forward.

He led them down the backslope of Jackson Mountain.

Ten

The shadows deepened as the sun settled westward. The men were tired and dispirited, bored with watching the hollow from their positions along the creek bank. Their vigilance was flagging, and among themselves, they began to grumble about the long delay. They wanted to pull out.

McLain knew they were disgruntled. They had climbed into the saddle before dawn and ridden twenty miles only to fall into an ambush. They looked beaten, and they were hungry as well, for he refused to allow them to build a cooking fire. Throughout the afternoon, he had held their rations to hardtack and dried apples, and turned a deaf ear to their complaints. He was waiting for dark to collect his dead.

Shortly after the fight, he had watched the Nighthawks withdraw up the mountain. They moved slowly, and despite the great distance, they appeared to be carrying dead and wounded. What he didn't know was whether or not they had left a rear guard in the treeline at the top of the hollow. Smoke from a campfire would have revealed his position, and he wasn't willing to risk another engagement. So far Chitto had outgeneraled him at every turn.

There was little he could do for his wounded. The man hit in the leg was propped up against the creek bank, and McLain felt reasonably certain he would survive. The bullet had passed through the fleshy part of his thigh without nicking an artery, and the bleeding had been staunched with a compress. The other man was more serious, shot through the lung, rarely conscious, wheezing a pinkish froth with every breath. McLain thought it unlikely that he could last the night.

The man's name was John Watson. McLain went to check on him, lifting the crude bandage covering his chest. The hole where the slug had exited was dark with blood, air whooshing softly every time he exhaled. He was young, perhaps twenty-three or twenty-four, his features leeched of color. As McLain replaced the bandage, his eyes rolled open and his expression seemed lucid. A reddish bubble seeped from the corner of his mouth.

"Marshal," he said on a labored breath, "how bad is it?"

McLain forced a smile. "You just rest easy. Save yourself for the ride home."

"You think I'm gonna make it?"

"Why, sure you'll make it. Don't worry yourself about that."

"Good . . . I won't."

Watson's eyes drooped closed. His ragged breathing grew harsher as McLain got to his feet. The other man, his pants leg soaked with blood, was seated nearby. He gave McLain a scornful look.

"You dodged the truth there. He's liable to draw his last breath any minute."

"All the more reason to lie," McLain said. "A little hope never hurt anybody."

"I hope to hell you're right. I'd sure hate to lose this leg."

"We'll get you to a doctor and you'll be just fine. You won't lose your leg."

"Guess that depends on how long till I see a sawbones, don't it? How long before you get us outta here?"

"Sometime after dark. Will you be able to ride?"

"You put a saddle on it and I'll ride forked lightning. Watson might not make it, but I will."

"Well, it won't be long now. You just hang on."

McLain walked to the creek bank. He glanced downstream, to where the horses were picketed, then stopped beside Joe Blackbird. The scout was partially concealed behind a tree, his stolid gaze fixed on the hollow. The slanting rays of the sun bathed the woodlands in a fiery glow, autumn leaves sparkling with color. The scene was somehow pastoral, hardly suited to a killing ground.

"What do you see?" McLain asked. "Have they pulled out?"

Blackbird shrugged. "Nothin' moving out there. They're likely gone."

"That sounds like maybe so, maybe not."

"Well, they might be on top the mountain. I tend to doubt there's anybody in them trees."

"But you're not certain?"

"No."

Blackbird was silent a moment. He finally nodded toward the distant treeline. "I think maybe I plugged Chitto this mornin'. Not certain about that either."

"You think?" McLain looked startled. "Why haven't you said something before now?"

" 'Cause things happened damned fast. Maybe it was Chitto, maybe not.''

"What makes you think it was?''

"When I shot him, he sorta stepped sideways, into a patch of sun. Then he fell back in them trees. I only saw him a second.''

"You know Chitto on sight, don't you?''

"Everybody in the Nation knows Chitto.''

"So are you sure or not?''

Blackbird nodded. "Pretty sure.''

"Try to remember,'' McLain said. "Any chance you killed him?''

"Nooo,'' Blackbird said slowly, playing it out in his mind. "Wasn't time to aim good and I took a real quick shot. Think maybe I just winged him.''

"Too bad,'' McLain said. "We might've gotten you that reward. But we'd have to be sure.''

"I got away with a whole skin. That's enough for me.''

The men along the creek bank listened with rapt attention. Alf Lungren, one of the army veterans, was thickset, somewhere in his late thirties, with the veined nose of a drinker. He pushed away from the embankment, a pugnacious scowl on his features. His eyes were beady.

"What the hell we waitin' for?'' he demanded. "Blackbird says there ain't no Injuns up there. Let's haul ass.''

"Not yet,'' McLain told him. "We don't leave without our dead.''

"Well, go on and get 'em. What's stoppin' you?''

"There might still be somebody in those trees. Joe doesn't know and neither do I. We'll wait till dark.''

"Wait by yourself,'' Lungren grated, turning to the

other men. ''What d'you say, boys? How many vote for heading home?''

A low mutter of approval passed through the men. McLain motioned them silent. ''We're not operating by vote here. You men were deputized, and you'll follow orders. Let's not hear any more about it.''

''In a pig's ass!'' Lungren rumbled. ''You led us smack-dab into an ambush and got us shot to pieces. Stuff your goddamn orders.''

''Lungren, I won't tolerate any nonsense. Get back to your post.''

''You got wax in your ears. I just told you we're through takin' orders. Get the hell outta my way.''

Lungren bulled into him with a shoulder. McLain pivoted aside, drawing his pistol, and struck out in a blurred motion. The heavy barrel of the Colt thunked into Lungren's skull, and he went down as though hammered into the ground. He was out cold.

''Anybody else?'' McLain said, wagging the snout of the pistol. ''Speak up or shut up.''

Joe Blackbird moved to his side. The scout held his Winchester at hip level, thumb curled over the hammer, his muddy eyes cold and alert. He stared at the men with an impassive smile.

A moment passed in tense silence. Then, one by one, the men turned back to their posts at the creek bank. McLain holstered his pistol, glancing around at the scout. A smile tugged at the corner of his mustache.

''Thanks for the assist, Joe.''

Blackbird grunted. ''What's a deputy for?''

McLain looked out across the hollow. A thought surfaced in the back of his mind, and he told himself that Lungren was right. He had led them into an ambush, and because of his rush to overtake the Nighthawks, three men were dead. He turned, his gaze drawn to John Watson.

Maybe four.

The land was cloaked in the fading light of sundown. Joseph Lynch rode out front, the Nighthawks trailing behind as they descended the reverse slope of the mountain. They had come less than two miles.

Chitto was the next rider in line. He was followed closely by Noah Adair, who had been assigned to watch him. On the steep descent, there were several times Chitto thought he might fall from the saddle. His head was woozy, the taste of bile thick in his throat, and he found it difficult to maintain his balance. But he was determined not to slow the Nighthawks, or burden them more than necessary. He somehow held himself erect.

To distract himself, Chitto tried to plan ahead. His wound was more serious than he would admit, and he warned himself against any display of weakness. The Nighthawks relied on him for leadership, and in many ways, they were as dependent as children. From the beginning, when he had formed the small band of Keetoowahs, the men had entrusted him with every decision in their fight against the *aniyonega*. His vision was their vision, and they looked to him for the wisdom to prevail. He worried they would lose the vision should he falter.

All of which forced him to consider the matter of Joseph Lynch. Long ago, he had selected Lynch as his second-in-command, and he'd never once regretted the decision. Lynch was capable, a forceful presence in his own right, and a man of unquestioned courage. Yet there was more to the struggle now than badgering turncoat Cherokees over land allotments, or engaging in gun battles with white lawmen. Only last night Chitto had devised the grand scheme of uniting all the tribes in the fight to overthrow white oppression and reclaim their birthright. He wondered if Lynch could rally the tribes and lead the fight without guidance. He thought so, but he wasn't altogether certain. And that kernel of doubt bothered him.

A sharp pain in his shoulder made him wince. His jaw muscles knotted, biting down on the pain, and he silently damned Joe Blackbird. He damned himself as well, for he knew he'd somehow given his position away, allowed Blackbird that split second necessary to get off the first shot. The wound couldn't have come at a worse time, for it made him human, with all the normal human frailties, in the eyes of the Nighthawks. Over the years his defiance of the whites had given him a mantle of invincibility, and now a single gunshot made him appear all too mortal. The vagaries of life had at last touched him, made him vulnerable. He vowed not to let it show.

Lynch called a halt at the bottom of the slope. Just ahead was Dry Creek, which flowed rapidly despite its name, and beyond were the heights of Gitting Down Mountain. He dismounted, instructing the men to water their horses, and walked back to Chitto. He searched the older man's face.

"How are you doing?"

"I am fine, Joseph. Do not concern yourself."

"You don't look so good."

Even in the chill of onrushing night, Chitto's features were covered by a sheen of sweat. The jouncing ride on horseback had clearly taken its toll, and there was little question that he was suffering. He tried to mask it with bravado.

"See to the men and horses, Joseph. You cluck around me like a mother hen."

Lynch was not fooled. "I was thinking we might camp here tonight. There's water and graze—"

"We will move on," Chitto interrupted. "I want more distance between us and the white men. They might be on our trail even now."

"I don't think so," Lynch persisted. "Not even Joe Blackbird could track in the dark."

The purple shadows of twilight were rapidly settling over the mountains. Lynch's point was well taken, and in any event, neither of them believed the lawmen would mount a pursuit. Chitto was stubbornly intent on reaching their stronghold at Doublehead Mountain, and the posse was merely an excuse. He would not halt so long as he could ride.

"I am in no mood to argue," Chitto said at length. "We have come maybe two miles, and that is not far enough. Get the men ready to move out."

When Lynch walked off, Chitto felt his energy drain away. He slumped forward, supporting himself on the saddlehorn with his good hand. Yet, even as his vitality deserted him, he was determined not to show weakness. As the men led their horses to the creek, he exerted a burst of willpower and forced himself to sit erect. He sensed the men were watching him, and he sat straighter. His shoulder flared with pain.

Unbidden, as if his mind was working tricks to divert him, his thoughts focused on an older wound. A wound so deep, and so grievous, that it would be with him all his days. In 1907, two long years ago, the new state of Oklahoma was inaugurated on the steps of the capitol in Guthrie. He recalled a ballyhooed part of the celebration was a symbolic marriage signifying the joint statehood of the two territories. A young Cherokee woman, almost white in appearance, wore an elegant doeskin dress, decorated with fancy quillwork. She was

wed, in a mock ceremony, to a dashing white businessman wearing formal morning attire. The union of red
and white, immortalized by newspaper cameras, was
complete.

The thought of it made Chitto forget his shoulder. He
took strength from rekindled anger, and his contempt
for the boundless hypocrisy of whites. Nor was his contempt any less for the Cherokee leaders who sanctioned
the union, and surrendered their honor along with the
hapless young woman. He suddenly felt revitalized,
feeding on an unholy broth of treachery and betrayal.
Old wounds, he told himself, were the stuff of vindi-
cation. A man forever fought the wrongs of his past.

"Are you all right?" Lynch asked, pausing beside
his horse. "You look like you were talking with the
spirits."

"Yes, maybe I was," Chitto said with a touch of
irony. "Do you know why we will win this fight of
ours, Joseph?"

"Why?"

"Because a man in the right cannot be beaten. A just
cause has a life of its own."

Lynch stared at him. "You're sure you want to go
on? I think you could use some rest."

"I will rest when we get to Doublehead Mountain."

"Whatever you say."

Shortly afterward the column moved out. Lynch led
them across the creek, ever deeper into the wilderness.
Their path lay through the most rugged terrain in the
mountains.

He wondered if Chitto would make it.

Eleven

The sky was ablaze with stars. Shafts of light filtered through the trees and lit the creek in a silvery glow. Somewhere in the woods an owl hooted, then the night was still.

The men sat wrapped in their greatcoats and mackinaws. A sharp wind out of the north left them chilled and huffing spurts of frost. Their manner was withdrawn, quietly antagonistic, and their eyes were hostile. They waited in brittle silence.

Alf Lungren, nursing a knot on his head, watched McLain with open malice. His defiance that afternoon had left him bruised and bleeding, and the lesson wasn't lost on the other men. Yet he was the only one willing to speak out, and he had appointed himself their ringleader. His voice grated now in the stillness.

"We're freezin' our asses off. You got no right to stop us from buildin' a fire."

McLain and Blackbird stood by the creek bank. Their attention was fixed on the open ground of the hollow, and the surrounding treeline. They exchanged a look, then McLain turned to the men. His eyes drilled into Lungren.

"I'll tell you just once more. Some of those Night-hawks could sneak up on us in the dark, and a fire would make everybody here a perfect target. You want to get shot?"

"Bullshit!" Lungren exploded. "Them Injuns are long gone. Nobody's gonna get shot."

"Why don't you take a stroll out there and put it to the test? Who knows, you might be right."

"Take your own goddamn stroll! All I want's a horse, so we can get the hell outta here."

McLain shook his head. "We stick together till we get back to Tahlequah. That's final."

"You'll get yours then," Lungren said shortly. "We're gonna tell the whole world how you waltzed straight into an ambush. You won't never live it down."

"Don't worry yourself about it, Lungren. I'll manage."

"Not after we get through with you. Wouldn't surprise me if you lose your tin star. Serve you right, too."

The men murmured their agreement. McLain knew he was in for a rough time, with four dead and one wounded. John Watson, the man shot through the lung, had died not quite an hour ago, as dusk turned to dark. There was little doubt that McLain would be held accountable for a manhunt gone wrong.

"Still a free country," he said. "You tell your story and I'll tell mine. But for now, we stick together."

"Bird dogs fly, too," Lungren muttered. "Least you could do is let us have a smoke. Where's the harm in a cigarette?"

"That'd be a dead giveaway in the dark. Don't you think I'd like a smoke myself? You'll just have to wait till we're on down the trail."

"Well, when's that gonna be? What're we waitin' for?"

McLain glanced at Blackbird with a questioning look. The scout turned, staring out at the hollow for a long moment, and finally shrugged. "Won't get any darker," he said. "Maybe there's somebody in them trees, maybe not. Only one way to find out."

"Guess so," McLain agreed, turning back to the men. "I can't manage this by myself. I need a volunteer."

The request was greeted by silence. The men stared at him with sullen expressions, and no one moved. After a moment, Lungren barked a harsh laugh. "Take Blackbird," he said sourly. "Anybody to blame for this mess besides you, it'd be him. Some goddamn scout!"

McLain weighed the risk. He thought there was some likelihood they would ride out the moment his back was turned. He had planned on leaving Blackbird behind, to guard the horses as well as the men. But he saw now that the problem would not be solved so easily. He fixed the men with a hard look.

"Let's get something straight," he said. "You boys are duly deputized until we get back to Tahlequah. Anybody who takes off will be in violation of his sworn duty."

"Yeah?" Lungren said in a surly voice. "So what?"

"You're federal deputies and that makes it a federal offense. Violation will get you a year in prison."

"You're bluffin'," Lungren said somewhat uncertainly. "You wouldn't have the gall to bring charges against nobody. Not after you got four men killed."

"Try me," McLain said bluntly. "You run and I'll arrest the whole lot of you. That goes double for you, Lungren."

''C'mon, for Chrissakes! Who said I was gonna run?''

''Just be here when I get back—all of you.''

Blackbird brought three horses from the picket line. McLain took the reins of one, and led the way from the shelter of the creek bank. They moved out into the hollow on foot, holding the horses between themselves and the woodlands on either side. Whether or not any of the Nighthawks still waited in the trees seemed to them a moot point. Neither of them wanted to be the next man killed.

The hollow glimmered beneath pale starlight. McLain took a fix on the center of the open ground, roughly following the line of their retreat after the gun battle that morning. Apart from the moan of the wind, there was absolute silence, broken occasionally by the scuff of a hoof on upturned stone. There was a sense of something eerie, something ghostly, about the darkened foothills bordering the hollow.

A half mile or so from the creek they came across the first body. The man lay twisted in a grotesque tableau of death, his arms splayed out and one leg crooked at a sharp angle. The horses shied, nostrils flared and eyes wide, spooked by the odor of a dead thing. McLain gentled them, holding tightly to the reins, while Blackbird got the body across the saddle. The dead man's hands and feet were securely lashed beneath the horse's belly.

On ahead, closer to the site of the ambush, they found the bodies of the other two men. One lay as though he had dropped into a deep sleep; but the second was splattered with caked blood from a wound through the heart. They went about the grim business of loading the bodies without a word spoken, lost in their own thoughts. McLain was thankful for the cold weather, which would preserve the bodies in some measure on the ride back to Tahlequah. Blackbird simply wanted to be gone from the field of dead.

Not quite an hour later they returned to the creek with their grisly cargo. The men were still hunkered in the shelter of the embankment, clearly dissuaded from pulling out on their own. In a gruff voice, brooking no argument, McLain ordered two of them to strap Watson's body aboard a horse. The deputy with the leg wound was assisted onto his horse, and the others quickly got themselves mounted. Four of them were assigned to lead the dead men's horses, and the fifth brought up the rear with the packhorses tied in tandem. They rode out in single column.

Blackbird led them west along the creek. Starlight rippled off the water, the glittery sparkle somehow a mockery of their solemn procession. Earlier that day, headed in the opposite direction, the men had been full of brag and bravado, spoiling for a fight. But now, carting away their dead, no one spoke of glory. Their pride lay soiled in Nigger Jake Hollow.

A mile or so downstream McLain rolled himself a smoke. He struck a match on his shattered saddlehorn, a reminder of how close he'd come to death, and lit up in a flare of light. He inhaled, savoring the acrid taste, his mind not on the dead but on the living. He wondered how badly Chitto Starr was wounded.

His gut instinct told him not badly enough.

The ravine was less than a quarter mile wide. A rocky stream marked the passageway through Gitting Down Mountain and the foothills to the southeast. Densely forested terrain rose steeply away on either side of the lowland.

Lynch rode at the head of the column. By the angle

of the stars, he judged the time to be somewhere around midnight. He calculated they had come five or six miles since departing the camp overlooking Nigger Jake Hollow. Under normal circumstances, beneath bright starlight, they would have traveled twice that distance. But there was nothing normal about tonight.

The ravine traced a winding path through the mountains. Lynch had purposely held the pace of the column to a sedate walk. The terrain was rocky, often rough going where thickets and heavy brush crowded the stream; but his concern was not for the horses, or the Nighthawks. His concern was for Chitto, who at times seemed to list in the saddle. He seriously considered stopping for the night.

Yet he doubted that he could win the argument. A look told the tale, and there was no question that riding horseback sent jolts of pain slicing through Chitto. For all that, the Nighthawks' leader was stubborn to a fault, immune to reason. His mind was set on reaching the stronghold at Doublehead Mountain, and he refused to admit the crippling nature of his injury. He was determined to travel throughout the night.

Over the last three years they had followed the route through the mountains any number of times. In all, building the stronghold and stocking it with provisions had taken the Nighthawks upwards of four months. Lynch knew every crook and turn in the trail, every landmark along the way. He estimated they were still some ten miles from Doublehead Mountain, and he dared not increase the pace. At best, they would arrive there somewhere around sunrise tomorrow morning. He grew increasingly concerned that Chitto would not last that long.

A short while later Lynch rode through the mouth of the ravine. Directly ahead, across a half mile of flatland, lay Sallisaw Creek. On the far side of the stream the terrain rose sharply, dominated by the heights of Beevale Mountain. The headwaters of the creek were off to the northeast, winding around Dahlonegah Mountain, and farther on, Fletcher Mountain. Their route to the stronghold followed the twisting path of the creek, which wound through open lowlands. The balance of the journey was easier, but nonetheless a ten-mile trek.

Lynch angled off to the northeast. He instinctively sighted on the North Star, brilliant as a sparkling diamond in the cloudless sky. At the northern edge of Beevale Mountain, he forded the creek onto a wide expanse of flatland. He debated a halt, however brief, to allow Chitto some momentary respite. While it would result in an argument, he decided to use the pretext of resting the horses. Given time, he might persuade Chitto to stop for the night. He thought it was worth a try.

The matter was resolved before he could signal a halt. On the far side of the creek Chitto slumped forward, dropped the reins, and toppled from the saddle. He hit the ground on his injured shoulder, facedown in the damp earth, and lay motionless. Noah Adair jumped off his horse, yelling an alarm as the other Nighthawks gained the shore. Lynch looked around, then hastily dismounted, and rushed to join Adair. They rolled Chitto onto his back.

In the bright starlight, they saw that Chitto's condition had worsened. He was unconscious, his breathing labored, his face and hair drenched with sweat. Adair put a hand to his forehead, and felt him burning with fever. Lynch called for a candle to be brought from the packs, and quickly lit it with a match. While Adair held the candle, he peeled Chitto's coat aside and gently lifted the bandage. The wound was reopened, matted with blood, splinters of bone visible in the candlelight.

A purplish bruise spread across the entire shoulder.

Chitto's eyelids fluttered open. He focused on the candle, his features contorted in a grimace, then looked at Lynch. "Where am I?"

"You fell off your horse," Lynch said. "You're hurt lots worse than we thought. You need a doctor."

"No doctor," Chitto said, steeling himself against the pain. "That would only lead the whites to us. You must tend to me, Joseph."

"I don't know how to treat anything this bad. If we let it go, you're liable to get blood poisoning. I won't take that risk."

"I still give the orders," Chitto said in a weak voice. "Treat it the best you can and leave the rest to me. I will heal myself."

Lynch thought them the words of a crazed man. But he saw nothing to be gained by arguing the matter on a creek bank in the middle of the night. He decided to settle for a compromise. "We are stopping here," he said staunchly. "Maybe you will be better in the morning. But we go no further tonight. Let that be the end of it."

"Until the morning," Chitto conceded, his vision suddenly blurred, unable to keep his eyes open. "We will talk of it then."

The Nighthawks were gathered around, watching somberly. Lynch turned to them. "Don't look so worried," he said, feigning casual confidence. "Chitto's got more lives than a cat. He'll be all right."

" 'Course he will," Doak Threepersons said earnestly. "Just got through saying he'd cure himself, didn't he? He'll do it, too."

Lynch ordered them to set up camp. He chose a site halfway up Beevale Mountain, hidden deep within the treeline. His choice was considered rather than random, with an eye to a well-concealed defensive position. Some dark inner voice told him they would be there awhile. He was convinced Chitto would not mount a horse tomorrow.

The men went about their work without further comment. But their mood was solemn, and despite his reassurances, Lynch could tell that they were worried. Everyone was thinking the same thing, and as though he could read their minds, he knew very few of them shared Threepersons's optimism. They had seen Chitto in the candlelight, and his condition spoke for itself. No man cured himself of a wound that bad.

The thought was uppermost in Lynch's mind as well. As he got Chitto positioned on a bed of blankets and dug into the medicine bag, he told himself there was little chance of recovery without a doctor. But at the same time, he was concerned for the men, and their survival. They were all wanted for murder, no less than Chitto, and the one great certainty was that the white lawmen would now come after them in force. The stronghold at Doublehead Mountain was their last refuge.

Lynch wondered if it might not also be their last stand. Should Chitto die, he would be forced to assume command of the Nighthawks. He was a realist, if nothing else, and his leadership had never been tested in battle. Some men were wily tacticians and some were simply warriors.

He had to hope he'd learned well from Chitto.

Twelve

Streetlamps flickered to life as dusk settled over Tahlequah. Stores and shops began closing, and the square filled with workingmen headed home for the night. Lights in the courthouse blinked out one by one.

McLain rode into town on the south road. Blackbird, his features inscrutable, was next in line. Somewhat like a funeral procession, the deputies were strung out behind them, leading the dead men's horses. The bodies were wrapped in blankets, for the journey had consumed the better part of two days, and the dead were now turning ripe. The faint odor of death lingered in their wake.

All along the street townspeople stopped, crowding the sidewalks. Their expressions were a mixture of shock and disbelief, and they seemed frozen in a moment of silence. As the procession neared the square, several cars braked to a halt, and larger crowds began collecting on streetcorners. A low murmur swept through their ranks as they counted the dead.

The men in the posse looked worn and haggard. Their features were etched with defeat, their eyes dulled by their ordeal in the wilderness. Just off the square, the wounded deputy was assisted from his horse, and bystanders carried him into the office of Dr. Chester Rinehart. The column proceeded on to the courthouse, where McLain signaled a halt. As he stepped out of the saddle, Ed Prather hurried down the walkway. His eyes darted over the shrouded bodies.

"Holy Christ," he said in a strained voice. "What happened?"

"We found Chitto," McLain said dryly. "Or maybe it was the other way 'round."

"You let him jump you again? You lost four men?"

"Four dead and one wounded. He was laying for us."

"Bushwhacked our ass!" Lungren snarled, glaring at the sheriff. "No need to run for office next election, Ed. You ain't likely to get many votes."

Prather looked startled. "What'd I do? I wasn't there."

"You roped us into the mess, that's what! We signed on because you told us this—" Lungren jabbed a finger at McLain. "This hotshot knows his business. He like to got us all killed!"

"C'mon now, Alf," Prather protested. "How was I to know? Hell, he's a federal marshal."

"Then the government must be hard up. He don't know beans from buckwheat about law work. And that's a puredee fact."

Lungren and the other men were still mounted. McLain stared at them a moment, his features curiously stoic. He motioned downstreet. "Lungren, you and your friends take those bodies over to the undertaker. After that, consider yourselves dismissed. You're no longer deputized."

"Thanks for nothin'," Lungren growled. "Glad to see the last of you. Ain't that right, boys?"

The men bobbed their heads in agreement. Lungren reined sharply around, and the others followed along behind. They left the packhorses standing in the street and led the dead men's horses across the east side of the square. A crowd of onlookers watched in hushed silence as they rode toward the funeral parlor.

"Jesus." Prather heaved a long sigh, glancing uneasily at the crowd. "Four more dead men and four new widows. What the hell am I gonna tell people?"

"Tell them the truth," McLain said. "Chitto Starr and the Nighthawks are a tough bunch. They're damned good fighters."

"So you say," Prather grumbled. "Come election time, all they'll remember is how many got killed. I'm liable to be up shit creek without a paddle."

McLain ignored the remark. He turned to Blackbird. "Joe, would you take these packhorses over to the livery stable? I'd be obliged."

"Take your horse, too," Blackbird said. "You want to keep your rifle?"

"Yeah." McLain pulled his Winchester from the scabbard. "Just so you know, you could be my scout anytime. You saved our bacon out there."

"Don't blame yourself too much, Marshal. Chitto's like an old fox. He knows lots of tricks."

"I'm not likely to forget." McLain smiled, shook his hand. "I'll see you around, Joe."

Blackbird leaned out of the saddle and collected the reins. He nodded, then led the horses toward the livery stable. Prather snorted with disgust.

"You and that Injun got awful chummy."

"His name's Joe Blackbird," McLain said curtly. "Don't call him an Injun again—not in front of me."

"What got your bowels in an uproar?"

''Figure it out for yourself. I need to use your telephone.''

Prather followed him into the courthouse. McLain went directly to the sheriff's private office and sat down behind the desk. He jiggled the phone hook, waiting for the operator, and gave her the number in Guthrie. A few moments later Fred Gilmore came on the line.

''Owen,'' he said tentatively. ''Where are you?''

''Tahlequah,'' McLain replied. ''I just got back.''

''I hope you're calling with good news.''

''I'd have to say it's all bad.''

McLain quickly briefed him on the aborted manhunt. He explained the ambush and the aftermath, noting that he'd lost four men. When he finished, there was a prolonged silence on the other end of the line. Finally, Gilmore cleared his throat.

''My God,'' he said in a stunned voice. ''It's a disaster.''

''I've got no excuses,'' McLain informed him. ''The only saving grace is that Chitto Starr was wounded. How bad is anybody's guess.''

''So you don't know if it was a mortal wound?''

''I'd tend to doubt it. 'Course, there's no question we killed two of his men. That evens things out a little.''

''Hardly,'' Gilmore retorted. ''We now have six dead lawmen. Or had you forgotten the two deputies killed before?''

''No,'' McLain said levelly. ''I haven't forgotten.''

''The newspapers are going to have a field day at my expense. They'll roast me over a bed of hot coals.''

''When all's said and done, I'm the one that's responsible. You could always throw me to the wolves.''

Gilmore was quiet for a long time. ''I want you back here as soon as possible, Owen. Leave first thing in the morning.''

"I'd like another chance," McLain said. "After this, I know Chitto better than anybody. He wouldn't trick me again."

"Do you really believe you could raise another posse there?"

"I'd damn sure give it a try."

"Come on home, Owen," Gilmore said wearily. "We'll talk about it when you get here."

"You're sure that's the way you want it?"

"Yes, Owen, I'm quite sure."

The line went dead. McLain replaced the receiver on the hook, staring hollowly at the telephone. When he looked up, Prather was watching him from the door, arms folded across his chest. His mouth widened into a smirk.

"Sounds like you got yourself in a fix."

"You'd like that, wouldn't you, Prather?"

"Hell, it'd plumb make my day."

"Yeah, I guess it would," McLain observed. "You could tell folks the whole thing was my fault."

Prather grinned. "You might just get me reelected, McLain."

"While you're out campaigning, be sure to tell them about your yellow streak. Yard wide and a mile deep."

"Who're you calling yellow?"

"I don't see anybody else standing there."

McLain got to his feet. He walked to the door, forcing Prather to step out of his way, and moved into the outer office. He felt a tinge of shame, even regret, aware that he was trading cheap, schoolboy insults merely to salve his anger. He reminded himself that Ed Prather, the yellow-belly sheriff of Cherokee County, was not the problem. The problem was that he'd made a fool of himself, and let Chitto Starr slip away. He thought the wolves would be waiting when he got to Guthrie.

Outside the courthouse he stopped to roll himself a cigarette. As he sprinkled tobacco into the creased paper, he saw a Cherokee hurrying up the walkway. The man was short and stout, with streaks of gray through his dark hair. He paused on the steps.

"Aren't you Marshal McLain?"

"What can I do for you?"

"I'm Enos Weaver, editor of the *Cherokee Advocate*. If you don't mind, I'd like to ask you a few questions."

McLain struck a match on his thumbnail. He lit up in a haze of smoke, snuffed the match, and dropped it on the steps. "I suppose you want to know about Chitto Starr?"

"Well, yes, it's big news," Weaver said. "I was on my way to see you and Sheriff Prather. Do you have a moment?"

"Fire away."

"I understand you lost four men out of your posse. Could you tell me how it happened?"

"We were ambushed," McLain said. "Chitto caught us in a cross fire from three sides. He knows those mountains pretty good."

Weaver scribbled furiously on a pad he'd pulled from his pocket. "Wasn't Joe Blackbird your scout?"

"Yes."

"Blackbird knows the mountains quite well, himself. After all, he was in the Light Horse for many years. How was it he led you into an ambush?"

"Have you ever been on a manhunt, Mr. Weaver?"

"Well, no, I haven't. Why do you ask?"

"The man you're hunting has all the advantage. He can lay for you at every crook and turn, especially in wild country. You won't know it till he springs the trap."

''I see.'' Weaver made a note in his pad. ''So you're saying it wasn't Blackbird's fault?''

''That's exactly what I'm saying,'' McLain acknowledged. ''Blackbird caught on at the last minute, or we would've all been killed. Chitto's a cagey old bird.''

''You keep referring to him as Chitto. Isn't that unusual, calling a wanted man by his first name? It sounds like you admire him.''

McLain took a drag, exhaled smoke. ''I respect a man who's willing to stand and fight. Chitto Starr would've made a good general.''

''So you do admire him?''

''I probably would if he wasn't wanted for murder.''

Weaver gave him a crafty look. ''All of this killing was started by Starr's resistance to land allotments. How do you feel about that?''

''Guess he's got a point,'' McLain said. ''If I was a Cherokee, I'd likely feel the same way as Chitto. He figures his people got a raw deal.''

''Do you share that view?''

''Let's just say I wouldn't call it a square deal.''

Weaver cocked his head. ''That's a curious statement for a U.S. Marshal. Do you think the government was in the wrong—about the land allotments?''

''Didn't say that.'' McLain hesitated, aware that he'd spoken out of turn. ''You asked about my personal opinion. I'm not talking as a marshal.''

''Yes, of course, I understand.'' Weaver hastily switched topics. ''Did you inflict any casualties on the Nighthawks?''

''We killed two, and Joe Blackbird wounded Chitto.''

''Now that is news! How seriously was Starr wounded?''

''The Nighthawks pulled out, so we don't really know. But I can tell you he was shot.''

"What's the next step? Will you go after him again?"

"Chitto Starr will be brought to justice. You can quote me on that."

"Oh, indeed I will. Thank you for your time, Marshal."

"Always happy to talk with the press."

Weaver was still jotting notes. McLain went down the walkway, admonishing himself for speaking so freely. Too late, he was reminded of the advice of some ancient wise man: I have often regretted my speech, but never my silence. He thought he'd better learn to button his lip.

On the opposite side of the square he stopped by the doctor's office. Chester Rinehart was portly, somewhere in his late fifties, with the unflappable air of a physician who found few mysteries in life. He nodded pleasantly as McLain came through the door, jerking his chin toward a room just off the outer office. The wounded man was stretched out on an operating table, his leg neatly bandaged. He appeared to be asleep.

"'Evening, Doc," McLain said. "How's the patient?"

"Doing quite nicely," Rinehart replied. "I knocked him out with ether before I operated. Recovered a .44-.40 slug, somewhat the worse for wear."

"So he won't lose the leg?"

"Not much risk of that. Although I doubt he'll appreciate your concern. He had some unkind things to say about you, Marshal."

"Doesn't surprise me," McLain said. "I'm not the most popular man in Tahlequah tonight."

Rinehart pursed his mouth. "I daresay you're right, what with four men dead. Tragic thing."

"Doc, you hit the nail on the head. Tragic."

"Do you think Chitto Starr will be caught?"

"That's the safest bet in town. He's a walking dead man."

"What do you mean?"

"Think of him as a snowball in hell. Fact is, I'd give odds on the snowball."

"You're saying it's no longer a matter of dead or alive?"

"Just dead, Doc. Just dead."

McLain left the physician to ponder the pronouncement. Outside, he turned upstreet and walked toward the hotel. As he neared the corner, he saw Jane Tenkiller step from the doorway of a millinery shop. She greeted him with a wan smile.

"I've been waiting for you."

"Waiting for me?" McLain repeated. "How'd you know where I was?"

"I saw you go into Dr. Rinehart's."

"Are you keeping tabs on me, Mrs. Tenkiller?"

"Yes, I suppose," she admitted. "I thought you might need a friend."

McLain laughed wryly. "Word gets around fast."

"Have supper with me. I will cook you a steak."

"Way things are, that might ruin your reputation."

"You forget." She gave him a bold look. "I am the widow of a bank robber. I have no reputation to protect."

"Mrs. Tenkiller—"

"Call me Jane."

"All right, then, Jane. You're sure about this?"

"Why else would I be here?"

She took his arm. McLain was at once baffled and flattered. But she was an attractive woman, and he wasn't one to turn down an invitation. Nor would he question her reasons.

He thought Jane Tenkiller was reason enough.

Thirteen

M<small>C</small>LAIN rode into Guthrie on October 26. Under a midday sun the streets were wedged with traffic, automobiles and trucks jockeying for position with buggies and horse-drawn wagons. The incessant honking of horns assaulted his ears, and the exhaust fumes seared his lungs. He had forgotten how dirty the air smelled.

After four days on the trail, he was covered with grime. His first thought was to report to the office; but he just as quickly changed his mind. He wanted a bath and a change of clothes, and he figured Fred Gilmore could wait a while longer. The phone call from Tahlequah, and Gilmore's concern with the political repercussions, still left a bitter aftertaste. He was in no hurry to renew the discussion.

On Division Avenue he dismounted outside Munson's Livery Stable. The establishment was one of the few in Guthrie that still catered to livestock, and offered no repair services for automobiles. He led his horse through the wide doors and into a musty rainbow of odors: manure and saddle leather mixed with the scent of hay. The dim interior, and the rich smell of horses, was a welcome relief from the frenetic clamor on the street. George Munson, the owner, walked forward to greet him.

"Well, Owen," he said amiably. "Back from the Nations, huh?"

"Just rode in," McLain said, somewhat taken aback. "How'd you know where I was?"

"The newspapers haven't talked about nothing else the last couple of days. You and that Indian—Chitto Starr?—you made the headlines."

"What'd they have to say?"

Munson ducked his head. "Guess I should've kept my big mouth shut. Figured you'd seen the papers."

"Go ahead," McLain said, a cold feeling along his backbone. "What's the bad news?"

"Not my words, you understand? Only tellin' you what I read."

"Give it to me straight, George."

"Pretty rank stuff." Munson scuffed at the floor with his shoe. "They're sayin' you let this Starr escape, and got five or six lawmen killed to boot. Flat rubbed your nose in it, Owen."

McLain wasn't all that surprised. He'd suspected Gilmore might use him as a scapegoat and toss him to the wolves. Politics was a dirty game, with devil take the hindmost. "Anything else?" he asked. "Did the paper call for my resignation?"

"Worse'n that," Munson mumbled. "One of the editorials said you ought to be fired. More or less nailed your hide to the wall."

"Anything from Marshal Gilmore?"

"Now that you mention it, not too much. The paper said he wasn't one to make hasty judgments. Something about him waitin' on a full report."

McLain handed him the gelding's reins. "Thanks for the tipoff, George. Glad I came by here first."

"Hope it all works out, Owen."

"You'll likely read about it in the papers."

McLain walked uptown to his boardinghouse. He filled the tub in the bathroom at the end of the hall, and soaked away the trail dust. Then, after stropping his razor, he shaved and trimmed his mustache with thin-bladed scissors. All the while he was wondering why Gilmore hadn't said more to the newspapers. Something about it didn't ring true.

In his room, he changed into a clean shirt and twill trousers. After strapping on his gun belt, he pinned the deputy marshal's badge to the pocket of his shirt. Studying himself in the mirror, he pondered whether he would still be wearing a badge at the end of the day. On the way out the door he grabbed his hat and shrugged into a dark corduroy jacket. He was ready to meet the wolves.

Downtown, he crossed the intersection of Harrison and Second. He took the stairs to the upper floor of the International Building, and entered the office. When he came through the door, Bob Newton looked up from his desk with a glum expression. He rolled his eyes in warning, and motioned McLain to the private office at the rear of the room. His doleful manner spoke louder than words.

Gilmore was seated behind his desk. He greeted McLain with a perfunctory nod. "Have a seat, Owen," he said, gesturing to a chair. "When did you get in?"

"About an hour ago," McLain said, seating himself. "Took time to clean up and change clothes."

"Forgive me if I dispense with the amenities and go straight to the heart of the matter. We have a serious problem."

''I heard what's been in the newspapers. Sounds like they're after my scalp.''

''To be more precise, your badge.'' Gilmore seemed jittery, unable to keep his hands still. ''I've been under intense pressure from Washington to terminate your commission. So far, I've refused.''

McLain thought there was more to it. ''Doesn't that put you between a rock and a hard spot?''

''Far more than you might imagine. Particularly after your tactless statements to that newspaper.''

''What newspaper?''

''The *Cherokee Advocate*.'' Gilmore leaned forward, clearly agitated. ''The Guthrie *Statesman* reprinted the entire article. What in God's name possessed you, Owen?''

''Which statements?'' McLain said, confused. ''Are you talking about Chitto Starr?''

''That certainly didn't help. Especially after he'd just killed four of your men. But your little bombshell about the land allotments! That was—lunacy.''

''Oh.''

''Oh, indeed!'' Gilmore flung out his hands. ''You are a federal marshal, Owen. You can't criticize the policy of the U.S. government—in the newspapers!''

''I made a mistake,'' McLain said lamely. ''I told the editor those were my personal views. I never thought he'd print it.''

''Well, it certainly made a splash in Washington. I was all but ordered to fire you.''

''How'd you get around it?''

''I told them you are my Chief Deputy and the best lawman in Oklahoma. To put it charitably, they were less than impressed.''

''So what happened?''

''I then played my trump card. Actually, it was the

only card I had left. I assured them you would be of invaluable assistance in the forthcoming campaign against Chitto Starr.''

McLain looked quizzical. "What campaign?"

"The one that will be announced tomorrow," Gilmore said, with no great enthusiasm. "Washington has taken the matter out of our hands. The governor mobilized the National Guard."

"The National Guard?" McLain said, dumbfounded. "To catch a dozen Indians?"

Gilmore nodded. "The Third Battalion of the First Oklahoma Cavalry. Under the command of Colonel Raymond Drummond."

"That's the nuttiest thing I ever heard. How the hell am I supposed to *assist* the cavalry?"

"The military places great stock in intelligence about the enemy. I sold them on the fact that you know more about Chitto Starr than any man alive. You are to brief Colonel Drummond on the disposition and tactics of the renegades—and in the process, save your job."

"When am I supposed to brief him?"

Gilmore got on the telephone. A moment later he was connected with the governor's office. "This is U.S. Marshal Gilmore," he said. "Please advise the governor I am on my way over with Deputy McLain. Thank you."

McLain followed him out the door. As they went through the duty room, McLain shook his head. "This takes the cake for stupid."

Gilmore laughed. "Wait till you meet Colonel Drummond."

Governor Charles Haskell was an imposing figure. He was solidly built, with an iron handshake and a commanding presence. By contrast, Colonel Raymond

Drummond was heavyset, on the sundown side of forty, with a paunch that strained the buttons on his crisp blue uniform. He looked like an overweight bandleader.

After a round of introductions, the governor got them seated at a conference table that overlooked the capitol grounds. His manner was cordial, but McLain detected a sense of unease with the situation. He seemed strung too tight, his features creased with deep-set worry lines. His gaze settled on McLain.

"Oklahoma is in crisis," he said in an orotund voice. "Has Marshal Gilmore explained the severity of our problem?"

"Just that you've called out the National Guard."

"Your unfortunate experience with Chitto Starr has inflamed the Five Civilized Tribes. We are on the verge of rebellion."

"First I've heard of that," McLain said. "What kind of rebellion, Governor?"

"A general uprising!" Haskell slapped the table with the flat of his hand. "This renegade band—what is it, the Nighthawks?—has shown the other tribes that the law can be broken, ignored. By armed force!"

"That's not exactly the case, Governor. We drove them into the mountains, wounded Chitto, and killed two of his men. They're on the run."

"At what price?" Haskell demanded. "Correct me if I'm wrong, but I believe six peace officers have been killed. To the Indians, that says the law can be flaunted, the land allotments overturned—perhaps a restoration of tribal law." He paused, fists clenched. "We are facing anarchy."

McLain appeared skeptical. "Have there been any incidents with the other tribes?"

"Not yet." Haskell said. "However, we are aware of a full-blood organization called the Four Mothers Society. We understand that it extends throughout all the tribes.''

"Four Mothers?'' McLain repeated. "That's a new one on me.''

"No doubt some arcane Indian mumbo jumbo. Our sources tell us that full-bloods are being actively recruited, and the membership already numbers in the hundreds. Perhaps thousands.''

"And they're talking rebellion?''

"Indeed!'' Haskell trumpeted. "All it requires is a leader to ignite an uprising across the whole of old Indian Territory. Chitto Starr is that man.''

"Maybe so,'' McLain said thoughtfully. "What do you want from me, Governor?''

"Information,'' Haskell informed him. "I have appointed Colonel Drummond to head the expedition. He needs to know anything you can tell him about Starr. Anything at all.''

"I'm glad to help however I can.''

"Well, then—'' The governor turned to Drummond. "Colonel, you're the military man here. Why don't you take over?''

"Very well.''

Drummond leaned forward, fleshy jowls spilling over his collar. He unrolled a map of eastern Oklahoma and spread it across the table. He nodded brusquely to McLain.

"Show me where you last made contact with Starr.''

"Here.'' McLain pointed to a spot on the map. "We saw him retreating over Jackson Mountain.''

"Starr was retreating?'' Drummond said, peering across the table. "I was given to understand that he all but decimated your posse. Why would he retreat?''

"I don't know,'' McLain admitted. "Maybe because he was wounded.''

"Do you have direct knowledge that he was seriously wounded?"

"Colonel, I know he was shot. That's about it."

"Well, no matter." Drummond rapped the map. "What was his line of withdrawal? Where would he be now?"

"Anywhere," McLain said. "That's raw wilderness out there. He could have headed in any direction."

"You're not exactly a fount of information, Mr. McLain. Do you know anything worthwhile?"

McLain flushed, stung by the sarcasm. "I've heard that he has a stronghold out in those mountains somewhere. But I don't know that for a fact, either."

Drummond heaved an exasperated sigh. "Facts are what I need, not supposition. How do you expect me to locate Starr?"

"For openers," McLain said tightly, "you ought to hire Joe Blackbird. He was my scout and he knows those mountains. He knows Chitto Starr, too."

"A scout who led you into an ambush? Not much of a recommendation, Mr. McLain."

"You've got it bassackwards, Colonel. Joe Blackbird's the only reason I'm here talking to you today. He saved our butts."

"I'm curious," Drummond said haughtily. "You were quoted in the newspaper as saying you have respect for Starr. Why is that?"

"Starr earned my respect," McLain noted. "He's smart, and he's a damn fine tactician. He knows when and where to fight."

"I rather doubt he'll be much of a problem. He has what, twelve or fourteen men? Hardly an imposing force."

"You're wrong there, Colonel. He's a hit-and-run fighter. He picks his spots."

"Does he?" Drummond's voice was laced with contempt. "The Third Battalion, which I command, has two hundred horse troopers, Mr. McLain. I think we can accommodate Starr and his Nighthawks."

McLain wagged his head. "You keep thinkin' like that and you'll get a lot of men killed. Chitto Starr will eat you piecemeal."

"Spoken by a man fresh from defeat. You have a high opinion of yourself, Mr. McLain."

"Yeah, but I'm a piker compared to you, Colonel."

Drummond's features went beet red. Before he could respond, Governor Haskell intervened. "I'm disappointed in you, McLain. I was led to believe you were willing to lend assistance."

"I have," McLain said flatly. "I gave your military wonder the best advice he'll ever get. Hire Joe Blackbird."

"Let me be blunt," Haskell snapped. "I don't appreciate your pugnacious attitude."

"Governor, you wanted honest advice and that's what you got. Underestimate Chitto Starr, and he'll make monkeys out of you and the National Guard. Guaranteed."

The meeting ended on that note. Governor Haskell dismissed them with an abrupt command, and they got to their feet in strained silence. Fred Gilmore could think of nothing to say.

Drummond was still glaring at McLain as they went out the door.

Fourteen

Gilmore looked like he could spit nails. He led the way down the capitol steps and strode angrily along Oklahoma Avenue. McLain kept pace, convinced too late that honesty was not always a virtue. He wished he'd thought of it back in the governor's office.

A gust of wind whipped down the street, and McLain tugged his hat tighter. He knew he might lose his badge by the time they reached the office, but he could think of nothing to redeem himself. They walked along in turgid silence, Gilmore staring straight ahead, his eyes distant. When they turned onto Harrison Avenue, McLain saw his only chance of easing the tension. He pointed to the Bluebell Café.

"How about a cup of coffee?" he said. "Today's my day to treat."

"Good idea," Gilmore agreed. "We need to have a talk, anyway."

The words somehow struck McLain as ominous in tone. The café was empty after the noon-hour rush, and they seated themselves at a table beside the window. A waitress took their order, and McLain rolled himself a smoke, wondering what he could say in his own defense. Gilmore fired up a cigar as the waitress returned with china mugs of coffee. He snuffed the match with a quick gesture.

"Let me ask you something," he said through a cloud of smoke. "You insulted the governor. You went out of your way to insult Drummond. Where the hell was your head?"

McLain stirred sugar into his coffee. "The trouble was, I told them the truth. They didn't like what they heard."

"Did it occur to you to soft-soap it a little? Try to play along to get along?"

"Drummond's the one that started it. Talk about a pompous sonovabitch. He got me hot, that's all."

"No, that's not all," Gilmore announced. "You're the one with your neck on the chopping block. You owed it to yourself to be more diplomatic."

"You're right," McLain conceded. "I owed it to you, too, and I let you down. Diplomacy never was my strong suit."

Gilmore tapped an ash off his cigar. "After this, I may not be able to save your job. You burned a lot of bridges today."

"Well, you'd have to fire me. I sure as hell won't quit."

"You just better hope the governor doesn't file a formal complaint. If he does, I'll have no choice in the matter."

McLain thought that sounded like a reprieve of sorts. He sipped coffee and took a drag on his cigarette, warning himself not to push it any further. He moved on to safer ground.

''Did you buy what the governor said about an uprising in the tribes?''

Gilmore nodded. ''That's been a powder keg since statehood. Lots of Indians believe we stole their land.''

''Well, he's right about one thing,'' McLain said. ''Chitto Starr could be the spark that sets it off. He'll fight to the bitter end.''

''You really believe Starr will give Drummond trouble?''

''I'd bet a bundle on it. Who is Drummond, anyway? I never heard of him.''

''Raymond Drummond,'' Gilmore said with a derisive look. ''He's a lawyer from Oklahoma City. A member of the governor's Council on Industrial Development.''

''So they're pals?'' McLain asked. ''The governor and Drummond?''

''I think it's more a matter of *quid pro quo*. One hand washes the other.''

''What's Drummond's military background?''

''Spanish-American War,'' Gilmore said, deadpan. ''Captain with the Quartermaster Corps.''

''Quartermaster?'' McLain echoed. ''He wasn't a line officer?''

''To my knowledge, Raymond Drummond never heard a shot fired in anger. I understand he wrangled a commission in the Quartermaster Corps just to say he served. Patriotism apparently has its limits.''

''How the hell'd he get to be a colonel in the cavalry?''

''Politics,'' Gilmore said simply. ''Drummond was instrumental in delivering the vote for the governor in Oklahoma County. Part of the payback was an appointment to the National Guard.''

McLain decided to skirt the issue of politics. Gilmore

was formerly an influential businessman from Lawton, with a retail background. He had worked diligently as co-chairman of the Oklahoma Republican Party to place William Howard Taft in the White House. His payback was the position of U.S. Marshal. *Quid pro quo*.

"Helluva note," McLain said at length. "A quarter-master captain promoted to colonel of the cavalry. I'd hate to be in Drummond's outfit."

"Oh?" Gilmore inquired. "Why do you say that?"

"Well, he's never been a line officer. What's he know about tactics, or commanding men in battle? Not much would be my guess."

"I suspect your guess would be pretty accurate. At best, he might have read a book on troop deployment."

"Yeah, maybe." McLain stubbed out his cigarette. "Flat lot of good that'll do him when he runs across the Nighthawks. He's in for a big surprise."

"You really believe that?" Gilmore said. "A battalion against a handful of renegades sounds like overwhelming odds. Even Drummond ought to be able to pull that off."

"Leadership means lots more than numbers. Chitto Starr will put him through a meat grinder."

"You have a great deal of respect for Starr, don't you?"

"So will Drummond before he's through."

After finishing their coffee, they walked over to the office. Bob Newton looked up from the telephone when they came through the door, and placed his hand over the mouthpiece. He motioned urgently to Gilmore.

"Ed Prather's on the line, and he's fit to be tied. He won't talk to anybody but you."

"Have him hang on," Gilmore said. "I'll take it in my office."

"Sheriff?" Newton said, unclamping his hand from

the mouthpiece. "Marshal Gilmore just walked in. He'll be with you in a second."

McLain wondered if there was news of Chitto Starr. He tagged along, waiting in the doorway as the marshal took a seat behind his desk. Gilmore lifted the receiver off the hook.

"This is Fred Gilmore," he said. "What can I do for you, Sheriff?"

A squawking sound, loud and testy, came over the line. Gilmore's expression darkened. "When did this happen?"

The receiver to his ear, he listened, nodding. "And he was definitely identified?"

A moment passed, the squawking sound even louder, and he nodded again. "I'll have someone there as quickly as possible." He paused, listening, his features set in a frown. "Who I send is my business, Sheriff. I'll let you know."

Gilmore replaced the receiver on the hook. He glanced up at McLain. "Are you familiar with a town called Proctor?"

"Farm town," McLain remarked. "About ten miles east of Tahlequah."

"Frank Starr robbed the bank there this afternoon."

"Well, I'll be damned. That's a new one for him."

"How do you mean?"

"Frank always steered clear of homeground. He's never pulled a job in Cherokee County before."

"Strange," Gilmore said thoughtfully. "What do you make of it?"

"Awful coincidental," McLain observed. "Chitto's off in those mountains south of Proctor. And so's the stronghold I told you about. Maybe Frank plans to meet him there."

"You know the Starrs better than anyone, Owen. I'm assigning you to the case."

"Won't that put you out on a limb?"

"Let me worry about Washington," Gilmore said. "You've got a chance to wipe the slate clean. Catch Frank and all will be forgiven. But if you don't . . ."

"I'll be out of a job."

"I suspect we both might be, Owen."

McLain nodded soberly. "I'm obliged for the chance. You won't regret it."

"Just bring me Frank Starr."

"You can count on it."

McLain turned out of the doorway. Gilmore leaned back in his chair, his fingers steepled into a tent. He considered whether he'd made a mistake, and just as quickly discarded the thought. From the look on McLain's face, he knew it was the right decision.

Frank Starr was as good as dead.

That evening McLain called for Amy shortly after dark. He had phoned that afternoon, and made a date to take her to the motion pictures. Alice Markham answered the door, apologizing for her daughter, who was still upstairs getting ready. She invited him to wait in the parlor.

John Markham rose from his chair as they entered the room. A merry blaze was dancing in the fireplace, but his mood was hardly cheery. He exchanged a handshake, motioning to the sofa, and McLain got himself seated. Alice sat down beside him, collecting her yarn and crochet hook, and resumed work on a sweater. A moment slipped past in uncomfortable silence.

"Well—" Markham cleared his throat. "I've been reading about you in the *Statesman*. Any new developments?"

"News of a sort," McLain said. "The governor called out the National Guard. A cavalry battalion's been ordered into the field against Chitto Starr."

"Yes, the rumor's been around town a few days now. No secrets at the capitol building. What about you?"

"I've been reassigned to Frank Starr. He robbed a bank over in Cherokee County today."

Markham looked surprised. "So you still have a job?"

"No worries there," McLain said, with a forced grin. "Marshal Gilmore doesn't pay much attention to the newspapers. Half of what they print is hogwash."

"Even if half were true, it sounded like you were in hot water. We thought you might be . . ."

"Not much chance they'd fire the Chief Deputy. You and Mrs. Markham can rest easy. I'm still gainfully employed."

Markham's expression was more disappointed than relieved. Before he could respond, Amy appeared in the doorway, radiant in a navy-blue dress with white piping at the collar and sleeves. Her hair shone, brushing her shoulders, and her eyes were alight with happiness. She kissed McLain on the cheek, bidding her parents good night, and led him out of the parlor. In the foyer, he helped her on with her coat.

Outside, the evening was crisp and frosty. She hugged his arm as they turned downtown. "Was father interrogating you about your job?"

"Well, nothing too strenuous. He just wanted to make sure I was still a prospective son-in-law."

"And what did you tell him?"

"Told him I'd take care of you in style."

She laughed gaily. "Honestly, Owen, you're just awful!"

"Yeah, I'm a regular card. Think I'll go into vaude-ville."

The Biograph Theater was Guthrie's latest symbol of the modern age. The marvel of motion pictures held audiences enthralled, and tonight's presentation drew a packed house. Bronco Billy Anderson, a former stage actor, played the lead role in *The Great Train Robbery*. A silent film, but nonetheless gripping, the action was accompanied by the frenzied pounding of an upright piano. The audience applauded the derring-do all the more because it was a western setting, with a timely theme. They knew a good deal about train robbers in Oklahoma.

After the motion picture, McLain took Amy to the Bon Ton Confectionery Shop for a treat. Apart from assorted candies, the Bon Ton was famous for its pastry and baked goods. McLain ordered a wedge of chocolate cake, and Amy, conscious of her figure, settled for an apple tart. Though McLain devoured his cake, she slowly became aware that his mood had changed. He was quieter than before, almost as if he was brooding on something. She gave him an inquisitive look.

"Penny for your thoughts."

"Nothing much," McLain said, licking the last of the chocolate off his fork. "Guess I was thinking about that picture show."

She stirred her coffee. "And?"

"Well, first, it reminded me I have to go after Frank Starr. But then, I got to thinking about Chitto and that ambush. You know, the way things went wrong."

"Do you blame yourself?"

"Nobody else to blame," McLain said soberly. "I was the one that took those men in there. They trusted me."

The words were less revealing than his downcast

manner. She saw now that he faulted himself for the
men killed, and with it came a lingering sense of guilt.
She was happy that he would talk of it, share the burden.
But absolution came from within, and seldom quickly.
She wasn't sure what to say.

"Nobody's perfect, Owen. You shouldn't let yourself
be weighed down by hindsight. You did what you
thought was right at the time."

"That's what I keep tellin' myself. Maybe it'll sink
in one of these days."

"I'm sure it will." She reached across the table,
squeezed his hand. "Things have a way of working out.
You'll see."

The touch of her hand brought another memory.
McLain remembered Jane Tenkiller touching him in the
same way, the night she had cooked him a steak. She
had smiled, staring across the table, invitation in her
eyes. Though he'd been tempted, he had politely refused
the offer, taking his leave shortly afterward. But now,
looking at Amy, he felt a stab of guilt. He'd wanted to
take Jane Tenkiller to bed.

"How about a walk?" he said, dropping bills on the
table. "We'll do a little window shopping and then head
on home. Maybe your folks will have turned in for the
night."

She gave him a teasing smile. "What's on your mind,
Mr. McLain?"

"Nothing a dark room and a cozy fire won't cure."

Fifteen

Joseph Lynch sat beneath a tree on Beevale Mountain. The sun was high, and farther back in the woods he could hear the drone of conversation as men went about their camp chores. But he stared out into space, brooding and thoughtful, his mind on other things. He contemplated the burden of leadership.

The Nighthawks had been camped on Beevale Mountain for a week. Lynch had selected a site on a narrow plateau, not quite halfway up the forward slope. There was adequate graze for the horses, and the spot afforded a vantage point overlooking Sallisaw Creek. His main concern was to occupy high ground, a good defensive position in the event they were attacked. He could not yet order a withdrawal deeper into the mountains.

In his view, Chitto was in no condition to be moved. The Nighthawk leader was improved, for his fever had broken their second day on Beevale Mountain. But he was weak, unable to stand, much less mount a horse, and in constant pain. His wound was healing poorly, despite daily treatment with herbal powders from the medicine bag. Still, he was lucid, clearheaded and stubborn, determined to reach the stronghold at Doublehead Mountain. He refused to listen to reason.

Lynch nonetheless prevailed in their arguments. Over the past several days he had asserted himself, equally adamant that they would not move on until Chitto could ride a horse. The men supported him with their silence, for they were no less concerned that Chitto's condition would worsen if he were moved. The men's silence was perhaps more persuasive than Lynch's rigid insistence that the Nighthawks remain camped at Beevale Mountain. Chitto wisely refrained from issuing an order that might be disobeyed. He knew the men were solidly behind Lynch.

For all that, Lynch never overstepped himself. No one doubted that the white lawmen would again take their trail, and he consulted with Chitto on matters of security. Before dawn every morning one of the Nighthawks was assigned to scout the ravine leading toward Gitting Down Mountain. Lynch and Chitto agreed that any pursuit would be along the line of their retreat from the fight at Nigger Jake Hollow. With a week gone by, the *aniyonega* were likely already in the field, tracking them even now. Their scout would give them adequate warning, and they would react as the situation developed. Until then, there was little to do but wait.

On other matters Lynch followed his own counsel. He was convinced that Chitto's condition was grave, and required medical care. Since he couldn't get Chitto to a doctor, he decided to bring a doctor to Chitto. Secretly, four days ago, he had sent Doak Threepersons to fetch Chitto's son, Will. He knew Chitto would have scotched the idea, but from his standpoint, the choice was clear. There was no certainty that Chitto would survive, and though he was chilled by the thought, he felt obligated to unite father and son. Were the situation reversed, he knew Chitto would have done the same for him. So he enlisted the Nighthawks in his scheme, and swore them to secrecy.

The plan was that Threepersons would spirit Will Starr out of Tahlequah at night. From there they would travel to Welling, a small farm town southeast of Tahlequah. The local doctor, Edward Keeler, was married to a Cherokee woman, and sympathetic to the Nighthawks' cause. There was no question as to his discretion, and little doubt that he would agree to help. Whatever small risk was entailed, Lynch was willing to take the gamble. Five days ago, when it became apparent they couldn't move on, he'd had no choice but to bury Eli Posey and Henry Ketch, the men killed at Nigger Jake Hollow. The memory was still fresh in his mind, and all the more reason to summon a doctor. He had no intention of burying Chitto.

Early that afternoon Lynch spotted movement at the mouth of the ravine. As he watched, Threepersons led Will Starr and Dr. Edward Keeler across the creek. He glanced back into camp and saw that Chitto was asleep, resting comfortably on a bed of blankets. Motioning the Nighthawks to silence, he made his way through the trees to the bottom of the mountain. He emerged from the woods as Threepersons and the two men dismounted from their horses. He greeted them with a warm smile.

"Will. Dr. Keeler." He shook their hands. "I am glad you are here."

Will gave him an anxious look. "How is my father?"

"Not good. We have done our best, but his wound is not healing. I thought I'd better send for you."

"Do you think he might . . ."

Will couldn't bring himself to say the word. "Your father's a tough man," Lynch said, glancing at the physician. "Maybe Dr. Keeler can tell us more."

Keeler was slim, in his early forties, with deep-set eyes and a droopy mustache. "I'll do whatever I can," he said. "Do I understand correctly that his shoulder was broken?"

"Not just broken," Lynch said uneasily. "The bullet blew it apart."

"You're right, that doesn't sound good. Let's have a look."

Lynch led them up the mountain. Threepersons followed with the horses, and a few minutes later they entered the camp. The commotion awoke Chitto, and his eyes fluttered open, disoriented a moment. His senses gradually returned, and he stared at his son in amazement. His voice was weak.

"Will," he said, blinking with confusion. "Where did you come from?"

"Joseph sent for us," Will said, kneeling at his side. "You remember Dr. Keeler, don't you?"

"Yes, I remember," Chitto said, licking his lips. "Been a long time, Doctor."

"A year or more." Keeler knelt down, placing his black bag on the ground. "Sorry it has to be under these circumstances."

Chitto glanced up at Lynch. "You are a sly one, Joseph. Why didn't you ask me about this?"

Lynch shrugged. "I knew you would not agree. You are too stubborn for your own good."

"So you keep telling me."

"Well, now that I'm here," Keeler said, moving closer. "Suppose I have a look at the problem."

"I feel fine," Chitto said grumpily. "You rode a long way for nothing."

"Let me be the judge of that."

Keeler lifted the blanket. When he peeled back the

bandage, he saw the muscles knot in Chitto's jaw. He took cotton wool and a small bottle of antiseptic from his bag, and began sponging away dried layers of herbal powder. Once the surface area was clean, he examined the wound at length. The shoulder was discolored, inflamed around the wound itself, tiny splinters of bone protruding from the bullet hole. He sat back on his haunches.

"I'll be frank," he said solemnly. "You need an operation, and very quickly, too. There's no alternative."

Chitto nodded. "Go ahead and operate."

"I'm just a country doctor. I wouldn't dare attempt anything that complicated. Particularly out here in the woods."

"Somebody has to do it," Will broke in. "You said there's no alternative."

"That's correct," Keeler replied. "I recommend Dr. Rinehart, in Tahlequah. He's a fine surgeon."

"No!" Chitto interrupted harshly. "You are not taking me back to Tahlequah."

Keeler frowned. "Herbal remedies aren't the answer. Infection has already set in, and it will only get worse." He paused, shook his head. "Without an operation, you have a small chance of recovery. Even if it somehow mended, you'd be crippled for life."

"Then I'll be crippled," Chitto said shortly. "I will not be captured by the *aniyonega* and hung by my neck. That is no way for a man to die."

"Father, listen to him," Will pleaded. "He's saying you have no choice. You must have an operation."

"You listen to me, my son. I am a free man, and I choose my own path. I will not be taken back to Tahlequah."

A leaden silence settled over the camp. The Nighthawks exchanged worried glances, and tried to pretend they hadn't overheard. Will shot Lynch a look of desperate appeal, but Lynch lowered his gaze. Finally, when no one spoke, Chitto motioned with his good arm. He nodded to Keeler.

"You are a friend to come all this way. Treat me as best you can and leave it in the hands of the spirits. I will not die."

"Joseph was right about you, Chitto. You are a stubborn man."

Keeler set to work. With a pair of tweezers, he extracted slivers of bone from the wound, delicately probing the puckered flesh. Chitto winced, his eyes bright with pain, and tried to distract himself. He looked at Will.

"Tell me the news," he said. "Have you heard anything of what the white lawmen plan?"

"Lawmen are no longer involved," Will told him. "Governor Haskell has called out the National Guard. A battalion of cavalry, according to the newspaper."

"A battalion?" Chitto repeated, taken aback. "To fight our small band?"

"The revolt has spread to the other tribes. The governor means to make an example of the Nighthawks."

"Are you talking about the land allotments?"

Will nodded. "People from the other tribes, and many Cherokees, are returning their land certificates to the government. Your victories over the white lawmen gave them courage."

"I knew it!" Chitto said, ignoring the doctor digging at his shoulder. "Have any of them formed organizations—like the Nighthawks?"

"There is now something called the Four Mothers Society. I understand it is a resistance movement among all the tribes. People are joining by the hundreds."

"Do you hear that, Joseph?" Chitto craned his neck

to look at Lynch. ''A resistance movement throughout all the Nations. Did I not tell you my vision was powerful?''

''Yes, and it came true,'' Lynch said, beaming a wide grin. ''We no longer fight alone. Just as you foretold.''

A murmur of excitement rippled through the Nighthawks. They began talking among themselves with great animation, their spirits suddenly restored. None had doubted Chitto's vision, but now it was real, a revolt among all the tribes. Their long struggle now seemed worthwhile, and they took renewed pride in themselves as warriors. Tales would be told about their exploits.

''Think of it,'' Chitto said, marveling to himself. ''A battalion of cavalry ordered into the field against the Nighthawks. We have taught fear to the *aniyonega*.''

''Hold still,'' Keeler said abruptly. ''I can't work when you're jiggling around. You'll start bleeding again.''

''With news like this, I have blood to spare. All I need.''

''A man in your condition has none to spare. Hold still.''

Keeler swabbed the wound with antiseptic. He then applied a fresh bandage and tied it off. Finished, he studied the loops of rope that bound Chitto's left arm. His expression was quizzical.

''Who thought this up?''

''That was me,'' Lynch admitted. ''Like you said, he's hard to hold still.''

''Good idea,'' Keeler observed. ''Keeps that shoulder immobilized to the extent possible. Seems to work.''

''How should I tend him after you're gone?''

Keeler and Lynch walked toward the fire, discussing treatment. Chitto was still buoyed by the news, vigor evident in his features. Will stared off into the woods a moment, then looked at his father. His eyes filled with emotion.

"I want to be with you when the soldiers come."

"What?" Chitto said, his reverie broken. "I'm sorry, my mind was elsewhere."

"The soldiers will come," Will repeated. "Here or somewhere else, they will find you. I want to fight beside you when it happens."

"You want to join the Nighthawks?"

"Yes."

Chitto searched his eyes. "You have never agreed with our methods, the use of force. Why would you join now?"

"You are my father," Will said simply. "My place is beside you."

"From the time you were a small boy you could never deceive me. Tell me the truth now. Why do you want to join?"

Will averted his gaze. "I think this will be your last fight. The soldiers are many and the Nighthawks are few. I belong with you."

Chitto felt a thick lump in his throat. He took a moment to compose himself. "You honor me more than I deserve, my son. But you have made another life for yourself. You must travel your own road."

"A man can change his mind. I choose your road."

"You would stay because of me, and I will not allow it. This is not your fight."

"That is for me to decide," Will persisted. "I will make it my fight."

"Hear me," Chitto said in a strong voice. "You will honor my wishes in this matter. Tomorrow, you must return to Tahlequah."

"You would enlist another Cherokee, any Cherokee! Why not me?"

"We will speak of this no more. Your place is not with the Nighthawks. Let that be an end to it."

The words were a command. Will saw that he could not win the argument. Nor could he disobey. "I will do as you say, but I still don't agree. My place is with you."

"I am tired," Chitto said, suddenly sapped of energy. "Let me rest awhile. We will talk later."

Their eyes met in silent communion, a final resolution. Then Will nodded, climbing to his feet, and joined the others at the fire. Chitto stared up into the sky, never more proud of his son than at that moment. He knew the boy wanted to stay with him, perhaps even die with him. But he would not permit it, for he had spoken the truth. This was not Will's fight.

Chitto was reminded that all men were mortal. History taught many lessons to those who were willing to learn from the past. One of the foremost was that the leader of a revolt often ended up a martyr to the cause. So in that respect, his son might well have a point. A telling point.

The cavalry battalion would find him, sooner if not later. For he would not run before superior numbers, or hide to await another day. Yet he had some inner sense that it would be his last fight, and that saddened him. Saddened him deeply.

He thought he would never see Will again.

Sixteen

A noonday sun filtered through trees gone lurid with autumn. Overhead a hawk floated past on smothered wings, and settled high on a stout limb not far from the road. Head cocked in a fierce glare, it looked down upon the intruders.

The Third Battalion was four days out of Guthrie. There were four companies, fifty troopers to a company, strung out along the road. The order of march was Company A through Company D, with guidon bearers, their pennants fluttering in the wind, positioned behind the troop commanders. The jangle of saddle gear echoed along the column.

Trucks and cars whizzing past laid down a furry coat of dust. The men rode in a column of twos, stretching almost a fifth of a mile from front to rear. Their uniforms were olive drab, with black, high-topped boots and wool greatcoats. They were caked with grime, stiff from four days in the saddle, and few of them engaged in the banter common to horse soldiers. There was little merriment in the Third Battalion.

Colonel Raymond Drummond was mounted on a bloodbay stallion that was too much horse for the man. He sat his saddle like a stone gargoyle, bouncing and thumping, his butt galled raw from the pounding of flesh against leather. On the first day out, the troopers saw right away that he was nothing of a horseman, hardly able to control his fiery mount. The stallion seemed to them all part of the lordly trappings of a lawyer playing at being a soldier. He was barely able to stay in the saddle.

McLain rode out front of the column. Through the governor, he had been ordered to accompany the battalion as far as Tahlequah. There he was to ensure that Drummond got off on good footing with Chief W. C. Rogers and Major David Lipe, leading figures in the Cherokee tribe. From all he could deduce, the governor had reconsidered, and arrived at the conclusion that his field commander needed help in the forthcoming campaign. Drummond was to enlist the cooperation of influential Cherokees.

For his part, McLain thought it was politics as usual. The mission was to capture or kill Chitto Starr, and stem the burgeoning revolt within the tribes. But the presence of the Third Battalion would be used to reinforce the governor's benevolent attitude toward Indians who behaved themselves. Chief Rogers and David Lipe would be held up as shining examples, and the message would go out. Those who wanted to prosper in the white man's world would embrace the notion of land allotments. Forever.

The governor's reassessment of things seemed to McLain somewhat misguided. For four days he had avoided Drummond, holding conversation to a minimum, and at night, camping off away from the troops. But he had watched the Third's commander at work, and quickly drawn some conclusions of his own. Drummond was arrogant, with an inflated opinion of himself, and operated under the belief that it took a martinet to run a military outfit properly. He enforced rigid discipline, harsh in his dealings with the company commanders and the men. His attitude was that of a slavemaster wielding a cat-o'-nine-tails.

To McLain, it was clear that Drummond had no understanding of command. His military experience was limited to desk work, and yet he strutted and postured like some bogus incarnation of Napoleon. McLain had spent four years in the cavalry himself, and he had served under sergeants, as well as officers, who grasped the cardinal rule of leadership. Soldiers responded to evenhanded discipline, strict so long as it was fair, but never to the lash. He had every confidence that Drummond's overbearing manner would offend, perhaps alienate, the Cherokee leaders. He was even more certain that the men of the Third Battalion considered Drummond a lard-assed imposter.

The men themselves were only slightly better. In McLain's view, they were ill-trained and lacked the cohesive spirit of a crack military outfit. Some of the noncoms were veterans of the Spanish-American War; but for the most part, the men were a mix of farm boys, shop clerks, and laborers. Few of them had been tested in battle, and their training consisted of two-week stints once a year. They served in the National Guard for the pay, extra spending money over their day jobs. None of them had ever expected to be called into the field.

As the column approached Tahlequah, McLain marked the date at October 31. He realized it was Halloween Eve, and thought it a note of unintended irony. There were ghosts and goblins in the Third Battalion's future, he wryly told himself, otherwise known as the

Nighthawks. Four days on the road had merely served to reinforce his first impression of Colonel Raymond Drummond. The one he'd formed during their acrimonious meeting in the governor's office. Chitto Starr would run the Third ragged.

A mile or so outside town Drummond ordered the battalion into bivouac. The companies wheeled off the road, into a large, open field beside a stream. Drummond sat his horse, overseeing the operation, his eyes darting here and there from beneath a wide-brimmed campaign hat. He was a stickler for by-the-book encampment, with companies aligned in straight, orderly rows. His adjutant, Lieutenant Perry Norton, was sent to harry any troop commander whose lines deviated from the geometric pattern. An accountant by trade, Norton was young, freckle-faced, and impressionable. He tried to ape Drummond's stern demeanor.

The bivouac slowly took shape. McLain waited on the road, watching with no great interest. After a while, he saw Drummond wave imperiously to his aide, snapping orders. Then, leaving Norton to supervise matters, Drummond reined his horse back toward the road. Even at a walk, he jounced in the saddle like a rubber ball. He nodded curtly to McLain.

"The day grows long, Mr. McLain. Let's be about our business."

"Sooner the better, Colonel."

Drummond took the road east into town. McLain fell in beside him, without further attempt at conversation. "Your ordeal is practically over," Drummond said after several moments of silence. "You've made it all too clear that you can't wait to be on your way."

"Guess I'm pretty transparent," McLain said dryly. "You see right through me, Colonel."

"You don't like me much, do you, McLain?"

"I'm not paid to like you."

Drummond pursed his mouth. "Do I detect a note of resentment?"

"Don't follow you," McLain said. "What's to resent?"

"The fact that I shall succeed where you—how shall I say it?—where you suffered considerable ignominy. A touch of sour grapes would be understandable."

"The Good Book says 'pride goeth before the fall.' Watch your step or Chitto Starr will whittle you down to size."

"I think not," Drummond said indignantly. "Although I have the distinct impression you'll be pulling for Starr. Am I correct, Mr. McLain?"

"I think not," McLain said, imitating his tone of voice. "You're not exactly my cup of tea, Colonel. All the same, I'm in your corner."

"How commendable."

"Yeah, that's me, commendable."

"Your merits aside—" Drummond made a dismissive gesture. "Tell me about these Cherokees we're to see."

The governor had arranged the meeting. Chief W. C. Rogers, who lived outside Tahlequah, was to meet them at Major David Lipe's office. The Cherokee leaders had readily agreed to the governor's request.

"I've never met Chief Rogers," McLain said. "I suspect he'll be cooperative, though."

"On what do you base that assessment?"

"Well, there at the end, he supported joint statehood and the land allotments. Guess he saw the handwriting on the wall."

"A wise man, I daresay." Drummond shifted in the saddle, trying to ease his sore rump. "Let me ask you something, Mr. McLain, just a matter of personal curi-

)sity. Do you really believe we stole the land from the Indians?''

McLain shot him a sideways glance. "That sounds like a loaded question, Colonel. Why do you ask?''

"Newspapers often misquote a man. Frankly, I couldn't imagine you saying anything so . . . intemperate.''

"What you started to say was, 'so stupid.' I've got to admit, I felt pretty damn dumb when it was printed.''

"So it's true, then?''

"That we stole the land?''

"Yes.''

"Colonel, I just got a sudden case of lockjaw. What's next on your list?''

Drummond seemed amused. "Tell me about Major Lipe.''

"A timber broker,'' McLain said. "Used to be head of the Light Horse Police. He's a man who bends with the wind.''

"A man of compromise, is that it?''

"Yeah, when it's to his favor.''

"You say that as though you disapprove. Are you offended by compromise, Mr. McLain?''

"Guess it all depends on whose ox gets gored.''

"Let's understand one another,'' Drummond said acidly. "You perform the introductions and I will conduct the meeting. Keep your opinions to yourself. Is that clear?''

"Don't worry about it,'' McLain said. "Chitto's your problem, and welcome to him. I'm after his brother.''

"Then I wish you luck, Mr. McLain. Based on your record, you'll need it.''

"You're the one that needs luck, Colonel. You'd better take along a rabbit's foot when you go hunting Chitto.''

"For the last time, keep your opinions to yourself!"

"Don't say I didn't warn you."

A short while later they rode into Tahlequah. Outside David Lipe's office they dismounted and tied their horses to a hitch rack. Drummond took a moment to brush himself off, tugging his uniform blouse down over his corpulent frame. McLain led the way into the office.

Lipe and Chief Rogers had been waiting all day. They were advised Drummond would arrive on October 31 and they had kept themselves available since that morning. McLain performed the introductions, and then, as instructed, left Drummond to conduct the meeting. He began rolling a smoke as the men got themselves seated around Lipe's desk. Drummond came straight to the point.

"You are no doubt aware that I have been ordered into the field against Chitto Starr. Governor Haskell felt you gentlemen might be of assistance."

Chief W. C. Rogers was a man of distinguished bearing. He was tall, with a leonine head of hair and quick alert eyes. "We, too, want Starr captured," he said. "How may we assist you, Colonel?"

"Several ways," Drummond said in a patronizing manner. "You are men of influence within the Cherokee tribe. I want you to use that influence to secure information as to Starr's whereabouts."

Rogers considered a moment. "That is no simple matter, Colonel. Our people are hesitant to betray a tribesman, even a renegade." He spread his hands. "That is their way."

"*Your* people," Drummond said tartly, "are citizens of Oklahoma. Are you telling me they won't cooperate?"

"I think it is unlikely."

"Then you should send out another message, Mr. Rogers. Anyone who protects Starr, or joins in the resistance against land allotments, will be considered enemies of the state. We deal harshly with our enemies."

"Few of our people support Starr," Rogers said calmly. "Most of them have accepted land allotments, even though they feel it was wrong. They are trying to be good citizens."

"Are they, indeed?" Drummond retorted. "The resistance movement is spreading throughout the Five Tribes. We hear the Cherokees actively support the revolt."

Rogers took a grip on himself. For a decade, he had fought to preserve the sovereignty of the Cherokee Nation. In the struggle, he had met many white men like Drummond, and he was always shocked by their brazen arrogance. He managed a tight smile.

"The Cherokees are not your enemy, Colonel. Chitto Starr is the problem, and the solution is to be rid of him. We all want that."

"Prove it," Drummond said bluntly. "I understand Starr has a mountain stronghold somewhere. How do I find it?"

"If I knew, I would tell you. We have heard that rumor ourselves. But no one seems to know the location."

"You give me platitudes and excuses. What I need, Mr. Rogers, are facts!"

"If I may—" Lipe intervened politely. "Marshal McLain used one of our most reliable men as a scout. If anyone can find Starr's stronghold, it would be Joe Blackbird." He tried to deflect Drummond's anger with an appeal to McLain. "Don't you agree, Marshal?"

"Yeah, I do." McLain took a drag on his cigarette,

exhaled smoke. "Fact is, I've already told the Colonel as much. He wasn't keen on the idea."

"With good reason," Drummond bridled. "He led you into an ambush."

"Not so," McLain corrected him. "I told you the way it happened. Blackbird wasn't at fault."

Drummond heaved a sigh of frustration. "All right, I'll agree to talk to him. But I'm making no promises. Where can he be found?"

"Right here," Lipe said quickly. "He works for me."

"Let's have a look at him, then. I don't have all day."

Lipe hurried out of the office. A few minutes later he returned with Joe Blackbird. Upon being introduced, Drummond made no offer to shake hands. He scrutinized Blackbird with a frown.

"Everyone tells me you're quite a scout. Do you think you can find Chitto Starr?"

"Maybe," Blackbird said. "His trail's pretty cold now."

"Where would you start?"

"Last place we saw him. Over by Jackson Mountain."

"Wasn't that where you were ambushed?" Drummond asked, not waiting for an answer. "How do I know you wouldn't get my troops ambushed?"

McLain woofed a laugh. "Don't let him get your goat, Joe. He knows you weren't to blame."

Blackbird nodded, his gaze shifting back to Drummond. "I'll scout for you because Major Lipe says so. You want somebody else, go ahead."

Drummond stared at him. "Your orders would come from me, Mr. Blackbird. Can you follow orders?"

"I do my job," Blackbird said flatly. "Never disobeyed an order yet."

"I can vouch for that," Lipe broke in. "And keep in mind, we want Starr stopped as bad as you, Colonel."

A moment of deliberation slipped past. Drummond glanced at Chief Rogers, who returned his gaze with an impassive stare. Finally, with a sigh of resignation, he got to his feet. He nodded at Blackbird.

"Consider yourself the new scout for the Third Cavalry."

Seventeen

"**I** warned you not to interfere."

"You'd better be glad I was there."

"What does that mean?"

"Just what it sounds like. You're lucky to have a scout."

"And you credit yourself with that, Mr. McLain?"

"No, you take credit. It'll look good in your report."

McLain paused at the edge of the boardwalk. Drummond moved to the hitch rack, unlooping the reins of his horse. His features were flushed, and when he turned, his eyes were pinpricks of anger. He glared at McLain.

"You are a most distasteful individual. I wonder that you've lasted in government service."

"Takes all kinds," McLain said with a crooked grin. "I've managed so far."

"By the grace of God," Drummond said gruffly. "Perhaps that will change after the governor hears of this incident. Your behavior was despicable."

"Be sure to ask the governor why he sent me along."

"Spare me your riddles, Mr. McLain. Say what you mean."

"Colonel, you could take lessons in dealing with Indians. That simple enough for you?"

Drummond's face purpled with rage. He started to speak, then his gaze went past McLain. "What is it, Mr. Blackbird?" he said crossly. "I thought we had concluded our business."

Joe Blackbird stood in the doorway of the office. "Nothin' much," he replied without inflection. "When do you want me to report? You didn't say."

"Didn't I?" Drummond appeared momentarily flustered by the lapse. "Well, the battalion is bivouacked a mile or so east of town. I'll expect you there by dark."

Blackbird merely nodded. Drummond finally realized that was all the answer he would receive. He clumsily hauled himself into the saddle, almost losing the stirrup as the stallion danced sideways. He reined sharply about and rode off at a slow trot. His backsides bounced as though wired to a spring.

"Humph," Blackbird grunted, amusement in his eyes. "Rides like a girl, don't he?"

McLain smiled. "Think what it'd be like at a gallop. He wouldn't last ten seconds."

"Why'd he ever pick a stallion? He ought to be ridin' a mare. A real old mare."

"I'd say it wouldn't make any difference, Joe. The man's built for a motorcar, not a horse."

"How'd he come to be in the cavalry?"

"Politics," McLain said. "He's pals with the governor. That tell you anything?"

Blackbird raised an eyebrow. "You sayin' he's not a soldier?"

"Not even close. He's a civilian decked out in a uniform. Never been near a battlefield in his life."

"And they sent him after Chitto Starr? Sounds like huntin' a bear with a switch."

"Watch yourself," McLain warned. "He's out to make a name for himself, and that's dangerous. He could get you killed."

Blackbird glanced at him. "You're not gonna be along?"

"You might say I was relieved of duty, Joe. They figured this was a job for the army. I've been assigned to Frank Starr."

"Heard he robbed the bank over at Proctor. Frank's a slippery devil, real smooth."

"Tell me about it," McLain said wearily. "I've been chasing him for two years. Haven't yet come close."

"Maybe this time." Blackbird hesitated, thoughtful a moment. "What's all this stuff about a revolt in the tribes? Where'd that get started?"

"Joe, it's all they're talkin' about in Guthrie. That's why they're so all-fired hot to nail Chitto. They think he could lead the tribes into a rebellion."

"Maybe there'll be some trouble with land allotments. But nobody's gonna get in a shootin' war. That'd just be dumb."

"Whoa, now," McLain said with a look of bafflement. "Are you tellin' me there's no talk of armed resistance?"

"Nothin' we've heard," Blackbird assured him. "Nobody's stupid enough to start a war they can't win. Chitto's out there all by himself."

"What about this Four Mothers Society?"

"That's about land allotments, not war. Chief Rogers says it's mostly hot air. All talk, no fight."

"I'll be goddamned," McLain said in amazement. "From what you say, the governor and everybody else is jumping at shadows. Chitto and the Nighthawks are the only war around.''

Blackbird jerked a thumb toward the courthouse. ''Sheriff Prather's the one that started that war.''

''I thought Chief Rogers was behind the warrant.''

''Don't know if he was or wasn't. But the sheriff could've waited till Chitto came into town and arrested him on the street. He didn't have to raid the Nighthawks' camp.''

''Yeah, he did,'' McLain said, with a sardonic undertone. ''The plan there was to get headlines in the newspaper. Prather's looking to the next election.''

''Guess so,'' Blackbird agreed. ''Whole lot of trouble over nothin'. Too damn bad.''

''Well, like I said, watch yourself with Drummond. He's another one looking to make headlines.''

''I'll keep my eye on him.''

''Keep both eyes on him, Joe.''

They shook hands and McLain stepped aboard his gelding. He reined around, waving to Blackbird, and rode toward the courthouse. As he crossed the town square, he thought back over their conversation, and his mood darkened. All of it seemed such a waste.

Chitto Starr, he reflected, had become little more than a pawn. Prather and Drummond, even the governor, were playing to the newspapers, chasing headlines. From what he'd just heard, the revolt itself was wildly exaggerated, perhaps a pure fabrication. In one fashion or another, everyone was looking to grease their own wheel, and Chitto was the only headline around. Politics as usual.

McLain left his horse at the hitch rack in front of the courthouse. Inside, he found two deputies seated at desks in the outer office. He nodded amiably, motioning them down as he moved across the room. Without knocking, he entered Prather's office and saw the sheriff standing by the window. Prather continued to stare out across the square.

"Figured I was your next stop," he said in a grouchy voice. "What were you doing over at Lipe's office?"

McLain took a chair. "Joe Blackbird signed on to scout for the army."

"So you got Drummond all squared away?"

"How'd you know his name?"

"I read the papers." Prather dropped into the chair behind his desk. "Way they write about him, you'd think he was Ulysses S. Grant."

McLain knuckled his mustache. "What's that I hear in your voice, Sheriff? You sound just a tad jealous."

"Why would I be jealous? So far as I'm concerned, Chitto Starr's all his. No skin off my nose."

"You made that pretty plain the last time I was here."

"Always the wiseacre, aren't you?" Prather tilted back in his chair. "So what's the colonel's grand strategy?"

"Don't know." McLain pulled out the makings, began rolling a cigarette. "He didn't say and I didn't ask."

"Yeah, that figures."

"Figures how?"

"You got whipped real good," Prather said with a mocking grin. "Makes sense you've had your share of Chitto and his Nighthawks."

McLain popped a match, lit up in a haze of smoke. "That's sort of the pot calling the kettle black. Chitto showed you a few tricks, too."

"Got a snappy answer for everything, don't you?"

"What say we move on with business? I assume you were notified I've been assigned to Frank Starr."

"Gilmore called me," Prather said peevishly. "Guess it's no secret I didn't want you here."

"What's new?" McLain remarked. "But I'm here and you're stuck with me. Let's talk about Starr."

"Go ahead and talk."

"It's been six days since he robbed the bank in Proctor. Anything on the grapevine as to his whereabouts?"

"Nope," Prather said. "He pulled his usual disappearing act."

McLain exhaled a plume of smoke. "How much did he get away with?"

"Little better'n three thousand."

"Frank never was greedy. Just looks to make a decent payday."

"Dirty sonovabitch," Prather grumbled. "Why'd he have to pull a job in my county?"

"I asked myself the same thing," McLain commented. "He's always stayed clear of homeground."

"You think it's got something to do with Chitto?"

"I'll ask Frank when I catch him."

"So what's your plan?"

"I'll need a couple of deputies," McLain said. "Your best men, good with a gun."

"Like hell!" Prather slammed forward in his chair. "You've got a way of getting men killed. Far as I'm concerned, this here's a federal case."

"Well, like you said, it's your county. You requested a U.S. Marshal and I got tapped for the job. But it's still your bailiwick."

"Don't make no nevermind. I won't do it!"

"Have you got anybody on Starr's trail?"

"You know damn well I called Gilmore."

"And then you sat on your thumb for six days. That's your story?"

Prather glowered at him. "What d'you mean—story?"

"The one you tell the newspapers," McLain said, smiling. "What'll folks think when they hear you won't protect your own county?" He paused, scrolling through the air with his cigarette. "Sheriff Turns Blind Eye to Bank Robbers. How's that for a headline?"

"You've got a way of rubbin' a man wrong, you know that?"

"What the hell, Ed, it's only your duty. You do believe in doing your duty . . . don't you?"

"Charley! Elmer!" Prather shouted in a rough voice. "Get your butts in here."

The deputies in the outer office crowded through the door. Charley Upgraff was wiry, with shifty eyes and a soup-strainer mustache. Elmer Swanson looked like a former prizefighter, square-jawed and beefy, with a flattened nose. Prather motioned across the desk.

"I'm assigning you boys to Marshal McLain. He's here to bring in Frank Starr."

The men exchanged a quick glance. Swanson squared his shoulders, his face screwed into a frown. "Why pick me and Charley just 'cause we're handy? Don't hardly seem fair."

"Don't give me any lip! The other boys will have to work double shifts with you two gone. Just do as you're told."

"Still don't seem right."

Prather ignored the comment. "They're all yours, McLain. Give 'em the lowdown."

McLain stubbed out his cigarette in an ashtray. He turned in his chair, holding their resentful stares. "We'll leave first thing in the morning. Get a packhorse and load up with supplies. We're liable to be gone awhile."

Upgraff groaned. "Where we headed?"

"We'll start out in Proctor. Try to get a lead on Starr."

The men shuffled out of the doorway with hangdog expressions. Prather followed them with his eyes, then looked back at McLain. His mouth quirked at the corners.

"You got what you wanted. Anything else?"

"Not unless you'd like to come along."

Prather grunted. "Don't hold your breath."

"In that case, I'll see you around, Sheriff."

Dusk was settling over the town as McLain emerged from the courthouse. A sickle moon, still faint in the fleeting light, rose higher in the southerly sky. He stood for a moment at the hitch rack, as though weighing some decision of considerable import. Finally, with an inward shrug, he walked his horse down to the livery stable. His step was chipper.

After stabling the gelding, McLain turned west along the street. There was no official reason to call on her, and he knew it was a matter of temptation overriding common sense. Still, with logic suspended, he told himself she might have heard something worthwhile. Any excuse seemed a good excuse as he knocked on her door. Jane Tenkiller opened it in a spill of light.

"Well, look at you!" Her eyes danced merrily. "I didn't know you were back in town."

"Just for the night," McLain said, almost tongue-tied. "I'm on the trail of Frank Starr."

"Come in out of the cold."

She pulled him through the door. McLain doffed his hat and took a seat beside her on the sofa. He was distinctly aware of her closeness, the musky smell of her. She turned to face him.

"I heard Frank robbed the bank in Proctor. I hope you catch him this time."

"Any news on where he might be holed up? I recall you mentioned a hideout in the mountains once before."

"All the news seems to be about Chitto. Is it true they've sent the army after him?"

"A whole battalion," McLain acknowledged. " 'Course, I'm not involved in that anymore. I'm after Frank."

"Oh, I'm glad," she said happily. "Maybe Chitto will get away."

"I wouldn't doubt but what he gives the army the slip."

"Better him than his brother. I wish I could help you with Frank."

"Yeah, me too," McLain said, unable to take his eyes off her. "Just thought I'd drop by on the chance you'd heard something. Guess that was wishful thinking on my part."

"I wonder," she said, with a sultry smile. "Do you like pork chops?"

"I'm mighty partial to pork chops."

"That's what I'm fixing for supper. Would you like to stay?"

McLain grinned. "Sure it's no trouble?"

"Don't be silly."

She rose, taking his hat from his hand. As she went past him, her skirt brushed his leg, and his mouth went pasty. He watched her hips as she dropped his hat on a chair and crossed the room. She looked back over her shoulder.

"Let me get things started in the kitchen. Then we'll talk some more."

He thought he could talk to her all night.

Eighteen

On November 2 the battalion sighted Jackson Mountain. The sun was high overhead, dulled by a muslin sky and thick clouds. A crisp wind drifted down out of the northwest.

Blackbird reined to a halt by the creek. He sat staring at Nigger Jake Hollow, and the mountain beyond. His mind flashed back to the ambush, and the drumming rattle of gunfire. Every detail was still vivid, and he mentally played it out again, wondering how it could have been averted. He thought there was nothing more he could have done.

Turning in the saddle, Blackbird looked back downstream. He watched as Colonel Raymond Drummond motioned the column to a halt, perhaps a quarter mile to the rear. The battalion was two days out of Tahlequah, moving at what Blackbird considered a snail's pace. He doubted they would ever overtake Chitto Starr.

Drummond rode forward with his aide, Lieutenant Norton. Neither of them were accomplished horsemen, their butts slapping leather at a trot. Blackbird thought

Norton looked like a freckle-faced kid, a toy soldier acting a part. They halted at the edge of the creek, Drummond sawing at the reins to control his stallion. His eyes were inquisitive.

"Why are we stopped, Mr. Blackbird?"

"That's Nigger Jake Hollow," Blackbird said, gesturing off to the south. "Figured you'd want to see where we was ambushed."

"Indeed." Drummond glanced at his aide. "The major tenet of military strategy is to know your enemy, and how he thinks. This could prove instructive, Norton."

Norton nodded eagerly. "Shall I take notes, sir?"

"No, no. Listen closely to Mr. Blackbird and pay attention to my critique. Learn by observation."

"Yessir."

"Very well, Mr. Blackbird," Drummond said importantly. "Proceed with your account of the encounter. Step-by-step, if you please."

"We rode through there," Blackbird said, motioning across the open ground. "Starr's tracks were on a beeline for that mountain. Jackson Mountain."

"And apart from the tracks, there was no sign of Starr's men?"

"Never saw nothin' till we got to the top end of the hollow."

"Continue."

Blackbird talked them through the ambush. From the moment he shot Chitto Starr, to the end of the gunfight, he estimated not more than five minutes had elapsed. He indicated the defensive position the posse had taken along the creek.

"Stayed here till dark," he concluded. "Then me and Marshal McLain brought in our dead."

"Let me understand," Drummond said, pointing to

the treeline bordering the hollow. "Starr's force was positioned there, there, and there. To your front and on both flanks, correct?"

"Had us boxed on three sides," Blackbird said. "Only way out was the way we come in . . . back here."

"And McLain ordered a retreat rather than a charge. Is that it?"

"We were outnumbered and caught on open ground. Smart thing to do was pull back."

"Hardly," Drummond said, directing his aide's attention with a thrust of his hand. "In battle, Lieutenant, one must seize the initiative. The correct tactic would have been to charge one of the enemy's salient points." He paused, waving grandly. "The line of attack in any direction was far shorter than the line of retreat."

Norton bobbed his head. "You're absolutely right, Colonel. By charging, McLain's men would have been exposed for a shorter period of time. No question of it."

"Far shorter than you think," Drummond amended. "Had he charged, that would have eliminated the interlocking fields of fire from the other salient points. They could scarcely fire on their own men."

"Of course!" Norton brayed, as though awakened to a revelation. "By firing on McLain's men, they would have directed fire on their own forces. A brilliant tactic, Colonel. Brilliant!"

"Elementary," Drummond said, preening with false modesty. "A lesson from any basic primer on tactics."

Blackbird watched them with a stoic expression. Yet he was inwardly filled with contempt, a growing sense of unease. A charge such as Drummond described would have gotten every man in the posse killed. The Nighthawks would have continued firing, even if it endangered some of their own, and the posse would have been wiped out before the charge was completed. It would have been a charge into the jaws of death itself.

Still, on second thought, Blackbird decided to say nothing. Drummond was not the type to be corrected by an Indian scout, particularly since he considered himself a master tactician. So far as knowing the enemy was concerned, Drummond clearly failed to grasp the essential lesson taught by Nigger Jake Hollow. Chitto Starr's tactics of hit-and-run applied only if there was somewhere to run. Having taken a stand, the Nighthawks would fight to the last man.

Drummond led the way back downstream. Through Norton, orders were relayed to company commanders along the column. The men were to dismount and take a half-hour noon break, which included tending to their horses. On the south bank, Drummond and the troop commanders gathered over a meal of cold rations and creek water. Blackbird, who generally kept to himself, found a comfortable rock upstream and sat down. He was gnawing on a piece of jerky when Sergeant Major Jack O'Neal walked forward. O'Neal took a nearby rock.

"What's up?" he asked, working on a hunk of hardtack. "You and the colonel see anything out there?"

Blackbird shrugged. "I showed him where me and that posse was ambushed. He figured out how we could've won the fight."

"Hindsight's a wonderful thing, Joe. Never fails."

O'Neal was the highest-ranking noncom in the battalion. He reported directly to Drummond and was responsible for dealing with the master sergeants who effectively ran the companies. A burly man, with a quick mind and a sharp eye, he was a blooded veteran of the Spanish-American War. He disapproved of Drummond's overly harsh discipline, and he detected a kindred soul in Blackbird. He had gone out of his way to make a friend of the scout.

"You should've heard him," Blackbird said, munching jerky. "His idea would've got everybody in the posse killed."

O'Neal glanced over his shoulder. No one was within earshot, but he nonetheless lowered his voice. "Like I've said before, the man's full of himself. He thinks he knows it all."

"Yeah, that's what worries me. He's liable to lead us over a cliff."

"All the more reason for you and me to keep our eyes open. We've got to bring the battalion through in one piece."

"How're we gonna do that?" Blackbird said doubtfully. "He's the one that gives the orders."

"Don't rightly know," O'Neal replied. "I'm just sayin' we've got to be ready if we get in a scrap. You still convinced Starr will stand and fight?"

"I'll find him and he'll fight. Trouble is, he'll pick the spot."

"Nothin' like a dirty little war, huh, Joe?"

"Sergeant Major!"

O'Neal jumped to his feet. Norton was standing a short distance away, motioning urgently. "Let's hop to it," he ordered. "The colonel wants to move out in five minutes."

"Yessir, Lieutenant," O'Neal said, muttering an aside under his breath. "Little pisswillie loves to give orders."

"Scout Blackbird!" Norton yelled. "Take your position out in front of the battalion."

Blackbird stood, stuffing the last bite of jerky in his mouth. Slowly, never once acknowledging the colonel's aide, he walked to his horse and stepped into the saddle.

He thought O'Neal was dead on the mark.

Pisswillies loved to give orders.

Late that afternoon Blackbird rounded the southern end
of Jackson Mountain. After scouting ahead, he had decided to bring the battalion through the lowlands to the
southeast. The detour avoided the steep slopes of the
mountain, but it had consumed the better part of the
afternoon. The sun steadily dropped westward.

Blackbird reined his gelding to a halt. Directly ahead
lay Dry Creek, which flowed through a wide notch between Jackson Mountain and Gitting Down Mountain.
He sat for a long moment, inspecting the wooded terrain
that rose steeply from the opposite shoreline. He saw
no movement, no telltale sign of men hiding in the trees;
but neither had he seen anything the day of the ambush
in Nigger Jake Hollow. He was determined to have a
closer look.

Dry Creek flowed generally east to west. Blackbird
nudged his horse and rode along the northern shoreline.
A mile or so upstream he found tracks descending Jackson Mountain and leading to a shallow ford in the creek.
The tracks were hardened by sun and frost, and he
judged the trail to be on the order of two weeks old.
From the depth of the impressions, he counted twelve
riders, with three packhorses and two spare mounts.
There was no question in his mind that the Nighthawks
had crossed the stream.

What lay on the opposite side was another question
entirely. Blackbird debated taking the battalion across
the stream without first having scouted Gitting Down
Mountain. Then, on second thought, he decided that
caution was the wiser choice, even though it meant further delay. He booted his horse into a lope and rode
west along the creek. The lead elements of the battalion

appeared at the base of Jackson Mountain as he pounded downstream. To avoid argument, he motioned for Drummond to order a halt, then immediately reined back around. He forded Dry Creek.

On the south bank, Blackbird again rode upstream. Some minutes later he located the spot where the Nighthawks had emerged from the creek. The trail angled off to the southeast, along a tributary that carved a rocky gorge between Gitting Down Mountain and Sanders Mountain. A short distance into the gorge, he suddenly hauled back on the reins and brought his gelding to a dead stop. He pulled the Winchester from the saddle scabbard, his eyes darting through the stands of timber on either side. Not ten yards ahead were the tracks of a horse—fresh tracks.

The silence was broken only by a faint rush of wind. After scanning the woods for a time, Blackbird slowly stepped out of the saddle. He walked forward, a thumb hooked over the hammer of the carbine. The tracks led to the edge of the tributary, and then doubled back into the dense timber at the bottom of Gitting Down Mountain. Someone had watered a horse, and from the sign, he placed the time at early that morning. He followed the tracks into the trees, and again came to an abrupt halt. The horse had been tied to a tall hickory, a mound of droppings heaped on the ground. The rider had dismounted.

Blackbird carefully studied the sign. The rider, who wore flat-heeled boots, had moved to the edge of the treeline. Looking north, the spot provided a perfect observation post along the tributary, and farther on, Dry Creek. Someone had been assigned to watch the Nighthawks' backtrail, and he had clearly spent the day hidden in thick timber. Blackbird inspected the bootprints leading back to the horse; he saw where the rider had mounted and ridden off through the trees to the south. He estimated the tracks were no more than an hour old.

A short while later Blackbird again forded Dry Creek. Downstream, the battalion was dismounted in the shadows of Jackson Mountain. At the head of the column, standing beside their horses, were Drummond, Norton, and Sergeant Major O'Neal. Drummond's eyes burned with impatience.

"Why are we stopped, Mr. Blackbird?"

"I found fresh sign," Blackbird said, as he swung down out of the saddle. "Somebody's watchin' the Nighthawks' backtrail."

"Are you certain?"

"No two ways about it."

"Tell me exactly what you found."

Blackbird quickly related the details. "Tracks were maybe an hour old," he concluded. "Way it looks to me, their scout sat there the whole day. Didn't pull out till a little bit before sundown."

"Indeed." Drummond assessed him with a look. "And what do you make of that, Mr. Blackbird?"

"I think Starr's camped back in those mountains. Maybe a couple of hours from here. No more."

"What leads you to that conclusion?"

"Not long till dark." Blackbird indicated the sun, which hovered on the western horizon. "Their scout took off to make it back to camp while it's still light."

"Assuming it is their scout," Drummond remarked. "Why would the Nighthawks be watching their backtrail after all this time?"

"Chitto Starr's no fool, Colonel. By now, he probably knows the army's after him."

"Come now, Mr. Blackbird, out here in the mountains? How would he know that?"

"You ever heard of the moccasin telegraph? Word gets around pretty quick."

Drummond deliberated a moment. "You may have a point," he allowed. "Why would Starr have halted his retreat and posted sentinels? Perhaps we've tracked him to his fabled stronghold."

"Of course!" Norton broke in, hands flapping with excitement. "There's no other reason for him to halt his retreat. You've put your thumb on it, Colonel!"

Drummond nodded wisely. "Gentlemen, we will bivouac here for the night. We march at dawn." He briskly rubbed his hands together. "I do believe we've found ourselves a fight."

Norton rushed off to inform the troop commanders. Sergeant Major O'Neal took Drummond's horse and fell in beside Blackbird. They walked toward the head of the column, silent until there was no fear of being overheard. O'Neal finally glanced around.

"Do you think the colonel's right?"

"About the stronghold?"

"Yeah."

"Don't know," Blackbird said. "But he's right about one thing. We'll find a fight tomorrow."

"Why?" O'Neal asked. "You figure that scout spotted us?"

"Way I read the sign, he was already gone. Not that it matters one way or another. Somebody will spot us tomorrow."

"So we're not likely to spring a surprise attack?"

Blackbird smiled. "Nobody's surprised Chitto Starr yet. Always been the other way 'round."

"Well, keep a sharp lookout," O'Neal said seriously. "We don't want any surprises for the Third."

"You have my word on that, Sergeant Major."

"What makes you sound so certain?"

Blackbird laughed. "I'd be the first one shot."

Nineteen

Proctor was a small farm town. The population was less than a thousand, and most people still drove buggies and wagons. Apart from the bank, the major business concerns were a general store, a mercantile, and a sawmill for the area's loggers. A single street bisected the backwoods community.

Gideon Brown was the town constable. A scarecrow of a man, he was loose and gangly with a wild thatch of wheat-colored hair. Yet he was a scrapper, tough as whang leather, the bane of drunks who got too rowdy on Saturday nights. His day job was at the mill, but he prided himself on his position as constable. The townspeople had elected him two years in a row.

The local jail was a stout log structure at the west end of the street. Brown stood talking with McLain, who had ridden into town early that morning. Elmer Swanson and Charley Upgraff, the Cherokee County deputies, lounged beside their horses, idly watching farm wagons roll past. On the ride over from Tahlequah, neither of them had expressed any great interest in the pursuit of Frank Starr and his gang. They thought it was a wild-goose chase.

"Gol-dang," Brown said, somewhat surprised himself. "Been a week since they robbed the bank, Marshal. How you figure to catch 'em?"

"Let me worry about that," McLain told him. "What I need from you is a starting point. Where were they last seen?"

"Me and some of the boys chased 'em a ways south of town. Lost their trail on Baron Creek."

"That'll have to be our starting point, then. Suppose you show me where you lost them."

"Yeah, I could do that," Brown said cagily. " 'Course, I'd expect you to take me along."

McLain eyed him narrowly. "These men are killers, Mr. Brown. I doubt we'll take them without a fight."

"Whyn't you call me Gideon? And don't worry about me holdin' up my part. I ain't no slouch with a gun."

"We're liable to be gone a good while. Aren't you a working man?"

"I got a duty, the same as you. It was my town they robbed."

McLain considered a moment. There were five men in Starr's gang, and Brown would even out the odds. He was impressed as well with the constable's determined manner. "All right, Gideon," he said. "Raise your right hand and I'll swear you in."

Twenty minutes later Gideon Brown led them south out of town. He was mounted on a sorrel gelding, loaned to him by the local livery stable. Holstered on his hip was an ancient Smith & Wesson .44 and he carried a Marlin lever-action rifle in his saddle scabbard. He looked proud as punch.

Toward mid-morning they halted along the banks of Baron Creek. The stream was some five miles south of

Proctor, flowing east to west through a wide stretch of flatlands. The terrain north and south was hilly, studded with rocks, and heavily forested. Brown indicated where he had lost the trail, after the gang had taken to the creek. Their tracks ended at the water's edge.

McLain searched the opposite shoreline. There was no sign of five riders along the bank, and he concluded that they had stuck to the water to elude pursuit. After pondering on it a moment, he had reservations that the gang would have headed west, in the direction of Tahlequah. Frank Starr was tricky, but not that tricky. He decided to look east.

Swanson and Upgraff, leading the packhorse, were assigned to ride the north bank. McLain, with Gideon Brown in tow, took the south bank. Though merely a hunch, McLain was still convinced that Starr would eventually turn south, into the refuge of the mountains and the rumored stronghold. Three miles upstream he found the first sign that his hunch was correct. A flat outcropping of rock, jutting into the water, extended along the shoreline. He signaled a halt.

McLain considered himself a decent tracker. Not in the same league as Joe Blackbird, or army scouts he'd met while serving in the cavalry. But over the years he had watched and learned from those who knew what to look for in the wilderness. He motioned the others to hold their positions and left his horse with Brown. On foot, he moved ashore onto the westward rim of the rocky ledge. He squatted down on his haunches.

The morning sun was still slanted eastward. A seasoned tracker, trying to cut sign, stationed himself between the suspected trail and the position of the sun. On rocky terrain the correct sun angle made the difference in spotting sign or missing it entirely. McLain was looking for scuff marks, or dislodged chips of stone, highlighted by the glare of the easterly sun. He squinted, peering some yards ahead, then rose and walked forward. Shiny scuff marks, unnatural to nature, told the tale. The gang had quit the water.

Standing, McLain crossed the outcropping. Where rock gave way to firm ground, he discovered that Starr had stopped to watch his backtrail. The spot was located at a bend in the creek, where a stand of timber bordered the shoreline. Hidden behind the trees, Starr and his gang had dismounted and waited, with an open field of fire far downstream. From there, with five rifles in action, they could have discouraged further pursuit. Or perhaps ended the chase.

McLain carefully inspected the spot. Farther into the trees he found where the gang had tied their horses on the day of the bank holdup. Hoofprints still scuffled the ground, with mounds of week-old horse droppings, indicating a wait of some duration. Nearer the creek, screened by the treeline, he saw where Starr had selected a vantage point with a field of fire covering the stream and the opposite shoreline. Imprints of boots were recorded in the earth beneath the trees.

"Come have a look," McLain yelled, motioning to Gideon Brown. "Good thing you lost the trail back downstream."

Brown dismounted and moved forward, leading the horses. Swanson and Upgraff splashed across the creek, and swung down from their saddles. The men stood collected in a knot, watching silently as McLain pointed out the sign. He swiped at his mustache with a humorless smile.

"Starr's a dirty piece of work. Him and his gang would've waited till you came along the creek. Then they'd have cut loose."

"Jesus H. Christmas!" Brown breathed. "Me and my

posse would've been blowed outta the water like sitting ducks.''

''Count your lucky stars,'' McLain said. ''They planned to bushwhack you and leave you for dead.''

Upgraff hawked, spat a wad of phlegm. ''I don't like this shit, McLain. How do we know they're not waitin' up the trail somewheres? Just like they did here.''

''Doesn't figure,'' McLain assured him. ''They wouldn't think anybody's on their trail, not after a week. They're feeling fat and sassy right about now.''

''What if you're wrong?'' Swanson chimed in. ''Who the hell says we gotta trust your word? You've got men killed before.''

''Let's get something straight,'' McLain said in a hard voice. ''You boys will toe the line, and I won't have any back talk about it. Understood?''

Upgraff and Swanson exchanged a glance. McLain's eyes bored into them, cold and implacable. They knew his reputation as a toughnut, and neither of them felt any urge to carry it further. They nodded in unison.

''Get mounted,'' McLain ordered. ''Lots of daylight left.''

The tracks leading from the trees proved McLain's assessment to be correct. All the sign indicated that the gang had ridden out at an easy trot, clearly in no hurry. They believed they had thrown off the law, and evidenced no fear of pursuit. But Frank Starr again proved himself a master of wile and trickery.

The trail followed the winding course of Baron Creek, due eastward. There had been no rain in several weeks, and the sign of five horses—churned earth through the flatlands—was simple to read. Yet the tracks never deviated, even though McLain kept expecting them to turn south into the mountains. He finally realized that he'd been fooled again. Frank Starr was headed somewhere else.

He followed the trail eastward at a steady lope.

Some miles farther on, the creek emptied into the Evansville River. The tracks angled off, skirting the river, which flowed in a southeasterly direction. The lowlands bordering the river were suitable to a fast pace, and the sign was plain to read. The trail wound along the snaky course of the river.

Ten miles or so to the southeast, the river took a sharp bend due eastward. Shortly before sundown McLain and his men crossed the line into Arkansas. He lost the trail where a wooden bridge spanned the river, and a farm road curled north and south. By now, he was no longer surprised with Frank Starr's devious nature, and he turned onto the south road. He knew where the gang had come to roost.

The town of Evansville was located half a mile across the state line. A backcountry crossroads with a small population, it was ostensibly a bustling little farm community. Yet the mainstay of commerce in Evansville was the sporting life, and a brisk trade in alcohol. Oklahoma was dry and Arkansas was wet, and there was steady traffic over the line by those in search of spirits. For some, it was an oasis in a parched land.

McLain was familiar with the town. Over the years he had apprehended any number of whiskey smugglers who made Evansville their base of supply. He led his men to Folsom's Bar & Grill, which was a combination saloon, whorehouse, and greasy-spoon café. Inside, he ordered a round of drinks, then left the men to themselves and walked to the end of the bar. He nodded to the owner, Davey Folsom.

"How's tricks, Davey?"

Folsom was a man of substantial girth, and no stranger to the law. His features clouded. "Long time no see, McLain. What brings you to our little metropolis?"

"I'm looking for some men. Thought you might have seen them."

"I see lots of men in my business."

"You wouldn't forget this bunch," McLain said. "Five men, all of them darker than your usual crowd. Indians."

"Doesn't ring any bells," Folsom said, feigning indifference. "Besides, it's against the law to sell liquor to Indians. I run a respectable joint."

"I'm not after you, Davey. I'm after information."

"Why would I put myself out for the law?"

"Maybe I could do you a favor one of these days. A man in your line of work needs all the markers he can get."

Folsom stared off into the middle distance a moment. He finally leaned into the bar, lowered his voice. "When the time comes, just remember you owe me," he said, waiting for McLain to nod. "The fellers you're asking about were here for five or six days. Stayed drunk the whole time and threw money around like they had it to burn. Damn near screwed my whores to death."

McLain held his gaze. "When did they leave?"

"Sometime yesterday, or so I heard. Every sporting house in town hated to see them go."

"Any idea where they were headed?"

"Not a clue," Folsom said. "Don't know and don't want to know. Lots safer that way."

"What about your girls?" McLain asked. "Maybe there was some pillow talk. Drunks like to brag."

"Whores like to gossip, too. Anything worth hearing, I would've heard it."

"Was Frank Starr partial to any one girl?"

Folsom looked at him with a closed expression. "Who said anything about Frank Starr?"

"I did," McLain countered. "That's who we're talking about."

"Not me."

"I thought we made a deal."

"I just went deaf, dumb, and blind."

"Are you still able to nod your head?"

"Try me and see."

"The gentleman in question was here—wasn't he?" Folsom nodded.

"Anything else?" McLain said. "Maybe some tidbit you picked up while he was in town?"

"I think you've pumped me dry, Marshal."

"I'd tend to doubt it. But something's better than nothing. I'm obliged, Davey."

"Don't forget next time I call you for help."

"I always look after my friends."

McLain moved back along the bar. He stopped and spoke with the deputies, who seemed pleased to hear they were spending the night in Evansville. He left them there, then went out the door, and turned upstreet. He walked to the town marshal's office.

Wiley Hogan was built like a fireplug, short and stout. He glanced up from his desk as McLain came through the door. His blunt features ticced in a smile. "Well, looky who's here. Been a while, McLain."

"Not long enough," McLain said shortly. "Still keep your ear to the ground, Wiley?"

"Guess that depends on who's askin'. What's on your mind?"

"I'm after Frank Starr, and don't try to weasel words

with me. I know he left town yesterday.''

Hogan drummed the desktop with his stubby fingers. He finally shrugged. ''I believe in live and let live. Starr hasn't pulled no jobs in my jurisdiction.''

''Lucky you,'' McLain said with veiled sarcasm. ''I'll ask you a question, and I want you to give it some serious thought. You ready?''

''Fire away.''

''Where was Starr headed when he left town?''

Hogan's eyes went blank. ''All I know is what I know,'' he said. ''Him and his boys rode out on the south road.''

''You're a poor liar,'' McLain said brusquely. ''Let's have the rest of it.''

''I wasn't finished,'' Hogan protested. ''Couple of miles out of town, you cross Grapevine Creek. They went thataway.''

''Whichaway?''

''Why, southwest, of course. That's where the creek runs.''

''How'd you come by all this information, Wiley?''

''I hear things,'' Hogan said. ''A farmer on his way into town saw them. He told anybody that'd listen.''

''Why would a farmer take any interest in a bunch of Indians?''

''Them boys painted the town red. Spent a goddamn ton of money. Everybody knew who they was.''

McLain thought it sounded like the truth. As he went out the door, he sensed he'd been right all along. There was no doubt of it now.

Frank Starr was headed into the mountains.

Twenty

"**M**r. Norton."

"Sir!"

"Is everything in order?"

"Yessir!"

Drummond squinted through the shroud of false dawn. In the murky light, he saw the battalion arrayed in marching order, the companies in column of fours. His stallion snorted frost, champing at the bit, and pranced sideways. He took a tight grip on the reins, feet planted firmly in the stirrups, and swung around facing Dry Creek. His right arm swept forward in a grand gesture.

Lieutenant Norton fell in behind him, trailed closely by Sergeant Major O'Neal. Drummond led the battalion across the creek, shoulders squared and proudly erect, his chin thrust out at a heroic angle. He imagined himself another Teddy Roosevelt, perhaps Jeb Stuart, marching to the call of battle. His one regret was that the Third lacked a band to render a stirring air. He thought "Garry Owen" would have done nicely.

On the opposite side of the creek, guidons snapping in the wind, the battalion wheeled east in columns of companies. Far upstream, Drummond saw Joe Blackbird pause at the junction of the tributary creek bordering Gitting Down Mountain. The scout raised his arm, a dim figure in faint light, and motioned southward into the gorge. As he disappeared into the shadows of the mountain, Drummond felt a tinge of unease, something approaching distrust. He still had reservations about Blackbird, setting a Cherokee to catch a Cherokee. The concept of the noble red man seemed to him illusory at best.

The murk turned to the dinge of dawn as the battalion neared Gitting Down Mountain. Drummond swung right into the gorge, looking back to check that the companies were holding the proscribed formation. A ripple of elation touched his backbone, and he thought he'd never been more proud than at that moment. The men sat straight in their saddles, their faces eager and expectant, and he had every confidence that they would uphold the honor of the Third. He fully intended to rout the Indian rabble before the morning was out. No quarter asked and none given.

"Sergeant Major."

O'Neal gigged his horse forward. "Sir!"

"At our first stop," Drummond said crisply, "pass the word through the ranks. We will take no prisoners."

"Beg pardon, Colonel?"

"You heard me, Sergeant Major. Not one of these damnable Nighthawks is to leave the field alive. Am I clear?"

"Yessir." O'Neal stared straight ahead, his features stony. "I'll pass along the word."

"Thank you, Sergeant Major." Drummond dismissed him with an imperious wave, and motioned Norton forward. "Do you believe in premonitions, Lieutenant?"

"Why—" Norton hesitated, somewhat startled. "Divining the future, sir? That sort of thing?"

"Precisely," Drummond said. "Upon awaking this morning, I saw it as though wrought in stone. We ride to glory today, Mr. Norton. Glory!"

"I agree, sir, most definitely. In fact, I've often thought we were destined to make history."

"Indeed?"

"Oh, yessir," Norton said expansively. "The Third will quell the last Indian uprising in America. Think of it, Colonel!"

"Well put, Mr. Norton." Drummond nodded approvingly. "When we return, remind me to use that in a quote with the press. I daresay it will have a certain ring in print."

"I'm sure you're right, sir. I'll be certain to remind you."

"Good, good. Thank you, Mr. Norton."

To the east, the sun crested the horizon. The heights of Gitting Down Mountain were limned in gold, silhouetted against the flare of sunrise. On the opposite side of the gorge, the wooded slope of Sanders Mountain was splashed with an explosion of color off autumn leaves. Light bounced off the walls of the gorge, revealing the men and horses of the battalion in dazzling splendor. The jangle of saddle gear marked their passage under a cloudless sky blushed rose by oncoming day.

A mile or so farther along Drummond abruptly signaled a halt. Some distance ahead Joe Blackbird rode toward them at a hard lope, hoofbeats clattering off the rocky streambed. The scout was bent low in the saddle, the chill wind whipping at the sleeves of his coat. Drummond's stallion skittered away, nostrils flared wide, as

Blackbird skidded to a stop. His gelding snorted spurts of steam, sides heaving from the long run. He motioned back to the south.

"Fresh tracks," he said. "Not too far ahead. They've spotted us."

Drummond frowned. "How can you be sure?"

"Saw where he stopped. Must have been the scout they post down by Dry Creek. He was coming this way."

"Yes, sunrise would be the time to post a sentinel. But you haven't answered my question, Mr. Blackbird. How do you know we were sighted?"

"I read the sign," Blackbird said simply. "He stopped where the creek makes a little bend. Kept his horse hidden behind the rocks until he rode off at a gallop. No doubt about it. He saw us."

"So it would seem." Drummond furrowed his brow. "It appears we have lost the element of surprise. But that hardly alters the course of things."

"Starr will be waiting for us now."

"How far does this gorge extend?"

"Maybe three miles," Blackbird said. "Could be four."

"I see." Drummond paused, thoughtful. "We can't afford to be trapped between these mountains. Do you think Starr has time to set an ambush?"

"Got all the time he needs. But what about this stronghold he's supposed to have? Wouldn't he make a stand there?"

"What's at the end of this gorge? What type of terrain?"

"Sallisaw Creek," Blackbird replied. "More mountains on the other side of the creek."

"You know the lay of the land, Mr. Blackbird. Where

might Starr have constructed this so-called stronghold?''

"Could be a fort of some kind. He'd likely pick high
ground.''

"Exactly my thought,'' Drummond concurred.
"Probably on a mountain overlooking the creek. What
was it—Sallisaw Creek?''

Blackbird deliberated a moment. "That'd make
sense. There's open ground all along the creek. Half a
mile some places, more other places.'' He hesitated,
nodding slowly. "Be a good spot for a fort.''

"Yes, indeed, a fundamental of military strategy.
Command the high ground and force your opponent to
attack uphill. Perhaps there's more to Chitto Starr than
I suspected.''

"Well, he's nobody's fool. He's proved that.''

"Mr. Norton!'' Drummond turned in his saddle.
"Bring the troop commanders forward on the double.
I'll have an Officers' Call right now.''

"Yessir!''

Norton wheeled around sharply, spurring his horse.
Within minutes the four troop commanders rode forward and dismounted where Drummond waited with
Blackbird and Sergeant Major O'Neal. Though the
troop commanders held the rank of captain, their civilian occupations were diverse. One was a haberdasher,
another was an oil contractor, the third was a stockbroker, and the fourth was a cattle rancher. Like their commander, their positions in the National Guard were the
result of political connections. None of them had ever
fought in a war.

"Gentlemen,'' Drummond said, addressing them in a
formal tone. "We will engage the enemy sometime late
this morning. Our scout, Mr. Blackbird, has been kind
enough to map the terrain. Here is our battle plan.''

Drummond directed their attention to a sketch drawn in the dirt. With a stick as a pointer, he indicated where the battalion would emerge from the gorge at Sallisaw Creek. A final scout by Blackbird would pinpoint the exact location of the renegades' stronghold. For now, he ordered Company A and Company B to form on line facing Beevale Mountain which was directly across the creek. Company C would secure the left flank, across an expanse of flatland fronting Dahlonegah Mountain, and Company D would be held in reserve. The precise order of attack would be determined once they were in position.

"There you have it," he concluded. "Any questions, gentlemen?"

Captain John Gryden, the stockbroker who commanded Company A, stepped forward. "Colonel, I gather you believe this stronghold to be located on Beevale Mountain. If so, will we attack mounted, or on foot?"

"That depends entirely on the disposition of the enemy forces. You will be informed once I have Scout Blackbird's final report. Unless you have further questions—no? That will be all, gentlemen."

The troop commanders snapped to attention, saluting smartly. When they rode off to rejoin their units, Drummond studied the rough sketch in the dirt a moment longer. Then, turning away, he walked Blackbird off a short distance. He nodded south into the gorge.

"Starr has a history of ambush," he said soberly. "Take your time as you scout ahead, Mr. Blackbird. We want no surprises today."

"I'll be on the lookout, Colonel. He won't jump us in this gorge."

"Well, then, let's move out. Good hunting, Mr. Blackbird."

Drummond strode back to where Norton and O'Neal waited. The Sergeant Major glanced at Blackbird, as if to solicit an opinion on the battle plan. Blackbird offered a bemused shrug, then stepped aboard his horse.

He rode south into the gorge.

The men went about their usual morning chores. After two weeks on Beevale Mountain, they had fallen into a routine that varied little from day to day. Some collected firewood, others tended the horses, and the best hunters kept the camp supplied with meat. A plump doe, killed only yesterday, hung from the branch of a tree.

Chitto watched as the men went about their work. He was stuffed with venison from the morning meal, and he felt remarkably well. Despite all the dire predictions, he was no longer running a fever and he was able to sit up most of the day. His arm was still strapped to his side, and any sudden movement sent a jolt of pain through his shoulder. But he was seated beneath a tree, propped against the trunk, idly contemplating the future. He thought that by tomorrow he might be able to mount a horse.

The sight of so many men did much to restore his vigor. Over the past week, one or two at a time, fourteen full-bloods had drifted into the camp. The Nighthawks' victories had inspired them to join the fight, and through Will Starr, Chitto's son, they had been directed with great secrecy to Beevale Mountain. They brought news of the army battalion, which had deterred many Cherokees from openly joining the revolt. But they brought word as well that small bands were forming in the other tribes, adopting the tactics of the Nighthawks. Though a full-scale rebellion seemed unlikely, there was renewed resistance to land allotments. Some men were willing to defy the government.

A sudden commotion intruded on Chitto's reverie. Ben Dewey, assigned to act as scout that morning, whipped his horse up the incline and rode into camp. He jumped out of the saddle, rushing forward, followed by Lynch and the rest of the men. His eyes were wild with excitement as he stopped before Chitto. He motioned off to the northwest.

"Soldiers!" he said in a loud voice. "Lots of soldiers headed this way. Joe Blackbird's their scout."

"Calm down," Chitto said softly. "You saw Blackbird?"

"Over by Gitting Down Mountain. He was a ways out front of the soldiers. I took off before he spotted me."

"How many soldiers?"

"Whole bunch," Dewey said, thinking back. "Couple of hundred, anyway. Maybe more."

"The battalion we keep hearing about," Chitto observed. "How long do you estimate before they get here?"

"They're moving pretty slow. I'd say at least two hours. Probably longer."

"We will be ready for them by then. You did well, Ben."

"Chitto—" Lynch started to speak, then turned to the men. "You men see to your equipment, and someone pour water on that fire. Chitto and I will talk about this."

The men dutifully broke apart, slowly drifted away. With Chitto injured, they were accustomed to taking orders from Lynch. When they spread out over the camp, he turned back to Chitto. His features were grave.

"What are you thinking?" he said. "We cannot fight that many soldiers. We must leave here."

"I will run no more," Chitto informed him. "Besides, I am unable to sit a horse. I will stay and fight.''

''We are outnumbered *eight* to one. How do you hope to win?''

''Leave if you wish, Joseph. I will not try to stop you.''

Lynch shook his head. ''Do you think I would desert you? The men would not follow me, anyway. You know that.''

''There's your answer,'' Chitto said quietly. ''We knew this time would come, and now it is here. We stand and fight.''

''And if we lose—what then?''

''I do not intend to lose.''

''So how do we win?''

''I have been studying this mountain, Joseph. What else was I to do with my time? Look down there.''

Chitto directed his attention to a defile, halfway down the mountain from their campsite. The defile was perhaps five feet deep, heavily screened by trees, and some thirty yards from the bottom of the slope. Not fifty yards away was Sallisaw Creek, which traced a winding path parallel to the face of the mountain. The stream was swift and wide.

''See that little gully?'' Chitto said. ''You take the men and hide there. When the soldiers come, they will have to slow down to ford the creek. You will have the high ground and they will be disorganized. That is when you open fire.''

Lynch scrutinized the terrain a moment. ''We can kill many men from there. But we cannot kill all of them. What if they keep coming?''

''Divide the men into two squads. If you must retreat, one squad gives covering fire while the other withdraws. Those who make it back to camp are to escape on their horses. Have them regroup at Doublehead Mountain.''

"You said yourself you cannot ride a horse. Do you think we would leave you?"

"I order you to leave me!" Chitto softened the command with a smile. "Save yourself and the men, live to fight another day. Respect my wishes in this, Joseph."

Some twenty minutes later Lynch led the men down the mountain. When he looked back, Chitto was where they had carried him for the final time. Two trees were bound by a common trunk, and the barrel of Chitto's rifle was wedged in the notch. From behind the tree, he could work the lever of his Winchester with one hand, the butt snugged into his right shoulder. He had a clear field of fire to the creek below.

Lynch already knew he was prepared to make his last stand.

Twenty-one

A ribbon of smoke spiraled skyward from the fire. The sun was high, but there was a sharp nip in the air. Jim Colbert fed sticks into the embers until a blaze caught. He walked to the creek with the coffeepot.

Frank Starr sat up in his bedroll. He rubbed sleep from his eyes and watched with dulled interest as Colbert filled the coffeepot with creek water. The other men lazed around in their blankets, yawning and scratching, still half asleep. They were stretched out on the ground, heads propped against their saddles, feet to the fire. To a man, they had slept with their boots on.

Starr levered himself to his feet. He was still suffering a hangover from their spree, and his head throbbed with a pulsing ache. For a moment, he wondered if he was getting too old for drunken benders; but the worrisome nature of the question only made his head hurt worse. He walked off a distance from the fire, unbuttoned his pants, and relieved himself. His eyes glazed with comfort as he splashed the ground.

The camp was located on a broad plain. From the

creek, grasslands gone tawny with frost rolled onward to distant mountains. Yesterday, when they rode out of Evansville, every man in the gang was woozy from the effects of their binge. At a slow trot, their teeth hurt from the jarring thud of hoofbeats on the hard-packed earth of the road south of town. By the time they crossed the line separating Arkansas from Oklahoma they were forced to slow to a sedate walk. They plodded west toward the mountains in dazed silence.

A night's sleep had revived Starr only by degree. He tucked himself away, buttoned his pants, and turned back to the camp. Colbert, who seemed sluggish but clear-eyed, placed the coffeepot at the edge of the fire. He began cutting a slab of bacon they'd bought in Evansville, and dropped the slices into their one frying pan. The smell of sizzling bacon wafted over the camp, and the men crawled out of their blankets with lethargic groans. One by one, they walked off to empty their bladders.

When they returned, Starr and Colbert were swilling coffee and licking bacon grease off their fingers. The men passed the coffeepot around, filling their tin cups, hunkered close to the warmth of the fire. After a few sips of coffee, they picked strips of bacon out of the hot frying pan and chewed in morose silence. Their bloodshot eyes slowly took on signs of life, and Redbird Smith wagged his head with a glum smile. His glance shifted from face to face.

"We're a poor lookin' bunch," he said to no one in particular. "I wonder any of us are still alive and kickin'."

"Who said we was?" Henry Brandon retorted, loosing a gaseous belch. "Way I feel, I must've woke up dead."

Colbert snorted a low chuckle. "You forked so many

whores you ought to be dead. Them girls was happy you left town."

"No, they wasn't," Brandon protested. "Them girls was sweet on me. They told me so."

"Don't make me laugh," Smith cut in. "They was sweet on your money, Henry. Didn't the fun stop when you went broke?"

Jack Fox looked at them. "Hell, we're all broke. Sittin' here drinking bad coffee and not a nickel between us." He darted a sidewise glance at Starr. "We need to think about pullin' another job."

"I've already got one planned," Starr said in a guttural voice. "But we're better off to lay low a week or so. Give the law time to lose interest."

"You think they haven't by now?" Fox asked. "Thought that's why we spent a week in Arkansas. I'd like a little money in my pocket, Frank."

"Jack's right," Smith added quickly. "You can't expect us to live on coffee and bacon. Let's hit a bank."

"Not just yet," Starr said stubbornly. "We'll loaf around Doublehead Mountain for a while. Just till things cool down."

Brandon groaned. "Not a woman within thirty miles of that place. Why not somewheres else?"

"Henry, you'll just have to keep your pecker in your pants. The mountain's the best hideout we ever had, and that's where we're headed. I don't want any more argument about it."

"If you'd told me, I would've brought along a couple of whores."

Starr shaded his eyes, studied the angle of the sun. "Quit bellyaching and get your gear together. Time to move out."

The men grumbled, but they began breaking camp. Within a half hour, their horses were saddled, bedrolls cinched in place, and the camp gear stowed in their saddlebags. Henry Brandon, denied his whores but not a last laugh, pulled out his pud and doused the fire in a shower of piss. Starr grinned at his antics, waiting until the fire was thoroughly watered, and signaled the men to get mounted. He led them southwest along the creek.

In the distance, Starr could make out the rounded knob of Taylor Mountain. From there, angling off to the south, it was another five or six miles to Doublehead Mountain. There was no particular rush, and given the condition of the men, not to mention himself, a moderate pace seemed best all around. He figured they would reach the stronghold, which was on the southern crest of the mountain, by late afternoon. He wondered if they would find Chitto there.

Some two weeks ago he had heard of the gun battle at Nigger Jake Hollow. At the time he'd thought it ironic that his brother, who often chided him about his outlaw ways, was now the most wanted man in Oklahoma. All in a matter of days, Chitto had fought three pitched battles and killed six *aniyonega* peace officers. Starr was impressed by his brother's tactical craft, and a certain gift for luring whites into an ambush. Chitto had proved to be an able general.

Which was a good thing for a man being chased by the army. The day after the bank robbery, when he'd led the gang into Arkansas, Starr remembered being dumbfounded by the news. The people in Evansville talked of nothing else, including the whores, astounded that the governor of Oklahoma had called out the National Guard. After hearing about it, Starr bought a newspaper and read that an entire cavalry battalion had been ordered into the field against his brother. He'd thought it a grand joke.

The idea of anyone trapping Chitto in the mountains

was laughable. Starr had hunted deer and bear with his brother in the wild country since childhood. They knew every twist and turn of the rugged slopes, the lattice-work of streams, no matter how isolated. Chitto would lead the army on a chase, and then vanish, taking refuge at Doublehead Mountain. The chance that the army would somehow track him to the stronghold was the chance of a snowflake on a hot summer day. No chance at all.

Still, for all that, there was one thing that worried Starr. According to the newspapers, Chitto had been wounded during the shootout at Nigger Jake Hollow. Whether it was true, or how bad the wound, was a matter of widespread speculation. But it was nonetheless a concern, and during the drinking and whoring in Evansville, the thought had never been far from Starr's mind. He considered it unlikely that anything short of a freak of nature could kill Chitto. Yet he was still troubled.

Starr saw no reason to discuss his concerns with the men. Their week-long sojourn in Arkansas had been more than enough to throw off the law. Nor was there any need to hide out before pulling another job. His arguments, at least where the men were concerned, amounted to little more than an excuse. There was only one reason to go to Doublehead Mountain.

He wanted to see Chitto again.

The tracks generally followed the creek. Wherever the stream curved, or made a sharp dogleg bend, the trail cut overland to shorten the distance. But the direction was always southwest.

McLain set a fast pace. He alternated between a steady trot and a ground-eating canter, holding to the quicker gait until the horses began to labor. Gideon

Brown rode directly behind him, quiet but alert, eager
to understand how he read the sign on the run. Swanson
and Upgraff trailed along a short distance to the rear,
leading the packhorse. Unlike Brown, neither of them
exhibited any great interest in the chase. They appeared
bored rather than eager.

The men had spent the night at a ramshackle hotel in
Evansville. Just before dawn McLain had routed them
out of bed, and led them to a café where he had arranged
an early breakfast. He told them to eat hearty, for it
would likely be their last decent meal in a long while.
By sunrise, they were at the creek south of town, where
Starr's gang had been sighted the day before. There,
scouting the ground on foot, McLain had found the
tracks of five horses. He set a hard pace toward the
western mountains.

By mid-morning, with the sun still at their backs, the
horses were beginning to tire. McLain signaled a halt
at a spot where the creek stretched onward in an irreg-
ular line. He stepped out of the saddle, motioning Swanson and Upgraff to hold their positions, and handed his
reins to Brown. The horses were slick with sweat,
blowing and snorting, their heads cocked toward the
smell of water. He waved in the direction of the creek.

"Horses need a breather," he said. "Walk them till
they cool down a little. Don't let them guzzle water."

"Hell, we know that," Upgraff said irritably. "We
ain't exactly green behind the ears."

"Do like you're told, Upgraff. I won't argue about
it."

"No, let's argue," Swanson butted in. "We've been
runnin' these horses near on four hours. And don't tell
me you slowed down now and then. They're still wore
out."

"How many manhunts have you been on, Swanson?"

"What the devil's that got to do with anything?"

"Just answer the question."

Swanson shrugged lamely. "I don't rightly recollect. Maybe one or two."

"Or maybe none," McLain said shortly. "Horses are lots tougher than you think. They'll go all day, and then some."

"What if they won't?" Upgraff insisted. "We're out in the goddamn middle of nowhere. What if we wind up on foot?"

"I've never yet ridden a horse into the ground. I don't intend to start now."

"Ask me, you've already got a good jump on it."

McLain took a grip on his temper. He understood that Swanson and Upgraff were disgruntled, and probably scared. He suspected that neither of them had ever tangled with anyone as deadly as Frank Starr. But he could not abide a whiner, or a sworn peace officer who tried to shirk duty. His mouth set in a hard line.

"Get your ears unplugged," he said roughly. "I'll say this just once more, and that's an end to it. Don't you ever again question my orders. Got it?"

Upgraff and Swanson averted their eyes. They looked everywhere but at him, and after a moment of turgid silence, he jerked a thumb toward the creek. "Water them slow and easy. We ride in thirty minutes."

Brown moved off, leading his horse and McLain's at a slow walk. He clearly understood the need to cool them down before allowing them to drink. Swanson and Upgraff followed along, their features fixed in hangdog looks. Neither of them spoke a word.

McLain walked ahead a few yards. He dropped to one knee beside the trail of the five outlaws. His hat

brim shielded his eyes against the sun, and he studied
the tracks, noting that the horses were being held to a
walk. He looked for the change of color caused when
the dry surface of the earth is disturbed to expose a
moister, lower surface. Heat increased the rate at which
tracks age, and he roughly calculated the time the hoofprints had been exposed to sunlight the day before. Then
he added in that morning, for the sun had now been out
some four hours. He was closing the gap.

"What'd you find?"

Brown halted a few steps away, still leading the
horses. He stared down at the tracks with the curiosity
of a man trying to decipher something written in code.
His eyes wrinkled at the corners. "We gainin' on
them?"

"Slow but sure." McLain rose to his feet. "They
passed here yesterday afternoon. I figure we're maybe
five hours behind. Not much more."

"Well, that's pretty good, wouldn't you say? What
with the start they had on us."

"We're lucky Starr doesn't have any notion he's being trailed. He's still holding to a walk."

"I'm itchin' to see his face when we pop up outta
nowhere."

McLain realized he'd taken a liking to Gideon
Brown. The constable was sharper than he appeared,
and eager to learn the tricks of tracking wanted men.
But there was something more, a willingness to endure
hardship coupled with a determination to punish those
who broke the law. All in all, McLain was glad to have
him along on the hunt. He thought Brown would hold
his own in a fight.

"Them boys back there?" Brown ducked his head
toward the creek. "They're plumb bent out of shape.
How'd they ever get a badge?"

McLain stared at the deputies, who were finishing watering their own mounts and the packhorse. "Old-fashioned politics," he said in a wry tone. "Not so much who you are as who you know, Gideon. They're probably related to the sheriff."

"You think they'll hold up their end when we catch Starr?"

"I'd like to hear your opinion, Gideon. What do you think?"

Brown gave the deputies a look of slow assessment. "Don't know that I'd peg 'em as fainthearts. They'll likely stick."

"I just suspect you're right. Most men do when the chips are down."

McLain shortly got them mounted. He was impressed by his brief conversation with Gideon Brown. The constable, much as he'd thought, would stick to the last.

He led them west at a fast trot.

Twenty-two

A noonday sun stood directly overhead. Flares of light bounced off the creek, and apart from the muted rush of water there was no sound. The mountain seemed cloaked in stillness.

Chitto sat hidden behind the forked tree. His rifle rested in the notch, the butt pressed against his good shoulder. He was stiff from sitting so long, unable to move except for flexing his legs from time to time. By the position of the sun, he judged he'd been seated there for three hours or more. He wondered what was keeping the army.

Earlier, when Ben Dewey returned from his scout, he had placed the army only two hours away. Chitto anticipated the cavalry battalion would proceed with caution, and the rough passageway through the ravine would slow them even more. But three hours seemed to him far too long, and a reason for concern. He was not comfortable with the unknown. Not where the *aniyonega* were concerned.

The plateau where the camp was situated afforded

unhampered observation of the creek. Some distance below Chitto saw the Nighthawks crouched in the gully, invisible to anyone approaching the mountain. By their deployment, he knew that Lynch had separated them into two squads, twelve men to a squad. He was pleased with the way Lynch had assumed command, the quick manner in which the men responded to his orders. He told himself that Lynch would make an excellent leader.

Chitto did not expect to leave the mountain alive. A battalion of cavalry was a formidable force, far too strong for the men hidden in the gully. With surprise on their side, he was confident the Nighthawks would fight well, and he knew they would inflict heavy casualties. But in the end, by sheer weight of numbers, the cavalry would overrun their position. The Nighthawks would be forced to retreat over the mountain, and he intended to cover their withdrawal. He would delay the cavalry, confident that he would kill many of them before they killed him. He thought it was a good way to die.

Better to go out fighting, he reminded himself, than to endure a slow death. He had survived this long only because he'd submitted to being immobilized, confined to camp. His shoulder would never heal without an operation, and one horseback ride would be enough to rekindle the infection. Yet a lingering death from blood poisoning still seemed preferable to capture and a hangman's rope. Far better to end it here, on his own terms, in the heat of a fight. Long ago, in the ancient time of the Cherokees, warriors went into battle shouting what he himself was thinking now. Today is a good day to die.

In some ways, he reflected, his death would be a good thing. History proved that a martyred leader often served a cause better in death than in life. People took heart and rallied to action when an underdog fell defending the rights of all men. Joseph Lynch and the Nighthawks would continue the fight, and in time, the Cherokees and the other tribes would join the struggle. He might die but his vision would live on. The legend was always greater than the man.

Chitto suddenly became aware of a strange stillness. The chatter of squirrels, the piping call of birds, was abruptly gone. All around him the woods were too quiet, oddly robbed of sound. His gaze went first to the Nighthawks, and then beyond, to the opposite side of the creek. He saw Joe Blackbird, mounted on a fine dun gelding, sitting motionless in the mouth of the ravine. For a moment his throat went dry as he watched the scout scan the expanse of open ground rolling onward to the mountain. He knew the army was not far behind.

Blackbird nudged his horse. His rifle was out of the scabbard, pointed skyward, the butt resting against his thigh. He rode at a slow walk across the half mile of open ground separating the rocky gorge from the creek. He was following the tracks of Ben Dewey's horse, fresh from that morning, raw earth churned at a gallop and easy to read. All the while his eyes were on the move, flitting upstream and downstream, and then back to Beevale Mountain. The absence of sound, the eerie stillness of the wooded slope, set his nerves on edge, made him all the more wary. He reined to a halt on the north side of the creek.

The stream was some thirty feet wide. On the opposite shore, Blackbird saw fresh tracks that disappeared into the brush at the base of the mountain. He methodically inspected the slope, from the bottom to the top, alert to any movement, the slightest sound, a glint of sunlight on metal. His every sense told him he was being watched, and he trusted instinct far more than his eyes. But he saw nothing man-made, no fortifications, no hint of a mountain stronghold. Nor did he see any men, and deep down in his gut, that bothered him most of all. He knew they were there.

From his perch on the mountain, Chitto observed the scout search the wooded slope. His respect mounted by the moment, for he felt certain Blackbird knew the Nighthawks were hidden within the trees. And still the scout invited death, sitting like a bronzed statue, eyes sweeping back and forth. Then, as though sprung from the ground, the lead elements of the cavalry battalion appeared in the mouth of the ravine. Blackbird sawed on the reins, digging hard with his heels, and kicked the dun gelding into a gallop. He pounded back across the open ground.

Chitto darted a quick glance down the slope. He spotted Lynch crawling through the gully, cautioning the men to keep down, and hold their fire. Satisfied that Lynch had the situation in hand, his gaze swung back across the creek. He saw mounted troopers spill out of the gorge, forming into companies, their guidons snapping in the wind. One company waited at the rear, clearly a reserve element, and another wheeled downstream to face Dahlonegah Mountain. The other two companies rode forward a short distance and halted on line, directly opposite Beevale Mountain. To their direct front, three men sat their horses as though viewing a parade. The soldier in the lead looked like a bloated toad nailed to a horse.

Blackbird skidded to a halt before the three men. Watching closely, Chitto saw the scout report to the fat one in the lead. His eyes narrowed in scrutiny, for he understood now that the heavyset man was the commander. He looked on as Blackbird motioned back toward the mountain, and appeared to be talking in a

strong voice. The fat one listened, staring intently across
the creek, and then seemed to wave Blackbird aside.
Chitto grasped instantly that Blackbird was arguing
against an attack, and the fat one was warding him off
like an irksome mosquito. He thought the cavalry commander was a fool, an arrogant fool.

Dismissed with another wave, Blackbird reined his
horse off to one side. The fat man rose in his stirrups,
arm thrust overhead, and looked back at the leaders of
the two companies waiting on line. The troop commanders acknowledged the signal, shouting an order,
and the mounted soldiers pulled carbines from their saddle scabbards. Then, with a grand gesture, the fat one
swept his arm toward the mountain. Chitto allowed himself a tight smile.

He had his fight.

Drummond signaled a canter. Behind him, Norton and
O'Neal and the two companies gigged their horses to a
faster gait. His rump slapping leather, Drummond directed his attention to the mountain. Blackbird had told
him the Nighthawks were there, waiting in ambush. The
scout had been unable to pinpoint their position, and
reported no sign of fortifications, or a stronghold. But
Drummond was intent on attack, and ignored the warning, ordering the troops forward. Having found the renegades, pride would not allow him to delay, or risk a
standoff. He meant to have his victory.

The mountain was now some three hundred yards to
his front. Drummond rapidly pumped his arm in the air
and led the charge at a full gallop. One hand on the
reins, the other anchored to the pommel, he struggled
to hold his seat in the saddle. His aim was to ford the
creek at a dead run, gaining the opposite bank as quickly
as possible. There, he planned to deploy the troops as

dismounted infantry, conducting the final assault on foot. His one concern was that the Nighthawks would break and run in the face of a full-scale attack. He was determined that none of them would escape.

From the mountain, Chitto watched the charge. The drumming hooves echoed off distant slopes, and despite himself, he was impressed by the sight of massed cavalry thundering forward. Across the flatlands, he saw Joe Blackbird waiting with the reserve elements, and he smiled to himself. The scout was wiser than the fat commander, electing to stay back rather than ride blindly into an unknown situation. Chitto was amazed that the fat man hadn't sent skirmishers ahead, to draw fire and reveal the Nighthawks' position. He waited for the cavalry to hit the creek.

Lynch waited as well. Crouched in the gully, he steeled himself to hold off, resisting the temptation to open fire. He had never seen a cavalry charge, much less one hurtling toward him in a wedge of dust and hooves. His stomach knotted in a tight ball, and he sensed the Nighthawks were gripped by their own fears. Doak Threepersons led one squad, and Noah Adair the other, and their eyes were glued to the horde of horsemen barreling forward. Yet they held their positions, screened by the brush and trees above the gully, nervously awaiting Lynch's order. His features taut, he stared across the creek.

On the opposite bank, Drummond's stallion plunged into the stream at a headlong gallop. Hardly an instant behind, the two troops of cavalry hit the water in a geysering splash. The creek was deeper than it looked, and their momentum was further broken by the force of the current. Their horses sank to their bellies, scrambling for footing on the rocky streambed, and the charge abruptly became a thrashing melee of men and animals.

Their attack bogged down before they reached midstream.

"*Fire!*" Lynch yelled above the din of voices. "*Fire!*"

The Nighthawks to his left and right leveled their rifles over the top of the gully. What they saw was a wild confusion of men and horses, swamped in the water, struggling against the swift current. Threepersons directed the fire of his squad into the cavalry company on the right, and Adair's squad covered the left flank. Their opening volley knocked twenty or more troopers out of the saddle, and sent bodies flying into the water. All of them were armed with repeating rifles, and since childhood, they had been shooting squirrels out of trees and deer on the run. Now they shot men trapped in a roiling stream.

Their second volley dropped another fifteen or twenty men in the creek. The troopers were fighting to control their horses, buffeted about by the current, confronted by a wall of gunfire a short distance up the slope. Though they tried to return fire, their Krag carbines were bolt-action, which required two hands to eject a spent shell and cycle a fresh cartridge. They were hard-pressed to hold on to their reins and operate their carbines at the same time, and most of them got off only one shot. The Nighthawks fired as fast as they could work the levers on their repeaters, and they laid down a withering barrage. The water ran red with blood.

Drummond never got his revolver out of the holster. His stallion squealed and thrashed, spooked by the blast of rifles to their front. A hail of bullets buzzed all around him as the Nighthawks tried to kill the cavalry leader. His hat went sailing, slugs pocked the sleeves of his coat; he was saved only by the furious gyrations of his horse. In the midst of the battle, Sergeant Major

O'Neal spotted the fiery streak of a muzzle flash half-way up the slope, and he winged a shot in return. But as his horse spun away, he saw that the Colonel had been hit, his right earlobe blown away. Drummond screamed, washed in his own blood, and jerked his stallion around. He spurred hard for the north bank.

Captain John Gryden, commanding Company A, caught a slug and fell backward out of his saddle. He dropped into the water as Drummond gained the shore and fled the carnage at a gallop. By now, the bodies of more than fifty troopers floated in the stream, battered beneath the hooves of horses gone mad with fright. The men saw their comrades fallen, a captain down, and the colonel deserting the field, and they broke. Disorganized, still under heavy fire, their terror was contagious, and they wheeled their horses in mass retreat. O'Neal tried to turn them back, stem the rout.

"Rally, boys!" he shouted. "Rally on me!"

Lieutenant Norton barreled past him at a dead lope. The troopers ignored his cries, urging their horses to flight back over the flatlands. A slug nicked O'Neal, searing his ribs, and he decided it was time to quit the fight. Low in the saddle, spurring his horse savagely, he pounded after the men in full retreat. Ahead, across the open ground, he saw Company D, the reserve element, riding to join the battle. But the troop commander saw Drummond and the fleeing men at virtually the same moment, and brought his company to a halt. Drummond galloped by them, motioning off to the north, and rode straight for the mouth of the ravine. The battalion, reduced to a rabble, trailed after their leader.

Blackbird was waiting outside the ravine when O'Neal reined to a halt. The sergeant major looked crazed. "That lard-gutted sonovabitch quit!" he snarled.

"You gotta help me regroup the men, Joe. I'm not done yet."

"You serious?" Blackbird said. "You're going back for more?"

"I'll track them bastards till hell freezes over! They can't kill my men and get away with it. You gonna help or not?"

"Well, why not?" Blackbird agreed. "I signed on for the duration."

On Beevale Mountain, Lynch watched as the scout and the soldier rode into the ravine. The suddenness of the victory left him astounded, and he attributed it to Chitto's shrewd judgment in tactics. He had lost six men killed, with three wounded, and he estimated the horse soldiers had lost at least five times that many. The thing that stuck with him most was the cowardice of the cavalry leader, and the wild scramble to retreat. He thought the Nighthawks had nothing more to fear from the army.

Still, he considered it prudent to take nothing for granted. He believed Chitto would agree that it was time to withdraw to Doublehead Mountain. The decision made, he ordered the men to collect the dead and wounded, and carry them back to the camp. He planned to treat the wounded, and bury his dead on the plateau, and move out by nightfall. He reminded himself to send out scouts to check on the cavalry, another lesson learned from Chitto. Never trust white men to do the sensible thing.

Lynch led the way up the slope. He walked into camp with a sense of exultation, expecting to share the moment with the Nighthawks' leader. Then, too suddenly to credit, he saw that victory had eluded them after all. Chitto lay slumped in a pool of blood behind the tree.

His left eye had been shot out.

Twenty-three

The men slouched in their saddles. A bright noonday sun warmed them, and the gentle sway of their horses lulled them into a drowsy stupor. They plodded along in single file.

Frank Starr blinked himself awake. He realized he'd almost fallen asleep, and scrubbed his face with a thorny hand. All morning he had held the pace to a walk, for his head still ached and his eyes felt dusted with sand. He thought a stiff drink would cure his ills, and his mouth watered at the thought. But he just as quickly set the notion aside, reminded that he never allowed the men to carry whiskey on the trail. He wished now he'd broken his own rule.

The sun hovered high in the sky. Starr unbuttoned his mackinaw, took a deep breath to clear his head. They were skirting the southern end of Taylor Mountain, and off in the distance he saw the twin spires of Doublehead Mountain. He debated an increase in pace, perhaps a moderate trot, which would put them at the stronghold in a couple of hours. Yet his bowels were unsettled, no less a concern than his throbbing head, and he doubted the men were in any better shape. He held to a walk.

A low, crackling sound reverberated off to the southwest. Starr snapped alert, sitting straighter in the saddle. He cocked an ear, his forehead wrinkled in concentration. There was a staccato, spitting noise to the sound, distinct yet far away. The men seemed jarred from their funk, staring into the distance with looks of curiosity and bemused uncertainty. Starr signaled a halt.

"You hear that?" Colbert asked.

"Yeah," Smith said in a baffled voice. "Sounds like thunder."

Colbert shaded his eyes. "No storm clouds out that way."

"Shut up!" Starr ordered. "I can't hear for you talking."

The men fell quiet, listening. The sound went on for three minutes, then four, a drumming rattle that was crisp but oddly muted. Finally, after what seemed five minutes or more, the reverberations faded into stark silence. They listened a moment longer, exchanging puzzled glances. The silence held.

"Could be gunshots," Smith ventured. "Sorta sounded that way."

Fox looked skeptical. "How far does gunfire carry?"

"Don't know," Smith admitted. "Guess it depends on the wind."

Colbert wet a finger, tested the air. "Wind's from the north. All that racket was off to the southwest."

"Tell you one thing," Henry Brandon said in a musing tone. "If that was guns, there was a helluva lot of shootin' going on. Lasted a good five minutes, maybe more."

"I think it was guns," Smith announced. "Noise

tends to echo off these mountains. 'Specially something that loud.''

The men became aware that Starr hadn't yet voiced an opinion. He was still staring into the distance, his eyes narrowed at the corners. "What d'you think, Frank?" Smith said. "Sound like guns to you?"

Starr nodded. "Yeah, it was guns, all right. Like Henry said, lots of guns."

"Well, who's doing the shootin'?" Fox demanded. "Long as it was, that'd have to be a damn war!"

"The army," Starr said flatly. "I got an idea they must've cornered Chitto."

"You're likely right," Colbert muttered. "I mean, that'd explain all the gunfire. Wasn't it a whole battalion after him?"

Starr lapsed into a prolonged silence. He recalled that Chitto had only twelve or fourteen men in his following. An image flashed through his mind, and he saw a battalion of cavalry swarming over the small band of Nighthawks. The cavalry's superiority in numbers would easily account for the short duration of the battle. Odds of seven or eight to one would make for a quick fight. He wondered if Chitto had escaped alive.

"Frank?"

Starr looked around. The men were watching him, and he realized he'd gotten lost in his own ruminations. "What're you thinkin'?" Colbert said. "You sort of drifted off there."

"Something's not right," Starr said, turning it over in his mind. "Chitto should've made it to Doublehead Mountain a week ago, maybe longer. That gunfire was lots farther away."

"No doubt about that," Colbert replied. "Question is, how far away?"

Starr's gaze searched the distant landscape. Before

them lay the headwaters of Sallisaw Creek, which flowed westerly through a broad expanse of open terrain. Some five miles ahead the creek curled around the northern edge of Fletcher Mountain and continued in a southwesterly direction past Dahlonegah Mountain. Puzzling on it, Starr imagined the volume of gunfire, and how it would echo north along the wooded slopes. The sound would easily carry across the open flatlands to their front.

"Eight miles, maybe a little more," he said in answer to Colbert's question. "Somewhere down around Dahlonegah, maybe even Beevale. That'd be my guess."

"Who the hell cares?" Fox blurted. "We've got no reason to tangle with the army. That's Chitto's worry, not ours."

"Try using your noggin, Jack." Starr motioned off to the west. "Suppose some of the Nighthawks managed to get away. What if they're headed for the hideout at Doublehead?"

"Suppose they are? So what?"

"I just suspect the army wouldn't be far behind. Think that'd be a good reason to stay clear of Doublehead?"

"Sure it would," Fox conceded. "So let's forget the whole thing. Go somewhere else."

"Not till we know what's what," Starr said. "Doublehead's the best hideout we ever had, and no guarantee the army will stumble across it. We'll stick around and see what happens."

"You mean, wait till the army shows up?"

"Not exactly."

Starr gave them a long look of assessment. He decided Colbert was the most alert of the bunch, with no lingering signs of a hangover. "Jim, here's what I want,'' he said. ''You scout down along Sallisaw Creek. Get the lay of things.''

Colbert nodded. ''You more interested in the Nighthawks or the army?''

''Where you find one, you're likely to find the other.''

''What if I find the Nighthawks first? You want me to make contact?''

Starr deliberated a moment. ''You'd best not,'' he said at length. ''Stay out of sight and keep your eyes open. I want to know if the army's trailing them.''

''What if the army's not after them?''

''Come on back here and make your report. I'll decide what to do then.''

Colbert rode off along the creek. Starr watched after him for a time, then turned to inspect Taylor Mountain. The base was heavily forested, the slope lifting gradually away from the flat plain. He sighted on a spot that was thick with trees, concealed from view in any direction. He signaled the men to move out.

''Let's find ourselves a place to lay up.''

''How long?'' Fox asked. ''We gonna make camp?''

''A fire wouldn't be the best idea, Jack. We'll wait to hear what Jim finds.''

''Damn the army anyway! I could sure use a cup of coffee.''

Brandon sighed heavily. ''Wish we'd brought along some whores.''

Starr ignored their comments. He led them toward the mountain, unable to shake a troubling thought. No matter how he tried, it stuck in his mind.

He had a bad feeling about Chitto.

The horses were lathered with sweat. McLain felt the need to press ahead, to overturn time and distance. But he knew he had to curb himself, and conserve the horses. He reduced the pace to a trot.

The tracks still followed the creek, angling southwest toward the mountains. They had been on the trail almost four hours, and the mid-afternoon sun was steadily tilting westward. Despite himself, McLain realized that he would soon be forced to call a halt, allow the horses a breather. He was particularly concerned about the packhorse, a black gelding that had seen better days. He thought the animal would never last the course.

One thought triggered another. His concern for the packhorse reminded McLain that he hadn't stopped for the noon meal. Instead, he had pushed on without a word to the men, intent on narrowing the gap. He sensed that Gideon Brown approved, for the constable seemed to thrive on hardship. Yet there were times when he felt the stares of Swanson and Upgraff drilling through his back. The deputies resented him, and there was no question that they resented his decision to press on during the noon hour. They had more appetite for food than for Frank Starr.

To his amazement, the image of pork chops suddenly popped into McLain's mind. He was momentarily at a loss, wondering if his mind was playing tricks on him. But then he realized that it had nothing to do with skipping a noon meal, and even less to do with food. His quick, mental flash of pork chops was more a thing of memory, some lingering remembrance of his last meal in Tahlequah. A hunger of a different sort, and far more pleasant to the taste. He was thinking of Jane Tenkiller.

She was considerably more than he'd bargained for. A widow less than a month, she apparently saw no reason for the sackcloth and ashes commonly associated with mourning. She was a spirited woman, intelligent and animated, willing to take happiness where she found it, and seemingly unbothered by convention. With no pretense or artifice, she had blithely played the role of seductress, and lured McLain into her bed. Not that he'd required coaxing, or struggled to escape her charms. He willingly allowed himself to be seduced.

Later that night, McLain had dragged himself from her bed. She was an ardent lover, wanton at times, and he'd been surprised by the fierceness of her hunger. She had begged him to stay the night, and finally extracted a promise that he would return on his next trip to town. Walking back to the hotel, he had told himself that it was nothing more than a dalliance, just one of those things. Though he was nagged by guilt, and damned himself for being unfaithful to Amy, he couldn't shake the sensation of something exotic, perhaps irresistible. He'd found himself lost in the fire of Jane Tenkiller's embrace. He knew he would return.

McLain smiled to himself, remembering. Then, slowly, the interlude faded, gave way to the time and place of the moment. Not far ahead, beside a copse of trees along the creek, he saw the remains of a campsite. The ashes of a fire were enclosed by a ring of stones, and the earth was a welter of bootprints. The trail led straight to the trees, and he knew he'd found Frank Starr's camp of the night before. He dismounted, handing his reins to Brown, and motioned the other men to stay back. He walked forward, searching the ground.

Two trees, perhaps twenty feet apart, bore the rub marks of a picket rope. In a line, stamped into the moist earth of the creek bank, were the hoofprints of five horses. After inspecting the droppings, he moved across to the campfire and knelt down. The ashes were cold, apparently doused with water, and he brushed away the top layer. He thrust his hand deep in the fire bed, and felt the flagging warmth of dead coals at the bottom. A fire told a tale all its own, and seldom lied. His mustache lifted in a faint smile.

At the edge of the camp, McLain found the trail leading off to the southwest. He walked along a few yards, then stooped down to examine the tracks. The hoofprints were baked by the sun, the rim and outer edges already dried to the natural color of the soil. But the bottom of the impressions, where hooves dug deepest into the ground, were lighter in shade, still slightly moist. He followed for another fifty yards, satisfying himself that Starr and the gang were holding their horses to a walk. The trail was on a beeline for the mountains.

Upon returning to the campsite, he waved the men forward. He waited until they dismounted, then motioned off to the southwest. "Tracks are pretty fresh," he said. "I figure we're about two hours behind."

"By golly!" Brown hooted. "We've cut their lead down next to nothin'. You think we'll catch 'em today?"

"Not likely," McLain told him. "We'd have to push our horses too hard. Tomorrow morning's a safer bet."

"How about some grub?" Upgraff said sourly. "I could eat a goddamn rock."

McLain looked at him. "You must've read my mind, Charley. Hobble the horses and put them out to graze. We'll stop here for an hour."

"What about us?" Swanson protested. "Can we build a fire?"

"Gideon will see to the fire. Whatever he can whip together, that's what we'll eat. You boys tend to the horses."

Swanson and Upgraff turned back to the horses. Brown hesitated, as if he had something on his mind. He finally nodded to the black gelding. "That packhorse is slowin' us down. I doubt he'll last much longer."

"I was thinking the same thing," McLain said. "We'll turn him loose when we stop tonight. Take what we can in our saddlebags."

"Travel light and travel fast. That the idea?"

"That's the idea."

"I wish't it was tomorrow already."

"We're close, Gideon. Damn close."

Brown wandered off to start a fire. McLain walked to the edge of the camp, staring down at the tracks a moment. Then his gaze went to the distant mountains, dark humps beneath the afternoon sun. Any vestige of doubt was now erased from his mind. Frank Starr was headed for the stronghold.

Yet his certainty raised a more troubling specter. He somehow had to overtake Starr and the gang before they reached the mountain stronghold. Once they joined forces with Chitto and the Nighthawks the odds would be thrown out of balance. Any chance of capturing them would go by the boards, probably forever. Which meant damn close wasn't close enough.

Some gut instinct told him that tomorrow was the last day. His last chance.

Twenty-four

A full moon bathed the land in a sallow glow. Cottony clouds drifted through an indigo sky ablaze with stars, and light rippled off the swift waters of the creek. Somewhere on the mountain an owl hooted, a solitary voice in the night.

Lynch stood watching the flatlands beyond the creek. Guards were posted along the base of the mountain, and directly behind him, the Nighthawks were preparing to break camp. He could hear the men talking softly among themselves, but he paid them scant attention. His mind was on the *aniyonega*.

Earlier, with the onset of dusk, Lynch had sent Ben Dewey to scout the ravine. When he returned, Dewey reported that the cavalry battalion had withdrawn to Dry Creek, on the north side of Gitting Down Mountain. The horse soldiers were camped on the far side of the creek, with fires lit and sentinels posted. All the sign indicated that they were bivouacked for the night.

The report allayed Lynch's concerns only by degree. He had no clear idea as to whether the army would mount another attack; but he felt certain they would return tomorrow, and return in force, to collect their dead. Which seemed all the more reason to stick with his original plan, and withdraw under the cover of darkness. He felt it was time for the Nighthawks to disengage, and if possible, elude the army. He meant to occupy the stronghold at Doublehead Mountain.

That morning, following the battle, Lynch had been forced to make some hard decisions. Chitto was gravely wounded, unconscious since being shot, and Lynch had assumed command of the Nighthawks. He doubted that Chitto would survive without an operation, and the closest surgeon was in Tahlequah. Yet his greater responsibility was to the men, and he dared not risk their capture, and ultimately, their execution on the gallows. He weighed the life of one man against the lives of many, and ordered preparations for a withdrawal. He thought Chitto would have approved his decision.

Still, even as he made the decision, Lynch refused to surrender hope. The quickest route of withdrawal, and by far the safest, would have been over the top of Beevale Mountain. But he was all too aware that Chitto's chances for survival across such rough terrain were diminished greatly, perhaps eliminated altogether. He chose instead to withdraw through the flatground along the creek, moving northeast past Dahlonegah Mountain. Though it was hardly the wisest choice, there was no hesitation in selecting the longer route. He knew Chitto would have done no less for him.

Turning back into the camp, Lynch crossed the clearing. He stopped where Chitto lay in dappled moonlight, the wound bandaged with an herbal compress. The whole thing seemed to him an aberration, a fluke that beggared all odds. Earlier in the day, after finding Chitto, he'd put it together piece by piece, like a puzzle.

A bullet fired by the soldiers had deflected off one of the trees Chitto was using for cover, leaving a telltale gouge in the bark. The slug then ricocheted off the receiver of Chitto's rifle, tearing out his left eye and a chunk of cheekbone. He appeared more dead than alive.

Chitto lay on a litter constructed of stout poles interlaced with rawhide webbing. The webbing was padded with blankets, and the litter would be used to transport Chitto down the mountain. Lynch had ordered the poles cut twelve feet long, so that the litter could be lashed to a horse and serve as a travois. The rig was springy, and Lynch thought it would cushion Chitto's head and shoulder on their trek through the night. He intended to drag Chitto to Doublehead Mountain on the travois—and get him there alive.

"We're about ready." Doak Threepersons moved forward from where the men waited with their horses. "When do you want to move out?"

"Let's get started," Lynch said. "Take four men and seal off the mouth of the ravine. Don't let anybody through."

"You think the army will have anybody out tonight?"

"Hard to say one way or another. They might have sent Joe Blackbird to scout our position. If he's there, kill him."

Threepersons nodded. "I'd like that job."

"Give us time to get past," Lynch went on. "Then you and your men stay back and act as rear guard. No need to take chances."

"We'll give you plenty of warning if anything happens."

"I know you will, Doak."

"How about Chitto?" Threepersons asked. "Will he make it awright?"

Lynch stared down at their fallen leader. "We'll just have to take it easy and hope for the best. He's in bad shape."

"I guess you know the men are plenty worried."

"Chitto's a hard man to kill. I'd judge he'll pull through."

"What if he don't?"

"Let's not borrow trouble. Things have a way of working out."

Threepersons gave him a strange look, then turned away. Lynch realized he'd fobbed off a question that he had been asking himself all day. Whether the Nighthawks would continue the fight without Chitto was clearly a matter of debate among the men. Should Chitto die he wasn't certain himself which way it would go. He only knew that he would never quit the fight, and those who believed would follow. As for the others . . .

A short time later Threepersons and his rear-guard contingent led their horses down the slope. Lynch gave them a ten-minute start, then motioned the other men forward and led them from the abandoned camp. Noah Adair trailed a distance behind, supervising four men who had been assigned to carry Chitto's litter. They picked their way along the rocky path, fearful of a misstep, wary of jostling the injured man. Their descent took the better part of an hour.

Lynch waited for them at the bottom of the mountain. He watched as they transformed the litter into a travois, lashing the upper ends of the poles over the shoulders of one of the spare mounts. When the job was done, he moved forward and knelt down, inspecting their handiwork. Chitto was still unconscious, wrapped in blankets, his features oddly jaundiced in the silvery moonlight. Finally, satisfied that all was in order, Lynch

walked to his horse and stepped into the saddle. He rode
to the head of the column.

Off in the distance, directly opposite their position,
was the mouth of the ravine. The moon went behind a
cloud as they started forward, cloaking them in shadow,
and Lynch took it as a good omen. He was no more
superstitious than the next man, but he thought it a fa-
vorable sign that their retreat began in a moment of
darkness. The gods, he told himself, were fickle but oftentimes benevolent, even protective. Perhaps their escape would go unnoted.

Then, in the next moment, bright moonlight flooded
the landscape. All around him, Lynch saw the bodies of
dead cavalrymen sprawled along the banks of the creek.
Whether a good omen or bad, he knew it was nonetheless a window into the future. He remembered Chitto
once saying that white men were at their worst in defeat;
that pride drove them to seek another fight. The wisdom
of the statement had been borne out, and Lynch had no
doubt that it would prove true in the days to come. The
army would soon be on their trail.

Yet there was nothing to be done tonight. His immediate goal was to reach the stronghold, and there was
a bright moon to light the way. Whatever the omens,
he'd learned that tomorrow was always another day. A
good tactician fought one fight at a time.

He led the Nighthawks from Beevale Mountain.

''I'm freezin' my ass off.''

''You've got lots of company.''

''We'll starve before we freeze.''

''C'mon, Frank, enough's enough.''

''I told you, no fire,'' Starr said. ''Not till Jim gets
back.''

The men were cold and hungry, and increasingly

quarrelsome. They sat inside the treeline, on the south side of Taylor Mountain, their horses snubbed to a picket rope. Without a fire, they were unable to fry bacon or boil coffee, and they huddled together in the chill night air. Their words billowed streams of frost.

"Well, dammit anyway," Smith complained. "How long you expect us to wait? Jim's been gone forever and a goddamn day."

"Leave it be," Starr warned him. "You're starting to get on my nerves. I don't want to hear any more."

There was a long moment of brittle silence. The men's features were visible in the moonlight, and they sat with their hands stuffed in the pockets of their mackinaws. The sharp tone in Starr's voice made them fearful of provoking his wrath. Brandon tried another tack.

"Maybe Jim's not comin' back."

"What're you talkin' about?" Fox said crossly. "Why wouldn't he come back?"

Brandon shrugged. "Maybe he got himself shot."

"Even if he did, why didn't we hear a gun? Answer me that."

"Maybe he was too far away. Like Redbird said, he's been gone a long time. For all we know, he got took prisoner by the army."

Starr was thinking the same thing. He stared up at the moon a moment, calculating the time at about eight o'clock. Colbert had been gone at least seven hours, and he was considerably more worried than he let on to the men. Several possibilities badgered his mind, and one of them was that Colbert had somehow been captured by the army. The prospect became more real with each passing moment.

Yet that wasn't Starr's most bothersome concern. Colbert was a loyal follower, and a good man in a tight situation; but he wasn't blood kin. For the last hour or

so, Starr had been dwelling on something of a more
personal nature, and the thought of it left him in a foul
mood. If Colbert had been captured, he dourly reflected,
then there was every likelihood that Chitto had been
taken prisoner as well. Or maybe worse, considering the
volume of gunfire they had heard around midday. Chitto
might be dead.

"You're barking up the wrong tree," Smith finally
said, glancing at Brandon. "Jim's a pretty slick scout,
not much better. He'd never let himself get caught."

"Then where is he?" Brandon countered. "A battalion of cavalry is an awful lot of men. We got no idea
how far they're spread out. Maybe he just stumbled into
them."

Fox snorted derisively. "You boys ought to get yourselves a crystal ball. Then we'd likely know what's
what."

"You got any better—"

"*Quiet!*" Starr hissed.

The men fell silent, startled by the harsh command.
Off in the distance, faint but growing louder, they heard
the thud of hoofbeats. Some moments later, on the north
side of the creek, a horseman materialized out of the
moonlight. He slowed to a walk, his features distinct in
the silty light, scanning the wooded mountainside. Starr
stepped out of the trees.

"Jim!" he called. "Over here."

Colbert crossed the open ground north of the creek.
He swung down from the saddle and led his horse into
the trees. The men crowded around, stamping their feet
against the cold. Jack Fox clapped him on the shoulder.

"Where the hell you been? We about gave you up
for lost."

"When'd I ever get lost?" Colbert said. "Just took
longer than I expected, that's all."

Starr looked prepared for the worst. "What took longer than you expected? What'd you find?"

"Found the Nighthawks," Colbert told him. "They cleared the north end of Fletcher Mountain about an hour ago. Saw 'em on the south side of Cherry Tree Creek."

"Saw them?" Starr repeated. "You didn't talk to them?"

Colbert wagged his head. "I was on this side of the creek. I started to yell out and then decided to stay hid in the trees. Somebody's followin' them."

"How do you know that?"

"Because they're travelin' with a rear guard. Nobody does that unless they're being followed. Thought I'd best let you know before we showed ourselves."

Starr nodded agreement. "Did you see Chitto?"

"Never got that close," Colbert said. "There was fifteen men out front, one being pulled on a travois. Guess he'd been wounded. Five men in the rear guard."

"Twenty men?" Starr said, dumbfounded. "Chitto never had that many men since he started. Where'd they come from?"

"Don't ask me, Frank. I'm just tellin' you what I saw. Maybe Chitto recruited some men."

"Yeah, I suppose that's possible. What about the army? See anything of them?"

"Nope," Colbert said, with a puzzled frown. "I hung around to see if that's who was followin' the Nighthawks. Never saw nobody."

"Don't mean a thing," Smith broke in. "You can bet the army's not too far behind. Why else would they put out a rear guard?"

"I just suspect it's so," Colbert said. "Way it looks to me, Chitto waited till nightfall to make his break.

Them army boys'll probably be hot on his trail come mornin'.''

"Something don't jibe," Starr said, thinking out loud. "All that shooting we heard this morning sounded like a war. How'd Chitto beat off a whole battalion?"

"You tell me," Colbert replied. "He's your brother."

Starr stared out into the moonlit night. Brother or not, he was confounded that Chitto and the Nighthawks had emerged intact from the battle. That morning, listening to the swell of gunfire, he'd considered it unlikely that any of the Keetoowahs would survive. His one hope had been that Chitto would somehow manage to escape, and elude capture. He was boggled by the thought that the entire band had survived the onslaught.

"Here's the way I see it," he said at length. "Chitto plans to fort up at Doublehead. Maybe the army will track him there, and maybe they won't." He paused, looking around at the men. "We'll wait till morning and find out."

"Why wait?" Fox said testily. "Let's just get the hell out of here. I don't want no part of the army."

"Told you once before," Starr said, his eyes cold in the moonlight. "Doublehead's too good a hideout to let it slide. We'll camp here and see what happens in the morning. I won't argue about it."

Jack Fox knew better than to push it further. He turned away, grumbling under his breath, and the other men joined him in setting up camp. Starr allowed them to build a small fire, adequate to boil coffee and fry bacon, but scarcely enough to warm their hands. They got busy collecting firewood.

None of them ventured another word about the army or the Nighthawks. But they were nonetheless of the same opinion about tomorrow morning. Starr's dark

mood merely confirmed what they had only suspected
until now.

He meant to satisfy himself that his brother would
live to fight another day.

Twenty-five

The broad plain shimmered under the radiance of moonglow. To the west, the mountains rose in stark relief against a starry sky, and a biting wind sliced out of the north with a low moan. Silvery beads of hoarfrost sparkled like chipped diamonds on the tawny grass.

McLain held the pace to a brisk walk. The tracks were visible in the moonlight, and he had no trouble following the trail. Off in the distance, where the plain ended and the mountains began, he saw a dark hump silhouetted against the sky. He didn't know the name of the mountain, but it was the first in a chain that stretched onward to the southwest. He thought they would find Frank Starr there.

Shortly before sundown, McLain had stopped to inspect the tracks. The sign was plain to read, and he judged they were no more than an hour behind the gang. He wanted to further close the gap, and there was little chance of losing the trail under the brilliance of a full moon. Yet the horses were worn from the day's chase, and he was wary of pushing them too hard through the night. He'd decided to press on at a walk.

Up ahead a tributary creek branched off to the south. A shelterbelt of trees bordered the stream, and the banks were fringed with grassland. McLain studied the position of the moon, estimating the time at somewhere around eight o'clock. He was leery of overtaking the gang at night, and he thought the creek was a good place to call a halt. There was water, plenty of firewood to ward off the chill, and abundant graze for the horses. He brought the men to a stop along the east bank.

The campsite he chose was beneath a copse of trees. By now, the men understood their assigned tasks and quickly went about their chores. After the horses were unsaddled, Swanson and Upgraff got them hobbled and put them out to graze. Brown meanwhile unloaded the packhorse, and McLain collected several armloads of firewood. Within a half hour, a blaze lit the night and the smell of salt pork and beans drifted across the camp. A small galvanized coffeepot steamed over a bed of coals.

The men gathered around the fire. They had been in the saddle since before sunrise, and their features were creased with fatigue. McLain poured coffee, passing out cups, while Swanson and Upgraff warmed themselves by the flames. Brown heaped plates from a cast-iron skillet, and handed them around to the men. They ate in dulled silence, scraping beans and chunks of salt pork from their plates with spoons. Afterward, Brown stuffed a pipe with tobacco and Swanson took a sack of Bull Durham from inside his coat. Upgraff poured himself another cup of coffee.

McLain rolled a smoke, lit up with a stick from the fire. He nodded to the empty skillet. "Hope you boys got your fill. That'll be our last meal for a while."

"What d'you mean?" Upgraff said, warming his

hands on the tin cup. "We still got grub in the packs."

"Starting tomorrow, we travel lean and light. I'm turning the packhorse loose."

"Why would you do a thing like that?"

"You might've noticed he's on his last legs. We can't be slowed down."

"Well, hell," Upgraff grumped. "We still got to eat."

McLain motioned to the packs. "Stuff some hardtack and dried fruit in your saddlebags. You won't starve."

Swanson watched the exchange with a narrow look. He took a drag on his cigarette, exhaled smoke. "Why're you worried about being slowed down? What's the sudden rush?"

"Frank Starr," McLain said. "We're less than an hour behind him and his gang. I plan to hit them first thing in the morning."

Swanson coughed smoke. "What's that mean—hit them?"

"I'd like to take them by surprise," McLain remarked. "We'll leave at dawn and set a fast pace. Might just catch them in their bedrolls."

"And if we don't?"

"Then we'll have a fight on our hands."

"How're we gonna sneak up and catch 'em off guard? We don't even know where they're camped."

"I'll find their camp come daylight. I tend to doubt they're expecting company."

"Maybe they'll run," Upgraff said hopefully. "Might turn out to be no fight at all."

Brown chuffed smoke from his pipe. "That's why we've gotta travel light. If they run, we'll be right on their heels. We can't let 'em get away now."

"When'd you get to be such an expert?" Swanson said gruffly. "I thought this was your first manhunt."

"Yours, too," Brown replied with a sly look. "Unless you've been keepin' secrets."

"Don't you worry yourself about me! I'll be there when the time comes."

"Never figured otherwise."

McLain understood that they were jumpy. Until now it had been little more than a long horseback ride. But they were suddenly confronted with the fact that tomorrow they would go up against armed men. He diverted their attention by pulling his Winchester from the scabbard, and a swatch of cloth from his saddlebags. They watched as he cranked the lever, emptying cartridges from the magazine onto his lap. He began swabbing the open breach with the cloth.

"Never hurts to check your weapons," he said casually. "When you need 'em, you want them to work."

"Sounds like good advice," Brown agreed. "Nothin' worse than a gun that won't shoot."

Swanson and Upgraff traded a glance as Brown pulled out his Marlin repeater. Before long, the four men were seated around the fire, busily swabbing grit from the innards of their carbines. McLain finished first, reloaded his Winchester, and set it aside. He shucked shells out of his Colt and tested the action. He began cleaning it with the cloth.

"Don't count on Starr and his boys to surrender," he said, working the hammer of the Colt. "They're wanted for murder, and they likely dread the idea of a hangman's noose. They'd rather go down fighting."

There was a prolonged moment of silence. Brown laid the Marlin over his saddle and upholstered his old Smith & Wesson. "I've never killed a man," he said in a quiet voice. "You got any pointers for a tyro like me?"

"Don't think," McLain told him. "A man who stops

to think generally gets his ticket punched. Don't think, don't hesitate, don't flinch from it. Just do it.''

"Get him before he gets you," Upgraff said, trying for an even tone. "First man off the mark wins the race. That the idea?"

"There's an old saying about such things," McLain observed. "Speed's fine but accuracy is final. Don't rush your first shot. Make it count."

Swanson cleared his throat. "What if the other man's shootin' at you? How do you take your time?"

"Charley, if he's still shooting at you, then it's likely you're not hit. You've got all the time in the world."

"Hope to hell I remember that tomorrow."

"You'll do just fine. You all will."

McLain shoved a cartridge into the first chamber of the Colt. Then he rotated the cylinder, skipping a chamber, and loaded four shells in succession. He lowered the hammer on the empty chamber, and smoothly holstered the pistol. The men watched him as though he were a magician performing some feat of legerdemain. They went back to cleaning their guns.

No one commented further on his advice. Nor were they uncertain as to what they'd heard. They were thinking instead of tomorrow, and there was one thought uppermost in their minds. A simple thought, but far more complex than it appeared. A motto to live by.

Make the first shot count.

The Nighthawks came to Doublehead Mountain late that night. The moon tipped westward as they halted at the base of the southern peak. Doak Threepersons and the rear-guard detail were only a short distance behind.

Lynch ordered the men to lead their horses up the steep slope. Their way was lighted by the moon, and they began the ascent in single file along a winding path.

After the travois was unhitched, Adair and three men carried Chitto up the mountainside. They topped the summit shortly after one o'clock in the morning.

The stronghold was a fortified redoubt just below the crest. A large chamber twenty feet square had been excavated with pickaxe and shovel from the northwest side of the slope. The open front of the chamber had then been sealed with a long wall, constructed of felled trees and shored with stone. A massive split-long door afforded entrance into the redoubt.

On the reverse slope a wide plateau had been cleared of trees. A corral had been built for livestock beside a stream that cascaded down the mountain. There was graze for the horses in a meadow at the base of the mountain, and the corral itself was hidden from view except from the southeast. The men unsaddled their horses in the waning moonlight and turned them into the corral. With their gear, they then trooped back to the redoubt.

A stone fire pit stood in the center of the chamber. Directly above, in the ceiling, a smoke hole had been bored through five feet of earth and rock. Some of the men quickly built a fire and took the damp chill off the room. Chitto was placed on his litter along the far wall, near the warmth of the fire. Candles were lighted, and the chamber was soon flooded in a cider glow. The men set about storing their gear and spreading blankets for the night. Their features were lined with weariness.

Lynch knelt down beside the litter. He placed a hand on Chitto's forehead, felt the radiated heat of a raging fever. He called to one of the men for a damp cloth and gently sponged away a sheen of sweat. As he worked, he wondered what more could be done, and drew a blank. He was about to rise when Chitto's good eye slowly rolled open. The eye fixed on him with dulled comprehension.

"Joseph." Chitto took a shallow breath. "What place is this?"

"Doublehead Mountain," Lynch said. "You are safe now."

"I don't remember much. I fired at their leader and— then it's gone . . . I wake up here."

"You were wounded. Even worse than before, I'm afraid. You lost an eye."

"Eye?" Chitto blinked, casting about with his one eye. "I thought I couldn't see you so good."

"Are you in pain?"

"Yes, my head hurts . . . hurts a lot."

Lynch was hardly surprised. He stared down at the disfigured face, still amazed that it was not a mortal wound. "I will change your bandage in the morning. Maybe it will feel better, then."

Chitto's voice was weak. "Did we defeat the soldiers?"

"Your plan was a good one. We drove them away and killed many. Fifty, maybe more."

"Will they follow us here?"

"We should know by tomorrow."

"Joseph."

"Yes?"

"Do not let them take me alive."

"Get some rest," Lynch said softly. "We will talk of it in the morning. Try to sleep now."

"I think I will. I am very tired."

Chitto's eye drooped closed. His breathing was even but labored, a raspy sound. Lynch got to his feet, aware that the men were watching him, awaiting a reaction. He nodded to them, offering reassurance with a forced smile, and walked to the door. He swung it open, the leather hinges creaking faintly, and stepped outside. The landscape was painted in pale moonlight.

Doublehead Mountain was aptly named. A low saddle of land, some two hundred feet below the peaks, separated the northern and southern summits. The stronghold, which was located on the face of the southern crown, commanded a sweeping view of the lowlands to the north and northwest, as well as the rest of the mountain. An assaulting force would have no choice but to attack uphill, and gun ports in the log wall of the stronghold provided clear fields of fire. A few defenders could hold the mountain against overwhelming odds.

Long ago, Chitto had selected the summit as their retreat of last resort. The Nighthawks had labored to hack the central chamber from the mountainside, and then buttressed the outer wall to withstand anything short of cannon fire. The stronghold was provisioned with dried meat and foodstuffs, stout barrels for drinking water, and sufficient ammunition to fight a siege. The fortified redoubt was all but impregnable, commanding the high ground, and easily defended. The Nighthawks could hold out a month or longer.

"What do you think?" Threepersons stepped through the door. "Will the army come after us?"

Lynch looked around. "There's no question of it in my mind, Doak. We've killed too many of them now. They'll come."

"I saw the look on your face after you talked to Chitto. What was it he asked you?"

"He doesn't want to be taken alive."

Threepersons considered a moment. "We can't move him again—can we?"

"Not without killing him."

"So we have nowhere to run from here. This is our last stand."

Lynch stared out into the night. ''We are at an end,'' he said wearily. ''Tomorrow, I will tell the men that those who stay invite certain death. There will be no dishonor for those who choose to leave.''

''And what will you do?''

''I will stay with Chitto.''

''Even if it means getting killed?''

''No man lives forever, Doak.''

''The men feel the same way,'' Threepersons said with conviction. ''They will not desert Chitto. Or you, either.''

Lynch nodded. ''Then we stand and fight one last time.''

Threepersons was silent. Finally, without saying anything more, he turned back through the door. Lynch continued staring out over the mountain, his emotions running strong. He knew Threepersons had spoken for all the men.

They were the Nighthawks, and they would not run. They would fight.

Twenty-six

They waited in a thick stand of trees beside Sallisaw Creek. A flare of light touched the horizon as dawn slowly gave way to sunrise, and the men nervously eyed oncoming day. To their direct front lay the northern slope of Doublehead Mountain.

Frank Starr was ready to travel. Before dawn he had rousted the men out of their bedrolls and ordered them to break camp. He allowed them to kindle a fire and make coffee, but he rushed them along. By full dawn they were mounted and on the move, riding south toward Sallisaw Creek. Colbert had been sent ahead to scout.

A private man, Starr rarely revealed himself to the gang. Sometime before dawn he'd awakened in a cold sweat, his every sense alert. There was no obvious cause for alarm; but some inner voice nonetheless told him to be on the move. He never questioned his instincts, especially one so powerful as to awaken him from a dead sleep. Over the years, reason had often led him astray, whereas instinct had kept him alive more times than he could count. He always listened to that inner voice.

What it told him now was not clear. Yet he somehow sensed danger, a need to break camp and be on the move by first light. He planned to react as circumstances dictated, and he waited impatiently for Colbert's report. If the army was on his brother's trail, Colbert would uncover sign to the south, along Cherry Tree Creek. In that event, Starr would turn north, put distance between himself and Doublehead Mountain. But if there were no sign of the army, he would head for the stronghold, perhaps outrun the sense of danger. The voice might have been telling him that all along.

"Wish Jim'd come on," Brandon complained, stamping his feet against the cold. "What's taking him so long?"

Smith grimaced sourly. "We could've cooked something to eat and still had time to spare. Don't know why we have to go hungry."

"Ask Frank," Brandon said, his words wrapped in frost. "He's the one that wanted to break camp so fast."

"Frank's not talking," Fox chimed in. "Keeps his secrets to himself, don't you, Frank?"

"No secret to it," Starr said. "Just time to move on, that's all. Why make a big thing of it?"

" 'Cause we're hungry," Smith said peevishly. "A man's got a right to eat."

"You're lucky you got coffee."

"Would you mind telling—"

Starr waved him silent. Off to the south, a horseman appeared in the quickening light. They watched, their bickering abruptly forgotten, as Jim Colbert rode toward them. A few moments later he forded the creek and reined to a halt. He stepped out of the saddle.

"What'd you find?" Starr demanded. "Any sign of the army?"

"Not a thing," Colbert said. "I checked back along Cherry Tree Creek a pretty good ways. Nobody in sight."

Starr looked puzzled. "I would've sworn they'd be on Chitto's trail. Wonder where they are?"

"Maybe they gave it up," Smith offered. "For all we know, Chitto could've whipped them real bad. They might be headed home."

"Well, they're not headed this way," Colbert said. "When it got light, I could see clear back to Fletcher Mountain. They're just not there."

"What about Doublehead?" Starr asked. "Did you circle back to the south?"

Colbert nodded. "That's what took me so long. I rode to within a mile or so of the hideout. The Nighthawks are there."

"You saw them?"

"Never got close enough. But I spotted smoke at the top of the mountain. They're there."

"Probably cooking breakfast," Fox said, glancing sideways at Starr. "Chitto don't make his men go hungry."

"Let it be!" Starr barked. "I've got more on my mind than your gut. I need time to think."

"What's there to think about, Frank? Jim already told you the army's nowhere in sight."

Starr ignored the comment. All along he'd been thinking that the source of his unease, what had awakened him that morning, was the army. Yet Colbert was the best scout in the gang, and he was forced to accept the fact that the army was nowhere near Doublehead Mountain. Which did far less to ease his mind than he would have expected. He still couldn't shake the sense that something was wrong.

For a moment he wavered, instinct telling him one

thing and the facts another. But then, chiding himself for indecision, he made a snap judgment. He had come this far because he felt some indefinable need to see Chitto, and the way was clear. He saw no reason not to go on.

"Mount up," he ordered. "We'll pay Chitto a call."

The men hastily got mounted. Starr led them out of the trees, resisting the temptation to look over his shoulder, and forded the creek. As they gained the opposite shore, shafts of light splintered the horizon in a fiery sunrise. Starr set the pace at a brisk trot.

They rode south toward Doublehead Mountain.

The embers in the fire were still hot. McLain stood, dusting off his hands, lost a moment in thought. The men sat their horses at the edge of the camp, watching him puzzle it out. He walked back to his gelding.

"Fire's still hot," he said, swinging into the saddle. "They're not far ahead."

Brown scratched his whiskery jaw. "Wonder why they pulled out so early?"

"I'd like to know myself, Gideon."

Swanson and Upgraff seemed no less surprised. The four men had been in the saddle since dawn, and they hardly expected to find the outlaws already gone. The horizon exploded in sunrise as they turned their horses from the camp, and paused at the fringe of the treeline. McLain found fresh tracks leading south.

Some ten minutes later they crossed Sallisaw Creek. McLain read the tracks on the run, certain now that the gang was less than a half hour ahead. To the immediate south lay a saddle-backed mountain with twin domes, and off to the west, a broad plain. The tracks skirted the northern base of the mountain, and then again angled southward across the flatlands. He held the pace to a ground-eating lope.

The sun rose above the mountain not quite twenty minutes later. As they topped a low swale in the grassland, McLain suddenly went rigid in the saddle. Off in the distance, perhaps a quarter mile to the south, he saw five riders moving at a steady trot. He motioned, directing the attention of Brown and the others, and got rapid nods of acknowledgement in return. The wind in his eyes, bent low in the saddle, he booted his gelding in the ribs. They pounded forward at a headlong gallop.

Up ahead, Frank Starr finally looked over his shoulder. What he saw froze his blood, and gave renewed faith to his darker instincts. He counted four riders, closing on him fast, and without being told, knew it was the law. He experienced a fleeting moment of wonder, dumbfounded that the law had tracked him into the wilderness. The men followed his gaze, their expressions a mix of alarm and disbelief, and looked back to him for direction. One arm overhead, he whipped it downward and pointed straight at the mountain. He gigged his horse into a dead run.

McLain saw the gangleader's signal. He naturally assumed that Starr and his men were making a run for the mountain, where they would take cover on the wooded slope. Had he looked up, he would have seen a tendril of smoke drifting windward from the southern summit. But he was intent on overtaking Starr, and failed to grasp that he was charging toward the Nighthawks' stronghold. He raked his gelding, whipping with the reins, determined to close the gap. He meant to engage the gang in a fight before they reached the mountain.

The race went to the fresher horses. McLain and his men had pushed their mounts to the limit over the past twenty-four hours. Starr and the gang were riding horses that had hardly broken a sweat since leaving Arkansas. Given a slight lead when the chase began, the outlaws were easily ahead by a hundred yards as they neared the mountain. Yet Starr had failed to take into account the steep banks on either side of Cherry Tree Creek. The gang was forced to rein up sharply when they hit the defile, or risk injury to their horses. They went down one side and up the other in a wild scramble, and their lead was wiped out. They barely made it into the trees.

A short distance behind, McLain assessed the situation at a glance. Should Starr choose to turn and fight, the trees afforded his gang protective cover. McLain made a spur-of-the-moment decision, and halted his men at the bottom of the creekbed. He jumped out of the saddle, pulling his Winchester from the scabbard, and took shelter behind the far bank. The men followed his example, shooing their horses downstream, and moved into position. As they shouldered their rifles, Starr's gang tried to boot their horses up the forward slope of the mountain. But in the heat of the chase, they had overrun the trail to the stronghold, and the grade was too steep at that point for man or horse. They bogged down some thirty yards within the treeline.

McLain drew a bead on Starr. He had been looking at wanted posters of the gangleader for two years, and finally had him in his sights. He fired just as Starr's thrashing horse lost footing, and whirled backward in a mad plunge on the slope. The slug struck the horse in the head, and it collapsed as though chopped off at the legs, dumping Starr from the saddle. McLain cursed, working the lever on his carbine, and fired as Starr rolled to a stop behind a tree. The bullet seared bark a few inches above Starr's head, and he burrowed into the ground beside the trunk. Bruised but unhurt, he quickly returned fire with his pistol.

Spread out along the creek, the other lawmen began popping off shots. The gang members quit their horses and scurried to find cover behind the trees. Redbird Smith was a beat too slow, and a slug from Brown's rifle sent him tumbling down the slope. Swanson and Upgraff blasted away, cranking the levers on their carbines with frantic speed. Their shots peppered trees, and kicked up spurts of dirt, but generally went wide of the mark. The remaining gang members finally got themselves untangled, and opened fire in a ragged volley. McLain removed his hat, presenting less of a target, his Winchester resting atop the creek bank. His eyes were fixed on one tree.

He waited for a clear shot at Frank Starr.

Lynch watched from the top of the mountain. Hidden in the timber, he had the old brass telescope glued to his eye. He slowly scanned the terrain below.

All around him, the Nighthawks were crouched behind trees. A short time before, when the gunfire awakened him, Lynch's first thought was that the soldiers were assaulting the stronghold. But then, even as he rolled out of his blankets, he realized the shots were coming from the bottom of the mountain. He grabbed his rifle and the spyglass, hurrying out the door, and led the men to the edge of the plateau. The gunfight below momentarily left him confounded.

A quick look through the spyglass told the tale. He saw Frank Starr and three of the gang, firing from the treeline near the bottom of the slope. The fourth gang member lay dead, along with a horse, and the other horses were scattered across the open ground. From the creek, four men—all of them *aniyonega*—were exchanging fire with Starr and the gang. He noted that one of the white men had wisely removed his hat.

Lynch centered the telescope on the bareheaded man
As the face came into focus, he recognized the white
lawman who had led a posse into the ambush at Nigger
Jake Hollow. Why the lawman had been pulled off the
Nighthawks and assigned to chase Frank Starr's gang
seemed to him a moot point. What was all too clear was
that Frank had failed to elude the lawmen, and whatever
his reasoning, he had led them to the stronghold. Lynch
had always thought that Frank's reputation as a will-o'-
the-wisp escape artist was somewhat overblown. Today
proved it.

A sense of disgust flooded over Lynch. For years, he
had tolerated Frank out of loyalty to Chitto. But he saw
now that Frank was willing to jeopardize the Nighthawks in order to save his own skin. He had little doubt
that Frank had made a run for the mountain, expecting
the Keetoowahs to join in the fight. All the worse, if the
army was trailing the Nighthawks, the gun battle raging
below would lead them directly to the stronghold. Disgust rapidly turned to anger, and he collapsed the telescope. He moved away from the tree.

Threepersons, who was waiting nearby, looked at
him. "What should we do?"

"Nothing," Lynch said. "Hold the men here."

"Where are you going?"

"To talk with Chitto."

Lynch entered the redoubt. The far side of the room
was in shadow, and he picked his way through blankets
scattered about on the floor. By the light of the fire, he
saw that Chitto's good eye was open. He knelt down
beside the litter.

"Joseph," Chitto said uncertainly. "Have the soldiers found us?"

"Not yet," Lynch replied. "Frank and his gang tried

to reach the mountain. They are in a fight with white lawmen. Down by the creek.''

"Frank?" Chitto appeared startled. "Why would Frank lead them here?"

"I am not worried about the lawmen. There are only four of them, and we can kill them quickly enough. But the sound of gunshots may draw the soldiers.''

"You are in charge now, Joseph. Why do you tell me this?''

Lynch's face was grave. "Last night you asked not to be taken alive. I said we would talk of it today. Is that still your wish?''

"Yes," Chitto said, his one eye gleaming. "I prefer an honorable death.''

"Frank needs help, and I will take some of the men to join the fight. But if the soldiers come, I may not return.''

"You are saying you may be killed.''

Lynch nodded. "I cannot ask the men I leave here to shoot you. They would refuse such an order.'' He pulled a pistol from his waistband. "You will have to do it yourself.''

"I understand.'' Chitto took the pistol with his good hand. "Of all the Nighthawks, I have been proudest of you, Joseph. You still do me honor.''

"Chitto, if we shouldn't meet again in this life—"

"Then I will greet you where the spirits dwell.''

Lynch was unable to speak. He got to his feet and turned away from the litter. The sound of shooting swelled as he crossed the room.

He felt a fierce eye follow him out the door.

Twenty-seven

McLain hugged the creek bank. A pistol barked and dirt flew just above his head. As though on command, three rifles boomed, and a slug ricocheted off a rock on the far side of the stream. The reverberation of gunshots echoed off mountain walls.

There was a momentary lull in the firing. McLain angrily swiped at his mustache, goaded by a sense of frustration. Starr's gang held the high ground, and continued to pour volley after volley down the slope. The snarl of bullets kept the lawmen pinned down, and left McLain in a quandary. He was caught betwixt and between.

The outlaws were unable to withdraw up the mountain. The steep grade would slow them to a crawl, and were they to try, their backs would have made inviting targets. By the same token, McLain and his men had no choice but to hold their position beneath the bulwark of the creek bank. A charge up the slope, in the face of rapid-fire repeating rifles, would have been suicidal. The fight was at a standoff.

McLain felt stymied. He had chased Starr across half of Oklahoma, into Arkansas, and back into a mountain wilderness. For the first time in two years, he'd run Starr to ground and finally had a chance to put the gang out of business. Nor was he mindless of the fact that he would be stripped of his badge, personally disgraced, if he allowed Starr to escape. Yet he was pinned down like a butterfly on a board, and unable to advance except at the risk of what he judged to be certain death. His frustration mounted as he chewed on the problem.

Still another volley pocked the earth above his head. Gideon Brown was hunkered down a few yards to his right, and a short distance beyond, Swanson and Upgraff were flattened against the creek bank. When the fight began, with the gang scrambling for cover, the lawmen had held a slight edge. But the advantage of high ground quickly reversed the odds, and McLain had never gotten a clear shot at Starr. Still, as he pondered on it now, he realized that he had to do something. He was slowly losing the fight.

"Gideon." He called out to Brown, scooted a yard closer. "We're getting nowhere fast. We've got to turn it around."

Brown bobbed his head in agreement. "I'm plumb tired of gettin' shot at. You got any ideas?"

"Way it sounds to me, they've fallen into a routine. Starr lets off one with his pistol, and the others cut loose with their rifles. It's like they're waiting on Starr to give the order to fire."

"Maybe they don't wanna run short of ammunition."

"Maybe so," McLain said. "Whatever it is, there's a little lull after they fire. Couple of minutes, sometimes more."

"Yeah, you're right," Brown said, thinking about it. "Bastards are timing their fire."

"Let's play their game, then. Quick as those rifles fire, we'll pop up and turn loose. Do it before they have time to reload."

"And if we do it fast enough, we might just catch somebody out in the open."

"That's the whole idea," McLain said. "I'd like to whittle down the odds, even if it's one at a time. Pass the word along to Swanson and Upgraff."

Brown moved downstream, hunched over to stay below the creek bank. He explained the plan to Swanson, who nodded rapidly, and in turn relayed the word to Upgraff. A minute or so later, the pistol roared, followed instantly by the crack of three rifles. McLain stood upright, vaguely aware that the other men were on their feet. He winged a shot at Starr, who ducked behind a tall oak. The slug thunked into the tree.

Brown fired and missed, and Upgraff's shot went wild. But the man to Swanson's immediate front was slower than the others, still partially exposed at the side of a tree. Swanson tripped the trigger, and the man staggered, dropping his rifle. His hands went to his throat, trying to stem a gout of blood, and his knees buckled. He fell face forward, crashing into the dirt, and tumbled down the slope. His body came to a stop wedged behind a boulder.

Starr popped out from the opposite side of his tree. He sighted quickly, arm locked and level, and his pistol spat a sheet of flame. Swanson grunted, drilled through the breastbone, a look of surprise etched on his face. He sat down heavily, his rifle clattering into the streambed, and slowly toppled onto his side. McLain fired a hurried shot as Starr again vanished behind the trunk of the oak. He cursed roundly, taking cover beneath the bank. His gaze was drawn to Swanson's body.

A good plan gone to hell, he told himself. And along

with it a man who in the end had found the heart to fight. One of theirs for one of ours seemed to him a poor trade. All the more so since it changed nothing.

They were still locked in a stalemate.

Lynch assembled eight men at the top of the mountain. He separated them into two squads, four men to a squad, all of them armed with rifles. Ben Dewey was in charge of one squad, and Noah Adair the other. They gathered as the sun rose full in the eastern quadrant of the sky.

Doak Threepersons, despite his protests, was being left behind. Lynch considered him a good leader, steady and smart, and he'd been given command of the remaining nine men. In the event the army attacked, and Lynch did not return, his orders were to lead the Nighthawks in defense of the stronghold. Should a retreat become necessary, he'd been told to look to the safety of his men, and not worry about Chitto. Chitto would take care of himself.

A sudden exchange of gunfire broke out below. Lynch nodded to Dewey and Adair, and led the men down the slope. The tactical maneuver would have been to split his squads, encircling the creek from east and west, and envelop the lawmen with an attack from the flanks. But he felt a pressing urgency to end the fight with dispatch, before the army was drawn to the rattle of guns. He planned a direct frontal assault.

Halfway down the mountain, Lynch signaled to his squad leaders. Dewey halted his squad in place, the men spread out on line to the right. Adair motioned his men onward, angling off to the left some ten yards. As Adair's squad advanced, Dewey's men opened fire, raking the creek with lead. Adair stopped a short distance ahead, waiting to screen Dewey's advance with covering fire. The plan was to keep the lawmen under constant fire, while advancing down the slope step by step. At the bottom of the mountain, in concert with Starr's men, the final assault would be launched. By Lynch's order, none of the lawmen were to be spared.

Far below, McLain cursed himself for a fool. The opening volley had taken him completely off guard, and the one that followed even more so. Crouched low in the creek, bullets whistling overhead like hailstones, he counted at least eight rifles. For a moment he was too stunned to react, or think, and he couldn't comprehend the sudden reinforcements to Starr's gang. But then, in the measured span between volleys, he sneaked a quick look over the creek bank. What he saw was an eyeful, and an eye-opener, nine Indians advancing down the slope under covering fire. As though blind, and abruptly cured, he realized what he'd overlooked in the heat of the chase. Frank Starr had led him to the mountain stronghold of the Nighthawks.

McLain took hold of himself. He had more immediate problems to deal with than his own folly. The Nighthawks were advancing steadily down the mountain, and he already saw how it would end. Once they joined forces with Starr's gang, he would be outnumbered four to one by a force that held the high ground. They were certain to attack, probably half providing covering fire while the other half stormed the creek. There was no question that they would overrun his position, and he seriously doubted they would take prisoners. His decision was not how to fight, but how to survive. He had to move now.

Still crouched low, he joined Brown and Upgraff. A bullet ricocheted off a rock with a high, whining sound. "Who's up there?" Upgraff said in a shaky voice. "Where'd they come from?"

"No time to explain," McLain said. "We've got to

get out of here, and damn quick. Otherwise we're dead.''

Brown stared at him. "Do we make a run for it?"

"We wouldn't get far on foot. Our only chance is the horses."

Their horses were somewhere downstream, spooked by the gunfire. He nodded to Upgraff. "Charley, I want you to go catch those horses. We'll stay here and give you covering fire. Just keep your head down—and move quick."

Upgraff swallowed hard. "How're you gonna know I've got the horses?"

"Fire three shots," McLain said. "We'll come running when we hear you fire. Now get going."

Upgraff scuttled off downstream. McLain glanced at Brown. "No time like the present, Gideon. Let's try to slow these boys down."

Brown needed no coaxing. They rose in unison from the creekbed and sprayed the mountainside with lead. Spent shells went flying, and they hardly bothered to aim, furiously cranking the levers on their weapons. The Nighthawks faltered, taken aback by the sudden burst of gunfire, slugs whizzing past them through the trees. Lynch shouted at them, his voice a deep bellow above the sharp crack of rifles, and ordered them to keep moving. Dewey's squad pressed forward, and Adair's men let loose another withering barrage. McLain and Brown ducked as bullets tore into the creek bank.

The Nighthawks were now some thirty yards above Starr and his gang. At first, when the firing broke out from their rear, the gang members thought they were being attacked from behind. Then they quickly realized that the shots were directed not at them, but at the lawmen in the creek. Starr was jubilant, his features split in a nutcracker grin, for the reinforcements would pull him out of a tight spot. He had felt certain his brother wouldn't let him down, and he searched the Nighthawks' ranks for Chitto's face. He saw, instead, that Lynch was leading the men.

There was a slight break in the gunfire as Ben Dewey's squad started to move forward. McLain was still waiting on the signal from Upgraff, and growing concerned that the horses had scattered too far downstream. While he reloaded his carbine, he kept one ear cocked to the action on the mountainside, all too aware that time was slipping away. He sensed the slack between volleys, and with it came the determination to buy every second possible. He nodded to Brown.

"Let's give them another dose. Don't hold anything back!"

Their hearts pumping, they again rose from beneath the creek bank. In that instant, Frank Starr's jubilance overcame caution and made him careless. He waved Lynch and the Nighthawks forward, completely unaware that he'd taken half a step from behind the tree. McLain saw him, quickly shifted aim and caught the sights, and shot him in the back of the head. The front of Starr's skull exploded in a reddish mist of brain matter and bone fragments. He dropped as though struck by a thunderbolt.

Lynch stopped in his tracks, stupefied. The Nighthawks were arrested as well, frozen in motion, suddenly uncertain as to whether he would press the attack. But then, shock replaced by anger, he motioned them on. Dewey's squad raised their rifles.

McLain and Brown dodged beneath the creek bank.

Sergeant Major Jack O'Neal rode to the sound of gunfire. Instilled with this oldest of military dictums during the war in Cuba, he'd been taught that a soldier was duty-bound to seek out the hottest part of a battlefield. He pumped his arm to signal a gallop.

Joe Blackbird rode at his side. To their rear, formed in column of twos, were twenty troopers from the Third Cavalry battalion. The men were volunteers, mostly veterans of the Spanish-American War, and itching for a fight with the renegade Cherokees. Like the sergeant major, their interest was not so much justice as retribution. They had a score to settle.

The patrol had departed Beevale Mountain shortly after dawn that morning. Their assignment was to reconnoiter the mountains to the east, and fix the position of their enemy, the Nighthawks. Blackbird, acting as their scout, had led them along Sallisaw Creek, skirting Fletcher Mountain, to where the tracks branched off on Cherry Tree Creek. By full sunrise they were within sight of a swaybacked monolith that Blackbird identified as Doublehead Mountain.

The gunfire swelled in volume as they charged across the open plain bordering the creek. To their direct front, O'Neal saw the orange-red wink of muzzle flashes near the base of the mountain. On a northerly wind, drifting leeward, he saw a column of smoke issuing from what appeared to be a timbered dugout just below the summit. One look told him it was the stronghold, and though he had no idea who the renegades were fighting, he was determined to join the scrap. He spurred his horse harder.

A few minutes later O'Neal spotted two men trapped in the creek, firing at the Nighthawks. Off to the west he saw another man, holding three horses, struggling to keep them from bolting. As he rode closer, the renegades abruptly ceased fire, staring at the mounted troopers, and then melted into the trees along the bottom of the slope. He led his men over the embankment with a sudden jolt, and leaped from the saddle before his horse stopped moving. He motioned wildly as Blackbird and the troopers swung to the ground.

"Get those horses downstream!" he yelled. "Take up firing positions along the bank!"

The troopers swatted their horses on the rumps, Krag carbines in hand, and rushed to take cover. O'Neal cast a glance at McLain, somewhat amazed to recognize the deputy U.S. Marshal who had accompanied the Third Battalion to Tahlequah. He was all the more astonished to find the lawman in a fight with the Nighthawks, on the verge of being overrun and killed. But the first order of business was to engage the enemy in battle. He turned back to his men.

"On my command!" he called out. "Fire at will!"

Twenty Krag carbines roared in a deafening blast. The troopers reloaded and fired another volley at shadowy figures on the wooded slope. McLain wrung Blackbird's hand, shouting to be heard over the gunfire, and the scout suddenly laughed. O'Neal had never seen Blackbird laugh, particularly in the midst of a battle. He looked at McLain.

"What's so goddamned funny, Marshal?"

"Something I never thought I'd see."

"And what's that?"

McLain grinned. "The cavalry to the rescue."

Twenty-eight

The Nighthawks were scattered throughout the trees. A steady barrage from the creek kept them flat on the ground, their heads down. The bullets buzzed through the woods like a swarm of angry bees.

Lynch was on his belly behind a tall hickory. He edged his head around the trunk just enough for a clear field of view. By rough count, he estimated there were twenty soldiers firing from the creek. A burly sergeant, whose voice sounded clearly above the crack of rifles, directed their fire. Their scout was an all-too-familiar face: Joe Blackbird.

The gunfight with the lawmen, just as Lynch feared, had drawn the soldiers to Doublehead Mountain. He silently damned Frank Starr, though he knew it was widely considered unlucky to curse the dead. He thought it probable that Blackbird would have eventually found the stronghold anyway, but the situation was now out of hand. The small force he'd led against the lawmen was dangerously exposed, outnumbered and outgunned. He had to pull back to the top of the mountain.

The barrage abruptly slacked off. Lynch saw the soldiers feverishly reloading their bolt-action rifles, which held only five rounds. He let go a shrill whistle, attracting the attention of Adair and Dewey, and motioned with hand signals. Farther down the slope, he gestured to the two remaining members of Starr's gang, Jim Colbert and Henry Brandon. He waved them on, and after a moment's hesitation, they jumped to their feet. They made a run for it.

Adair's squad opened fire. They raked the creek with three spaced volleys, hitting one soldier and forcing the others to dive for cover. Dewey pulled back with his squad some thirty yards, and turned to fire as Adair and his men retreated from their positions. The soldiers, under a blistering tirade from their sergeant, quickly rejoined the action with a rattling fusillade. Henry Brandon dropped to his knees, clutching his chest, dusted on both sides by a slug. He fell facedown in the dirt.

The withdrawal went along in fits and starts. One squad moved up the slope for twenty or thirty yards, while the other provided covering fire. The soldiers returned volley for volley, their Krags blasting a drumming tattoo from the creek. Dewey lost two men, cut down as they retreated through the trees, and Adair lost one. Jim Colbert dodged and weaved, the lone survivor of the gang, and finally joined forces with Dewey's squad. The roll of gunfire echoed out across the mountains.

Some twenty minutes later the Nighthawks finally gained the summit. Their numbers were reduced by three dead, not counting Brandon, and four had been wounded. Lynch found Threepersons waiting at the top, with the nine men who had remained behind to guard the stronghold. As the last of the retreating force spilled onto the plateau, he took a quick head count. He began issuing orders.

"Noah! Ben!" he called to the squad leaders. "Get your men inside and tend your wounded. Anyone not wounded, I want him manning a gun port."

Adair and Dewey led their men to the redoubt. One of the wounded had to be carried, and the other three hobbled along under their own power. Colbert, thankful to be alive, followed them inside. Lynch turned back to Threepersons.

"I kept my men here," Threepersons said tentatively. "Thought that's how you'd want it."

"You were right," Lynch assured him. "Down there, you would have just gotten in the way. We had to move fast."

"Do you think the soldiers will attack?"

"I'm not sure what they'll do, Doak."

Lynch stared down the slope. He saw the soldiers still positioned at the creek bank, their rifles trained on the mountain. The sergeant was huddled with Blackbird and the white lawman, gesturing wildly at the summit. He watched a moment longer, then his gaze shifted to the open plain beyond Cherry Tree Creek. He was looking for horsemen, or a dust column, anything to indicate the cavalry battalion was advancing to join the fight. He saw nothing.

"These men were sent to find us," he said, pointing to the troopers below. "Maybe they will wait for the other horse soldiers before they attack."

"Do you want my men inside or out here?"

"For the time being, keep them out here. Post men on a line across this side of the mountain. Watch for movement from any direction—especially the north-west.''

''You think the others will come from there?''

''I expected to see them before now.''

''What about the ones in the creek?''

''Let me know at the first sign of movement. I will be inside.''

Lynch entered the redoubt. His first concern was for the wounded, and he moved among the men being treated by Adair and Dewey. One was shot in the hand, another in the arm, and the third a painful but not too serious bullet hole through the right buttock. The fourth man, who had been carried inside, was shot through the stomach, and appeared close to death. Lynch looked on a moment, then glanced at Colbert, who was manning one of the gun ports. Colbert was unable to meet his stare.

After satisfying himself about the wounded, Lynch walked to the rear of the room. Chitto was awake, his one eye alert despite the sweat beading his forehead. His fever was clearly running strong, and his jaw muscles were knotted in pain. He took a shallow breath as Lynch knelt at his side.

''I heard the men talking, Joseph. They say the soldiers have found us.''

Lynch nodded. ''What looks like a patrol, maybe twenty soldiers. Blackbird is with them.''

''A scouting patrol,'' Chitto said softly. ''That means the others are not far behind.''

''I have seen nothing of them yet. But they will probably be here before long.''

''How many men did we lose?''

''Three,'' Lynch said. ''Four wounded, one pretty bad.''

''I saw Jim Colbert over there.'' Chitto made a listless gesture with his good hand. ''Why doesn't he come talk to me? What happened to Frank?''

''Frank and three of his men were killed. The white marshal shot him just before the soldiers showed up. The same marshal we ambushed at Nigger Jake Hollow.''

Chitto was silent a moment. ''Did Frank die fighting?''

Lynch shaded the truth. ''You would have been proud of him. He fought to the end.''

''I always told him the law would get him one day. He wouldn't listen.''

''Frank was his own man.''

''Yes.'' Chitto seemed to drift off, then his eye snapped around. ''Too many have died, Joseph. I want you to take the men and leave this place. Help them save themselves.''

Lynch shook his head. ''I will not leave you, and that is my final word on it. Do not ask me again.''

''And what of the men?''

''They know they are free to go. But they stay because they choose to stay. They are Nighthawks.''

Chitto's features sagged. ''Before this day is out, I will be with Frank. I am dying, Joseph. I would like you to live.''

''You forget,'' Lynch said with a slight smile. ''I am a Nighthawk, too. I choose to stay.''

''You are a stubborn man.''

''You taught me well.''

''Maybe too well.''

Chitto suddenly seemed drained. His eye fluttered, then closed, and he fell into a fevered sleep. Lynch levered himself erect, staring down with a subdued expression, and finally walked to the door. A shaft of sunlight struck him in the face, and he realized the morning was not yet half gone. His mouth crooked in a rueful smile.

He thought it would be a long day.

"Fifty-three dead?"

"Not to mention our wounded."

"I warned Drummond about Chitto."

"The colonel's not big on advice."

"All the same . . . fifty-three."

McLain looked staggered. He was seated near the creek beside Joe Blackbird and Sergeant Major O'Neal. Half the troopers stood at the embankment, their carbines trained on the mountain. The others, along with Brown and Upgraff, sat close to the stream, conversing in low tones. Some fifteen minutes had elapsed since their skirmish with the Nighthawks.

O'Neal had just finished his account of the fight at Beevale Mountain. As he spoke, McLain's expression had gone from stunned disbelief to a look of dumbfounded shock. He realized the battle had taken place only yesterday, as he and his men were tracking Frank Starr. The enormity of the defeat still left him shaking his head, and not just at the losses. He was oddly impressed that Chitto had trapped an entire battalion.

"So anyway," O'Neal went on. "The company commanders convinced Drummond to come back this morning and collect our dead. He was all for leaving them to the buzzards—the lily-livered bastard!"

"You should've seen it," Blackbird added. "One smell of them dead men and he puked his guts out. Couldn't wait to take off."

"Take off?" McLain repeated. "Where'd he go?"

"Tahlequah," O'Neal said. "Great leader that he is, he plans to regroup and reorganize. He pulled the battalion out of the field."

"You mean he quit the fight?"

"I doubt we'll see the colonel anytime soon."

"What about reinforcements?" McLain asked. "Don't tell me he sent you after the Nighthawks with just twenty men?"

O'Neal looked amused. "I had to do some fancy talking to get this patrol. Drummond wasn't keen on the idea, was he, Joe?"

"Not a little bit," Blackbird acknowledged. "He'd like to just forget Chitto and the Nighthawks."

McLain glanced from one to the other. "So how'd you get him to go along?"

"We lied," O'Neal said with a grin. "We were supposed to reconnoiter and report back to Tahlequah. Our orders were to avoid engaging the enemy."

"Well, I'm damn glad you showed up. Another couple of minutes and it would've been too late."

"Yeah, it's funny how things work out. Guess you never expected Starr to lead you into a hornet's nest."

"Have to tell you, I thought we were goners."

McLain looked upstream. Elmer Swanson and the trooper killed in the skirmish were laid out on the ground beside the creek. His gaze shifted to the mountain slope, where the bodies of Frank Starr and three gang members lay sprawled in death. Farther up, he saw the crumpled forms of three Nighthawks, killed during their withdrawal. He shook his head.

"We got Frank," he said slowly. "Question is, how do we get Chitto?"

O'Neal nodded soberly. "For what it's worth, we've got them outnumbered. We're twenty-four altogether, counting you and your men."

"How many you think they have left?"

"I'd say maybe fifteen or sixteen. What's your count, Joe?"

"Eighteen," Blackbird said, calculating in his head. "Tracked twenty here from Beevale Mountain, and killed three. Add one of Starr's men and that makes eighteen."

"Maybe not," O'Neal remarked. "Unless I miss my guess, they've got some wounded up there. Our boys popped 'em pretty good."

McLain agreed with the assessment. The troopers were armed with the Krag carbine, which fired a .30-40 cartridge. The 220 grain bullet was accurate out to four hundred yards, and the Nighthawks' withdrawal had been something of a turkey shoot. He thought it likely they'd suffered casualties.

"Got one wounded, anyway," Blackbird conceded. "Dragged him all the way here on a travois. Might be Chitto himself."

"That's right," McLain said quickly. "You shot Chitto that day at Nigger Jake Hollow. I wonder how bad he's hurt."

"I'd say bad enough," Blackbird allowed. "Wouldn't be in a travois if he wasn't bad off. 'Course, we don't know it's Chitto. Could be anybody."

"Chitto or not," O'Neal said, "they're still in good hands. Did you see the one directing things when they pulled back? Bastard was cool as an icicle. Knew his business."

"His name's Joseph Lynch," Blackbird said. "Tough old devil, just like Chitto."

"Which brings us back to the question," McLain commented. "How do we put an end to this thing? Got any ideas, Sergeant Major?"

O'Neal stared up at the mountain. "That fortification of theirs commands the high ground. We'd play hell taking it with a frontal assault."

"You've got my vote there. I'm not anxious to

harge their stronghold. So what's the alternative?''

''Just about now I'd like to have a few sticks of dynamite. That'd at least flush 'em out in the open.''

''Dynamite's likely in short supply out here.''

''Yeah, I know,'' O'Neal muttered. ''The alternative
would be to split our forces and attack from the flanks.
don't much care for that idea, either.''

''Why not?'' McLain asked.

''Because they'd be forted up and it'd turn into a
niping contest. We just reduce our exposure a little by
coming in from the flanks.''

''What if we starve them out?''

''I don't follow you.''

''Suppose we captured their horses?'' McLain said,
motioning off to the south. ''They've got to have their
horses hidden out there somewhere. And without
horses—''

''They're stuck!'' O'Neal finished the thought. ''By
God, it might just work. They'd have to surrender or
starve.''

''What about it, Joe?'' McLain looked around at
Blackbird. ''Think you could find their horses?''

''Wouldn't hurt to have a look.''

Blackbird disappeared into the woods at the base of
the mountain. McLain rolled himself a smoke, popped
a match on his thumbnail. He lit up, staring over the
flame at O'Neal. ''What's your opinion of things, Sergeant Major? Have we got the Nighthawks, or do they
have us?''

O'Neal laughed. ''I'd have to say it's a toss-up, Marshal. A flip of the coin.''

Twenty-nine

Joe Blackbird returned within the hour. He whistle softly to alert the troopers before stepping out of th trees. His coat was unbuttoned, and despite a bris wind, his dark hair glistened with sweat. He appeare to have been moving fast.

McLain and O'Neal walked forward to meet him. Fo the last hour they had watched the mountain in a cor of silence. There was no visible movement at the sum mit, and neither of them had hatched a plan to take th stronghold. They waited now for Blackbird's report.

"I found the horses," he said, breathing deeply fro his run through the woods. "They built a corral on th back side of the mountain. Creek and a meadow dow below."

O'Neal grinned. "Damn good work, Joe. Did yo spot any Nighthawks?"

"Didn't see anybody," Blackbird said. " 'Cours they probably water and graze the horses at night. B safer that way."

"Chitto's clever," McLain said in an admiring ton

"Never thought anyone would scout the back of the mountain. Got himself a dandy back door."

O'Neal looked quizzical. "You talking about an escape hole?"

"That'd be my guess," McLain said. "What do you think, Joe?"

Blackbird nodded. "They'll slip off after it gets dark. Leave us watching the front door."

"And nobody there," McLain added. "By the time we got wise, they'd be long gone. Chitto doesn't miss a trick."

"To hell with that!" O'Neal fumed. "We'll run their goddamned horses off. Slam that back door shut."

"Suppose we don't," McLain said. "Maybe there's a better way."

"What's that mean?" O'Neal demanded. "You're the one that came up with the idea. Capture their horses and starve them out. Wasn't that what you said?"

"Yeah, but I just had a better idea. Suppose we could get them to surrender, instead?"

"Surrender?" O'Neal said blankly. "How the Christ would we do that?"

"Give them a choice," McLain told him. "Either they surrender or we shoot their horses. Indians are partial to their horses, am I right, Joe?"

Blackbird detected something strange about McLain, a silent appeal of some sort. He decided to go along. "No man likes to see his horse shot."

"But why shoot 'em?" O'Neal asked. "Why not just run them off?"

McLain spread his hands. "For all we know, they've got somebody watching those horses. Try to run them off and we're liable to wind up in a fight." He paused, underscoring the words. "Why risk getting more of your troopers killed?"

"So you're saying we sit back and pick their horses off at long range. That the idea?"

"Two birds with one stone. We avoid a fight and it still closes the back door. But I don't think it'll go that far."

"You really think they'll surrender just to save their horses?"

"I think it's worth a try."

O'Neal considered a moment. "Hell, why not?" he said. "We've got nothing to lose by killing their horses. I doubt they'd try to escape on foot."

"Not with us mounted," McLain noted. "They wouldn't stand a chance."

"You're a devious man, McLain. Worst that can happen is that we starve them out. So we win either way."

"That's how it looks to me."

"First step's to close the back door," O'Neal said, eyes narrowed in thought. "I'll send Joe and nine men to cover the horses. That leaves plenty here in case the Nighthawks start anything on this end. I count fourteen, including you and your men."

"Thirteen," McLain corrected him. "Somebody has to carry the message."

"What message?"

"Our ultimatum that they surrender."

O'Neal stared at him. "Why do I get the feeling you've picked yourself for the job?"

"Only makes sense," McLain said, with a touch of guile. "You're the military man here, and that puts you in command. You're the one to stay."

"What if they don't like the message? You ever think they might shoot you?"

"Whichever way it works out, I still nominate myself."

"You've got more guts than a bear, McLain."

O'Neal walked off to organize the raiding party. Blackbird studied the ground a moment, then looked up. "I got a hunch the sergeant's right," he said, with some conviction. "You're a devious man, Marshal."

"Why would you say that, Joe?"

"You mean to take Chitto alive, don't you?"

"I wouldn't mind," McLain said. "How about you?"

"Whoever you talk to, you'd better talk fast. They're not gonna like the message about the horses."

Blackbird moved away to join O'Neal, who was collecting a squad of troopers. Gideon Brown turned from the embankment, where he'd been watching the mountain. He approached McLain, the Marlin repeater tucked in the crook of his arm. His features were curiously downcast.

"Couldn't help overhearing," he said, with an apologetic shrug. "Sounds like you've set yourself in harm's way. You mind me askin' why?"

"I suppose I'm a natural-born volunteer. What makes you ask?"

"Our job was to get Frank Starr, and we've done that. Why stick your neck out any more?"

McLain smiled. "Well, Gideon, I guess Blackbird pegged it right."

"How's that?"

"I want Chitto Starr alive."

Lynch was summoned from the redoubt. The sun was at its zenith, directly overhead in a noonday sky. He found Doak Threepersons crouched beside a tree, staring intently downslope. Threepersons pointed with his finger.

"Somebody's on his way up here."

A lone figure was visible far down the mountain.

Lynch pulled out the brass telescope, extended it to full length, and placed it to his eye. When he got it focused, he saw a man carrying a stick with a white handkerchief tied to the end. He grunted softly to himself, recognizing the lawman they had almost killed that morning. As he watched, the lawman stopped at the halfway point, waving the stick back and forth. The handkerchief fluttered in the wind.

"A truce flag," Lynch said, collapsing the telescope. "They want to talk."

Threepersons frowned. "Maybe it's a trick."

"I think this is an honorable man. I will go see what he wants."

"What if he shoots you?"

"Then you can shoot him."

Lynch walked off down the mountain. He thought it prudent to take his rifle, even though the lawman appeared to be unarmed. Then, on second thought, he decided the lawman probably had a pistol beneath his coat. Not that it mattered either way, for he fully expected the cavalry battalion to arrive at any moment. Whether he was killed now or later seemed a matter of small consequence. He was resigned to how it would end.

Halfway down the mountain, he halted before McLain. They inspected one another a moment, their expressions stolid, revealing nothing. Lynch saw that the lawman was armed, the bulge of a holstered pistol apparent beneath his mackinaw. McLain stood with the butt of the stick planted in the ground, the handkerchief snapping in the wind. He finally nodded.

"You are Joseph Lynch."

"How do you know me?"

"You were identified by Joe Blackbird."

"That traitor!" Lynch said derisively. "Why are you here? Do you speak for the soldiers?"

"I bring a message," McLain said, prepared to bluff his way through. "The cavalry battalion will be here by tomorrow morning. We won't let you escape before they arrive."

"Then you have climbed this mountain for nothing. The Nighthawks do not intend to escape. We make our stand here."

"You've run before. The soldiers believe you will run again when it grows dark. They demand your surrender."

"That is foolish talk," Lynch said, his eyes hard. "Tell them we will never surrender."

McLain shrugged. "You might change your mind between now and dark. The soldiers won't risk letting you escape this time." He jerked a thumb over his shoulder. "See that man down there?"

Lynch looked past him. On the creek bank, he saw the leader of the horse soldiers, holding a rifle. He glanced back at McLain. "What about him?"

"Unless you surrender, he will fire that rifle. We have soldiers on the other side of the mountain, waiting for his signal. They will kill your horses."

"How did you find our horses?"

"Joe Blackbird's a good scout."

"Go ahead and kill them," Lynch said stoically. "I told you we will run no more."

"You can't win," McLain said. "After we kill your horses, we'll starve you into surrender. Why put your men through that?"

"I have given you my answer."

"Look, I know Chitto's wounded. Otherwise you wouldn't be standing here talking to me. Do you want him to die out here on this mountain?"

Lynch studied him a moment. "You have been trying

to kill Chitto for a long time. What does it matter to you where he dies?''

''Haven't enough men been killed?'' McLain said earnestly. ''Let me ask you something, Mr. Lynch. Did Chitto order you to fight to the death?''

''The Nighthawks are free men. Chitto would never order a thing like that.''

''So what would it take to convince you to end it here?''

Lynch considered the thought. ''You would have to let our men go. Give them back their lives.''

''Would you and Chitto be willing to surrender?''

''You need someone to hang, is that it?''

McLain nodded soberly. ''That's the only way to save your men.''

''Then hang me,'' Lynch said, with an enigmatic smile. ''I do not think you will hang Chitto.''

''Why not?''

''Come with me and I will show you. Maybe it is time you met Chitto for yourself.''

McLain dropped the truce flag on the ground. He turned, waving his arms in a crisscross motion, signaling O'Neal to hold off. A moment passed while he waited for the sergeant major to signal back.

Then he followed Joseph Lynch up the mountain.

Chitto was burning with fever. His features were strangely composed, almost peaceful. McLain looked down at the disfigured face, and understood why the government would never hang Chitto Starr. He was near death.

''I didn't lie to you,'' Lynch said. ''He will not live to see a white man's court.''

''No, I guess not,'' McLain replied hollowly. ''He looks in bad shape.''

"A soldier shot him in the eye at Beevale Mountain. There was never much hope after that. We knew he would not last long."

"Not many men would have lasted this long."

"Chitto always said he was a hard man to kill."

McLain glanced around the room. The Nighthawks at the gun ports returned his look with flat stares. He thought the army would have paid dearly in an attempt to take the stronghold. The deal he'd struck with Lynch seemed to him the better choice.

Chitto moaned, and the room went quiet. His eye rolled open, slowly settled on Lynch. His voice sounded parched. "Joseph."

Lynch knelt at his side. "I have brought you a visitor. The lawman we fought at Nigger Jake Hollow."

"Mr. Starr," McLain said, kneeling down. "I'm Owen McLain."

"I remember you," Chitto said weakly. "You are a good fighter."

"Not as good as you, Mr. Starr. You've fought the army to a standstill."

Chitto blinked, his vision blurred. "Why are you here?"

"Let me explain," Lynch said, bending closer. "The marshal wants to end the fighting. I have agreed that you and I will surrender here, today. In exchange, our men will go free."

"Free." Chitto seemed to seize on the word. "I think you got the best of him."

"I had a good teacher."

"But what of you, Joseph? They will hang you."

"I am not important. Someone will take my place, just as I took yours. So long as there are Nighthawks, we will not have lost the fight."

"Yes." Chitto took a wheezing breath. "We fooled

them after all, Joseph. The Nighthawks will outlive us
. . . go on.''

Lynch wondered if Doak Threepersons would pick
up the mantle of leadership. He thought it more likely
that the Nighthawks would fall apart and go their separate ways. But they would be free, and alive.

"I am tired.'' Chitto's eye glazed, then closed. "I
will rest now, Joseph.''

Lynch glanced at McLain. "He once told me that a
cause has a life all its own. Perhaps he was right.''

"One thing's for sure,'' McLain said quietly. "No
one will forget his name.''

Chitto died at three o'clock that afternoon. By then
McLain had convinced O'Neal that they'd got the best
of the bargain. No more men would die, either white or
red, and the Nighthawks were to abandon their stronghold. Blackbird and the squad of soliders were recalled
from the back side of the mountain, and the cavalry
patrol settled in to wait. O'Neal put a detail to work
digging graves.

On the summit, Chitto's body was wrapped in blankets and securely lashed to the travois. Lynch, with
McLain at his side, escorted four Nighthawks who carried the litter to the bottom of the mountain. There, the
troopers took charge of the body and began securing the
travois to a horse. While McLain looked on, Lynch
shook hands with his old comrades, and then stepped
aside. The men turned back to the slope.

Shortly afterward, Doak Threepersons led the Nighthawks south from the stronghold. On the opposite side
of the mountain the cavalry patrol rode northwest, toward the headwaters of Cherry Tree Creek. McLain
joined O'Neal at the head of the column, and they
agreed to camp somewhere along the stream at sundown. For now, they both felt a strong need to be gone

from the place where Frank Starr and his gang lay buried. A killing ground best put behind them.

Their own dead, Elmer Swanson and the trooper killed at the creek, were wrapped in blankets and strapped aboard horses. Joseph Lynch, hands tightly bound and guarded by troopers, rode behind the travois bearing Chitto's body. A short distance up the trail he twisted around in the saddle and took a last look at Doublehead Mountain. The westerly sun crowned the twin peaks in an aura of gold, and for a moment he was reminded of better times. But memory quickly faded to a harder truth.

He thought the Nighthawks were no more.

Thirty

The cavalry patrol rode into Tahlequah three days later. All along the street shops emptied and onlookers spilled onto the sidewalks. They watched in hushed silence as the column filed past.

Sergeant Major O'Neal, with McLain at his side, led the way across the square. The travois, clearly bearing the body of a dead man, at first claimed the attention of the crowds. But then someone recognized Joseph Lynch, and a low murmur of conversation swept through the onlookers. Their whispers quickly turned to speculation that the dead man was Chitto Starr.

On the southeast corner of the square, McLain turned and nodded to Charley Upgraff. The deputy peeled off from the column, assisted by four troopers, and rode toward the funeral parlor with the bodies. Will Starr, hurrying out of the hardware store, saw Lynch and then the travois. Some inner dread told him more than the murmured buzz of those standing nearby. He rushed across the street.

O'Neal brought the column to a halt in front of the

courthouse. McLain stepped out of the saddle as the troopers were ordered to dismount. Blackbird and Gideon Brown joined him at the hitch rack, and O'Neal walked forward. By then the crowd had swelled to five hundred or more, ganged around in jostling excitement. The door of the courthouse burst open.

Sheriff Ed Prather, followed by a deputy, bustled down the walkway. Behind him, a gaggle of the courthouse crowd pushed through the doorway and followed along. His eyes went from McLain to the soldiers, and out over the massed throng of townspeople. His expression was at once curious and confused, for he saw nothing to justify such a large crowd. He stopped at the hitch rack, nodding to McLain.

"See you got back," he said without ceremony. "Where's Swanson and Upgraff?"

"Swanson's dead," McLain informed him. "Turned out to be a first-class lawman. Got killed in a fight with Frank Starr's gang."

"What about Starr?"

"Him and his gang are buried out in the mountains. They won't be robbing any more banks."

"Well now, that's good news. I never thought you'd pull it off."

Before McLain could respond, Prather looked past him with a startled expression. "Godalmighty," he said. "Is that Joseph Lynch I see there?"

"Yeah, that's him," McLain said, glancing back to where Lynch stood guarded by the troopers. "Way things worked out, we got Chitto Starr, too. Upgraff just took his body over to the undertaker."

"Glory hallelujah!" Prather crowed uproariously. "You finally killed that red nigger!"

McLain hit him. The punch struck Prather on the jaw and dumped him flat on his back, out cold. The crowd looked on in a stilled tableau, their mouths slack with amazement. O'Neal shook his head, staring down at the unconscious lawman. He tried to keep a straight face.

"You pack quite a wallop, Marshal."

McLain grinned, rubbing his knuckles. "I've been wanting to do that for a long time. Maybe it'll teach him to mind his mouth."

Prather's deputy was torn between attending to his boss or coming to his defense. McLain nailed him with a hard stare. "What's your name, Deputy?"

The man swallowed. "Pete Henkle."

"Here's what you do, Henkle. Take Mr. Lynch and lock him in your jail. See to it that he gets good treatment. I'll pick him up in the morning."

"What about the sheriff?"

"Tend to him after you're finished with Mr. Lynch."

"Before that," O'Neal said, halting the deputy with an upraised palm. "I'm looking for the Third Cavalry Battalion. Where are they camped?"

Henkle appeared flummoxed. "Why, they're probably in Guthrie by now. They got ordered back a couple of days ago."

"Who ordered them back?"

"Well, I'd guess it was the governor. Just after he fired that colonel."

"Colonel Drummond?" O'Neal said incredulously. "He relieved the colonel of command?"

"I don't know about relieved," Henkle replied. "But he damn sure fired him. One of the captains took the battalion back to Guthrie."

Henkle stepped around the sheriff and walked toward Lynch. O'Neal glanced at McLain, wagged his head. "I'll be damned," he muttered. "There's a God in heaven after all."

McLain smiled. "I think it's called justice."

O'Neal decided to camp outside town for the night. They agreed to meet in the morning, after McLain collected Lynch, and proceed on to Guthrie. When the patrol rode away, McLain followed Henkle into the courthouse and got Lynch locked in a jail cell. Then he placed a telephone call to Fred Gilmore, standing at the window in the sheriff's office. Outside, he saw some of the crowd help Prather to his feet.

Gilmore was elated. At first, he couldn't comprehend that both Chitto Starr and Frank Starr had been killed. After he calmed down, McLain explained how he'd accomplished Lynch's surrender, in exchange for letting the Nighthawks go free. But Gilmore took it in stride, excited by the prospect of placing the second-in-command on trial for murder. McLain got the feeling he was already writing the headlines.

Prather stumbled into the office as McLain was on his way out. The sheriff was holding his jaw, and he gave McLain a dirty look. "I oughta arrest you for assaulting a peace officer."

McLain laughed. "Don't try it unless you're feeling lucky."

Outside the courthouse McLain came to an abrupt halt. The crowd had drifted off, but Jane Tenkiller was waiting by the steps. She gave him a sloe-eyed smile.

"You're certainly the talk of the town. I'm glad you made it back in one piece."

"Not near as glad as me."

"I was thinking," she said in a throaty voice. "Maybe you'd like to come to supper. We could celebrate."

"I've been thinking myself," McLain said, with a rueful shrug. "Last time, I plumb forgot I'm soon to be a married man. You've got a way of turning a fellow's head." He smiled gently. "Guess I'll have to pass."

She wrinkled her nose. "You're not married yet."

"All the same, it's not in the cards."

"If you change your mind . . ."

"I'd like to, but don't leave a light in the window. I've just gone blind."

She watched as he went down the walkway. He felt an overpowering urge to turn back, but he forced himself to keep walking. At the hitch rack, he stopped to shake hands with Joe Blackbird and Gideon Brown. There was small likelihood that they would ride together again, and yet he felt a deep camaraderie with both men. He promised to look them up whenever he was in Cherokee country.

Across the square, McLain entered the funeral parlor. He found Will Starr seated in the anteroom, his features stark. The young man got to his feet, managed a faint smile. He stuck out his hand.

"Thank you for bringing my father home. I know you could have left him out there."

"No, I couldn't," McLain said, returning his handshake. "Your father was a brave man. He deserved a decent burial."

"Were you with him when he died?"

McLain nodded. "That's why I came by to see you. I thought of something you might want to carve on his gravestone. A tribute to what he really was."

"What is that?"

McLain gave the words eloquence. "The Last Warrior."

"Yes, he was," Will Starr said, his voice choked. "A warrior to the end."

They talked for a short while longer. Then McLain walked from the funeral parlor and turned back toward the square. He thought Chitto Starr would have been leased by what he'd done. For it was a fitting eulogy. The Last Warrior.

Four days later the patrol rode into Guthrie. McLain was determined to finish his business without drawing a crowd. Everywhere they'd stopped along the way, the curious had turned out to gawk at their prisoner. He was tired of the sideshow.

By keeping to back streets, he led the patrol to the federal jail without attracting attention. A holdover from the territorial days, the building was used to house federal prisoners until they were brought to trial. There, he filled out the paperwork and got Joseph Lynch lodged in a cell. When the door swung closed, he waited for the jailor to turn the key. He nodded to Lynch.

"Guess that does it," he said. "You'll probably be arraigned tomorrow. I'll drop by in the morning."

Lynch looked at him through the bars. "How long will it be before I'm brought to trial?"

"I'd say it'll be pretty speedy. The government won't waste any time."

"A cage is no place for a man who has lived free. I think I will welcome the noose."

"I understand," McLain said. "You fought a good fight, Mr. Lynch. Too bad it has to end this way."

Lynch smiled. "For a white man you have more heart than most, Marshal. I will not forget that you let the Nighthawks go free."

"Things have a way of working out."

McLain shook his hand. On the way through the cell block, he thought Joseph Lynch and Chitto Starr were birds of a feather. Neither of them feared death so much as they feared the loss of freedom. The troopers were standing by their horses when he emerged from the jail. O'Neal waited at the head of the column.

"All squared away, Marshal?"

"Looks like our job's finished, Sergeant Major. He locked up tight."

"Well then," O'Neal said. "I'd best take these boy along to the capitol. Get somebody to discharge us from duty."

McLain extended his hand. "You're a helluva so dier, Jack. Thanks for saving my bacon."

"No thanks needed, Owen." O'Neal clasped his han in a firm grip. "I'm proud to have served with you."

"Let's not do it again anytime soon."

"By God, you've got my vote on that!"

O'Neal led his patrol toward Oklahoma Avenu McLain cut across town and left his gelding at Mur son's Livery Stable. He walked over to Harrison an Second, acutely aware of the automobiles and clangin trolley cars after so long in the wilderness. At the I ternational Building, he climbed the stairs and foun Bob Newton seated at a desk in the outer office. Th deputy pounded his shoulder with wild congratulation

Fred Gilmore hurried out of his office. He wrun McLain's hand with a wide jack-o'-lantern grin. "We come back, Owen!" he said effusively. "A magnificer job well done. You're the man of the hour!"

"I wasn't alone," McLain said, shrugging it off. ' had lots of help."

"Don't go modest on me! You're the man who kille Frank Starr and brought down Chitto Starr. The gov ernor thinks you saved Oklahoma. You're a hero!"

McLain started to feel uncomfortable. Before h could respond, Gilmore glanced around the offic "Where's your prisoner? Joseph Lynch?"

"I dropped him off at the jail. Didn't see any nee to bring him here."

"On the contrary," Gilmore said, still grinning

"You captured the Nighthawk second only to Chitto Starr. We have to call the newspaper and arrange photographs." His head dipped in a conspiratorial nod. "We'll make the front page with this."

McLain saw where it was leading. A photograph of Gilmore, beaming proudly, with Joseph Lynch in the middle and himself on the other side. Somewhat like trophy hunters displaying their prize. The thought made him uneasy.

"Maybe tomorrow," he said, determined that it would never happen. "Feels like a month of Sundays since I had a bath. Think I'll go get cleaned up."

"Of course!" Gilmore said, with jocular good humor. "We want you looking tip-top and spruce as a goose. It's not every day you get your picture on the front page."

McLain left after another round of handshakes. He realized it was politics as usual, and Gilmore meant to make the most of Joseph Lynch. But he had little use for the limelight, particularly with a man who would shortly be hanged. He decided to make himself scarce for the next few days.

Later that afternoon, bathed and shaved, he rang the bell at the Markham home. Amy threw open the door and hurled herself into his arms, showering him with kisses. Her eyes were bright with excitement, and she could hardly contain herself. She hugged him tightly around the neck.

"You're here!" she cried, pulling him into the foyer and kicking the door closed. "I was worried sick until we heard you were all right. And then I couldn't wait for you to get home!"

McLain chuckled. "Maybe I ought to go away more often."

"Don't you dare!" she said, hugging him fiercely.

"Oh, Owen, you're famous, absolutely famous. Daddy thinks you hung the moon! He says the governor is going to give you a medal."

"Not me," McLain protested. "I don't take medals for killing men. Let him give it to someone else."

She searched his face. "You admired Chitto Starr very much, didn't you?"

"I admire any man who'll die for what he believes."

"Well, I'm sorry it had to end so badly. But you're home and you're safe, and that's what matters to me. Just you."

McLain peered down the hallway. "Are your folks home?"

"Daddy's still at the office and Mother's at a charity bazaar. Why?"

"You remember what you said about us getting married? How a girl has to have a proper engagement?"

"Yes . . ."

"I'm not feeling proper." McLain drew her closer, her breasts pressed against his chest. "You understand what I mean? I can't wait till June."

"Omigod!" She felt him hard against her thigh, and her resolve weakened. "Ummm . . . I don't know— maybe we *should* get married."

"I think the sooner the better."

"Daddy will be furious."

"He'll get over it."

McLain pulled her into a tight embrace. But even as he kissed her, his mind flashed back to Doublehead Mountain. He saw again the dead and dying, heard the rattle of gunfire, and knew why he couldn't wait. Life was fleeting, a thing to be celebrated, and he'd said it himself a moment ago. The sooner the better.

They would be married before Christmas.

In 1889, Bill Tilghman joined the historic land rush that transformed a raw frontier into Oklahoma Territory. A lawman by trade, he set aside his badge to make his fortune in the boomtowns. Yet Tilghman was called into service once more, on a bold, relentless journey that would make his name a legend for all time—in an epic confrontation with outlaw Bill Doolin.

OUTLAW KINGDOM

MATT BRAUN

OUTLAW KINGDOM
Matt Braun
_____ 95618-5 $5.99 U.S./$7.99 CAN.

BEFORE THE LEGEND, THERE WAS THE MAN...

AND A POWERFUL DESTINY TO FULFILL.

On October 26, 1881, three outlaws lay dead in a dusty vacant lot in Tombstone, Arizona. Standing over them—Colts smoking—were Wyatt Earp, his two brothers Morgan and Virgil, and a gun-slinging gambler named Doc Holliday. The shootout at the O.K. Corral was over—but for Earp, the fight had just begun...

WYATT EARP

MATT BRAUN

WYATT EARP
Matt Braun
_____ 95325-9 $5.50 U.S./$6.99 CAN.